A Love Child's Journey

Ckay Duncan

Copyright © 2009 Colleen K. Duncan

Published and distributed in the United States by
Ckay Duncan Publishing
www.ckayduncan.com

Edited by: S. Rains and Heather McCoy

Cover Photograph/ Cover design by: Matt McCoy

Graphic design: Mustang Graphics Designers

All rights reserved. No part of this book may be reproduced by any mechanical, photographic, or electronic process, nor may it be stored in a retrieval system without permission in writing, except by a reviewer who may quote brief passages in a review.

ISBN 13: 978-0-9823689-0-9

ISBN 10: 0-9823689-0-9

Printed in the United States of America

In Loving Memory

of

My birth mother Carolyn who never stopped loving me and my dear friend Terry whose kindness will live forever in my heart.

"Spread love wherever you go…

Let no one ever come to you without leaving happier."

Mother Teresa

AUTHOR'S NOTE

Although fiction, this book is based on a real journey and real events. Names, places and identifying details, occupations or professions, geographic facts (cities and streets) have been changed.

Acknowledgements

Never in my wildest dreams did I understand the magnitude of all the people that would willingly open their hearts for me during my search. For that, I'm filled with gratitude.

To my brother Mark Hobson, thank you for pushing me to find the truth. My sister Susan DeLane-WOW, what a ride! Thank you for your great verbiage on the back cover, being by my side-through tears, laughter and crazy adventures. Carolyn would be pleased with the power of three.

To my extraordinary mother Irene Coker, my love for you is as long as I am old. Thank you for your support, unconditional love, companionship and amazing help with the back of my book.

To my little guy that started it all, Matt McCoy, you grew into an exceptional man, husband and father. Thank you for the perfect cover picture and I'm so grateful for your editing, input, superb computer knowledge and patience with your not so computer savvy mother. To my beautiful daughter-in-law Heather McCoy, thank you for your ideas, editing and encouragement, you're the best. To my precious grandchildren Emerson and Hudson McCoy, thank you both for sacrificing your grandma time so I could write. I love you all more than words can describe.

Bonnie B., you have a special place craved in my heart. Michael Mansur, what a profound connection. Thank you for your intuitive insight and continual guidance. To Anjuli, thank you for your intuitive help and reassurance. I'm truly grateful to you both.

A deep appreciation to my editor Sally Rains, thank you for your friendship, time, expertise and swift editing.

To Joyce Scott an amazing author, a heartfelt thanks to you for sharing the birth mother's side. The connection I feel toward you is pure love and admiration.

To Karen Jansz, thank you for kindness and taking the time to read my story.

My deepest gratitude goes to Shelly Gadberry, Chris Vasquez, Elizabeth Bomke, Karen Newcomb, Sharon Meyer, Geri Lennon, my baby sister Wendy DuBose–You're the best, niece Emily DuBose, sister-in-law Melody Elledge, Bobbie Christensen author of Writing, Publishing & Marketing Your 1st Book (or 7th),

Becky Pate and Merry at Central Plains Book Mfg., Rick at Mustang Graphics, and Mollie Milland at Ocean Shore Printing.

Thank you to all the kind and wonderful people who offered their help during my search.

I give my thanks and humble gratefulness to God, my guides and all the Angels that helped with divine guidance throughout my search.

Last, but by far not the least, my wonderful husband Jerry Duncan, without your love, patience and constant encouragement, would I have endured such a project. Through thick and thin you've been by my side and always believed in me. I love you.

This Incarnated World

Is it important for you
to know my existence?

Or only the fact that you
participated in my creation.

Where I am and who I am
may not merge with your Earthly plan.

But my physical essence releases the wonder
to know the details of mine.

And in my heart I know that when we
shed our human layers, the meeting will be
nothing less than divine.

So let the course be set knowing that someday
your plan will intertwine with mine.

Ckay Duncan

A Love Child's Journey

Chapter One

The day I decided to tell my parents was probably an ordinary day. Whatever the weather was doing I didn't notice. I drove to their house in a daze.

What should I say? How would they react? I tried to prepare myself but couldn't focus. Driving familiar streets on autopilot, I had no idea how the journey I was about to take would affect them. But I was determined to take it.

When I parked in front of their house my dad's truck was gone. I felt a tiny bit of relief. Mom was easier to approach and deal with. She was a mother; she would understand. So why was I still nervous?

I was a mother myself, my young son asleep in the car seat beside me. I looked down at his dark hair and olive skin, just like mine. I had to do this right. I didn't want to hurt my parents or imply that I didn't love them or was disappointed in life. Nothing could be further from the truth.

Carrying baby, diaper bag and purse, I headed for the porch that stretched the entire length of their two-story house. Mom held the screen door open. A powder blue robe bulked up her slender body while accentuating her sky blues eyes. Always cold, most days she wore a robe over her clothing. She had pinned her long hair high on her head, which increased the height of her already tall structure. Average in height, she had five inches on me and I wore the current hairstyle, a Dorothy Hamill cut but having thick hair added nothing to my height and I didn't intend to pin it up.

Her skin looked pale against mine and my dark brown hair seemed black against her blonde. We were like night and day in our appearance, but our love was mutual. I rolled my brown eyes at her whenever she reminded me how fortunate I was to have larger breasts than her. Her generation considered big breasts a great asset. Sure, some guys liked to look at them, and I assured her I'd be more than happy to give them to her if I could. I figured it was like everything else in this world: if you have it, you don't want it and if you don't have it, you want it.

After the usual soda and chitchat, the time had come.

Uncomfortable and hesitant, I said, "Mom, you know I love you and dad more than anything… but I've been thinking about it a lot and… I want to find my birth mother… Would you be okay with that?"

"Of course," she said with enthusiasm. "We know you love us. Besides, I think that would be interesting. I've often wondered about her and what she was like."

I couldn't have hoped for a better response. The disagreements we had while I was growing up had just been erased by one fully supportive comment. A heavy sigh silently eked from my mouth and the tension in my body began to relax.

Hugging her, I said, "Thanks Mom."

She held me at arms length, "If I were you, I'd want to know. I hope you can find her."

I sat down in the chair opposite as she rocked my son, "Mom, remember that single sheet of paper with my birth parents' personal statistics listed on it? You showed it to me when I was about fourteen."

Mom thought for a moment. "Yes, I have it filed away somewhere, but I think I can find it."

Recalling only bits and pieces of the information, I was anxious to see it again. But Mom's filing system was like no other. I crossed my fingers while she searched. That paper would contain important clues. For me, becoming a mother seemed to transform statistical information into a real person.

Mom returning from her room said, "Here it is, right where I thought it would be."

"That's a little scary," I quipped teasing her.

"I could put it back," she said playfully.

"No," I said quickly, "Just teasing. Can I make a copy?"

"Certainly. It's about you, but I would like it back," she said.

She leaned over my shoulder as I silently read the capitalized heading, BACKGROUND INFORMATION. There in print was the physical information about my birth and brief descriptions of the two individuals who created me. No first or last names, no city or state, only short physical descriptions, my birth mother's date of birth and my birth father's year of birth, my birth father being eight years older. The information about my birth father was vague, but for some unknown reason, at that time, I wasn't too concerned with him.

My birth mother's eyes were blue; she had blonde hair, 5'4" and described as being a very attractive person with above average intelligence. Reading that made me feel good. Not that it should have mattered, but I was glad to hear that maybe genetically I could be somewhat intelligent. Call it a boost of confidence for unknown possibilities. I wished I had inherited her blues eyes.

One thing that bothered me was her age at my birth. At thirteen, she was almost a baby having a baby. I couldn't help but wonder how my birth parents had come to know each other. Were they boyfriend and girlfriend? Why had she been with a man so much older? And why would he want an adolescent? I didn't get to go out on my first date until I was a senior in high school. And, that took a lot of begging and pleading. At thirteen, I was still beating up boys. How did she get into her predicament? Not that I didn't know how one gets pregnant, but I wanted to know what led up to her pregnancy. My mind raced with all kinds of questions.

Glancing at Mom, I wondered what she was thinking.

"Sad. She was so young," I said.

"Yes, but I'm glad we have you. Her blue eyes were tearing up."

"Me too, and I wonder… did they love my each other? Why is his information so vague?"

Mom shook her head, "It is curious."

"You know... I remember information on some television program about a closed adoption law. A law passed in the late fifties. It allows either birth mother or child to write a letter and have it put in the child's folder at the adoption agency. That way if either one contacts the agency, the letter's there for them. I thought that would be a great place to start. What do you think?"

"It's a place to begin. Yours was a closed adoption and that meant the adopted child and adopted parents had no right to any personal information regarding birth parents. Closed adoptions were standard in the fifties."

"All I can do is check it out. Thanks for your support, Mom." I hugged her tightly and gathered up my son.

Headed for home, I was still apprehensive about finding my birth mother. But when I looked over at my son, I knew I was doing the right thing. Maybe she needed to know that I was okay. The next day I'd make the call.

*   *   *

Relieved that Mom supported my decision, I hoped Dad would too.

My mind wandered on the drive home. When I was fourteen and saw my background information for the first time, I remembered it saying something about my birth mother being very attractive. As a young teen, I was into movie stars; Chad Everett was my dream guy. Since movie stars were attractive, she could have been a movie star. What fourteen-year-old female wouldn't want a movie star for her mysterious birth mother? That's where my head was then, somewhere between untainted and la la land. With no understanding of the adult predicament she had endured, my own teenage years seemed insignificant and mundane.

*   *   *

The birth of my son and my love for him made it difficult to fathom the thought of giving him up for adoption. I realized my birth mother probably had no choice. In those days at her age, there had been no other acceptable path but adoption. I applauded her for enduring the heartbreak and pain in hopes her baby would have a good life.

My parents considered me a special gift, although they may have questioned that during my teen years. At some point, I acquired the nickname Snip. But I never thought of myself as snippy, and thankfully, my parents had overlooked that character flaw. If the thought of giving Snip back had crossed their minds, (not that they could have), they kept it to themselves.

If I had given up my son, I'd want to know that he was okay and in a loving family.

I felt that my birth mother needed to know I was okay. She needed to know that her circumstances and possible heartbreaks were appreciated. I wanted to thank her.

I wondered what she looked like, if she had other children and how I came about. I wanted to hear her talk and watch her interaction with others. I wanted to see her being herself.

*   *   *

As far back as I could remember I had known I was adopted. To me the word adoption meant special, but I wasn't the only special child in my family. My older brother and my little sister were adopted too. Our little brother was the exception, a mid life surprise to my mom who delivered him at forty-one.

My big brother had been adopted first. Tall, lean and mean summed him up. At times, I'd thought my parents should have given him back, but they overlooked his flaws too. He had a different take on things. I think he felt abandoned. I once asked him if he ever thought about his birth mother. He stared down at me with his dark intense eyes and said, "If she didn't want me, why would I want to know her?"

The remark irritated me. His insensitivity swept over me like a cold wind. Did being a woman and a mother enhance the empathy I had for his birth mother? What created his lack of compassion? Possibly because he went to another family before my parents got him and maybe deep in his soul he remembers. How could he judge her, knowing nothing about her? But maybe he did think about her. And maybe it was easier to think she didn't want him. A pang of sorrow drifted through my heart as I thought of the woman I would most likely never know.

*　　　　　*　　　　　*

Like me, my little sister knew she was adopted. She seemed okay with it and hadn't asked many questions.

My little brother was a miracle and a blessing. My sister was a blessing via the adoption agency. There was no doubt, my parents ordered her. Mom wanted a blonde blue-eyed child, and she got one. The day my baby sister arrived, I got to miss school without being sick.

On Sacramento Adoption Agency's fifteenth anniversary they chose our family to appear on local television, as my parents had been one of the first couples to adopt from them.

The day of the taping, we were all nervous. Some of my nervousness came from the pink frilly dress I wore. The oversized bow under my chin looked like a clown's giant bow tie for a big performance, and I hadn't planned to perform. I was more of a jeans and T-shirt girl. But if it made Mom happy and was appropriate for the occasion, why not?

The camera crew had us lined up on the couch. My stomach churned, making it difficult to sit still. The idea of being on television sounded better than it really was. There were moments when I wanted to rip that bow off, but I didn't. Both parents were within arms reach of me.

The newsman questioned my parents first, and then turned to me, "Colette, what do your friends think about you being adopted?"

What was that suppose to mean? I didn't go around telling people I'd been adopted. I rarely thought about it. Annoyed I said, "Most of my friends don't know. We don't talk about it. They wouldn't care, anyway." He moved on to my older brother. Maybe some of my snippiness showed, but at twelve, there wasn't much to say about it. We were all relieved when the interview ended.

*   *   *

I thought about what might happen if I found my birth mother. Would I be welcome in her life and did I want to be part of hers? Would it stir up aching and painful memories that may be buried deep inside her? What if she wasn't the loving person I imagined? I was excited and frightened at the possibility of her wanting something from me I might be unable to give. I had my own family, and a mom and dad that I loved deeply. I wasn't looking for a replacement but I had plenty of room in my heart to add another. What if instead of a movie star, she was a call girl? She could be anything and I'd be okay with it. I didn't need to judge her or her lifestyle.

What if she didn't want to see me? Could I deal with that rejection? I had no idea but I would respect her decision. I'd be disappointed and hurt, but would have no choice except to honor her privacy. I had no desire to upset her current life. I'd have to wait and see. Her situation wasn't the only one on my mind. Although my Mom had been supportive, I didn't want to hurt my parents. My loyalty to them was as strong as a loving dog's and sometimes, a sense of betrayal tugged at my heart.

*   *   *

I felt uncomfortable calling the adoption agency. I had no idea what to say or ask for. I hoped the person who answered would be sympathetic. Nervous I dialed the number. My stomach felt like the Boy Scouts were having a knot-tying contest in it. Sweat beaded on my forehead as I twisted the phone cord around my fingers. The ringing stopped.

A cheerful woman said, "Good morning, Sacramento County Adoption Agency."

"Good morning... Are there any new laws that would help an adopted person locate their biological parents?" I said it in a rush, like the first horse leaving the starting gate.

After a brief silence, she replied, "You said that so fast, I want to be sure what you're asking. You want to know if there is laws that will help someone who has been adopted find their biological parent. Is that right?"

"Yes," I said with relief, looking down at the twisted phone cord that would take me an hour to untangle.

She sounded nice, as she answered, "No, there are no new laws. The agency is unable to give out names, addresses and personal information regarding biological parents."

Frustrated and trying to untangle the phone cord, I said, "I thought there was a law passed that information can be put in the adoptee's folder."

"Yes, either side is welcome to put information in their folders."

"Has there ever been a meeting arranged between two sides?"

"There have been, but the agency didn't set up the actual meetings, although they do have a protocol before such meetings can take place."

That was a comforting thought. I knew by her soothing words that she'd had this conversation with others and I appreciated her kindness and help. By now, she knew I had been adopted.

"Would you like to speak with the social worker?" she offered.

"Yes, that would be nice," I said.

"She's out of the office until this afternoon. I'll leave a message for her to call you."

"I'd appreciate that, thank you." I gave her my telephone numbers for work and home and said good-bye. The call disappointed me and I decided to leave the untangling of the cord for later. The remainder of the afternoon I ran like a gazelle whenever the phone rang, but none of the calls was the one I'd been waiting for. Patience was a virtue I would later learn.

The next day I left for work, hoping to hear from the social worker. When the call came in late morning, my heart pounded and my nervous voice crackled as if I was speaking in front of a large crowd.

Her soft voice said, "Hi, this is Marilyn from the Sacramento Adoption Agency."

I clutched the telephone as if I could pull her through the receiver that instant and have her right in front of me.

I eagerly said, "Yes Marilyn I've been waiting for your call."

"I know you have questions. Let's schedule an appointment for you. By then I'll have time to review your file and answer whatever questions I can."

Grateful that she was going to see me, but I had secretly wanted her to say more. The first available appointment was the following week. I'd wished it were sooner. Looking on the bright side, I told myself it would give me more time to think of questions. I was fooling myself, but it sounded good at the time. Asking a lot of questions doesn't mean they'll be answered.

*   *   *

The week passed quicker than I anticipated. I had taken off work early for my appointment. My mind raced with questions during the drive to the adoption agency. After parking, I sat motionless staring at the short flight of stairs that led to their door. Would my secure world change forever once I entered? Were my hopes too high? Was I opening Pandora's box? The unknown answers created a sense of excitement tangled with fear. Opening the car door, I eased my way out. I felt more like a steel rod clinging to the magnetic force of my car, a force too strong to separate. I leaned against the car wishing for a saltine cracker to calm my nervous stomach when I caught a glimpse of my son's car seat. It hit me like a hammer to my head and brought me to my senses. A reminder of why I was doing this.

The walk across the parking lot was a blur. I stopped at the bottom of the entry stairs. There were only five steps. I counted them. But it felt like the bottom of Mt. Everest. A trek I had to endure. Wishing again for a cracker, I stepped up each stair with a slow steady momentum. At the top, I paused by the door. Wiping the moisture from my forehead, I knew a dreaded trip to the dentist would be a welcome exchange. That being a comforting thought was somewhat disturbing. My heart beating like a drum, I opened the door and went in.

I'm not sure how long I sat in the waiting area listening for my name to be called. I began visualizing what would soon take place. I hoped there was a letter for me. What would it say? Would it answer my questions? Would she want to see me?

Hearing my name, I jumped up. There in front of me stood a plump kind-faced elderly woman.

Extending her hand, she gently asked, "Colette?"

Shaking her soft hand, I answered, "Yes."

"I'm Marilyn. Glad to meet you. Come with me back to my office."

Walking down the narrow hallway, a wave of comfort rolled over me. Marilyn was a soothing individual and I knew she'd had many walks down this hallway with adoptees, anticipating whatever lay ahead. I sat down across the desk from her and noticed a large folder with my first and maiden name on it. There in front of me was all the information I wanted but knew I couldn't have or see.

In a crazy moment, I thought of grabbing it and running. What would they do, besides arrest me and put me in jail? I dropped that thought. Being in arm's length of something so secretive was like putting candy in front of a child and saying don't eat, just look.

I forced myself to relax and ease back into the uncomfortable chair. Marilyn opened the folder slowly. I wished I had Superman's powerful vision and a photographic mind. I could see, read and copy that whole folder in an instant. Again I relaxed, glad that Marilyn was not telepathic. She would have considered me unstable, if not crazy.

My heart pounded and my hands were moist. Sweat would soon be dripping down the sides of my face. We stared at each other waiting for one of us to speak.

Nervous, I started. "Marilyn, after having my own child, I began thinking of my birth mother more often. You know… about how difficult the situation must have been for her. The love she must have had to want something better for me than what she felt she had to offer. I want to thank her and let her know my life is good. I hoped there might be a letter for me."

In a sympathetic voice, she said, "I went through your file… I'm sorry, but I didn't see a letter."

Saddened but not discouraged, I realized my birth mother might not have been aware that she could leave a letter. But what

I heard next hadn't been one of the scenarios that played in my head. It was totally unexpected.

Her soft voice somber, she said, "You were conceived by rape."

Disappointment and shock rushed over me.

"That's awful," I exclaimed. "I better drop the idea of finding her. Who would want to see the results of the worst thing that could happen to a woman?"

Marilyn glanced up at me, then back to the papers.

"Your birth mother and her sister were adopted by their aunt and uncle when she was two and her sister ten months. Your birth mother spent her younger years in a travel trailer as her father worked in the construction business and the family moved a great deal." Marilyn read to me without looking up.

I tried to listen to every word she said, but the word 'rape' echoed loudly in my mind over the others. That explained the vague description of my birth father.

Marilyn continued, "Your birth mother's parents were outraged when they discovered that she was four months pregnant."

Marilyn looked up at me then fell silent reading to herself.

What was she reading? What is it she can't say?

I waited quietly for her to tell me more. I almost said—say something. I felt suspended in mid air waiting for someone to let me down.

"Her parents were so embarrassed and ashamed that they immediately moved her to a home for unwed mothers. The treatment she received from them was anything but kind," she added.

Marilyn looked up and waited for me to say something. It saddened me to hear that. Not only because she was my birth mother, but also she was a child who needed love, comfort and reassurance from the people she loved. I didn't understand her parent's behavior but my heart felt her pain. They just dropped her off with strangers.

"Marilyn, how could they do that to their child, a baby herself?"

"You have to remember it was in the fifties," she answered. "Being pregnant and unmarried was not acceptable. That didn't make it right, but that's how it was."

I looked at Marilyn. "I don't think I should pursue this."

She looked straight into my eyes and said, "I think you should."

Her response took me by surprise. She must know something about the situation she couldn't tell me. Otherwise, why would she encourage me to pursue it? In the hour I spent with her, she seemed sincere and trustworthy. Not the type to encourage something she thought wasn't right. But... What was the secret she couldn't share? I had to know.

A Love Child's Journey

Chapter Two

The next day I went to work and requested a day off. I needed some time during the week. My husband wouldn't be happy at my using up vacation time. He was unhappy about the search, but I was determined to proceed. It had been a long time since I felt confident with the direction my life was taking.

Giddy with excitement, I drove downtown to the library. It felt like hunting for a map that would lead me to a hidden treasure. I was optimistic. I would look for information on rapes in early 1955. Two large newspapers were in circulation at that time. There had to be something printed.

On my rare drives downtown, I would usually be nervous about traffic, but I was searching old newspapers in my mind until I reached the library. Then panic hit me. Where could I park? Where are all the parking spots people just drive into? The parked cars were in an unbroken line. I circled the block, my hands starting to sweat. I was gripping the steering wheel so tightly a pry bar wouldn't have loosened my fingers. I circled the block a second time, hoping for two open spots. Just drive in and park, that's all I wanted. I remembered my driving test nine years earlier. I hadn't parallel parked since then. But I had done it then and I could do it now.

Then I recalled that during my test there were no cars in front of or behind me. And that was before I almost hit an armored car. The instructor hadn't yet become uncomfortable enough to scrunch part of the passenger seat between the cheeks of his butt. A memory I tried to forget. I circled the block again looking for a large opening. My focus had switched. I was racing pirates to the shore for a small opening between two huge rocks and I was going to get there first. Finally I found an open space. With a few forwards and backs, turns and in and outs, I had parked. My fingers loosened and let go of the steering wheel. I stepped out of the car to admire my accomplishment. It may not have been the best job, but I was pleased.

I turned and noticed the parking meter, which only took quarters. I had bills, not quarters. Where would I get change? If I didn't put something in the meter, I'd get a parking ticket. Between the loose change at the bottom of my purse and the glove compartment, I found enough quarters to fill the entire time slot on the machine. I walked to the library with confidence and eagerness.

The size and structure of the library captivated me. The huge old building had large uniform windows across its front. The day being cloudy lights inside glowed dimly through the magnificent windows. I could have been a scholar or a student entering a massive building of knowledge and when I left, I'd be wearing a cap and gown and holding a precious parchment validating my journey.

I pulled open the heavy glass doors enough to squeeze through. In the large entry way my body straightened with a sense of instantly acquired knowledge. I hadn't even opened a book and already I felt smarter. The first floor of the library was enormous; rows of bookshelves neatly lined down the length of the room. To my right stood wooden cabinets of card catalogs. The air was still and slightly stale. A few people at the reading tables glanced up as I walked across the noisy tiled floor to the carpeted area. I had an urge to run to the carpet, but that would have captured everyone's attention. And I could have easily slipped in the heels I wore. Then all the intelligence I acquired on walking through the door would have poured out onto the floor. I hurried instead and still maintained my composure.

The assistant at the information desk sent me upstairs to the microfiche department. Fortunately, the floor was carpet to the elevator.

"May I help you?" asked the assistant at the microfiche desk.

"I hope so. I'm looking for local newspapers that were in circulation in the early part of 1955."

"Oh yes, we have them. Have a seat at one of the viewers and I'll bring the film and show you how to use the machine."

I thanked her and headed for the viewer.

She brought me microfilm for both newspapers that covered the first three months of 1955. After she showed me how to work the machine, I began my search, confident that something would show up.

The old newspaper structure was different and everything was in black and white. The clothing seemed plain and women's hair flipped a perfect curl on the ends. It must have taken whole cans of hairspray to keep them in place. Police officers looked just like the ones on old television shows. After hours of reading and searching, I found only two rape articles. The information was vague, and didn't connect to me, but I wrote it down anyway. Emotionally drained and disappointed, I headed out the library's large glass doors. I knew that a lot of rapes weren't reported, but I needed a direction for my search. And I still didn't have one.

As the heavy glass door closed behind me, I began my own little pity party walking to my car. The only good thing about the day was my parallel parking. Nearing my car, a yellow piece of paper under my wiper caught my eye. I looked at the parking meter with its bright red background reading, "EXPIRED".

I couldn't believe it. A parking ticket! Completely wrapped up in my search, I forgot about the meter. So much for the great parking job.

*   *   *

The next day I called the adoption agency and left a message for Marilyn to call me. As the day lingered, my doubts became stronger. Maybe I wasn't meant to find my birth mother. Maybe it was for the best. I tried to convince myself of that. Waves of disappointment made it difficult to focus on my work. At least it was one of my easier workdays.

The day was almost over when I finally heard from her.

"Marilyn, I think I need to let this search go. I went to the library yesterday looking for rapes in this area, and found two. From their stories, neither one could have been my mother. I don't know where to go from here," I said disappointed.

"I understand your frustration and I'm glad to see you're trying, but what makes you think you have the right area?" she asked.

"I don't know. I just assumed that I was adopted in this area and must be from this area." It sounded lame and I felt sheepish.

"You can't assume anything. Life doesn't work that way."

"You're right, I know. So... she wasn't from this area," I said, waiting for confirmation.

"No."

I waited for her to say something else, but she didn't. I wanted to hear the rest. Where do I start searching?

"Marilyn, is the place close to here?"

"Not too far."

"What's not too far?" I asked, wishing I had a map to spout off the names of different cities and towns.

"It's north from here," she said calmly.

The tip excited me until I realized there are numerous towns and cities north of Sacramento. I wanted to reach through the phone and pull the name out of her mouth. But I knew patience and respect were the keys here.

I took a deep breath. "From my house, which freeway or highway would I take?" I asked.

There was silence on the line. What was she thinking? Would she go out on a limb and give me another hint? Did she feel that strongly about me finding my birth mother? Was she reading my file again before deciding? Did she think I was a person who could handle this situation? I didn't know, but the silence was deafening.

"You're certain you want to find your birth mother?" She asked with authority.

"I do. Yes, very much. I need to thank her, Marilyn." I hoped she believed me.

"Oildale." she said.

"Did you say Oildale?"

"Yes."

"The town of Oildale, she lived in Oildale," I asked with excitement, barely believing what I had just heard.

"Yes," she said sharply.

I knew by her tone not to ask for more, but I was happy to have a place to start. I thanked her and said I would keep in touch. Excitement was bubbling inside me, but I kept my composure. She encouraged me to keep her informed. After hanging up I ran out of my office and yelled to my co-workers that were aware of my search, "I have a town."

*   *   *

My evening routine of preparing dinner and getting my family ready for the next morning made thinking about my next move impossible. I was looking forward to work in the morning. I could concentrate on my search while doing my job too.

The next morning I parked at work and walked to the entrance. I had a town. It was a positive direction for my search. Inside the large windowed building, I passed employees who probably wondered why I looked so happy that early. It was 6:30 A.M. The smile on my face must have had them guessing. They probably thought I had a romantic evening and was still wearing the afterglow, but I was contemplating my next move.

"Good morning, Sandy" I said cheerfully entering the accounting department. I really liked my boss and she was supportive about my search and very lenient with my telephone time, which I appreciated.

She looked up from her desk. "Good morning to you."

"You weren't here yesterday and didn't get to hear my news. I have a town," I said with excitement.

"You do? That's great! Where is it and how did you get it?"

I hesitated before saying, "Well, I got it from the social worker."

The last thing I wanted to do was jeopardize Marilyn's job, but I figured she knew I'd be sharing my information. The guilty thought left me as I took a deep breath.

"So...what's the name of this town or do I have to guess?"

That's why she's the boss. Even in general discussions she speaks with authority. She was always kind, but there was no question, she was in charge. I respected that.

"Oildale."

"Wow, that's interesting. My close friend Janice and her husband graduated from Oildale High School."

"You've got to be kidding."

That was an amazing connection. My boss had close friends that went to the same high school as my birth mother. Before that connection, I hadn't given much thought on divine help. Nevertheless, at that moment, and maybe only for a moment, I wondered.

Sandy was two years younger than my birth mother; her friends had to be in high school around the same time. Wouldn't it be something if they knew each other?

"Sandy, maybe they might remember hearing about a rape. The student body couldn't have been that large."

"I'm not too sure about that. My class was pretty big. But I can give her a call for you and ask. One thing I do know. She has yearbooks."

I couldn't believe it. The morning just kept getting better.

"Do you think she'd let you borrow them and you could bring them to work with you?"

Looking down at her paperwork, she picked up a pencil and made a note. "All I can do is ask."

It was time to start work. "Thanks, that would be great," I said with appreciation.

At my desk I thought about the conversation with Sandy. Who would have thought my boss's friends went to the same high school as my birth mother. (Contentment swept through me with the reassurance I needed). I began believing this search was meant to be.

*   *   *

It had been two days since my conversation with Sandy. It was the end of the accounting cycle and a very busy time for her and the whole accounting department. However, it took all the inner strength I could muster to keep from running up to her and shouting HEY, WHAT ABOUT THOSE YEARBOOKS? I knew she understood the importance of them and would get to it when she could. That same afternoon before I left work she called me over to her desk.

"I called Janice last night. She didn't remember any rapes, but said you're welcome to look at her yearbooks. She'll be coming to our area in about a week to visit her mom. She'll drop them by my house," Sandy said hurriedly.

"That's fantastic! I know you've been busy, so I didn't want to bother you, but I was wondering if you had talked to her yet."

I was disappointed that her friend hadn't heard about any rapes, but glad they talked. My jaw muscles were sore from gritting my teeth for the last two days while waiting for news.

"I know and I'm sorry, but you know how busy it gets at the end of the month."

"Of course and thanks for calling her. Have a nice night. I'll see you tomorrow."

Outside I felt unsettled, yet excited as I walked to my car. What good were the yearbooks if I didn't have a name? I could see if I looked like anyone. First, I could eliminate all boys. That made me chuckle silently. I knew it was a fact that none of the boys was my mother. But what if I didn't look like her? I had to have a name. I needed to go to Oildale.

*   *   *

The following week I took Wednesday off work and made my first trip to Oildale. Their library might be a good starting place, although I didn't have much luck with the other one.

On the drive, I thought of what to look for at the library making the time pass quickly. There weren't that many choices. I'd look through their old newspapers for rape reports. The idea didn't inspire confidence but it couldn't hurt to look. I reminded myself that an open mind would be more productive, remembering again that the majority of rapes went unreported. Maybe the library would have old yearbooks. I'd been patiently waiting for my boss to show up with her friend's yearbooks, but an early peek would be exciting.

At the library, I didn't have to parallel park and there were no meters. The town was older but not that different from the one I lived in. After parking, I turned off the ignition and sat mesmerized by the library building. An old single story structure, which showed its age. Large trees huddled around it, but hadn't protected it from nature's harshness. I wondered how many times my birth mother had entered the tattered building. Was it a place she loved or she loathed?

On my walk to the front door, I looked down at the old sidewalk. I bet she walked this very sidewalk. Did she step on the cracks or jump over them, or was she too mature to care about the cracks in an old sidewalk? It didn't matter. All I knew was that I'd come one step closer in a town that was once her home.

I glanced through the glass door. The library was small, with rows of shelves stocked full of books. I watched an elderly woman bustling around straightening misplaced books. It looked quiet and empty except for a lone patron reading at a table.

Both heads turned as I entered. I didn't know if I made too much noise coming through the door or if they were just surprised to see someone else in the library. I smiled and walked toward the woman.

"Can I help you?" she asked quietly.

"I hope so."

"Are you looking for a specific book?"

"No Ma'am. I'm on a different search. I'm trying to find my birth mother. She went to Oildale High School in the mid-fifties. I don't know her first or last name but her father worked in the construction business." I took a deep breath and whispered, "There's a chance she was raped."

She slowly shook her head. Her wide eyes made me turn around to see if something or someone frightened her behind me. I couldn't see this woman's thoughts, but her body language gave me a good idea. I was hoping for anything I could get, even sympathy. I wanted her to know I was desperate. I didn't like sharing the idea of rape, but that's what I had been told.

Regaining her composure, she said, "I've worked at this library for years and lived here all my adult life but this is a first for me. No one else has ever come here with a quest like yours. Not that I remember anyway."

I was glad to hear that she'd lived in Oildale a long time. She would know some of the history of the town and might have ideas I hadn't thought of. I sensed wheels turning inside her head. It was comforting to have found someone for a little brainstorming. She could have said she was the librarian, not an investigator, but she didn't. I appreciated her kindness. Fresh ideas would be welcomed.

"I was thinking about old newspapers and maybe school yearbooks," I said.

"Good ideas, and you might also check out construction companies. I don't believe there were many around at that time. If I were you, I'd go to the City Hall and ask them which companies were working construction in the area at that time. It's just a thought. I'll get the yearbooks for you. You can start with them."

She walked to the back of the library. City Hall was a good idea. Everything was on public record and I was happy to have another place to check out. With the name or names of construction companies, maybe I could get my hand on a list of employees. My job as a payroll clerk sent a chilling flash through my wishful thinking. Confidential information on employees was not available to the public. But I would cross that bridge when I came to it. I watched the librarian walk toward me with a grin and a stack of books.

Handing me the yearbooks, she said, "I hope you find something."

I knew from her smile that it was heartfelt and I appreciated her help.

For a moment, I stood staring at the yearbooks. Somewhere in at least one of them was a picture of my birth mother. It gave me a sense of moving forward. I sat down, both excited and fearful.

21

What if I actually found her picture? What would I do then? Was it a good or bad thing? At the sound of metal rubbing metal, I looked up to see the library door closing behind the other patron. He had left. I turned back to the yearbooks and organized them by year. She would have started her freshman class a few of months before I was born. I didn't think they allowed pregnant girls in public schools at that time, married or not. My school didn't. Did her parents keep her home or did she go to a continuation school that allowed pregnant girls to attend? Did continuation schools exist in 1955? I started with the freshman. It was interesting looking at the differences in the clothing styles from my own yearbook. These girls had full skirts, tight sweaters and scarves tied neatly around their necks. No one in my class would have been caught dead in an outfit like that. Soon I realized these yearbooks, unlike mine, had group pictures. Except for the senior pictures.

It was difficult to see individual details in the group pictures. I knew she was in one of them. I looked at each group for some resemblance to myself. Then I remembered that she was a blue-eyed blonde. Very different from me, I was a brown-eyed brunette. But all the pictures were in black and white. Some people had lighter hair, but there was no way to tell eye color. The faces were too small to detect moles. I had very distinct moles on my face. My dad told me they were beauty marks. I liked hearing that. It made me feel beautiful.

Without a name, finding anything in the yearbooks was a long shot. But the pictures intrigued me. I tried to imagine which teenagers were her friends. Did she feel close enough to any of them or have a special friend to share her secret? Did she like sports? After experiencing something as grownup as childbirth, maybe high school was something to get through, not enjoy. To a lot of people, the high school years are some of their best memories of growing up. But she had been raped before she had finished the eighth grade. My heart felt heavy with sadness for her. I wished she had never been raped, but then, of course, I wouldn't be here. All the more reason to find her and thank her for giving me life. And for having the courage to give me up for adoption so a family could love me the way she wanted me loved.

I wanted her to know that something wonderful came out of it. Not that I was all that wonderful, but I sure did feel loved. My adopted parents were more than anyone could have asked for. She needed to know that the ultimate sacrifice of a mother—giving—up her baby—was the best of all gifts to another woman longing for a child. And the gift she wanted her child to have, a stable home with loving parents did happen.

I checked the wall clock. If I wanted to stop by City Hall before going home, I'd have to look at old newspapers another time. That was a long shot, anyhow. As I put my coat on, the librarian walked over to me.

"How did you do with the yearbooks?" she asked.

"Honestly, I can't really tell too much from the pictures." Did I sound as defeated as I felt?

"It would be helpful if you had a name."

"Yes, I know. But I don't have that yet." I looked at the clock again.

"Oh my, if you're going to City Hall you better hurry."

"Thank you so much for your help. My boss's friend has these yearbooks too, so I'll be able to look at them again. I can take a closer look then."

Who was I kidding? I went through all the books with close scrutiny and came up with nothing. It was all I could do for now.

She gave me a quick smile as I left the library. A kind woman, she seemed to take great pride in her job. I hurried back to my car over the cracked sidewalk that I earlier strolled over. The Librarian gave me directions to City Hall, but by the time I got there, the office had already closed. It disappointed me. I would come back another day or give them a call. Exhausted and melancholy, I sat in my car in the empty parking lot. I didn't know what else to do and didn't feel like thinking about it anymore that day. I would call Marilyn and tell her what I didn't find and ask more questions. Which questions, I wasn't sure. But tomorrow was another day.

A Love Child's Journey

Chapter Three

The next morning I was in no hurry to go to work, I was exhausted from the day before. I knew I had to change my attitude or I wouldn't get anywhere in my search. But it was hard to be optimistic while looking for someone without a name. The librarian had been patient and understanding. Did I seem crazy to her at first? Oh yes, can you help me? I'm looking for my mother. She's blonde, blue-eyed and beautiful. Can you help me find her? Oh and there is a possibility that she was raped and her father worked in construction. I couldn't believe this woman didn't laugh at me or call the police. Time to snap out of my self-pity and think of questions to ask Marilyn. I bundled up my son, grabbed his diaper bag and headed for my car. Backing out of the driveway, my sleepy eyed son in the back seat was so precious I couldn't imagine anyone else loving him as much as I did. Considering my own life however, I knew it was possible. I had been loved, cherished and I always felt safe. Especially after my dad made sure there were no spiders on my walls at bedtime. My birth mother didn't know the love I received. The only way she would know was for me to find her and tell her.

*   *   *

After dropping my son off at his babysitters, I turned on the car radio for some upbeat music on my way to work. I flipped through the stations, pleased to hear a favorite song playing. It was about a guy on a horse that didn't have a name. The longer I listened to that song, the more I thought about my search. The horse may not have had a name, but at least the guy had the horse. I didn't have a name or the horse. That made me laugh. It felt better than crying.

I had a busy day at work, but now and then thought about new areas to direct my search. I'd decided not to contact Marilyn for the time being. I wanted to exhaust all my options before calling her and wasn't sure that I had. I needed to show her I was very serious about this journey. How amazing that she encouraged my search, knowing about the rape. But I was glad she did. At lunchtime, I sat alone to eat without my co-workers thinking of a search plan. But that didn't last long.

"What, you don't like us anymore?" Darla yelled across the lunchroom in her New Jersey accent.

"Yeah, why are you sitting over there?" Sally piped in.

"Okay, Okay," I said, picking up my lunch and walking to their table.

"Why were you sitting by yourself?" Darla asked.

"Well... I need to come up with some new ideas for my search." I looked down at my half-eaten sandwich.

"Hey, how was your trip yesterday? Did you find out anything?" Sally asked, interested. Assertive but always kind, fashion was her talent.

"I'd say she didn't get much or we would have heard about it this morning," said Darla.

It was like the morning news when I entered the accounting department every morning. I shared every new bit of information I had. Everyone had been busy this morning and I hadn't felt like sharing bad news. Or worse yet, no news.

"I didn't find anything. I looked at old yearbooks. The same yearbooks Sandy's friend has. I didn't make it to the City Hall before they closed," I said, disappointed.

They knew I'd been waiting to see the yearbooks.

"How did it feel being in the town where your birth mother lived or maybe still does?" asked Sally, eyes wide with wonder.

"Yeah, that part felt good, I have to admit," I said.

"What were you looking for at the City Hall?" asked Darla.

"Names of construction companies that worked in the area at that time. Her family moved around a lot, so I figured there had to be some project going on in Oildale at that time for them to be there."

"What about the Oildale Dam?" Sally said loud and excited.

"I thought about that and wondered when the dam was built."

"So that's one thing you have to check out," she said optimistic.

"We're on a roll now," added Darla with confidence.

Lunchtime was over and we headed back to our desks. The time had passed quickly for all of us. Sally and Darla were eager to help. They both let me know they would be thinking of ideas for me. I was glad I hadn't eaten my lunch alone. On my afternoon break I would call the City Hall in Oildale and ask them about the dam and construction companies.

*   *   *

It was just about time for afternoon break when I heard a loud clip clop coming toward me. Who was running in high heels? The company had the floor polished often, which meant anyone running in high heels was definitely taking their life in their own hands. Due to the confidentiality of my work, I sat behind a partitioned wall, with a half door. I couldn't see who was running. Out of curiosity I got up and walked to the door. Sally braked to a sudden stop and held on tight to my door until she regained her balance.

"Are you okay?" I asked her.

"Yes, I'm fine. Hey, I have another idea for you."

"Sure," I said quietly. I could see Sandy, looking at us from her desk, but she didn't give me the get busy look. She knew it was close to break time. I think Sally running concerned her. I turned my attention back to Sally.

"What's your idea? I asked, pleased that she had already found one.

By now, I'd settle for anything. I hadn't come up with any new ideas since lunch. I was thinking about it. Probably too hard. Sally's face was lit up like a Christmas tree.

"What about your birth certificate?" She said with an ear-to-ear grin.

"My birth certificate? It has my adopted parents' name on it."

"But what about the doctors' names and the place where you were born?"

"I can't remember the details, but that's a good idea. I didn't think about my birth certificate because it changed when I was adopted. I don't think they'd change the other information, only the mother and father's name," I said, hopeful.

Sally pleased, "I'll keep thinking." You need to call Oildale City Hall."

"Thanks Sal, I really appreciate it."

She smiled and walked back to her desk.

I called information and got the number. I sat there a minute planning the right questions to ask, hoping for a new lead. When I dialed the number, my heart pounded listening to each ring at the other end.

"Good afternoon, Oildale City Hall," said a young woman.

"Yes, I'm looking for some information about construction companies that would have been working in Oildale in the mid-1950's," I blurted. So much for planning.

"Boy, I don't know the answer to that question, but let me see if I can find someone to help you," she said.

It seemed like I was on hold forever. Break time would be over soon. And I'd hoped I wouldn't be interrupted or forced to hang up with a work-related issue. A voice finally came on the line.

"Yes, you wanted the names of construction companies operating in Oildale in the-mid 50's," asked a woman who sounded much older than the first.

"Yes ma'am and could you tell me if that's when the dam was built?'

"The dam was built before then. I do remember hearing of a company called Walton Construction. They built the water tunnels in the area. May I ask why you need this information?" she sounded puzzled.

"Well... I'm trying to find my birth mother and her father worked in the construction business in Oildale in 1955. I thought if I could get the names of the construction companies, I might be able to get a list of their employees," I said, a little hesitant.

Her tone softened. "I see. Like I said, I heard of Walton Construction, but for the others I'll have to check our archives. Give me a few days and call me back, maybe I'll have some names for you. Ask for Doris."

I thanked her and hung up, pleased that she was willing to help. Staring at the blank wall in front of me, I replayed the events of my search. Everyone tried to help me. The information wasn't much greater now than at the beginning of the day, but I felt better. And I had the name of one Construction Company. But that wasn't why I felt so good. It was the kindness shown me. I was truly fortunate and full of appreciation.

* * *

I couldn't wait for my son's bedtime. I wanted to study my birth certificate without interruptions. My certificate seemed small compared to his. The information looked the same, but the paper was black with white writing. I studied it closely, wondering what my original birth certificate said. What did they put in the father's space? Probably "unknown" since my birth mother had been raped. What did the hospitals do with original birth certificates? Did they send them to the County's Vital Statistics office? Did I have a name before my adoption? What was my first name? Would I have preferred it to the one I have? Not that I didn't like my first name, it just wasn't a common one. What name would I have wanted? I always liked the name Jancy when I was younger.

I was in a foster home for two months before my adoption; they must have called me something. Some foster homes had more than one baby at a time. I couldn't imagine them calling us Baby One or Baby Two because if Baby One left, Baby Two would become Baby One. Okay, that was silly, but I really wanted to know my original name, especially the last name. That was the key. That would make my search so much easier. I wrote down the name of the doctor who delivered me along with the aide's name. I was so tired I decided to continue in the morning. I put everything down and headed for bed.

*   *   *

I left for work early the next morning. I didn't have the Sacramento phone book, but my work place did. I wanted a chance to search for the names before starting work. Settling down at my desk, I opened the book to the doctor's name and found a listing. Butterflies tickled the lining of my stomach. I wrote down the phone number and address. There were only initials, so I couldn't tell if it was a man or a woman doctor. I found two listings with the same name as the aide. I couldn't believe it. I had two more leads to check out. I sat back in my chair and sighed.

"Did you find out anything else?" Sally yelled over the partition. It startled me.

My heart began beating at a rapid tempo. I was so engrossed I hadn't heard anyone enter the large office.

"Sally, you scared me. I didn't hear you come in."

Not at all concerned, she said, "Sorry. But did you find anything else?

Sally stood outside my half-door. I walked over to her. She wasn't allowed in my work area. I opened the door and followed her to her desk, thankful that she didn't break into a run.

"Okay, what did you find out?" she asked with excitement.

"Not that much, but I do have some leads."

"Did you look at your birth certificate?"

"Yes. Like I said before, it has my adopted parents' name on it, but I did get the doctor and the aide's name off it," I said, pleased with my find.

"No kidding? Did you find them in the phone book?" she asked, her excitement growing.

"Yes, that's what I was thinking about when you scared the life out of me."

"Yeah, sorry about that. So what are you going to do?"

"Think about it! How many babies do you think this doctor has delivered? It's been twenty-five years since I was born. Do you really think the doctor is going to remember either my birth mother or me?" I felt discouraged.

"Well, remember she was a rape victim and she was pretty."

"Yes, but I wonder if the doctor even knew about the rape. And you and I both know that you don't exactly look your best while you're in labor with a baby."

"You're right about that," she agreed.

We were both silent. I had names and a number, but the odds of a doctor remembering my birth mother were like finding the needle in a special haystack. I wondered if the doctor ever had anyone ask that question. I probably wouldn't even be able to talk to the doctor but maybe I should try.

"I need to get busy and work, Sally."

"Yeah, me too."

I hurried back to my desk. I needed to gather the leads I had, and think of some new questions and give Marilyn a call. But for now I needed to get busy and work.

*   *   *

The day passed quickly. It had been a busy day and I was thankful. Having a lot of work to do made it easy for me not to dwell on the progress of my search. I got into my car and took a deep breath; I was looking forward to the drive home. I needed some quiet time. I thought about my search with the yearbooks and the woman I talked to from Oildale City Hall. I thought about the doctor's name on my birth certificate.

"Okay," I said out loud. "I have three leads, but I want more questions to ask Marilyn."

I was facing forward, but I had a strong urge to glance around and see if anyone was looking at me. I knew they couldn't hear me, but they could see my lips moving and my hand waving about. My hands moved every time I talked, even if I was driving. I looked around there was no one near me. Talking gave order to my thoughts, but I decided to just think and not speak.

The questions I would ask Marilyn had to be answered with either a yes or no. Her hands were tied with legal obligations and I would never expect her to jeopardize her job. Thinking about the yearbooks, I wondered if my birth mother's sister was in high school during the same times. I knew she was younger, but how much younger? That would be a good place to start with Marilyn. Asking questions about my biological mother's relationship with her sister and maybe her parents. That satisfied me.

Pulling into my babysitter's driveway, I decided not to think about my search at all and just enjoy my family. Tomorrow was a new day. I would call Marilyn first thing in the morning.

*   *   *

Refreshed, I walked toward my office building in the morning. I had a great night with my family and a good night's sleep. I usually had a hard time turning off the day's events when I went to bed at night, but not last night. Today I was ready to move forward. I couldn't wait to call Marilyn. I had put it off longer than I wanted because I didn't want to bother her too much. Her job began an hour later than mine. The hands on the clock seemed to stand still. I was like a kid waiting for recess, listening for the bell and preparing to be the first to grab the only basketball.

I tried to busy myself with my usual morning tasks, but found myself sitting motionless while thinking about my upcoming conversation with Marilyn. I prepared a short list of questions, but was unsure if I would get any answers.

Startled by the sudden ringing of my phone, I jumped like a frightened deer as I leaped to answer it, "Good morning, Payroll Department."

"Good morning to you, this is Marilyn," she said with a cheery inflection.

I was so thrilled to hear her voice on the other end I almost fell off my office chair, "I was just about to call you. I can't believe it's you," I said with excitement.

"I'm glad I can make someone happy so early in the day. I've been thinking about you too. I hadn't heard from you and was wondering how your search is going."

My stomach began to ache. It almost mirrored the first time I saw her. I didn't know if it was fear of asking my questions or the painstaking response I might get. I studied my first question, and then looked down at my wastebasket in case my stomach rebelled.

"I do have some questions for you," I said, taking a deep breath to calm my nerves.

"I'll do the best I can with them." She sounded calm.

She had a soothing way of communicating. That's why she did so well in her line of work. I decided to update her before plunging into my questions.

"I went to the Oildale library a few days ago. I looked at old yearbooks, but didn't see anyone in them that looked like me. And without a name it seemed useless." I reviewed my list of questions.

"That would be difficult," she said with compassion.

"I called City Hall and asked about the names of different construction companies working at that time. I got one name- Walton Construction Company. Does that sound familiar?" I boldly asked.

"Yes," she said without pausing.

My heart pounded. Did she say yes? Of course she did. Maybe that's the company I'm looking for, but I had to be sure.

"Would Walton Construction be the company I'm looking for?" I squinted my eyes as if she could see me asking such a brazen question.

"Yes," she quickly said.

I knew by her speedy response to move on to the next question. I wanted to spin around on my office chair, but then I would have really needed the trashcan.

"I was looking at my birth certificate and noticed the doctor's name and the aide's name. Would contacting those individuals be helpful to me?" I asked with doubt.

"No," she said sharply.

Okay, I got a no. Should I ask something else or stay on this birth certificate issue. I hoped she would let me know when to move on.

"Is there a good reason why I shouldn't try and contact the doctor?"

"Yes."

"Can you tell me that?" I was getting into the flow of this question and answer game. I wanted to be the winner. I wanted answers to all my questions. To win the game, I needed wise and concise questions and no giving up at unwanted answers.

"You were born in a home for unwed mothers called Fairhaven," she conceded.

I couldn't believe my ears. She told me where I was born. If I jumped up and down, I wouldn't be able to continue my questions. The phone might fall on the floor and we'd be disconnected. I had to restrain myself. I didn't want her to feel uneasy about giving me information. I loved the answers I was receiving in this game. One thing I understood was not to dwell too much on the answers. Just move on to the next. So I did.

"I know that my birth mother had a sister, but I don't know their age differences. Do you know it?" I asked my last question with confidence.

"I'm not sure. I'll have to get your file out and check. Can you hold on a minute?"

"Sure." I could hold forever for the answers I needed.

I heard her lay the phone receiver down on her desk. Flicking my pencil back and forth in a nervous rhythm, I heard her voice, but she was muttering to herself. I over-heard her say "Lacy... May.... as though searching for a file. I couldn't believe it. Then again in a slow precise tone, "Lacy... May... here it is," I heard her say. I was so excited. The sensation of a super ball inside me started bouncing from the top of my head to the bottom of my toes, back and forth. I wanted to run and leap and yell wildly. I calmed down as I heard her pick up the phone.

"Okay, your birth mother was just over a year older than her sister," she said, a little winded.

"So she was most likely about a year behind in school," I added knowing better than to mention what I just overheard. Was my birth mother's name Lacy and her sister's name May or the other way around? It was on the tip of my tongue, but I knew that wouldn't work. That wasn't part of the game.

"Yes, that would be correct, one year behind your biological mother," she said.

"Thanks for your help, Marilyn. I'll check out these new leads and keep you informed. Talk with you soon," I said, as if I'd heard nothing more than her responses to my questions.

I couldn't hang up the phone fast enough before jumping up and down. After a quick hop I ran to my door and yelled, "I have two names."

It didn't matter who heard me; in fact, I wanted everyone to hear me.

I yelled again. "I have two names. I'm not sure if it's two people or just one, but I have names."

Everyone in the office clapped and cheered. I was elated. I finally had names. Only first names, but nonetheless it was a big step forward in my search.

The rest of the day was a blur. I thought about the names I had overheard, the place where I was born and the company name that employed my birth mother's father. It was a great day. Grabbing my purse to go home, the list of questions that I had for Marilyn fell. Glancing at it, I realized I had forgotten a few questions. The excitement of hearing the names stopped me. A childish belief that she had the ability to reach in my ears and take back the names scared me. After that, I wanted to end the call. I would think of more questions and call her in a few days. For now, I had new leads to concentrate on.

A Love Child's Journey

Chapter Four

I spent the next few days contemplating what to do with the information I had. It was like the excitement of becoming engaged and writing my soon-to-be new name on every blank piece of paper that crossed my path. Only it wasn't *my* name I was writing.

It was *Mrs. Lacy Whatever, Lacy Whatever, Lacy May Whatever, Mrs. Lacy May Whatever* and so on. I wrote each variation in large, small, blocked and slanted letters. I hadn't yet tried curlicues or calligraphy. Sometimes I wondered how she felt about her name and what sort of handwriting she had. I liked her name. Was it a nickname or shortened from something else?

The names were the best leads I had since the beginning of my search, but I wasn't sure what to do next. I had the first name of my birth mother and possibly her middle name or her sister's first name. I had the name of the place where I was born and the name of the construction company that employed her father. I wondered which direction would bring me closer to finding her.

Either the cramping of my hand from writing or the fact that I needed to do something moved me forward in my search. I decided to make another trip to Oildale. That's where she had lived, gone to school and been raped.

Oildale City Hall would be my first stop. Maybe someone there would have information on Walton Construction. Then I'd go by the library and look at the yearbooks again. I had all but given up on getting them from my boss's friend. I also needed to find out if the high school kept information on students dating back to the mid-fifties. I was eager to get going on my search.

The last few days had seemed like a treadmill; walking-but getting nowhere. I wanted to jump off and charge ahead.

Passing Sandy's desk at the end of my workweek, I asked for the following Wednesday off. All week I looked forward to the weekend. But I was hoping this one would pass like a jet stream —— I wanted it to be the following week. Better yet, I wanted it to be Wednesday.

*   *   *

On Monday morning rays of a rising sun lit the sky as I drove to work. It was going to be a beautiful day. March had arrived and I was ready for spring. The weekend had been pleasant; lunch with my mom was always enjoyable. I kept her updated on my search, and it was nice to sit down and mull things over with her. She agreed with my idea of going back to Oildale. Her reassurance boosted my confidence.

In the accounting office, Sandy was busy working. Her position called for long hours. I guess that's one of the disadvantages of being a boss.

"Good morning." She said in a cheery voice. "Did you have a nice weekend?"

"Actually, I did. How about you?" I wondered why she was so perky this early in the morning.

"Yep, me too. A friend of mine I hadn't seen in a while stopped by and we had a nice visit."

I opened the half door to my workspace. "I am glad to hear that."

"She brought me something, too."

It hit me like a brick. I knew why she was so chipper. I looked back at her desk, then at her. She grinned.

I slammed through my office half door like a sprinter at the finish line. There they were on my desk.

"The yearbooks" I said, trying to curb my excitement. "You got them."

"Yeah, I was beginning to wonder if she was ever going to bring them. I'm sorry it took so long. I know you've been anxious to see them."

"You couldn't have done any more than you did. I'm just glad to have them. It saves me a trip to the library when I go back again. Thank you so much and I'll be careful with them."

"I know you will, that's why you have them. Now, I've got to get back to work."

With fifteen minutes before work started, I sat down and opened the 1956/1957 yearbook.

I went to the sophomores first. I'd planned to write down all the sophomore girls with a first initial of L and their last names.

Then, I'd go through all the freshmen girls with a first initial of M and their last names. Maybe I could find matching last names for two girls. I still wasn't sure if May was the name of Lacy's sister, but it was a place to start.

If that didn't work, I'd add all the freshmen and sophomore girls to the list. I stared at the pictures wishing she would pop out like a paper doll. She had to be on one those pages, but I didn't know which one.

It was going to take me a long time to go through them. I'd have to do it at home; there wouldn't be time at work. One of these days I'd be able to open the yearbook and turn right to her page.

I flipped to the faculty, wondering if any of the younger teachers still taught there. I would ask at the high school. Right after City Hall.

*   *   *

I thought Wednesday would never come, but it did. I'd hoped for a nice day to make the drive easier, but it was overcast and cloudy. I didn't let that influence me. I was determined to come back home with something, anything of value. I planned to arrive at City Hall when they first opened, but sporadic bouts of rain slowed me down.

I couldn't remember the name of the woman I spoke with, but I remembered her voice. I forgot to call and make sure she'd be working. I'd deal with that when I got there.

A little off schedule because of the weather, I arrived at City Hall. When I was there before, mine was the only car on the lot. Now half the spaces were full. A good sign. I grabbed my notebook and umbrella and headed for the door.

"Is it raining hard?" asked a young woman inside the building.

"Not too bad." Closing my umbrella, I said, "More of a continuous drizzle."

"I'm tired of the rain," she said. "I'm ready for spring."

"Me too."

"Can I help you?"

"I hope so. I called a couple of weeks ago and asked about construction companies working in Oildale in the mid-fifties. I believe I spoke with you first, and then another woman. She gave me the name of Walton Construction. I forgot her name. I'm looking for more information regarding that company."

"Have a seat. I know who she is."

"Thank you."

I looked at city maps on the walls and old pictures of the dam construction. Not a job I'd want to do.

"Walton Construction was the one you needed?" said an older woman approaching me.

I recognized her voice. "Yes. I really appreciate your help. I was wondering if you or someone else knows where I can get more information about that company?"

"They built most of the water tunnels. When I was inquiring, I was told you should check with the Oildale Water Resources. I have a name and number for you." She handed me a slip of paper.

"That's great, thanks."

"Good luck on your search."

"Thank you."

When I walked out the door, the rain had stopped. I was disappointed at not getting more information on Walton

Construction but grateful for a new lead. I'd forgotten to ask her name.

I looked at the name on the paper and decided to call him later, after going to the high school. If I didn't get there before lunch, the person I needed to speak with might be gone or busy eating. I hurried out and took off.

*   *   *

I parked in a visitor area at the high school. For a moment, I stared at the old building. My birth mother had gone there, but I wasn't thinking about that. Schools are like trees. They seem to last forever. Is it what they represent or the sturdiness of their structure?

This school gave the impression of not having changed in recent years. It was old. Did it look the same as when my birth mother was a student?

I got out and found the administration office. It was full of students and busy staff. Some students were waiting; some helping and a few seemed angry or unhappy to be there.

Eight years had passed since I graduated from high school, but I began to have the same uneasy feeling I used to get when I walked into the office. That was where the girls and boy's Dean, Vice Principal and Principal had their offices. Places most students didn't care to visit.

I walked over to the desk with a 'secretary' sign on it.
The woman sitting at it was busy talking on the telephone, so I stepped back and waited.

"May I help you?" she asked hanging up the phone.

I hadn't thought about what to say or how much to say about my search. I hesitated then said, "I hope so."

She was middle-aged, and seemed to take her job seriously and looked very busy. Would she be compassionate and sensitive? She had to deal with teenagers on a daily basis. My optimistic attitude began to fade.

"I'm searching for my mother who was a student here either late in 1955 or the beginning of 1956. I don't know if you keep records from that far back or if there are any teachers still here who taught back then."

"Yes, we do keep records of all past students. They're on film, but we have them. I think you need to speak with Mr. Palmer. He's been here years." She picked up her ringing telephone, motioning for me to wait.

I waited for her to finish the call, wondering what she thought. I couldn't tell. Who was Mr. Palmer? She finished her call, but didn't hang up.

"I'll try and get hold of Mr. Palmer. Have a seat and I'll see if I can locate him."

"Who's Mr. Palmer?"

"He's the principal. I should be able to catch him before he leaves for lunch."

The Principal! No one wants to see him. You only see the principal when you're in trouble.

I walked slowly toward four chairs attached together lined up against the wall. All the students but one had left.

He sat slumped on the far right chair, legs extended out as far as they could reach. His attitude spilled over onto the areas surrounding him. I detoured around his leg barrier and sat on the chair farthest from him. When I smiled at him, he didn't react.

Here I was, sitting in the office waiting for the principal. I felt like sinking down in my own chair. My heart thumped like a loud drum. I glanced at the sullen student, could he hear my heart thumping or feel its vibration through the chairs? He didn't move a muscle, didn't even blink. I assumed he was alive.

I had to remind myself that I was there for information, not for being in trouble. Two female students passing by looked my way and whispered together. Surely they knew I was a visitor? I looked down for a quick button, zipper and nylon check. Now the person I waited for couldn't get there fast enough.

To my surprise, the sullen student suddenly sat up in his chair and pulled in his legs. I followed his gaze.

Walking toward us was a middle-aged man with a confident gait. I straightened up too. It was catching. The suit he wore looked like funeral garb. His stark white shirt and dark tie only strengthened that image. Maybe it helped intimidate rowdy students. Some students might think they were going to their own funeral if they had to go and see him. The suit fitted his position.

"I hope you haven't waited long. I'm Mr. Palmer, the principal," he said with a pleasant smile.

"No, not long. Thank you for seeing me," I realized I forgot to introduce myself.

"Let's go to my office," he said.

I reached down to pick up my purse.

"I'll talk with you later," he said to the sullen student.

I followed him down a narrow hallway. He stopped and looked back at me. A checkpoint I guess, making sure I followed him. How many students had run the other way? My nervousness settled. He opened a door and ushered me inside. I better be direct with such a right-to-the point person.

"My secretary said you're searching for your mother who was a student here some time ago," he said, waving me to a chair and sitting in the one beside me. I was glad he didn't sit on the other side of the desk.

"Yes, she would have been a freshman in the 1955/1956 school year. She had a sister a year younger. I know her first name and her sister's first name or maybe her first and middle name. I'm not sure which but I know her father was employed with Walton Construction," I said.

"I see."

"The secretary told me you keep all the student records on film."

"Yes, that's right."

"And I was wondering if there are any teachers still here who taught back then?"

"I'd just started teaching at that time, but I don't recall most of the students. There are a few others who taught then, but I doubt if their memories are any better. "

"What about the information you have on film?

"Yes, we do have film, but everything's in alphabetical order. If you have a last name, I can find information on her.

"That's the problem; I don't have a last name."

"Then I have one possibility: Mrs. Kelly. She lives in the area. Maybe you'd like to talk with her?"

41

"I'll talk with anyone. Who is she?"

"She was the girls' dean back then."

"I'd love to speak with her. Do you think there's a possibility I could see her today while I'm still in town?"

"She doesn't live far from here and she doesn't get around too well so she's usually home. Let me give her a call."

"Thanks. I really appreciate that. But first, there's something I want to tell you. I'm adopted and the woman I'm looking for is my birth mother."

He nodded, "And what will you do if you find her?"

A good question. "Meet her, I hope, if I can. Maybe get to know her. If she's not interested, at least I'll have tried."

"That's sensible and you seem determined. I wish you luck."

"There's more."

He looked surprised. "Oh?"

"I was conceived by rape."

He looked away, then back. "I'm sorry to hear that."

"It's okay. I'm glad to be alive. And my adopted family's wonderful. I'm very fortunate."

He smiled. "You have a great attitude. I hope your mother appreciates you when you find her. I'll make that call I promised."

He searched for the telephone number. I was disappointed that I couldn't access the records but maybe I'd get some information from this Mrs. Kelly. The girls' dean would have known about unusual events, especially a rape.

I watched him dial the number, crossing my fingers. He began talking on the phone and then smiled at me, a good sign. My tension drained.

He hung up. "She'll talk with you. She asked that you give her about an hour before coming by." He smiled.

"That's great. Thank you so much for your help." I reached out to shake his hand.

"Oh, I almost forget." He shook my hand. "You said Walton Construction, right?"

"Yes."

"One of my neighbors worked for them. If you want, I can check with him to see if he knows anything."

"That would be wonderful."

He gave me the address, phone number and directions to Mrs. Kelly's house. His help amazed me. The principal, the one person in school I would least expect to be kind and understanding. Underneath that scary title and mortician's suit was a caring man.

I gave him my name and phone number. He walked me out to the main office, and said goodbye. Then he turned and walked toward the sullen student. What a guy! One minute a Clark Kent, and the next a Superman. I was glad to have met him.

*   *   *

I stopped at a small hamburger stand for lunch. I was glad Mrs. Kelly wanted me to wait an hour. All my running around had made me hungry. I took my time and reviewed the day's events while eating. After checking my watch, I headed for Mrs. Kelly's house.

The principal was right. She lived very close to the school. The drizzly rain had stopped and the sun was trying to peek through overcast clouds but it wasn't cold out. I parked by her house and could see her sitting on her front porch bench. She probably spent a lot of hours on that bench. The house was small but quaint. A picket fence bordered her property and flowers had started blooming along her walkway.

She was smiling and wore a nice dress. That's why she needed an hour. She had to dress up for company.

In her mid to late 80's, her hair was snow white, but it was obvious that she went to the beauty shop on a regular basis. She probably didn't have many visitors.

"Thank you for seeing me, Mrs. Kelly," I said, walking up to the porch.

"Oh, you're welcome. Have a seat. She pointed to a small chair across from her.

I thought she'd invite me inside, but realized this is where she felt most comfortable. She didn't know me. For all she knew, I could have been a crazy woman, especially if she had talked with the local librarian I met.

I explained my situation, hoping she would recall something. But I could see by the disappointment on her face there wasn't much to get.

"I'm sorry dear, I don't recollect hearing of any rapes. They don't always get reported, of course. A few girls got pregnant every now and then, but I don't recall their names." She looked apologetic at letting down the lone visitor she was more than happy to have.

"That's all right. It was a long time ago," I tried to sound upbeat.

It would have been rude to leave so soon. A lovely woman, she had dressed for company, so I went along with it.

We spent an hour together with me listening to her stories about life as a girl's dean. Her face lit up with each new story.

"Mrs. Kelly, it's time for me to head home," I finally said, trying not to disappoint her too much.

"I know. I'm sorry if I bored you with all my old stories, dear." She sounded embarrassed.

"Don't be silly. They were wonderful. Thank you for sharing them with me." I bent down to hug a woman who must have been a pillar of strength in her earlier years, but was now frail and lonely.

I turned to wave goodbye from her walkway. She had seen my birth mother at school, maybe just in passing, but I was sure of it. But that memory was mixed in with all the others. I was so close, yet still so far away from finding her.

* * *

It had been a full day and I was tired. I had two new leads. I should have been excited but I couldn't muster up much enthusiasm. It was a somber drive back home.

I would call Marilyn in the morning and tell her what I didn't find. My search still felt like a dog chasing its tail, around and around, going nowhere. Maybe a good night's sleep would give me new ideas and rekindle my enthusiasm.

A Love Child's Journey

Chapter Five

Staying awake on my way to work was an effort. I'd hoped for a good night's sleep, but as hard as I tried not to think about my next conversation with Marilyn, the more it stayed on my mind. All this detective work was draining the energy needed for my own family. I wanted to cut to the chase. I wanted my mother's full name. My patience was fading, I was tired and I didn't know if my leads would get me anywhere.

The principals' neighbor worked for Walton Construction, but he could have been working on a different job site. Even if he knew my mother's father, he may not have known the family. In which case he wouldn't know if she was raped or even pregnant, for that matter. That type of information didn't usually leak outside of families.

On the upside, maybe he did know the family or knew of a rape. If not, he might recall a worker who had two teenage daughters.

That gave me a little hope.

In the accounting office, everyone stared at me, as if I was a doctor fresh from the delivery room, and were waiting to hear the sex of the new baby.

"Sooo...how did your trip go?" Sally asked, becoming the spokesperson for the office.

"Well, I spent most of my time in the principal's office."

They laughed. "What, were you being bad?" asked Sally. "Demanding answers and stepping on toes?"

"It felt like it. No, actually he was very kind. He was a new teacher at the same time my mother attended school."

"Did he know her or about any rapes?" Sally asked.

"No, he said he didn't remember hearing anything like that. He said when someone became pregnant, all the teachers knew. They gossiped just like the students."

Sally snickered, "Yeah, I know how that is. It's not much different here."

"You're right. I bet everyone here knows I'm trying to find my birth mother." I laughed.

"So what are you going to do now?"

"I still have the yearbooks to go through and compare last names."

"That's going to be time consuming."

"I know. I think I'll call Marilyn again. I need to think of new questions that she can answer with a yes or no."

Sally turned. "That's kind of hard. I'm getting the look from Sandy. We better get to work."

"Right. I was running late when I got here."

Sitting down at my desk, I tried to think of the right questions for Marilyn. One thing I wanted to know was if Lacy May was the name of one individual or two. She could tell me that if I asked it right.

I'd tell her about my last trip to Oildale, the principal and Mrs. Kelly. She wants to know of my progress. I think she just wants to know if I'm really making an effort to find my mother.

*   *   *

After the afternoon break, my sleepless night caught up with me. It was difficult to concentrate, but I wanted to talk to Marilyn. I hoped she hadn't left for the day.

I decided to play it by ear.

"Good afternoon, this is Marilyn."

"Hi Marilyn, it's Colette."

"I was hoping to hear from you soon. How's your search going?"

"I went to Oildale and met with the school principal and a woman who was the girl's dean in the fifties."

"Did you get any information that was helpful?"

"No, not directly. I couldn't access the school records without a last name and they didn't know of any rapes. But the principal has a neighbor who worked for Walton Construction and I got a contact for the Oildale Water Resources. Nothing propels me forward."

"You sound disappointed."

"I am a little. I do have the Oildale high school yearbooks. I can go through each year and write down all the girls' last names to see if I come up with sisters a year apart."

"Sounds like a lot of work," she said with sympathy.

I straightened up, detecting pity in her voice. Maybe this was my chance. Clutching the telephone, my pulse started beating in my ear.

Think. Ask questions.

Worried she would hang up, I blurted, "I do have some questions for you."

"Sure, I'll give you what I can."

"Are Lacy and May the names of two different people?" I asked, knowing never to mention I overheard them.

"No," she said without hesitation.

My heart raced with excitement. Time for my next question.

"Is Lacy May my mother's name?" I closed my eyes, waiting for a response.

"Yes," she said with another quick response.

Thrilled to finally know her name, I had trouble sitting still. Now what to ask? Can you please tell the last part of that name too? Wishful thinking.

I knew not to dwell on the names too much. It was something I had overheard by *accident*.

"I guess I'll go through the yearbooks. The first name will narrow it down a lot. That's the best lead I have at this time. The only real lead," I added, hoping she still felt sorry for me.

Crying came to my mind. Maybe I should just start bawling. Preoccupied with my own pity and thinking up more questions, I wasn't listening when Marilyn began talking. I didn't quite catch her last words.

"Excuse me, Marilyn, I didn't quite hear what you just said." I had a hunch she'd given me some kind of clue.

Would she repeat it? Upset, I took a deep breath, holding the phone receiver so hard against my ear, it should have come out the other ear. I didn't want to miss the slightest sound.

My hand made a circular motion as if silently encouraging her to speak. My palms were sweaty and I was afraid I'd have a heart attack. Seconds that seemed like hours passed. Good thing she couldn't see my impatient behavior through the telephone. She would have hung up.

"Catches fish!" she said.

Hesitating for a moment, I repeated, "Did you say catches fish?"

"Yes, the name you're looking for—catches fish."

"What? Catches fish, catches fish?" What did that mean? I was thinking hard, but nothing came.

I was numb. It could be the biggest clue of my search and I had no idea what it was. Maybe Marilyn thought I was overwhelmed or just not too smart. My stomach churned, my head spun. The wastebasket was handy. I was thinking too hard. Any minute I might lose my lunch. I scooted the wastebasket closer.

"Get a dictionary!" Marilyn said.

A dictionary. Of course. This is accounting; we do numbers, not letters.

"Could you please hold for a moment, Marilyn?' I need to get a dictionary. Not giving her a chance to respond, I nervously jabbed the hold button.

Shaking, I leaped up and stumbled before catching my balance.

"I NEED A DICTIONARY, I NEED A DICTIONARY!" I yelled with the same intensity as if I was yelling FIRE.

Everyone seemed to notice my state of panic, and all focus turned toward me.

"I have a clue from Marilyn and I need a dictionary," I said, lowering my voice. Now!"

Sally responding to the urgency. "What's the word you need to look up?"

"Catches fish," I shouted.

Almost everyone, including Sandy, yelled in unison, "A Fisherman."

Not even taking the time to thank them, I dashed back to the phone as if I had to disarm a bomb and the seconds were ticking away.

Winded, I picked up the telephone and blurted, "A fisherman."

There was no response. Did she hang up? Did I have her on hold too long or was that all she wanted to say?

I looked down at the telephone and realized I hadn't taken her off hold.

My heart pounded hard as I pushed the hold button, "Marilyn, are you there?"

"Yes, I'm here."

Relieved to hear her voice, I regained my composure "a fisherman?"

"Yes."

"The name I'm looking for is Fisherman?"

"Yes."

I didn't want to stop there. I wanted the whole name confirmed. What did I have to lose? It was her choice. I needed confirmation of the entire name.

"So... Lacy May Fisherman is the name I want?"

"Yes."

Her silence told me the conversation was over.

"Thank you Marilyn. I'll keep you updated on my progress."

My feet stomped up and down as I hung up the telephone. I turned to see the whole accounting department standing at my door.

"I have the whole name!" I yelled, running to hug Sally and anyone else within arm's length.

Everyone, including Sandy, was happy and excited at the new information.

"What'll you do now?" asked Sally.

"I can't wait to get home and check the yearbooks to see what she looks like."

Everyone looked at Sandy.

"Okay... Okay, the day's almost over, anyway. Go home. I'll clean off your desk." Sandy told me, aware of everyone's intensity.

I gave her a big hug, "Thank you."

I grabbed my purse and started running out of the office.

"WALK," I heard Sandy yell. It sounded just like a schoolteacher.

Oblivious to the sound of my clopping high heels, I stopped, turned and smiled.

Getting home to the yearbooks was filling my mind, not safety. But she was right. I walked quickly. Then once out of her sight, I ran to my car.

*   *   *

The distance wasn't far from the babysitter's house to mine, but after picking up my son the drive home seemed to take hours. In my house, I passed the yearbooks sitting on the counter. Take care of the baby first then look second. My heart skipped a beat. Relieved that we were the only ones home, I slowed down to savor the moments.

Ordinarily I'd be tearing the yearbook pages searching for her name, but instead I stared at them. Would I be able to guess the right girl? Was she the beauty I had pictured? Did it matter? Would she look older than the other girls after enduring childbirth? Or did she look like any other teenager? My son was fine and I had all the time I needed.

Slowly I opened the yearbook to what would have been her sophomore year. It didn't take long to find her. I thought I'd be excited and eager, but I was sad.

My toddler tapped my leg. I reached down and picked him up as tears welled up in my eyes. My emotions somewhat surprised me. I hugged my son as if I was hugging myself for her. That's what it's all about. She wasn't able to do this for me, but I wanted her to know I had all the hugs I needed.

I lowered my wiggling son to the floor and he scooted away to play. Her face was beautiful, but she looked so young, heart breaking young. My heart suddenly seemed to weigh a ton. Tears streamed down my face. She was smiling but behind that smile, there had to be tremendous pain and sadness. How could she be happy? After the violation of rape, her baby was taken away. Not that she was ready to be a mother—still a child herself—but that baby was a part of her. I'm that baby.

My thoughts took a turn. Raped and pregnant, maybe she didn't want to remember any of it. I erased that thought. I didn't think Marilyn would have encouraged me to find her if there were indications that Lacy wanted to forget my existence.

I studied the photo, but couldn't see anything of me in her. I double-checked to make sure I was looking at the right person. None of our features matched. I didn't recognize a thing. I would never have guessed her to be my mother. But that didn't matter. I had her picture and her name.

I checked the other yearbooks and found her picture one more time. She looked about the same.

What was her life like now? Was she married? Did she have other children? Had she kept my existence a secret? I didn't want to cause her any problems. I vowed to myself that if she didn't want to see me, I'd respect that. As hard as it sounded, that's how it would be.

The ringing telephone startled me. I didn't feel like talking, but answered anyway.

Sally's voice was so loud and shrill the neighbors could have heard her. "Did you find her?"

"Yes, I did."

"You don't seem very excited. Is she ugly?"

"The opposite," I said, laughing.

"Then why are you so down? You have her name and picture. You should be ecstatic." She sounded puzzled.

"I know, but... I feel sad. I've been waiting and wanting this for so long, and in one day she suddenly became real."

"Well, last time I saw you, you looked pretty real."

51

"Thanks for trying to cheer me up. It's like I'm so happy she had me, but so sad she had to go through what she did to have me. Does that make sense?"

"Yeah, it does, but you can't change any of that."

"I know but I'm not sure how I'm supposed to feel." I watched my son toddle across the floor.

"I don't think there's anything wrong with the way you feel. You just need to sort it out."

"Yeah, you're right."

"So what's your next move?"

"You didn't give me much sorting time."

"Come on. Don't drag your feet. You must have an idea."

I did feel a little more enthusiastic, "Well... tomorrow I'll call the high school principal. He said if I had a name he could find her records."

"Wow, that should get you a lot of information."

"I hope so."

"I'll see you at work tomorrow."

"Sally?"

"Yeah?"

"Thanks for calling."

"You're welcome. See you tomorrow."

I felt better. I needed the reassurance that everything would be fine. I also needed to call mom and tell her the news. She's the one who usually kept me grounded during my search. Hearing her voice would do me good.

I called but no one answered. It was a relief. I should have been excited but wasn't and didn't feel like acting. I needed time to think. I had no regrets about my search, but I wanted to understand my feelings. How was I supposed to feel? I would call my mom and Mr. Palmer tomorrow.

*   *   *

I took the yearbooks to work with me. If I hadn't, I'd probably have been sent home to get them. One by one everyone wanted to see her picture. I didn't mind. They had been so encouraging and helpful.

I called my mom and she was more excited than me. She couldn't wait to see the picture. It amazed her that I had the full name. It amazed me too. I'd been searching for less than two months. Now I had the identity of the woman who gave birth to me. But I still had no idea who she was. I wanted to continue my search.

In the morning, I called Mr. Palmer's office, but he wasn't in. I left a call back message with the secretary.

The day dragged on forever. It was just about quitting time when my phone rang.

"Is this Colette?"

"Yes... Mr. Palmer?"

"Yes it is. Sorry I couldn't get back to you sooner. I've been in meetings all day."

"I have a name."

"You do? That's great."

"Her name's Lacy May Fisherman. I found her in the 1956 yearbook and in the 1958 yearbook. Maybe she skipped some school, I'm not sure though."

"Give me a couple of days. I'll have my staff go back through the records on microfilm. It might take some time."

"That's okay. I appreciate your time and help."

"I'm glad to help. I understand that this is important for you. I'll be talking with you soon."

"Thank you. I'm looking forward to hearing from you."

What information would he find? There should be her parent's names and her address while in school. That would give me a definite direction in my search but I'd have to wait and see.

A Love Child's Journey

Chapter Six

A week had passed since I spoke with Mr. Palmer. He'd said it could take a few days, and the few days passed a few days ago. I'd already looked in the phone book and written down the entire Fisherman's I could find. There were sixteen in all, but none of them had the first name of Lacy or the initial L. But there might be spelling variations like *Fischerman*. Her last name was probably no longer Fisherman, anyway.
    A co-worker in data processing had friends who lived in Oildale. She offered to call and ask them to check their phone book for all Fishermans in that area.
    This search was testing my patience and perseverance. I had to rely on so many people, but without those people I wouldn't be where I was in my search. I received a lot of information in a very short period of time. I really appreciated the extra help but had to remind myself of that every so often.

*   *   *

    The following day I decided not to work on my search at all. That didn't last. My phone rang not long after I arrived at work.
  "Is this Colette?"
  "Yes."

"This is Mr. Palmer from Oildale High School. I have some information for you."

I could hardly contain my excitement. "You do?"

"Yes, do you have a pen?"

Of course I had a pen, pencils, you name it, I worked in accounting. I couldn't remember if I told him that. "Yes I do."

"Her mother's name is Wilma Fisherman and her father's name is Rodney. She has a sister named Laura Fay, who was a year behind her in school."

Wow, I had three more names. I couldn't believe I was getting all this vital information. Thrilled at the potential, I hardly knew how to act or what to say.

"Thank you *so* much Mr. Palmer."

"There's more."

He has more. I always hoped for more, but I'm so used to getting less. "You have more?"

"I do. Her first day of enrollment was January 20, 1956. She left November 19, 1957, and returned on September 8, 1958. Her last day at Oildale High was April 15, 1959."

"So... she didn't graduate from there?"

"It doesn't appear as though she did."

"I wonder why she left and then came back. Did her family move because of her father's work?"

"That's possible, but I'm not showing any transfers from another high school. I do show that there was a request to send her records to Idaho State College on January 15, 1975."

"That wasn't that long ago. Is there a name where they sent it to?"

"No, just to the administration department at the college."

He gave me her last year class schedule and the names of her teachers. The information might not help with my search, but it was interesting to find out the type of classes she had taken. I thanked him again and promised to keep in touch as my search progressed. It amazed me how willing he was to help. He was a busy guy, a principal, and a man with a kind heart.

I had new names and a new state. First I'd concentrate on her parents. Unless her current last name was still the same, I wouldn't know where or how to start hunting for her.

When I peeked over my door at the office, everyone was busy working. I'd tell them at break.

* * *

"Hey, you going on break?" Sally asked, peering over my door.

"Sure, I'll be right there."

I clutched the piece of paper with the information from Mr. Palmer and headed for the break room. I felt like skipping. I'd been keeping the new information to myself for a whole hour and a half and was about to explode. I didn't know I could go that long without talking.

When I entered the break room, everyone was talking. I nonchalantly walked over and slapped my piece of paper down in the middle of them. They all tried to grab it like vultures swooping down on a fresh kill.

"You have new names?" Sally asked, consumed with excitement.

Blowing on my fingers tips, I polished them on my chest in an arrogant manner. "I do."

Sally laughed at my cockiness. "You heard back from the principal?"

"I did, and I have three new names."

Reading my paper, Sally shouted, "You got the mother, father and the sister's name?"

"Yep!"

She handed the paper to a co-worker. "What's your next move?"

"Well, Darla in data processing has friends that live in Oildale. They have the Oildale telephone book and she…

Sally interrupted, "Heck with that, we have an Oildale telephone book right here at the switchboard."

Before I could respond, Sally was out of sight. No one uttered a word; eyes were on the doorway waiting for her to return.

Sally rushed into the break room like a lightning bolt, telephone book in hand. She slapped it down on the table and turned to the F's.

Stopping on a page, her index finger scanned up and down, then pointed. "There's a Wilma B. Fisherman," she shouted.

Everyone at our table screamed. The rest of the employees in the break room turned and stared at us. I smiled and mouthed sorry over the racket.

"There's even a telephone number and an address," Sally shrieked.

"Not so loud," I told her.

"NOT SO..." The noise died down a little.... "Loud. Aren't you excited?"

"Of course I am, but I think we're disturbing everyone else in the break room."

"So what? This is important! Copy it down."

I was so excited my hands shook but I wrote down the address and phone number, "Sally, I don't know if this Wilma is the Wilma I'm looking for."

"Come on, how many Wilma Fisherman's live in Oildale?" Sally protested.

"You're right, but I'm afraid to get my hopes up. Besides, I want to find Lacy first. I need to talk to her."

"Oh man, look at the time." Someone said. "We've been here long enough for two breaks."

We returned the phone book on our way back to work. We all knew Sandy was not going to be happy with us.

Sally walked in first and we followed her in.

"Colette has three new names." Sally said immediately.

Sandy nodded.

"I have an address too." I added, continuing toward my workspace.

Sandy didn't look up. "Good."

The room fell quiet as everyone started working. I sat at my desk and stared at the address. If the woman were Lacy's mother, then she'd be my grandmother. I wondered what kind of mother she'd been, but remembered she hadn't treated Lacy very well while Lacy was in Fairhaven, according to Marilyn. How could a mother be cruel to a daughter who'd been raped? I folded the paper and put it in my purse. It was time to work.

*   *   *

That evening I shared the new information with my husband. He had no interest in the details but listened anyway. I was glad I had my mom and co-workers to talk with. They all supported the search, unlike my husband. I hurried to get everyone fed and ready for bed. I couldn't wait to tell my mom about the new finds. Once everyone was in bed, I called her.

"Hi Mom, I hope it's not too late."

"No, I'm just sitting here doing some book work."

"Hey, guess what?"

"What?"

"I got the names of Lacy's mother, father and sister. Can you believe that?"

"Oh honey, that's great!"

"I was so surprised. The father's name is Rodney, her mother's name is Wilma and her sister's name is Linda Fay."

"So what are you going to do now?"

"Wilma's in the telephone book. Well... I think it's her. I'd like to know her approximate age to see if she's old enough to be Lacy's mother."

"Wilma's an old-fashion name. Hey, why don't you ask your policeman friend to run some sort of check on her? Maybe you could find out something from that."

"That's not a bad idea. Maybe he could run Lacy's too."

"Can't hurt to try."

"Great ideas, Mom. I feel so good when I talk with you. Sometimes this whole thing gets a little overwhelming. I don't know what I'd do without your encouragement. I'm sure glad you picked me to adopt."

"Me too! I love you. Let me know what you find out."

"I will and I love you too."

Mom and I didn't always see eye to eye, but I loved her and knew if I'd been in Lacy's situation Mom would've been right there for me. That's what being a mother is all about. She might not like the situation, but she'd love and protect her child regardless. Unfortunately, it appeared that Lacy's mother didn't see it that way.

If only I could find Lacy's current name and whereabouts. Tomorrow I'd call my friend at the police station and see what he could find out.

*   *   *

I hadn't talked to my friend at the police station for some time, but I knew if he could help me, he would. I called and left him a message as soon as I got to work.

Right before lunch, I finally heard from him. I explained the situation and gave him Wilma and Lacy's names. He said he'd see what he could do. I thanked him and went back to work.

Later that afternoon, he called. I didn't know what to expect, but I hoped the Wilma in Oildale was Lacy's mother. I didn't want my excitement to end in disappointment.

"I ran Wilma Fisherman's name and it came up in Oildale with the same address you gave me. Her date of birth is Feb. 23, 1917."

"The age range fits. What about Lacy, were you able to find anything?"

"I didn't get anything on her. Nothing in California anyway. It's the only state I could run, and it took a lot to get approval for it. The department has been clamping down on running checks on individuals unless it's police work."

"I understand. Thanks so much for checking this out for me."

"I bet this lady's your grandmother. I got to go, but let me know how things are going."

"I will. Talk with you soon. Thanks again for your help."

Grandmother, that sounded odd, but biologically it was the right word to call her. I had only one other grandmother and she lived in Missouri. I'd seen her less than ten times before she died.

I reflected on the new information. So what do I have? I'm unable to locate Lacy, but I might know where her mother lives. Although the mother may not want to be reminded of her daughter's rape. Yet the grandmother was one who knew I existed. I wanted to be discreet, but I had to go see her. She might know where Lacy lives.

How should I approach the woman? I had to be tactful about the whole thing, but had no idea what to say or how to say it. I didn't want to go alone. She might refuse to see me once I'm there. Did she ever wonder what I was like and what kind of person I became? What if she meets me at the door with a shotgun and tells me to leave? Or worse yet, shoots me? I had no idea what to expect. I wanted Mom along when I meet this grandmother. I wasn't sure why. I was a married adult with a child, but I still needed her there with me.

"Cooper residents," my little sister answered on the phone.

"Hi, Cindy. Can I talk with Mom?" The receiver hit the table with a bang. I could hear her yell "Mom! It's Colette."

"Hi honey," Mom said a few moments later.

"Hey Mom. I took your advice and asked my friend at the police department to check the names for me. He and I both think the Wilma Fisherman in Oildale is Lacy's mother. Her age fits and like you said, the name is an older one. So... do you want to take a ride tomorrow after I get off work?"

"You're going to drive there and see her?"

"I'm thinking about it. If you'll go with me."

"If that's what you want to do."

"Great. I'll see you when I get off work. Love you."

"Okay, I'll be ready. Love you too."

*   *   *

It took forever for my workday to end. Everyone was excited for me. They kept reminding me of questions to ask as I left the office. You'd think I was taking a trip around the world, but it was only a few hours drive. It was strange to realize that she lived so close.

Before long Mom and I were on our way to Oildale. Fruit trees lined the roadway. Neither of us said much during the drive.

"Do you know what you're going to say to her?" Mom asked breaking the comfortable silence.

"Not exactly. I've rehearsed this so many times in my mind, and now that it's here I'm at a loss for words. I know you might find that hard to believe, but it's true."

"No, I understand. I've been thinking about what I'd say if I were you." She didn't comment on my loss of words.

"What would you say?"

"I have no idea."

I laughed. "That wasn't the answer I expected."

"Well…Okay. How about introducing yourself?" She tried not to laugh.

We both giggled.

"So I should just go up to the door and say, Hi, I'm Colette, the baby your daughter gave up when she was raped at thirteen and you sent her to a home for unwed mothers. Would you mind telling me where I can find her?"

"Something like that, but without the sarcasm."

"I know. That's my nervous energy running amok. I'll figure it out when I get there."

The rest of the trip passed quietly. My stomach churned. What should I say to her? I had dreamed of this day but didn't know if I was ready. I wished it were Lacy. What Marilyn told me about her mother wasn't kind. What would I do if she refused to tell me where Lacy lived? I decided to rely on what I'd been taught all my life: be polite, kind and careful. Or better yet, let Mom go to the door first.

"The first Oildale exit is coming up," Mom said.

At her words, my stomach went on a roller coaster ride, "I see it. I'll exit and we'll take a look at the directions Darla gave me."

"Good idea."

I pulled off into a small shopping center and studied the directions. My stomach still ached. We'd taken the right exit and weren't far from her address. I was excited yet apprehensive. I had to remind myself that this woman wasn't Lacy. If she shut the door in my face, it was her choice and I had to respect that rejection. I could always throw myself on the ground begging and sobbing. Not that I'd ever done that before, but there's a first for everything. Okay, drop those thoughts. For all I knew, she just might welcome me warmly and offer milk and cookies. That's what Grandmas do in storybooks, except for the wolf in Little Red Riding Hood.

"Turn left here," Mom said.

I turned onto a gravel road and stopped. "Do you see any street numbers?"

"Move up a little bit. There's one right here. Maybe her house is further up."

We crept slowly up the gravel road and stopped suddenly. "I think it's this driveway here." I said. "It's hard to make out the street number on this post."

"It looks like a mobile home," Mom said, peering over my shoulder.

"It's pretty dark up there and scary looking." I hesitated.

"Oh, it's fine. Drive on up."

I edged my way on the dirt driveway to the front of a mobile home and parked. It was older, but large. Shrubbery engulfed its perimeter, leaving the door entrance clear. Its eerie appearance made me shiver. "Doesn't look like anyone's home."

"How can you tell? Get out and go knock on the door," Mom said.

"I'm not getting out. You go knock on the door."

"I'm not knocking on the door."

"We're not even sure it's the right house. I'll back down so we can double check the house number."

"I'm pretty sure it's the right house," she said.

Ignoring her comment, I backed down to the numbers on the post and flashed my headlights on them.

"It's the correct address."

"I thought so," she said.

"I just wanted to be sure," I stated, driving slowly back up the dirt driveway and parking.

Mom sat staring straight ahead. "Are you going to knock on the door?"

"Can't you knock on the door for me?" I pleaded.

"No! This is *YOUR* search."

"But you're my Mom. You're supposed to protect me."

"From what? You haven't even got out of the car yet."

"I know.... I don't think anyone's home."

"I don't either. There are no lights on."

"Oh, I see. You're just as afraid as I am, aren't you?" I snickered.

She began to laugh. "I guess I am. I think it would be better if we came back in the daylight, don't you?"

"Yeah, I agree. At least in the daylight we'll be able to see where to run and who we're running from."

We laughed together backing down to the main road, and teased each other about our cowardice all the way home. I hadn't verified if the Wilma who lived in the mobile home was Lacy's mother, but Mom and I had a memorable trip. I realized that the trip was about enjoying my Mom. The following day would bring me new ideas. Or at least a name of someone who wasn't a coward, and would actually get out of the car and knock on the door at Wilma's on my next trip. Someone besides me, that is.

A Love Child's Journey

Chapter Seven

When I arrived at work the following day, my coworkers surrounded me like a swarm of bees. They were waiting to hear about Wilma.

Sally the unofficial spokesperson for the group, jumped right in.

"Well, is it her? Is she your grandmother?"

All eyes were on me in anticipation.

"I don't know."

"What do you mean, you don't know?" she asked.

"It didn't look like anyone was home," I said, embarrassed.

Sally looked puzzled. "You mean no one answered the door?"

"No. I didn't knock on the door, but I'm pretty certain no one was home."

Everyone let out a loud cackle, including Sally.

"It was really spooky and dark," I explained.

"So…you drove all the way up there and you didn't even knock on the door?"

"Nope, didn't even get out of the car."

Still laughing, everyone headed for her desk. The mystery was still unsolved. Eventually I would find out if this Wilma was my grandmother, but I needed to muster up a little more courage.

* * *

Later that afternoon on my way to data processing to drop off my payroll cards, I ran into Darla.

"I hear you didn't have much luck in Oildale yesterday," she said, teasing.

"Boy, news travels fast. I got there but I didn't go up to the door. I'll never live that one down."

"Well, you know, I'm going to Oildale this weekend," she said.

"Really?"

"Yeah, and I'm fairly sure I'll have time to stop by and check out that address for you. I'm going to have lunch with some friends."

"Oh Darla, I'd appreciate it so much if you have time. Let me go get the address. Do you have my phone number?"

"I don't think so. You better give it to me."

"I'll be right back."

I was so grateful that Darla was going to check out this address for me. I should be the one doing it, but I was relieved at her offer. That was enough courage for me.

Elated I got the address and my phone number for Darla. We went over the questions she would ask and I told her to call me if she had any information. She said she would.

I had to deal with a lot of playful heckling the remainder of the day, but I left work excited that I might hear good news from Darla over the weekend.

* * *

Saturday passed the usual way with housework, but it gave me time to consider my fears and feelings. Was it about rejection? I wasn't certain. It was something that I might have to deal with. No matter how much I convinced myself to respect the wishes of Lacy and her family, I knew I'd be disappointed if they weren't receptive to me. A jabbing pain rolled around my stomach.

I thought about my first visit with Marilyn, at the beginning of my search. I remembered her reading to me that Lacy's mother was unkind to her while she was pregnant with me. If she was that unhappy with a daughter who'd been raped, how was she going to treat me, the outcome of that situation? She might be more than unkind to me. However, our age difference alone left me confident of outrunning her. But it would be more difficult to outrun harsh and hurtful words. Was "that" the reason I didn't want to get out of the car?

I was finishing up dinner dishes when the phone rang.

"Hello," I said catching my breath after running to answer it.

"Hi Colette, this is Darla."

My heart went into overdrive, "Hi Darla. Did you find out anything?"

"I did," she said in a smug tone.

I was jumping up and down and searching the counter top for a pen and paper. "What'd you find out?"

"Wilma wasn't home, but her neighbor gave me the telephone number of a friend who takes care of things for Wilma when she's in Yuma."

"She's in Yuma? Like in Yuma, Arizona? That's not what I was expecting to hear."

"Hold on, I'm not through telling you everything."

"I'm listening!"

"Okay, so I called her friend and she gave me some information."

"You called her friend?" I said, screaming for joy.

"She said that Wilma should be back from Yuma in a couple of days. She also said that Wilma's daughter Lacy's last name is Snider and her granddaughter, Allaine lives in Idaho."

I calmed down. "This is the right Wilma, isn't it?"

"Sounds like it to me. She gave me her granddaughter's last name, address and telephone number."

"You've got to be kidding? I can't believe you got all this information. Who did you say you were when you called Wilma's friend?"

"I just said I was a friend of Lacy's, I was in town and thought I'd look her up. She didn't question it."

I wrote down all the information along with the granddaughter's last name and address. Thanking Darla for all her help, I said I owed her big time and promised to keep her posted so she wouldn't have to hear it secondhand at work.

After hanging up I just sat there thinking. I have my birth mother's current name and her daughter's name. I have another sister. WOW! It was a little overwhelming. I wondered about Allaine's age. Did we resemble each other? But most important, I wondered if she knew about me.

I decided to wait until the next day to share my new information with everyone. I had to decide what to do next. Discretion was now important in my search. Being so close to finding Lacy, made me apprehensive. I felt confident I was meant to find her. But what would happen when we met? Well, I hadn't found her yet, so I better concentrate on that first. My son was tugging on my pant leg. Smiling I picked him up and kissed his chubby little cheek. He was more important, for now. A nice family night and a restful sleep should help guide me to the next step in my search. I set my new information to the side.

*   *   *

A good sleep didn't fall in line with the nice family night I had envisioned. I tossed and turned, torn between calling Lacy's daughter or continuing to try and find Lacy, now that I had her last name.

It would be so much easier if I could call up her daughter, other daughter that is, and say, hey, where's your Mom? That's what I wanted but would it be right? After thinking about it half a day, I decided to call her daughter and pretend I was a friend of Lacy's from California. Hopefully… she'd tell me where to find her.

I paced from the kitchen to the front room carrying a small wastebasket, certain that any moment my nervous stomach would toss out my breakfast. I couldn't even think about lunch. Each time I decided to make the call, I would chicken out and give myself another half-an-hour. Either my arms were getting tired or I was afraid the day would soon be over, but after taking four half-hour extensions, I decided, enough was enough. I dialed the number.

I'd already decided to call myself Sue. I didn't know why I picked that name and didn't care. The last name had been a little harder. Jones came to mind but that was too common. Making up a last name shouldn't have been that difficult. I was a payroll clerk and dealt with almost 400 people on a weekly basis by their last names. I picked Brady, which probably came from watching the Brady Bunch when I was younger. Sue Brady sounded good.

I felt numb as the other end of the line began to ring. I didn't want to make a mistake. I wanted to be sure I had the right number. With each ring, my heart beat so hard it scared me.

The ringing stopped.

"Hello," said a young woman.

"Ah...Hello. I'm looking for Lacy Snider," I said.

"She doesn't live here anymore," she said and slammed down the receiver.

Not sure what to do, I sat listening to the hum of the disconnected telephone.

She *did* say that Lacy didn't live there any more, so she had to know her. It was a good bet she was Lacy's daughter.

My first rejection. Well, sort of. She didn't give me a chance to use my fake name. Maybe she thought I was a bill collector of something. Technically neither Sue Brady nor I had been rejected.

I hung up, wondering what kind of relationship Lacy and her daughter had. I smiled at thoughts of the trip Mom and I took to Oildale. I was so fortunate and happy with the relationship Mom and I shared. Although disappointed, it would be silly for me to take the hang up personally. But calling her back might not be the best thing to do right now. So I didn't.

*   *   *

I got to work earlier than usual. I wanted to share the events of my weekend first thing, and hear everyone's ideas on what to do. There were plenty of ideas about what I should do floating around the office.

I ran into Sally at the coffee machine.

"Did you hear from Darla this weekend?" she asked.

"Yes." I said, dropping my quarters in the coffee machine.

"Is it the right Wilma?" she gasped.
"We're pretty certain she is."
"What's she like? Is she nice?"
"She wasn't there, but Darla spoke with Wilma's neighbor and a friend."
"So Darla didn't see her?"
"No, but she got Lacy's last name and her daughter's name, address and phone number."
"Wow! That means you have another sister! Did you call her?"
"I tried, but she hung up."
"She hung up? Did you tell her who you were?'
"Of course not! Anyway, she didn't give me a chance to tell her who I wasn't."
"What?"
"Well, I made up a fake name. Remember, I have to be discreet. I don't want to cause their family any problems."
"Yeah, I know. So what'll you do now?"
"I'm not sure. Lacy's last name is Snider and Wilma will be back from Yuma in a few of days."
"She was in Yuma?'
"Yeah. It wouldn't have mattered if I'd gotten out of the car. She wasn't home," I snickered.
"Why don't you call Wilma and tell her who you are? She does know about you."
"Yeah… I've been thinking about that. But I wanted to talk to Lacy first. It's such a personal situation and I wanted it to be her decision whether or not to see me."
"I understand that."

We walked to our desks without saying much. Sally understood how important it was for me to do the right thing and I appreciated that. I could listen to everyone, but I knew the direction had to come from me. I could call my friend at the police station again, but I doubted that Lacy lived in California and it was difficult enough for him the first time. I had to do some soul searching for the next step. I considered calling Marilyn, but knew what she would say—*Just call*. She's encouraged me all along. I didn't want to call her again until after I found Lacy.

Wilma wouldn't be back for a few days. I had some time to think about it.

Darla and I repeated the story all day long to different people. Everyone gave his or her opinion on what to do, and if I'd taken a poll, calling Wilma would have won by a landslide.

*   *   *

The week flew by and Friday arrived faster than I wanted. Everyone left me alone and didn't bug me about calling Wilma. But every time I passed Sally, she smiled and pretended to dial a telephone with one finger. It made me laugh, but by the fifth repeat, I wanted to rip her arm off. I decided against it, knowing her heart was in the right place. A few times, I gave her a playful evil eye, but it didn't faze her.

"Hey, you ready to go to lunch?" she yelled.

"I guess."

"Why are you so mopey?" she asked.

"All I think about is calling this Wilma."

"Then call her."

"It's not that easy. What'll I say…? I'm still not absolutely sure I even have the right person."

"Want me to call her?"

"You…what would you say?"

"I don't know, but I'll think of something."

"See? It's not so easy."

Sally tapped her fingers together, "I got it."

"What?"

"I'll pretend I was in Lacy's graduating class and say I'm searching for missing people for our class reunion."

"Is it time for her reunion? She left school and returned a couple different times. I'm not sure what year she graduated. I'm not even sure if she graduated."

"All the better. If Wilma questions me, I can say it must be a mistake."

"That's a great idea. Hey, I still have all the names I wrote down from the yearbook. You can say you're one of them."

"That works for me. Let's go eat lunch. I'm starving."

Over lunch we talked about what Sally would say and how to respond to different questions. We both agreed that for most of her conversation she would have to wing it. We came up with a date and time for the reunion. I told her I'd call later from home with a name she could use.

I wanted the workday to end right then. Excitement rather than the usual fear swept through me. A welcome change.

At the end of the day I hurried home. I wanted to call Sally right away. Her making that call for me was such a relief. I found a few names I liked and left the final choice to her.

"Hello." Sally said as she answered.

"Hey Sally. I have some names." I began reading them to her.

"I like Carol. It was a popular name then," she said.

"You're right. Okay. Wilma should be back from Yuma by now, so you can call her anytime." I hoped she'd do it immediately.

"I know. I have a full weekend, so it'll be Sunday night before I'll have time to sit down and call her without being interrupted. Don't worry; I'll call you right after I talk with her. I promise."

It was going to be a long weekend. I was thankful that Sally would be making the call instead of me. Psyching myself up for these cold calls to people at the heart of my search might have made a basket case out of me.

The waiting wasn't easy, but Sunday evening finally crawled around.

I was like a child on Christmas Eve waiting for bedtime and Santa. Each hour ticked by without a call. I knew she'd ring me if she had something to tell. Maybe Wilma wasn't home from Yuma yet. Disappointed, I decided to go to bed.

I'd just drifted off to sleep when the phone rang. I was glad my husband was still at work. He wouldn't be happy with anyone calling so late.

"Hey, it's Sal. I can't talk long, but I did speak with Wilma and she told me a lot."

"She did? What did she say?"

"She's the right Wilma, but I can't talk. The baby's not feeling well. I think she's teething. Dave watched her while I called.

He's ready for me to take over. I've got to go. I'll tell you tomorrow."

I heard her baby crying, and quickly said, "Okay Sal. Thanks."

She hung up. I sat on the edge of the bed with phone, wishing she were still on the other end. I wanted so much to hear what Wilma had told her, but I'd have to wait for tomorrow. How could I get back to sleep after that?

A Love Child's Journey

Chapter Eight

I pulled into the employee parking lot excited to see Sally's car. I'd been so hyped up the night before that I didn't think I'd get any sleep. But before I knew it, I was out like a light. I parked, gathered my purse and made a beeline for the door. Anyone who noticed would have thought I was either late or had too much morning coffee.

I hurried to the cafeteria but she wasn't there. Like a hound dog on a hunt, I continued to track her. I headed for the accounting department; she had to be there. But she wasn't.

I went to my desk and had her paged, then stared at my phone as if my glare would make it ring.

The glare must have worked; before long Sally called me.

"I knew it would be you. I'll be right there," she said.

"Where are you? First you made me wait all weekend, and then you called me last night and made me wait until this morning. Then I get here and can't find you and have to wait again."

She laughed. "Relax, I'm out in production, I'm on my way."

I hung up and began fidgeting with paper clips. What information did she have?

She showed up at my door waving a piece of paper in the air. "You're going to be pleased with what I have for you."

"I better be. I had to wait long enough," I joked.

"Yeah, I know. Sorry. I'll be glad when my daughter's teething is over."

"I know how that is. So how did our idea about the class reunion work?"

"Wilma didn't question it; she just kept talking. I wrote as fast as I could. I didn't want to miss anything. I wanted to ask her to slow down but decided not to."

"What did she say?"

"She didn't think Lacy would make it to the reunion because she was in a terrible car accident in 1975."

My heart sank at those words, "Did she die?"

Sally was reading from her paper, "No, she didn't die, but she was in a coma for three months. She went off a 54-foot cliff in a VW and broke just about every bone in her body. She uses a walker."

"Oh, man," I said with a sigh.

She continued reading. "She had some brain damage and has seizures."

It wasn't what I expected or wanted to hear. But it didn't matter; I still wanted to see her. Whether she understood what I'd say to her or not. Having brain damage, she may have forgotten that I existed. No point in dwelling on her condition. My quest was to find her, thank her and tell her that I was fine. I would like the opportunity to know what type of person she was. I wanted to see if I shared any of her mannerisms or feelings. Or maybe I just wanted to look for any of me in her.

"What else did she say?"

"She has two children, Allaine-22 and Mitch-20. Allaine has a baby boy. Lacy's last name now is Ritch, but she's with a guy named Rob Lewis."

"Yeah, I remember the conversation I *didn't* have with her daughter Allaine."

"Oh, yeah, the hang up." Sally said, snickering.

"I wonder what Wilma meant when she said that Lacy's name is now Ritch? It sounds like she may have had a few different last names. Did you get that impression?"

"It did make me wonder why she said it that way."

"Anything else?"

"Wilma said that she herself married a guy named Herb Dalton and they go to Yuma, Arizona during the winter months. She said they're home now until next winter."

"Did she say where Lacy currently lives?"

"She did, well kind of. She knows the town, but doesn't know her address or phone number."

"Where is it?'

"Cloverdale, California," Sally stated with a smile.

"Cloverdale...where's Cloverdale?"

"It's between Santa Rosa and Ukiah."

"That's a doable trip."

Sally picked up the telephone. "Yeah. Let's call information and see if there's a listing for Rob or Robert Lewis."

I nodded and she called. Her facial expressions told me she wasn't getting the information we wanted.

She hung up. "No listing for a Rob Lewis."

"I figured that would be too easy."

Sally glanced at her watch. "We better get to work."

I looked up at the wall clock, "You're right. Thanks for calling Wilma for me."

She headed for her desk, "No problem. It gave me a little adrenaline rush."

* * *

I kept busy all afternoon but don't remember what I did. How could I get Lacy's address and phone number? I was so close. I even thought about driving to Cloverdale and going house to house. It was probably a small town and I was desperate. But even I could see how ludicrous that would be.

I decided to call my friend at the police station again. I didn't like taking advantage of his position, but I was stuck. I had exhausted all my ideas. His help was all I had left, except going right to Wilma. I wasn't ready for that. Not yet. I looked at the time and dialed his work extension. It was late. He might be gone for the day. I was glad when I heard his voice.

"Hey. This is Colette."

"I figured I'd hear from you again," he said in a good-natured way.

"Could I please ask... one... more... favor?" I pleaded.

"What do you need?"

"I found the town that Lacy's in and the guy's name she's living with, but I can't find either a phone number or address."

"What's the guy's name?"

"Robert Lewis." I spelled the last name. "And her name's Lacy Ritch." I spelled that too. "They live in Cloverdale, California."

"Well, at least they're in California. I'll see what I can do and get back to you in the morning."

"Thank you so much."

Relief flooded me as I hung up the phone. If there were anything to find, he'd find it, especially since they were in California. I was almost there. A great way to end the workday.

*   *   *

On the drive home I thought about Sally's information. Lacy had a son and daughter. I wondered what her son's last name was, not that I would contact him. He might not know anything about me. Lacy had her other two children at a very young age too. She was seventeen at Allaine's birth and nineteen at Mitch's. Did being pregnant bring back memories of carrying me? It must have. But were they feelings of joy or sorrow? I wasn't sure I wanted to know.

How disabled had she become from to her accident? She must be tough to have survived rolling down 54 feet in a Volkswagen. My vision of her looking like a movie star was fading. That was a childish idea from years earlier. My only hope was that she wouldn't be too damaged to remember giving birth to me.

*   *   *

The following morning was hectic. I'd been delivering paychecks to department managers when I heard my name paged. Hoping it was my friend from the police department, I found the nearest phone.

"Colette. I found a couple Robert Lewis', but they all come up with Los Angeles addresses. Nothing in Cloverdale."

Disappointment consumed me. "What about Lacy's name?"

"No luck there either. I found a J. L. Ritch. Are you sure her last name is Ritch?"

"Well... I thought it was."

"Sorry I couldn't come up with anything in Cloverdale. They must be new to that area."

"Sounds like it. Thanks for trying."

I finished delivering paychecks and headed back to my office. The switchboard operator handed me a message in passing. It was from Marilyn at the adoption agency. It had been a few weeks since we'd talked. I'd wanted to wait and get in touch with her after finding Lacy. Oh well, maybe she'd have some helpful ideas.

Forcing myself to smile, I dialed her number.

"This is Marilyn."

"Hi Marilyn, this is Colette."

"Oh, I'm glad you got back to me so soon. How's your search going?"

"When you called earlier, I was on the line with my police officer contact. He didn't have much luck. He was my last hope of finding Lacy without seeing her mother first."

"What's wrong with seeing her mother first? She does know about you."

"I know, but I have a feeling she wouldn't be happy to see me. I wanted to try Lacy first, but guess that's not going to happen."

"I understand your feelings, but if the mother's your only lead to Lacy, I'd take it. You have her address and number, right?"

"Yes."

"Well... call her."

"Looks like I don't have much choice."

"Let me know how it goes."

"Okay, thanks Marilyn. I'll be talking with you soon."

She was right. I didn't have any choice but to call Wilma. But first I had to think about what I'd say to her.

Sally leaned over my door and told me everyone was going to lunch. Eating was the last thing on my mind, but maybe I could get some ideas from the lunch group. They never seem short on words.

*   *   *

I was given everyone's opinion of what greeting to use and what to say. It all came down to just telling her I was the baby Lacy gave up for adoption. Then let the conversation go from there, providing she didn't hang up on me. It was that simple. But was it too blunt?

I didn't eat much lunch and became more terrified as time passed. Everyone had decided I should call her at the afternoon break. That would give me about two and a half hours to make myself thoroughly sick.

Wilma might be irritated at me having the nerve to call, but my reluctance didn't stem from that possibility. I worried about her not giving me a chance to explain my intentions and being unable to tell her I was a good person. The fear that maybe she didn't want to know the person created by her daughter's rape. It was difficult. I didn't realize I'd have so much inner turmoil. It was a reminder not to predict how people displayed their emotions, only how I reacted to them.

The afternoon break rolled around faster than I wanted. Everyone stood at my door waiting for me to make the call. I felt like a bride having second thoughts—all her bridesmaids encircling her to prevent her escape. Running did enter my mind, but I wouldn't get far.

"We know the perfect place for you to make your call," Sally said.

My voice was shaky, "Where's that?"

"The back switchboard room. No one will interrupt you in there."

"You're right about that, but will I be able to hear anything?" The place was noisy.

"Just talk loud," joked Sally.

My stomach in knots, I grabbed the telephone number and some notes I'd scratched down of what to say and ask. Then I headed to the switchboard room, passing the group of supportive co-workers on my way. I couldn't remember ever being more nervous in my life, but my heart lightened as I passed each one of them. The warmth of their smiles gave me courage.

My courage disappeared when I passed the switchboard operator and entered the room behind her. It was noisy but private, with a telephone in back and a place to sit down and write. A handy wastebasket in case I *lost* my lunch. Good thing I hadn't eaten much. I began dialing. When I got to the last number I kept my finger on it, not letting it complete the turn for a while. Finally I let it go. It only rang two times and stopped. My whole body went numb.

"Hello," said an elderly woman.

"Um...is this Wilma Fisherman?"

"Yes, who's calling?"

"Ah... well... my name's Colette."

"Do I know you?"

Taking a deep breath, I said, "Um.... Yes, I think so. I'm the, um... I'm the person Lacy gave up for adoption."

"You are?"

"Yes, I am."

"You mean you're that baby girl from Sacramento?"

"Yes, that's me."

"Well, for heaven sakes. What a wonderful surprise. Do you live in Sacramento?"

"No, I live on the outskirts," I said with relief.

"You didn't go far? Have you lived in the same area all your life?"

"Yes," I said, over hearing the loud clicking noises from the switchboard.

"I'd love to see you. I live in Oildale."

"You're not that far," I said, remembering the trip Mom and I took. "I'd like to come and see you too."

"This week would be fine for me. What about you?"

"It would have to be on the weekend since I work during the week."

"Let me give you directions."

"I'd appreciate that," I said. No way would I tell her I had made the trip before. We both assured each other how anxious we were to meet and said goodbye.

Hanging up, I let out a big sigh. I still felt numb, but my blood had started circulating again. When I walked out of the switchboard room I ran right into Sally.

"How'd it go?" she asked with excitement.

"Have you been waiting here the whole time?"

"I couldn't stand it. I had to. So…?"

"I'm going to go see her on Saturday."

"Really? So she was receptive?"

"Yes, she's just as excited to see me as I am to see her."

"Did you ask her about Lacy?"

"No, I'll wait until I see her."

"Probably a good idea."

We headed back to our desks; stopping to share the outcome with everyone we passed. Thankfully, there wasn't much time left in the workday. It was difficult to concentrate on my job.

*   *   *

The next two evenings I spent at my parent's house going through my school pictures and other family photos. I thought Wilma might want to see pictures of me growing up. Mom was so helpful. She had to make sure I felt comfortable going alone, and I did. I'm not sure she was convinced after my behavior on our previous trip to Oildale. But I assured her Wilma sounded pleasant and as anxious to see me, as I was to meet her.

Excited and nervous, I went to bed Friday night more or less prepared to meet the first person in my biological family. I called Wilma. Not that I had any other choice. I hoped she felt the same excitement, but wouldn't know until our meeting the following day.

A Love Child's Journey

Chapter Nine

The alarm went off at 6:00 AM, but I had been awake for the last hour. I mulled over what to ask Wilma and how she might respond. Would she answer my questions? Most important, would she be honest? While feeding my family breakfast, my mind drifted. Preoccupied with getting ready for the journey, time passed and before I knew it I was on my way.

Anxious and apprehensive, I wondered if Wilma had contacted Lacy. Maybe she wanted to meet me first, a mother's protective action for a daughter. Our brief talk was all she knew about me. What I'd heard about her frightened me. She sounded fine on the telephone, but you never know.

By the time I reached Oildale, my thoughts were in order. Well, the best I could manage. I stopped at a gas station to freshen up. The outfit I chose to wear looked good; not that I had so many to choose from. The way my hand shook applying lipstick, I was lucky not to leave the restroom with clown lips. Back in the car, I gave myself a once over in the rearview mirror. I was ready to meet Wilma.

The dirt road to her house wasn't as scary in daylight. I saw her standing outside the front door as my car crept up her driveway. She must have been looking out her window and waiting. A good sign. Either she was eager to see me, or as nervous as me about our meeting. My heart had a fierce rhythm. I swear my car doors expanded with each throb.

After parking the car I avoided my usual once-over glance in the rearview mirror. I didn't want her to think I had any doubts about my appearance.

She was wearing a light colored dress, pretty but it didn't do much for her hefty frame. She resembled a wrestler. I wouldn't want to tangle with her but was confident I could outrun her. It was early spring, the weather cool but pleasant. I wanted to study her looks longer, but it would be rude to stare. The scowl on her face didn't give me the warm fuzzy feeling I had hoped for. Actually, she looked a little scary. There was no resemblance to the picture of Lacy. I gathered my photos and stepped out of the car.

"You don't look like anyone in this family," she said in a stern tone.

"Is… that a good thing…? Or a bad thing?" I asked, wondering what she meant. It wasn't the greeting I'd expected. Nothing like, did you have trouble finding my house? Or, how was your drive?

"It's a good thing," she said in the same stern voice

I knew right then, it would be an interesting visit. She had seemed eager to meet me and very pleased that I didn't look like anyone in her family. If Lacy had been raped, wouldn't Wilma want me to look like someone in her family, rather than the rapist family? An uneasy feeling lurched over me. Why would she make a comment like that?

Not sure what to say, I smiled and followed her up the steps. I had to be careful with my words.

Inside the large doublewide mobile home, family photos lined one wall above a hutch. Remembering the yearbook pictures, I spotted Lacy. She was stunning. Wilma was right, I didn't look like her, but I wished I did. Lacy's blue eyes mirrored two sparkling sapphires surrounded by flawless makeup. Wilma pointed out pictures of Lacy's two children, Mitch and Allaine. They didn't look like her either. There was a picture of Lacy's sister Laura. But they didn't look like sisters. Wilma picked up a family picture of her late husband, Rodney. She stared daggers at his face, and then banged the picture face down on the hutch. I waited for the shattered tinkle of glass, but nothing happened. She regained her composure, and then motioned for me to sit on the couch. I was glad when she sat in the chair across from me instead of the couch. She made me uneasy.

To break the tension, I asked, "Does Laura have any children?"

"Yes, she does, but I haven't seen them since they were small," she retorted.

Well, that question didn't do much for the tension. For lack of anything else to say, I asked, "Does Laura live somewhere else?"

"I believe she's in Oregon, but I don't know where her children are. Mike is Allaine's age. And Nora, I don't know where Laura came up with that name, Nora is Mitch's age. Then she has a younger son named Barry."

"So you haven't seen them since they were little?"

"No, Laura was jealous of the fact that I was raising Lacy's two kids. Laura was always in Lacy's shadow. She wasn't as pretty as her sister. Rodney worshiped Lacy, but didn't really want Laura."

I understood why Laura was so jealous, but I intended to keep that thought to myself.

Wilma continued, "When we took Lacy, we had to take Laura too. They had a brother, Larry, but my brother wouldn't let him go. One Christmas when Lacy was sixteen she ran away to San Francisco, Rodney said that with Lacy being gone there was no reason to have Christmas and Laura told him—but Daddy, I'm still here."

Sadness filled my heart for Laura's unimportance in her family.

"Lacy and Laura were your brother's children?"

"Only Lacy and Larry belonged to my older brother. Laura's father was my uncle's child. The kid's mother left my brother and married my uncle."

"Their mother didn't want them?"

"No, she was only concerned about herself and her men. She had a baby that died, you know."

"That's too bad."

Wilma gazed toward the window. "Probably for the best."

"How old was Lacy when you got her?"

"She just turned two and Laura was ten months."

"Lacy was very special to both you and your husband?"

"Oh yes. She was such a beautiful girl. I couldn't take her anywhere without people stopping me and telling me how beautiful she was."

Playing it safe with my words, I said, "Yes, she is pretty."

Wilma's kind smile instantly turned into an exasperated frown. "Rodney liked Lacy so much because of Lacy's mother, Rachael. He wanted her and the whole time we were there to pick up the kids, she flirted with him."

It was time to change the direction of the conversation.

"May I ask why you raised Lacy's children?"

I studied her face as she carefully chose her next words.

"Lacy wasn't interested in being a mother. She always said she was a woman first, then a mother."

That comment made me think that I didn't get my maternal instincts from her.

"You know, Allaine and Mitch have different fathers," she said. "Allaine's father was a Mexican that owned a jewelry shop in the bay area. When Lacy ran away, he snagged her up and got her pregnant."

"Wow," was the only word that seemed safe. I sensed that she had a problem with Allaine's father being Hispanic as well as getting Lacy pregnant too.

It made me wonder what she thought of me with my dark hair and olive skin. I didn't know what nationality my biological father was, but I didn't think it was Hispanic, which was probably a good thing. Wilma herself had dark hair and olive skin.

Wilma didn't skip a beat. "Mitch's father was a bar owner in Las Vegas. He died when Mitch was a baby. He was married to another woman anyway. Lacy didn't have time to raise babies, so she brought them to me."

"That had to be hard on you," I said.

"It was hard, but it was better than having them exposed to her lifestyle."

"Her lifestyle?" I repeated.

"Her flying to Las Vegas, Los Angeles and San Francisco. She made so much money that she hid it behind light switches. She's been married five or six times. I can't keep up with them. She was even married while she was working. Of course now, her body isn't the same."

Without her using the actual word, it seemed that Lacy's occupation had been that of a call girl. Wilma didn't hide her disgust. It wasn't an occupation that came to mind when I wondered what Lacy had done for a living. Married five or six times, no wonder it was difficult finding her.

Wilma showed me pictures of Lacy and Laura along with Mitch and Allaine. Lacy and Laura didn't smile much.

With the picture gazing done, I decided to brave the question I wanted to ask.

Not sure how she would respond, I asked, "Wilma please tell me about Lacy's rape."

She lowered her head and stared at the floor, "I wasn't in Forest Glen when it happened. I had to get Laura away from Lacy. Laura had always been in Lacy's shadow for too long. I thought it best to move to Oildale with her while Lacy stayed with her father. He was finishing up his job. Then he and Lacy would join us. So I wasn't there when it happened."

"What did Lacy say happened?"

"She said a traveling dress salesman came to the door and she let him in. She went in the back room to try on a dress and he raped her. All Lacy remembered was the red hair on his arms," she said, still looking down at the floor.

"Did she tell you right away?"

Lifting her head, she looked aloof, "No... but I saw her panties... I should have known then... that something had happened to her."

I didn't know what to say. Wilma was uncomfortable talking about it, but I needed to know. Why did she mention seeing Lacy's panties? My heart ached for Lacy having to go through that.

"You know... Lacy was a good girl until that happened to her and she became pregnant. Then we had to put her in a home for unwed mothers."

Her comment confused me. Why would Lacy no longer be a good girl when someone raped her? It wasn't her fault. Did Wilma feel any girl was no good after something like that happened, or did Wilma hold her responsible for it? I thought back to Marilyn's conversation at the adoption agency, how Wilma wasn't kind to her daughter during the pregnancy. I felt uneasy, but couldn't leave before finding out if she knew how to get hold of Lacy.

"You know, Lacy was able to hold you the next day after she had you. She thought you looked like Laura."

I was surprised. "I thought they took the babies away before the mother woke up."

"The aide that was working thought Lacy was keeping you, so she brought you to her. That's how she knew she had a girl."

After spending two hours with Wilma, I was glad Lacy had decided to give me up.

I listened to all the information about Lacy's accident and the illness that caused her father, Rodney's death.

Ready to leave and desperate for current information on Lacy, I bit the bullet and asked, "Wilma, can you get in touch with Lacy?"

"Well, I know she's in Cloverdale... maybe Allaine will know how to get a message to her."

"I'd really appreciate it if you could."

"I know she would love to see you."

I liked hearing that. I gave Wilma my address and phone number and thanked her for the visit. She asked me to come again. I smiled and waved goodbye. Backing down her driveway in daylight was much easier. I didn't mention I'd been to her house once before.

*   *   *

I couldn't wait to start home, but first I needed a soda. She never did offer me milk and cookies or even water. I'm glad she didn't. Spending time with her half convinced me she might have given me something to make me sick. I was the illegitimate child that ruined her daughter's life.

It was a frightening thought that Wilma could have been my main caregiver.

After finishing my soda, I headed home. How strange that Wilma spoke in a manner that made me a different person from the baby girl given away in Sacramento.

*   *   *

Consumed with thoughts of Lacy, the drive didn't take long. I couldn't stop thinking of the fear she must have felt. Raped and pregnant with no emotional support must have been unbearable. I wondered what the home for unwed mothers had been like. Did they treat her well or make her feel ashamed? A chill rushed over me as I thought of her pregnant and unmarried. At thirteen, I didn't understand anything about my body. I hadn't even started my period. If I'd become pregnant as she did, I would have been clueless.

I wondered how many girls lived at the home. What did they do while waiting to have their babies? How painful had it been to endure such a mature situation? How did they cope after leaving the home, especially if they left empty-handed? I suppose, giving up their babies was the right decision for many of them, if it was their decision. But, I wondered if it was. They all carried those babies for nine months and felt the first stirrings of another life. Their separations had to be heartbreaking, even at the age of fourteen.

There was something odd about Lacy's rape. Wilma's immediate comment about me not looking like anyone in her family was strange, and so was her being happy about it. After all, it wasn't my fault. Caution came to mind after that remark. She didn't say what happened after finding out that their daughter had been raped. I sensed there was more information than what she told me. Maybe that's why Marilyn encouraged me to pursue this search. She knew more than I did, but I couldn't ask her to reveal it. That was the unspoken understanding we shared.

Wilma gave the impression of wanting to share the news of my visit. I hoped she'd share it with Lacy, but the two of them didn't seem to have much contact. It didn't look like Wilma saw much of Laura either. The way she talked of being a doting mother didn't fit if both her daughters were no longer interested in her.

The woman struck me as someone you wouldn't want to upset; her mood might change suddenly.

I was more confident of her calling Lacy's daughter Allaine, the most likely source for Lacy's location. I'd wait a few days before calling Wilma to ask if she'd contacted Lacy. It was an interesting trip and I was glad I went. I knew it would be just a matter of time before I met Lacy, so for now I had to be patient and wait.

*   *   *

I hadn't been home long when the telephone rang.
Emotionally drained, I pushed myself to answer. "Hello."
A male voice said, "Is this Colette?"
"Yes it is."
"You don't know me. I'm Mitch, Lacy's son and... your brother."
My tiredness instantly vanished, "Oh...Hi." Hearing brother sounded odd, but that's what he was.
"I hope you don't mind that I called," he said, polite but serious.
"No, not at all. I'm glad. I guess you talked to your grandmother."
Hesitating, "No, I haven't talked to her in a while, but I did talk with my sister, Allaine."
"I'm surprised to hear from you so soon."
"Yeah... I thought about waiting until tomorrow, but I couldn't. My sister and I have always known about you and I swore one day I'd find you."
What a warm thing to say. I liked him.
"Thank you."
"I'd like to meet you soon."
"Yes, me too. I can't wait to meet Lacy."
"Well... there's a problem with that."
"What do you mean by a problem?" I asked.
"Mom's biggest dream was to someday meet you... but since Nammie, or Wilma as you know her, has talked with you, Mom now doesn't feel comfortable about meeting with you."

Confused, I said, "But I tried to find her first."

"I know, but she knows Nammie told you about her and her lifestyle. They don't talk much."

"I gathered that. I don't care what Nannie, Nammie or whatever you call her said. I didn't find Lacy to judge her. I want to tell her I'm okay and thank her. I gathered that your grandmother is... well... scary."

"That's putting it mildly. You don't realize it yet, but you're the lucky one."

"What do you mean?"

"She used to dress me in white clothes and send me out to play then threaten to spank me if I got dirty. Boys and white clothes don't mix. Her spankings were more like beatings. She had a large wooden paddle that hung in the kitchen. It was off the wall more than on."

"I'm sorry." Unsure how to respond to his remark."

"She stayed up late into the early morning, and if she found something or thought of something she didn't like that I'd done, I'd wake up to her beating me with the paddle. Boys aren't her favorite."

Listening, I was speechless. I knew right then that he was right. I was the lucky one, even if I was a girl.

"I remember one time when Grampy, or Rodney to you, was painting the kitchen and didn't move the paddle, just painted over it. Allaine and I thought it was pretty funny, but of course Nammie wasn't too happy."

I laughed with him, but couldn't imagine living like that. Had Lacy been aware of these things or was she too busy with her own life?

"Well... do you think you can talk Lacy into seeing me?"

I hoped I didn't sound as frustrated as I felt.

"I tried, but she didn't want you to think badly of her without getting to know her. She wanted you to form your own opinion after she had a chance to talk with you."

Disappointed, I said, "I do that with everyone I meet."

"She doesn't know that. What I'd do is write her a letter and tell her how you feel. Maybe she'll get a better idea of the person you are. I mean, you sound pretty normal, and coming from our family that's a good thing."

"Okay. I guess it's better to write than call her."

"She doesn't have a telephone anyway."

"Then the letter will have to do. Do you have her address?"

He gave me the address and we shared some more information about ourselves and a few more Wilma stories. The more he talked, the more frightened I became of Wilma. She was very abusive, if his stories were true. And I had no reason to doubt them. I'd have to think about it before visiting her again. He said he'd be calling me soon to plan a time and place to meet. I enjoyed talking with Mitch. He seemed like a nice person. But I was disappointed that Lacy felt uncomfortable talking with me after I'd seen Wilma. If I'd had a choice, I would've gladly skipped Wilma completely, but at the time I was out of leads. In a round about way, it did get me to Lacy. Well, kind of. It might turn out to have been the wrong thing to do, but at least I got to speak with Mitch. He seemed to have a good relationship with our mother. I was too tired to think about what to say to her anyway. Tomorrow I'd write her. Tonight I needed sleep.

A Love Child's Journey

Chapter Ten

My mind wrote all night long. I didn't have much luck with sleep. I had to be careful with my words so as not to ruin what might be my one chance of convincing Lacy to see me. I understood her feelings. She had waited and hoped all these years to see her first child, only to have someone interfere and mar her image. It wasn't about whether it was true or not; she wanted to relate to me from the mother image.

It was important to get across that her image wasn't my focus and wouldn't keep me from seeing her. I found her occupation intriguing, but knew nothing about it. Prostitution was an entirely different world, alien to me. I would have to know her better before approaching that subject. Lots better. I organized my thoughts and started my letter:

Dear Lacy,

I understand your not wanting to see me after I talked with Wilma first. I wanted you to be first, but I ran out of leads. I didn't want to disrupt your family. But going to them was the only way to find you. I was unaware of the fact that everyone in your family knew about me. First and foremost, please do not think I found you to judge either you or your lifestyle. I have no right to do that, and I wouldn't. I haven't walked in your shoes, so how could I know. I just wanted to thank you and get to know you and see what you looked like. I want you to know me too. My life has been great, but it would be nice to know who brought me into this world. I'm sorry that you had to endure so much at such a young age, but I'm glad you had me. Please find it in your heart to give me this opportunity.

I added a second page and told her about my life growing up and my family. I wanted her to understand me a little and hoped to ease any ill feelings she might have. I finished my letter and took it to the post office. It was Sunday, so it would take a few days before she received it. Now all I had to do was wait.

Later that day I called Mom and filled her in on my visit with Wilma and the call from Mitch. She was very happy for me and thrilled that she didn't have to make another drive to Wilma's place.

*   *   *

At work the next day, everyone was anxious to hear about my visit with Wilma. It amazed me how far I'd come in less than two months. Everyone had been so helpful. I wanted to call Marilyn, but wanted to have already visited with Lacy before that.

Time seemed to stand still as I waited to hear from my birth mother. When I got home from work on Thursday, I was surprised to find a letter from her. A cheerful sensation fluttered through me. Not knowing what she thought of my letter, I hoped I would continue to be thrilled after opening hers.

The first thing I noticed was her nice handwriting. I opened it as if it was a birthday gift, careful not to tear the handwritten address. Her letter was written on stationery paper and dated March 3, 1980. The first few pages brought tears to my eyes:

Dear Colette,

I just received your most welcoming letter. Never in my wildest dreams did I ever visualize seeing you again. I hope very much that I can become your friend. Of course you will always be my daughter, even though you may call me by my first name since your Mom and Dad are yours for the rest of your life. You must have developed your love and courage from them to exercise your right to find your birthmother. To me, a mother is someone who is always there, through happiness and strife, not just delivering a child. The circumstances of your birth are something I would like to explain to you because it was against what I wanted, but it appears to have turned out for the best. I wasn't supposed to see you, but one of the girls staying there to have a baby was working as an aide and didn't realize I wasn't keeping my child, so she brought you to me the next morning. You were beautiful (I thought you looked like my sister). I inspected your body to make sure you had all your fingers and toes. You weighed 7lbs 10ozs. Those things and your date of birth are all I have ever known.

In the next pages, she explained that she was bothered by my seeing Wilma first, but decided that it really didn't matter in the scheme of things. She told me about her accident and explained that it was her fault. She'd been drinking before driving her Volkswagen. She swerved and went off a cliff. The car rolled but fortunately she was thrown out of it. A lot of her bones were broken, but no one else was hurt. As a result she was slightly disabled and walked with a limp. She said Mitch and Allaine had always known they had an older sister and both were anxious to meet me. Finally, at the end of her letter, she invited me to come and visit her. That's what I'd been waiting to read.

She seemed to express herself in a motherly way. She did all the things a new mother would have done after having a baby, even at fourteen: inspecting her baby and cuddling it. That's what I did with my son.

The letter made me feel more at ease with her and pleased that she remembered details about me from so long ago. I couldn't wait to meet her. She didn't sound mentally disabled at all, as Wilma had hinted. My uneasiness about Wilma grew deeper, especially after Mitch's stories. Could I trust anything she'd told me?

Now willing to see me, I had no way of getting a hold of Lacy. I'd have to wait for Mitch to call me.

*   *   *

I ran to answer the ringing telephone. "Hello."
"Hi, this is Mitch." It was as if he had read my mind.
"I hoped you'd call soon."
"Well... I knew what day Mom sent the letter to you and figured you'd have it."
"I got it today. She wants to see me."
"She sure does. Do you have a rig?"
"A rig?" I said, puzzled by the question. I associated a rig with an eighteen-wheeler and I didn't have one of those.
"You know, a truck or a car."
"Oh... yeah I have both."
"Can you drive to Cloverdale on Saturday?"
"Sure, but I'm not sure where it is." I said.
"It's not too far north from Santa Rosa. There's a little burger place on the main drag when you get into town. I'll meet you there. We can talk and then I'll take you to Mom's place."
"Sounds good."
 He gave me directions and we decided on the time to meet and said goodbye. I couldn't believe it. In two days I was going to meet my birth mother and my half-brother. This is what I'd been waiting for.
Wanting to share my news, I called Mom.
 She was pleased and happy for me. She offered to watch my son, but I told her I thought Lacy might want to see him too. She agreed but asked me to be careful. I told her I'd call her after my visit. I still had to get through one more day at work and two more nights of sleep.

*   *   *

 Preoccupied by my upcoming meeting with Lacy made it difficult to get to sleep. What should I say? I'd take some pictures of me to share, but I was unsure what we'd talk about. I didn't think she'd want to talk about her rape, although I was very curious about it. I'm the result, but she might consider it too personal to discuss. Would seeing me stir up emotions and memories she had tried to forget? I wondered if she was thinking about these things too. I felt uneasy but excited. I'd have to wait and let the encounter play itself out. Quieting my thoughts, I eventually fell asleep.

*   *   *

Anxious to get to work and share my news, I left home earlier than usual. I wanted the day to be over, so I figured if I started it sooner, it would end sooner. At least in my mind. My co-workers were overjoyed with my news. Sally couldn't contain herself. Every time she walked by, she reminded me to be polite and respectful when I met Lacy. I *thanked* her each time. I didn't need to be reminded of my manners. Manners were tattooed in my mind and on my butt by my parents since I was very young, but her intentions were good. I don't think she had any better idea of what to say than I did. But I agreed with her, being polite goes a long way when all else fails. Starting the day early didn't make it end any sooner, but at last the workday was over.

Leaving the building, I began making a mental list of things to pack for my trip to Cloverdale. It was about a three-hour drive. I wanted to be prepared with snacks, drinks, bottles, diapers, and of course my pictures. One-minute pangs of excitement rushed through me, the next minute my heart beat so fast that I had to speed the car to catch up with it. In the past I had handled just about anything that came my way, but this situation created a rash of emotions I hadn't experienced. Fear of rejection swallowed up my confidence. I tried to erase it from my thoughts, but it only stayed away temporarily.

*   *   *

It was a beautiful spring day and by mid-morning my son and I were on our way to Cloverdale. He was a few months shy of the terrible twos, but a comfort to have with me. I could express my feelings and say anything and he'd have no idea what I was talking about. He loved me no matter what, the ideal audience. Traffic was light, but being nervous I ate all my snacks within the first hour on the road. My son's snacks didn't look as appetizing, so I left them alone. The remaining time I spent pointing out things to entertain him and keep my mind busy.

At Cloverdale I slowed to look for the meeting place. It didn't take long. A guy sat on a picnic table outside an old hamburger stand. It was probably Mitch. My heart began to pick up speed. I'd seen pictures of him as a small boy, but nothing current. When I drove closer he stood up, a tall slender young man with coarse bushy hair. He had a serious expression for a guy who wasn't yet twenty years old. Did his seriousness mean Lacy didn't want to see me? I'd hoped so much for a joyous outcome. I took a deep breath to avoid hyperventilating. Not that I ever had, but there's always a first.

His eyes stayed on me as I parked. Uncomfortable with his scrutiny, I wondered what he was thinking. He gave me a quick smile before the serious expression returned. I guess I was on display. I returned his smile, and then turned my attention to my sleeping son. He was tired and needed the nap. I was relieved we could leave my toddler in the truck and sit outside next to it. Still being watched I gracefully began my exit from the truck. That is if slithering down instead of hopping down is graceful.

Approaching me, he said, "Colette, right?"

I extended my hand to him. "Yes, nice to finally meet you, Mitch."

His voice had a deep soft tone, pleasant and comforting.

He laughed and shook my hand. "Yeah, same here. Did you have trouble finding this place?"

"No, not at all. Would you like something to drink?" I asked looking for a distraction to calm my nerves.

"No, I'm fine."

I pointed to the takeout window of the hamburger joint. "I need to get something to drink."

He sat down at the picnic table. "Go ahead. I'll wait here."

I nodded and walked toward the window. I sensed him staring at me, most likely sizing me up. It was a little unnerving, but I was doing the same to him. In my quick glimpse, I didn't see much resemblance between us. We both had brown hair and eyes, but my hair was darker. His facial features were very different from mine. I'd been hoping we looked more alike, but we did have different fathers.

Returning with a soda in hand, I sat down on the other side of the picnic table. There we were eye to eye. His demeanor was very controlled and serious, and appeared mature for his age. I almost was expecting him to start spewing off current events from the newspaper, which was never good news.

"Is something wrong?" I asked.

"No... no, not at all," he said.

"She still wants to see me, right?" I asked with apprehension.

His look intensified, "Oh yeah, but you need to understand some things about her before you do."

"Sure. I don't have any expectations."

"I know... I figured you heard from Nammie that Mom was a call girl. She's not proud of it, but that's what she did. She's also been married a lot of times and she was in a bad car accident..."

I interrupted him. "I know about these things and it's okay. I mean, it's her life and it doesn't seem like her life has been too great. Or yours either, for that matter."

Staring at Mitch and guessing how hard his early life must have been, I realized just how lucky I was to be adopted out.

Another deep laugh rolled out of his mouth. "I had to grow up fast, that's for sure, but Mom's different since her accident. She was so beautiful and confident. She didn't take crap from anyone. She was in a coma for a long time. She had to learn to talk and walk again... But that's another story. She did suffer some brain damage."

"She seems to write fine and it made sense," I said.

"Most people wouldn't even know, but she is different. A little kinder, but she drinks too much now."

I nodded, not knowing what to say.

He continued. "She's always said her life wasn't too bad before she got pregnant with you. After living with Nammie, I find that hard to believe, but that's what she says."

"Yeah, your grandmother was kind of... uh... she seemed... well, weird," I said, hoping I wasn't too abrasive.

He let out a loud deep laugh, "She's weird alright, and she's a wacko case and should be in the loony bin."

We both laughed. Laughing at the expense of his grandmother relaxed both of us.

"You know what the first thing she said to me was?"

"Nothing would surprise me coming from her," he said.

"She said I didn't look like anyone in her family and it was good that I didn't. I thought with Lacy being raped, that she'd want me to look like someone in the family." I was still confused by her comment.

His serious scowl returned, "Did she mention Grampy or Rodney to you?"

"Yeah, she told me about his death and that he visited Lacy when she had her car accident."

"She didn't say anything about Grampy and Mom?"

"No, she just said she and Rodney couldn't have children and they thought it was Rodney who couldn't father, but later found out it was her," I sensed what he was going to say next.

"Well... the story is you're supposed to be Grampy's child," he said in a matter of fact tone.

"Your grandfather's. Lacy's dad might be my father? Like incest?" I asked.

"That's what Mom says. Every time Allaine and I saw a girl your age with red hair and freckles, we wondered if it was you. Grampy had red hair, freckles, hazel green eyes and he wore long sleeve shirts to protect his ghostly complexion."

"As you can see, I have dark hair, brown eyes and my complexion is more to the olive side. According to my adoption paper, Lacy is fair, blonde and blue eyed."

"She has red hair now. The good thing is that Mom and Grampy aren't biologically related, so you don't have to worry about being goofy or anything like that." He giggled. "Remember Mom was adopted too."

"I guess that's a comfort. Although if I was goofy or whatever, I probably wouldn't be aware of it," I remarked.

"I do see some of Mom in you. After watching you it's interesting that even though you haven't been around Mom, you have many of her mannerisms. You have a larger nose than Allaine and I, but you don't look like Grampy. He was just plain ugly."

"Well, your Grandmother didn't think I looked like him or Lacy," I added.

"Yeah, but that's the story. Mom won't talk about it. In fact, that subject is off limits with her. You can ask her about her call girl jobs and she'll tell you more than you want to hear, but nothing to do with your conception," he said sadly.

"How did your Grandmother find out?" I asked.

"When Mom was about twenty-three years old or so, she got drunk at some bar and called up Nammie and said, "do you want to know who the father of that baby girl is, it's your husband's," Mitch said softly.

"Wow, I knew some of the things she said didn't add up when I was talking with her, but I wasn't sure what it was about. Your Grandmother told me about seeing Lacy's panties and about the dress salesman who came to the door and raped Lacy when she was trying on a dress.

"That's the story Mom and Grampy came up with," Mitch said.

"I'm confused. In the letter she wrote me, she said that I was conceived by rape."

"You were. Grampy, her father, had sex with her when she was thirteen years old. That's rape when you mess with your own child who's only thirteen. It's sick and he messed up her life," Mitch said with anger.

Empathy and sadness filled my heart. Mitch was right it was rape. I was glad to be alive, but I couldn't fathom going through such an ordeal. Mitch seemed to have Lacy's best interest at heart and was very protective of her. I assured him I wouldn't say anything to hurt or upset her in any way. If Mitch's grandfather —— Lacy's dad —— was my dad, it was just too weird. I didn't think Mitch was convinced of it, but he did seem positive that his grandfather had sex with Lacy.

He showed me a picture of his own dad, the Las Vegas bar owner. It was amazing how much he looked like him. Mitch said his dad was married and had a family, but died shortly after Mitch's birth. Allaine's dad lived in San Francisco but didn't see Allaine much. He too was married with a family when he got Lacy pregnant. He had divorced and married Lacy for a short time. It didn't last long so they had it annulled and he then went back to his wife. Mitch stated that Allaine's father was Hispanic and she looked a lot like him too, but had some of Lacy's features like me.

I checked on my sleeping son and we talked some more. Allaine stayed with Nammie until she was fourteen, but Mitch had gone to live with Lacy when he was nine. They moved to and from a lot of different towns and places. It was unsettling to listen to, but Mitch seemed unfazed by it. I only remember moving once as a child and it was difficult. I couldn't imagine moving around so much all the time.

I shared the pictures I brought to show Lacy and talked about my life with my family. Mitch listened intently to everything I said. He seemed to enjoy our visit as much as me.

"Well, I think we better get over to Mom's. She's going to be wondering what happened to us; we've been talking for over an hour. She's so nervous that this waiting is probably driving her crazy."

"I didn't realize we'd been talking so long, but it's hard to cover so much in a short time."

Mitch sounded serious again. "Here's what we'll do. You follow me in your rig to her house and then I'll take you in and introduce you to Mom and Rob, her husband. They just got married about a month ago. Rob and I will leave so you two can talk."

Not sure about his sense of humor I decided not to salute him, I said, "Sounds good."

The car he stepped in appeared to have been around for a while and time had taken a toll on it, but it started right up. Not worried about being lady like, I hopped in the truck. My son stirred, but continued to sleep. Mitch waited as I pulled in behind him.

Visiting with Mitch relaxed me and I wanted to know more about Lacy's life, but my anxiety began to return stronger than ever. In the time it takes to drive a few blocks, I would be meeting my birth mother. I looked at my son and smiled.

A Love Child's Journey

Chapter Eleven

I pulled up behind Mitch and parked my truck. Looking around, I took a moment to relax. Setting back on a small hill was what looked like a row of old motel units. Their patchy lawns sloped down to the sidewalk with a cement walkway leading up to each door. I'd never been inside anything like this before. But it was Lacy's home and I came to see her, regardless of how or where she lived.

I picked up my sleeping son and waited for Mitch to take the lead. Holding my baby made me feel that I could handle anything. I had my child and that's what mattered, a protective mother increasing her inner strength.

Mitch asked, "Are you ready for this?"

"As ready as I'll ever be." I thought the sound of my thumping heart would wake the baby.

"Do you want me to carry him for you?" asked Mitch.

Not wanting to let go of my security blanket, I said, "Oh no, I'm fine; I carry him all the time. But thanks for asking."

"It's kind of a steep climb up the yard," he pointed out.

"I'm fine."

"Okay."

"Is this a motel?" I asked.

"No, they're Kitchenettes. They usually have a small kitchen area, living area and one bedroom. They're not the best place to live, but at least it's a roof over her head."

"Yeah, that's good." I didn't know what else to say.

When we got to the top of the yard sweat beaded my forehead. It wasn't from climbing the hill, but from the encounter ahead. Drops of sweat started running down the sides of my face. Mitch must have noticed and stopped walking to let me recover. He smiled as we moved on toward one of the doors. I felt numb. Everything began to blur. Mitch stopped and gestured that this was her place. I nodded. If I hadn't been holding my son, I felt that I might sink down through a crack in the walkway.

I knew the minute I walked through that door my life would change. But I wasn't sure if it would be a change for the better or worse.

Mitch tapped his knuckles a few times on the door, and then walked in. I followed.

"Here she is," he announced to a woman sitting on the couch.

I couldn't focus on her.

She looked at me and said, "You're beautiful."

"Thank you." I managed to say, feeling like a deer blinded by headlights. Everything seemed vague.

When I looked at her, my eyes went right to her boobs. I hoped she didn't notice. They were big! Not that I was intrigued with boobs, but now I knew where mine came from. There's one connection. I liked that, although I often wished mine were smaller.

She asked something about the drive to Cloverdale. I pretended to be listening, but was comparing her to images from the photos at Wilma's. Her hair red instead of light brown and her front teeth slightly gapped, probably from her accident. But her sapphire blue eyes were as stunning as in her old photos. Her makeup seemed professionally done. A little heavier, but still she was a beauty. I traced every part of her face, but couldn't see any resemblance between us. How I wished I had her blue eyes.

Mitch introduced me to Rob, Lacy's husband and the men left. The room was bigger than it looked from the outside. There were two couches, one on each side of the room. A few pictures hung on the white walls, throw pillows sat neatly on the couches. Nothing looked new, but everything was clean and nice. I sat on the couch opposite of Lacy, laying my son down beside me.

"So that's your Chase?" she asked.

"Yes, he's been sleeping for awhile. I keep thinking he'll wake up soon, but he hasn't. I'm glad he's still asleep; this way we can talk."

"You want a soda or something?"

"No thanks, I had one while Mitch and I were talking."

"I'm glad you two had some time to get to know each other."

"He's a real nice guy."

"Yes, he is. I want Allaine to meet you too."

"I'd like that. I brought some pictures to show you, if you'd like to see them."

"Of course I would love to see them."

She didn't try to move from the couch, so I took the pictures to her. I remembered that she had a leg or foot problem. My impression was that she didn't want me to see her disability.

"Here I am at two months. This was taken the day my parents brought me home from the adoption agency."

"You mean your parents didn't get you until you were two months old?"

Surprised at her surprise I said, "Babies had to be close to two months old before they went to live with their adopted family."

"Where did they keep you?"

"I was in a foster home."

"Then they lied to me at Fairhaven. They told me you'd go right to a loving home, not foster care." She looked somber.

Trying to lighten the mood, I said, "I don't think it hurt me."

"Well, that's a good thing," she added.

She looked through the remaining pictures while I told her about each one, but she wasn't paying much attention. Finding out I'd been placed in a foster home had upset her.

She asked about my parents and said she'd like to meet them and thank them for doing such a loving job of raising me. She didn't mention her line of work or her mother. She talked in a very motherly way and I could tell she didn't want me to know the unsavory details of her life. She did say she had wanted to keep me. She also told me that she ran away about a year after my birth to try and get me back from the Fairhaven home. Her voice had been loud while we talked, but softened when she told me that. I could feel the ache in her heart. If she had found me and somehow gotten me back, it would've been heart wrenching for Mom. Would I have ended up in Wilma's care? I shuddered at the thought. It all worked out for the best for Mom and me but I'm not sure it did for Lacy.

My son woke up, and I realized she wasn't into children. Although kind, she showed no real interest in him. I didn't inherit my love of children from her. That was okay. Everyone's different.

But I've often thought about what characteristics are inherited and which ones we get from our environment. After spending time with Lacy, I wondered if they'd not only lied to her at Fairhaven, but also switched babies. She and I were so different.

My son was being good, but I probably should have left him home. Lacy was very selective in her conversation and made it clear that her life was not an open book for the asking. I told her I respected that, but after telling her all about my life, I ran out of things to say. The conversation didn't exactly lag, but it was surface talk. I knew I couldn't ask her anything about my father, whoever he was. It disappointed me, but didn't seem that important at the time. I wasn't sure what else to ask or avoid asking so we talked about current events and other safe boring things.

I was glad when Mitch and Rob returned. I told everyone it was time for me to head home. Lacy didn't get up to say goodbye, but I walked over and hugged her.

She hugged me back to the point of near asphyxiation, saying, "I've wanted to do this for so many years. Thank you for finding me."

"You're so welcome."

Carrying Chase and my things, I left her with an invitation to come and stay at my house. That way she could meet my family. She said she'd like that. Mitch walked me to my truck.

"Did you have a good visit?" he asked.

"Yes, it was nice." I pointed to my breast. "Now I know where these came from."

'Well... I hate to be the one to burst your bubble, but hers aren't real."

"What?"

He laughed. "She didn't have much on top so she had a boob job."

"Oh, well... I guess that theory didn't work out."

Hugging me, he said, "It's been nice meeting you, Sis."

I liked him calling me Sis. "Same here."

"I'll be giving you a call. Don't forget to write Mom. And me too."

"Okay."

It was a relief to be back on the road heading home. I needed time to get used to everything. Sometimes I felt surreal. I had worked toward this encounter for only two months, yet the search had consumed my daily thoughts and routine to the point of obsession. This made it seem like a much longer time, but in retrospect, no time at all. I didn't get a lot of information about my origin, but at least she now knows what happened to her first child. She knows I was loved and had a wonderful family. Where it will go from here, I have no idea, but she does want to visit me again. And I want to meet Allaine and see Mitch again. As to the grandmother, that's something else. I can wait a while on that.

I looked over at my son and said, "I'm glad you came with me today."

He smiled, exposing chewed bits of cracker in his mouth. How could I not love that?

After my first visit with Lacy, I was sure I'd made the right decision to find her.

It was late when I got home. I put Chase to bed, exhausted I headed for mine.

*   *   *

I hadn't been up long when the telephone rang.

"Hello."

"It's your Mom," she said as if I didn't recognize her voice.

I chuckled. "I was going to call you, but I haven't been up that long."

"I couldn't wait any more. You know your father; he wakes me up at the crack of dawn."

"Yeah, how well I remember."

"Did you have a nice visit with Lacy?" Her voice was eager.

"I did. I really enjoyed Mitch too."

"Now that you've seen her when she's older, do you think you look like her?" She sounded curious.

"Actually, I don't think I look like her at all, not at this time in her life. But get this, the story is that Lacy's adopted father is my father."

"Really. Is that what she said?"

"No, she didn't even mention it and made it clear I shouldn't ask about her past because she doesn't talk about that with anyone. Mitch is the one who told me."

"She was molested by her own father?"

"Actually he was her adopted father. But, yes it seems so; Mitch said I don't look like him at all. He said the man had red hair and was very fair and just plain ugly."

"Well, that doesn't sound at all like you."

"I hope not. Lacy did tell me she'd like to meet you and Dad. Would that be okay?"

"I'd like to meet her too, but I'm not sure about your Dad. I'll talk with him. I think he'll be okay with it, though," she added.

"She wants to thank you both. She seems to think you did a pretty good job of raising me," I boasted.

"Well, we got the job done," she laughed.

"She lives in a Kitchenette with no telephone. I'm not big on writing, but I guess that's the only way I'll be able to communicate with her for now."

"What did she think of Chase?" she asked.

"Well… I wouldn't say she was big on kids. He was great and a comfort to have with me, but I should have left him home with you."

"Everyone's different," she reminded me.

"That's true."

"Let me know when she'll be visiting you. I'll make sure your dad behaves himself."

"I'll let you know as soon as I know. Oh, I almost forgot. Lacy said that when I was about a year old she ran away to Fairhaven home to try and get me back."

"Yes. The adoption agency notified us about that, but we heard nothing more. She couldn't have supported you without her parents' help and they wouldn't help her."

"Wow. That had to make you a little uneasy though." I didn't remember ever hearing that story.

"It did, but nothing came of it."

"Well, I'll stop by to see you in a couple of days."

"Sounds good to me. Love you honey."

"Love you too Mom."

I was thankful Mom didn't seem hurt by my finding Lacy. She and Dad knew how much I appreciated them adopting me. I couldn't fathom living the life of Mitch's childhood, but he seems to have survived it well. He told me Lacy signed papers for him to quit high school at sixteen. She must not have thought of education as important. Lacy occasionally drank with Mitch and they'd lived with some abusive men. The thought of quitting high school never entered my mind and my mom didn't drink, let alone drink with her children.

I don't think the grandmother would have treated me well at all, especially if she found out I was her husband's daughter. But she seemed convinced I wasn't his when she saw me. I couldn't imagine why Lacy would say he was if it wasn't true. I didn't worry about it. I wanted to get to know Lacy. I figured the father part would fall into place later.

*   *   *

Monday was a busy day for payroll so I went to work an hour earlier than usual. I knew that once the accounting staff arrived, they'd bombard me with questions about my visit. It surprised me that Sally hadn't called over the weekend.

Soon the echo of high heels entered the large accounting office.

"Are you there?" Sally yelled.

"If you're talking to me, I'm here," I yelled back.

She continued yelling. "Everyone's waiting in the break room to hear how your visit went."

"I'll be there soon," I shouted, not realizing she had arrived at my door.

"You know, it was all I could do to keep from calling you this weekend, and now you're working. We want the scoop!" she stomped her foot in fake anger.

"I wanted to get some work done before I start talking. It's Monday and payroll time. Sandy's been so lenient with me. I thought I'd work a little harder to show her how much I appreciate her looking the other way when I was working on my search instead of doing my job."

"Okay, you've worked some, now it's time to talk some. Come on!" she insisted with a cocky toss of her head.

"All right." I said, giving in. "Let's go to the break room."

The moment I entered, everyone swarmed around me. I smiled, realizing that this moment would probably be the closest I'd ever get to celebrity status. The only difference was that I knew all the people gathering around me. I was pleased that they cared.

I gave them a moment-by-moment update. They enjoyed the part about Lacy's large breasts, which turned out to be fake. But everyone fell silent when I told them her adopted father had molested her and I was the result.

"That's horrible," Sally exclaimed.

"Yeah. According to Mitch, Lacy's son, the dress salesman that raped her was a story made up by Lacy and her father.

"What did she tell you?" Sally asked.

"Nothing. She put it in a nice way, but made it clear that her past was not up for discussion."

"They didn't arrest him or report him to the police?" asked Sally.

"I guess not. According to Mitch, the grandmother didn't find out about it until ten years after it happened."

"And she stayed with her husband, after knowing what he did to their daughter?" questioned Sally.

"She did. However, when I met the grandmother, she said I didn't look like anyone in her family and she was pleased at that. So maybe it wasn't him but someone else. Who knows?"

"Well, at least you and your birth mother got to meet and that's the main thing. Now you can call her and talk with her," said Sally.

"If she had a telephone? She's hoping to get one soon," I said.

"No telephone? You'll have to write her then," Sally stated.

"Yeah, I guess. I'm not sure where it'll go from here, but I'm glad I found her. Thank you guys for all your help. I couldn't have done it without you."

It was a quiet walk back to the accounting department. They were happy for me, but somber. At that moment, I realized that everyone who gathered around me had taken my journey alongside me. I was truly fortunate to be surrounded by such wonderful supportive people.

* * *

Later that afternoon I called the adoption agency and gave Marilyn all the details. I hadn't talked to her for a while and she was happy to hear about my progress and success. She asked if I could come in and see her one more time. I wanted to see her too. She said she'd call in a week or so and arrange our meeting.

Exhausted, I couldn't wait to get home. For the past two months, I'd been on an emotional roller coaster. I needed to catch up on rest. Although tired, I appreciated how short a time it took to find Lacy.

From what I'd heard, some people search for years. Others search but never find their birth parents. I had been very lucky.

My telephone rang, as I was about to leave the office at the end of the day.

I didn't want to answer it, but the switchboard operator would just page me if I didn't.

"Payroll," I said.

"Colette?"

"Yes," I answered.

"This is Lacy. I'm sorry to bother you at work," she said, apologetic.

I was shocked —— I hadn't recognized her voice. She was the last person I expected to hear on the other end, "No, it's fine. I was just getting ready to go home."

"My neighbor's letting me use her telephone, so I have to be quick. Rob needs to come to Sacramento Friday after next. I thought if you weren't busy that weekend, I could visit you then. If that works out for you."

Detecting apprehension in her voice, I said, "That should be fine... You could stay over Friday night and then Saturday you can meet my parents."

"That would be great. Rob can drop me off Friday afternoon and pick me up Saturday evening. Could you mail me the directions to your house?"

Trying hard not to sound hesitant, I said, "I'll get them in the mail tomorrow."

"Sounds good. I'll call you before I leave. I'm really looking forward to seeing you again."

"Me too."

When I hung up, I felt numb. This took me by surprise. I hadn't expected to hear from her so soon. I hoped my husband wouldn't be mad. He hadn't supported my search for Lacy and now she was coming to stay at our house on short notice. That wouldn't go over big. But I wanted her to come and meet my parents, so he'd just have to cope. I told myself it would all work out. That sounded good, but was it true?

I had to call Mom and tell her Lacy would be here in a couple of weeks, but that could wait until tomorrow. I was still getting over the shock of my first meeting with my biological mother. I wasn't yet ready to deal with her coming to my house.

But ready or not, she was going to visit me in two weeks.

A Love Child's Journey

Chapter Twelve

I had taken a vacation day for the Friday when Lacy would arrive. My mom and dad were excited about meeting her. Fortunately my husband would be working that Friday night and all day Saturday, which reduced some of my tension. He could meet Lacy in passing with very little exchange. He wouldn't have time to say something embarrassing or make her feel uncomfortable. Not much could make me any more uncomfortable than I was. I just met her two weeks ago and now she was coming to spend the night at my house. I really didn't know much about her. According to her son, Lacy had been a call girl, drinks and smokes too much, but she did deliver me twenty-five years ago. Her own mother, who biologically is her aunt sounded kind of crazy. There wasn't much comfort in that. Our lifestyles have been very different. But I was intrigued by hers and wanted to know more about it. Maybe she wanted to know more about mine.

*   *   *

I spent the morning cleaning and by afternoon I was ready for company. Our usual houseguest was either a girl or boy about ten or eleven spending the night with my stepchildren. Except having to share a room for the night, both kids were excited about meeting Lacy.

Later they both raced each other to the door when the doorbell rang. My heart sank with the same apprehension as when I first met my birth mother.

Holding a small overnight bag in her hand, Lacy said, "You two must be Randy and Julie?"

Simultaneously they both said, "Yes."

It was the first time I'd seen her standing up. She stepped forward with her good foot, and then slowly dragged the other foot up beside it. Her drop foot gave the appearance that one leg was shorter than the other. Not wanting to focus on her walking, I turned with a "Let's sit over here" and led her to the dining table, pulling out a chair for her.

"Did you have any trouble finding the house?" I asked, turning to seat myself as she did the same.

She placed her bag on the floor, "No, you gave great directions."

"Good," I said, then motioned the kids to take their little brother in the other room and play. Reluctantly, Julie picked up Chase and they headed for her room.

I pointed to the doorway off the dining room. "Randy is going to sleep in his sister's room tonight so you can have his room."

"I could sleep on the couch," she offered.

"No, he'll be fine. He can sleep on the floor in a sleeping bag. He likes that kind of thing. It's like camping out."

"It's nice to see you again so soon. Where's your husband?"

"He had to work tonight and he has to be back at work at seven in the morning. His work shifts change all the time."

"That must be hard."

"He has one weekend off a month, which makes it difficult to do family things."

"He's okay with me being here?"

Trying to sound convinced, I immediately said, "Oh, of course."

"Do you mind if I smoke?" she asked.

I didn't mind, but my husband hated cigarette smell. "No…let me find you an ashtray."

113

My husband didn't let anyone smoke in our house, but I could spray air freshener around before he got home. Looking in our cabinets, the best thing I found for an ashtray was an old ceramic saucer.

"I can't find an ashtray," I said, "Will this do?"

I handed her the saucer.

"That's fine."

"Would you like something to drink?"

"Do you have coffee?"

"Sure, I'll make you some. I'm going to fix dinner soon. Are you hungry?"

"No, Rob and I stopped and ate before he dropped me off."

I made her coffee, and she asked for a glass with ice in it. Then she poured her cup of coffee over the ice. I'd never seen anyone pour hot coffee over ice before, but I was new to coffee drinking. What did I know?

Later she watched me fix dinner and feed the kids. She asked Randy and Julie their birth dates. She said she wanted everyone's birth dates because she was into numerology. I had heard of that, but wasn't familiar with it. I gave her my husband's and Chase's birthdays. Conversation didn't go far from current activity at my house. I was glad she took some interest in the kids.

Bedtime for them finally rolled around. She gave each one a good night hug. Fearing it might be awkward without the kids around, I secretly wished they'd put up their usual fuss about going to bed, but they didn't. I tucked them in, thanked them for being polite, and then returned to the dining room.

"Would you like some more coffee?" I asked Lacy.

"That would be great. How long have you had Randy and Julie with you?"

"We got custody of them almost three years ago."

"Do they understand who I am?"

"Yeah, for the most part. Randy will be eleven and Julie ten next month. I haven't gone into a lot of detail, but they're old enough to understand."

"That's good. I was wondering about it and wasn't too sure if I should say anything about who I was or not."

"I concentrated on my search at work most of the time, but they heard me on the telephone talking with my friends about it. I've had to be careful because now and then they see my little sister who's thirteen. She's adopted too and knows it, but thirteen is that age when you start wondering who you are and where you came from. My parents and I think it's best to wait until she's a little older before telling her more about her biological background."

"I understand. Remember, I was adopted too."

I so much wanted to ask how she felt about it. But I didn't want to go against her wishes. That was part of the past and her past was off limits. Frustrated, I didn't ask.

I told her I'd show her where I grew up and we could drive by my parent's former roller skating rink before going to their house. She seemed interested in the plan, but said she was getting tired and felt ready for bed. She took a long drag from her cigarette and put it out in the makeshift ashtray.

"Do you get up early?" she asked.

"Yes, but not by choice."

"I forgot kids like to get up early."

"Yes, they do."

She stood up. "Well, I like to get up early myself, so I'll see you in the morning."

"Okay. Good night."

She slowly walked up and hugged me, "Good night honey," she softy said.

It was a gentle hug.

"Sleep tight." I left out the bed bugs line. I wasn't sure about her sense of humor.

She slowly made her way to the bedroom and shut the door. I busied myself in the kitchen waiting for the beam of light under her door to go out. Then I emptied the saucer full of cigarette butts into an old tin can, doused them in water and took it outside to the garbage can. I hoped she would fall asleep quickly and not hear me spraying the air freshener around the room like a frantic teenager trying to hide the remnants of a party from her parents. I used the entire spray can and hoped the smell would be gone in a few hours. Otherwise I'd have to think of something to tell my husband that would explain her smoking in our house.

* * *

The air freshener didn't let me down. By morning I couldn't smell any smoke and neither did my husband. He got up, ate and left for work without saying a word. I let out a big sigh of relief.

Within minutes of his leaving, Lacy ambled out of the bedroom holding her cigarette pack. She sat in the same chair at the dining table as the night before.

"Did you sleep okay?" I asked, handing her the old saucer with reluctance.

"I did."

"Would you like some coffee?"

"Yes, thank you."

"Do you want some ice with it too?"

She laughed. "No, I like my coffee hot in the morning."

Reaching for a cup from the cabinet, I heard the flick of her cigarette lighter. I had to find more air freshener today. As I put the coffee cup in front of her, a strange smell made its way to my nose. I looked at her and realized she wasn't smoking a cigarette. It was marijuana. Holy crap! She was smoking pot in my house.

"I hope you don't mind, but I'm just so nervous."

"Ye...ah."

I wanted to slap myself. All I could say was yeah! I had kids sleeping down the hall. But Randy and Julie probably knew more about pot than I did. Especially with their previous surroundings before we got custody. It's not that I hadn't tried pot before, but I was a responsible adult now, with kids. I should've said something else and probably would have if not for the politeness and respect your elders that had been tattooed on my butt since childhood. I couldn't visualize Mom sitting at my dining room table smoking marijuana. Most elders didn't do that sort of thing. I quietly prayed the kids wouldn't wake up.

"This helps me relax," she said, carefully snuffing out the marijuana joint.

Maybe it helped *HER* relax, but she about gave me a heart attack.

"I think I need to spray some air freshener," I said, searching the cabinets.

"Do you need some help?"

You could've not lit that thing without asking, I thought, but bit my tongue. "No, I can get it."

What a relief when I spotted another can of spray in the corner of the cabinet. I sprayed more than necessary and it didn't smell much better than the marijuana, but a floral scent was more acceptable.

Her lack of consideration disappointed me. Was she deliberately shocking me with her behavior? It worked. I was more embarrassed than shocked... but didn't want her to know. She was definitely nervous, but so was I. Taking deep breaths usually calmed me down. I had plenty of paper bags she could have breathed in. Lighting a joint was way down the on the list of solutions.

The kids woke shortly after I finished spraying the room but it didn't faze them as they began their Saturday morning ritual of cartoons and cereal. For that I was thankful.

*   *   *

Randy and Julie politely ignored Lacy's limp, but would sometimes glance at her from behind. Chase was young and oblivious to her disability. She looked nice. Her makeup was impeccable. I wished I could apply makeup like that. I was lucky to keep lipstick inside the outline of my lips. Maybe I'd pick up some pointers from her in time.

I bundled the kids into the back seat of the car while Lacy seated herself up front. We dropped the older two off at their friends and then headed up town to show Lacy my parents' roller rink.

"Here it is. This is where I spent most of my years growing up," I proudly stated.

"It looks large. Is it still a roller skating rink?"

"No, my folks leased it to a group of individuals who rent the space to different businesses."

"Do you miss the skating rink?"

"Sometimes, but I used to get tired of it."

Lighting another cigarette, she said, "I could see how that could happen."

I had one more place to show her. By the time we got to my parents' I'd probably smell like an astray. I hoped my dad wouldn't tell me "You Stink!" in his usual blunt way. Not in front of Lacy anyway. He had no problem speaking his mind if he wasn't happy or something bothered him. But I was counting on him to ignore the cigarette smell.

After leaving the skating rink, I headed toward the home where I lived until I was twelve.

"I'd like to show you where I spent my first twelve years of my life."

"Sure, I'd like to see it."

"It's a little different now, but you'll be able to get an idea how it was. My dad built it, and he and my mom planted every kind of fruit tree imaginable on the property."

"How much property?"

"Three acres. It has a small creek that runs along the back property line."

"Did you have animals?"

"Yes, all kinds: chickens, horses and a Jersey cow. My dad made my older brother and I milk it every day at 5:30 in the morning before school. My brother would squirt the cat and me with the milk. I haven't cared for milk much since."

Laughing, she said, "I don't think I could get up that early."

"We didn't have a choice. My dad insisted it would help build our character. I told him I didn't have one friend, who milked a cow, and he said, "But *they* do!""

"Your dad sounds like he has a good sense of humor."

"I guess you could call it that. But it wasn't very funny at 5:30 in the morning."

After we drove by my old house, I headed for my parents' place. Lacy looked calm, but the amount she smoked in a short period of time told me differently. I was more nervous about their reactions. I had no idea what she might say to them or what they might say to her. I'd explained to them earlier that she wanted to thank them. I wondered if they were nervous too.

I parked in front of their house, and Lacy rubbed her hands down the top of her slacks, as if they were clammy. I was edgy and she seemed anxious. She was about to meet the people who raised her daughter. In the short time I'd known her; it was apparent she liked to maintain her composure and was doing a good job of it.

Hoping to ease the tension, I said, "This house is very different from the one we just left."

"Yes, but it's nice and a big house too, just older."

"Moving was an adjustment. They've made a lot of improvements."

"You haven't moved much, have you?" she asked. "I can't even count the number of times I've moved and had to start all over again."

"I don't know how you did it."

"I usually didn't have a choice," she confessed.

The bright sun began heating up the inside of the car and Chase wanted out. Without a word I got out and took my time releasing him from his car seat. It gave Lacy enough time to get herself out and ready. Silently we all walked slowly to the front door. Chase pulled on my arm the whole way. I wondered if she was feeling like I felt when I walked up to her door. She was older, but I can't imagine the feeling being any different.

I looked at her and smiled, then tapped on the door.

Dad opened the door, Mom standing near him, as he said, "Hey, come on in."

They both hugged Chase and me as we entered. Then I introduced everyone.

"Mom and Dad this is Lacy."

Extending a hand to each of them, Lacy said, "Hi, I'm so glad to finally meet you both."

"Same here," Dad said. He bent down and gave her a hug. Tall, but muscular, Dad wasn't someone to be messed with. When he talked, all of us kids stood at attention.

Mom hugged her too and then motioned us to have a seat at the table.

"Lacy, would you like some coffee? Mom asked.

"Yes I would, please."

I was waiting for her to ask for ice in a glass, but she didn't. I didn't think she'd ask for an ashtray either. My little sister came in and sat down by me. I introduced Lacy to her as a friend. She had no idea what was going on, but I wondered what she would think if she knew who Lacy really was. We sipped coffee waiting for my sister to leave the room. Never enjoying hanging around grownups, she disappeared into her room.

Suddenly Lacy cut to the chase. "I think you've done a wonderful job with Colette."

"Yeah, she's a pretty good gal," Mom said.

"Well, she can get a bit snippy," added Dad. "That's how she got her nick name. Right, Snip?"

Everyone laughed. Dad continued to tell her that my favorite word was 'SO' and I had always looked for the money tree when I was young.

Interrupting, I said, "What do you mean when I was young? I'm still looking for it."

The tension eased and conversation flowed with light humor, me being the source of the amusement. I laughed right along with them. Listening I realized how important this meeting was not only for Lacy, but for my parents as well. I was so proud of their kindness to Lacy, especially my dad. Mom was a mother, she understood, but Dad was a different story. He was the protector and didn't want anyone hurting his girl. He hadn't been sure that finding Lacy was a good idea. I'd expected him to be more guarded than he was. I couldn't have loved my parents more at that moment. In front of me was the woman who brought me into this world and the two people who made my world. I couldn't have asked for a better reunion.

I hadn't been paying attention. Silence brought me back to the conversation. I glanced at Mom and Dad. They were looking at Lacy as if waiting for her to finish something.

Holding back tears, Lacy said, "I know she's your daughter for always to keep, but I can't thank you both enough for taking such good care of my baby. It's such a relief to know that she had a good home and wonderful parents who love her."

On the verge of tears herself, Mom said, "You are so welcome, but she was a very special gift that we got from you."

Trying to lighten the mood, Dad said, "Yeah, we even like the snippy part."

It worked and we all laughed. The conversation returned to surface talk. I sensed that Lacy was either ready to go or needed a cigarette. Maybe both.

"I've got to get home and fix lunch," I said. I found Chase and my sister watching cartoons. Chase didn't want to go until I promised him French fries for lunch. He was hungry. Then he couldn't leave fast enough. I kissed my sister goodbye.

My parents walked us to the door and gave all three of us a hug good bye. To my relief, Dad didn't say a word about the cigarette smell. That alone made a wonderful visit.

Mom walked us to the car.

Giving her another hug, I whispered, "Thank you."

Whispering back, she said, "You're welcome."

Chase banged a toy on his car seat, chanting "Fy! Fy! Fy!" French fries were his favorite. By the end of the street Lacy had lit a cigarette.

Taking a drag like an anteater sucking up ants, she smiled, "Boy, I needed this."

Thankful that it was a cigarette rather than a joint, I said, "I bet you did."

"Your parents are wonderful people. Now I know why you are who you are. I'm happy with your looks because I had some part in that."

"Yeah... I wish I'd gotten your blue eyes though."

"Allaine and Mitch didn't get them either. They each look like their Dads."

I waited for her to say something about me looking like my dad, but she didn't. I looked more like her than Mitch and Allaine did, but it was slight. I decided not to say anything, but I did wonder if she thought I resembled my dad.

I glanced in the rearview mirror—Chase was asleep. Rounding the corner to my house, we could see Lacy's husband, Rob, standing outside their car. It didn't look much different from Mitch's car, but it got her here and I hoped it would get them home.

"I didn't expect him here this early. Did you?" I asked Lacy.

121

She looked relieved to see him. "No, but his business must have finished up early."

"I haven't even fed you lunch. Maybe Rob would like to come in and eat something too."

"Nah, he'll want to stop on the way and grab something quick."

Feeling she was ready to go, I didn't argue. "Maybe next time?"

"That sounds good and maybe next time I can meet your husband too."

Truthfully, I hoped he'd be working next time too, but said, "Yes, I'd like that."

"Thank you for letting me stay and allowing me to meet your mom and dad. That meant so much."

"I'm glad they got to meet you too and I'm thrilled that I was able to visit with you."

"I need to get my overnight bag from inside," she said.

It would take her a lot longer than me to get it. "I'll get it for you," I offered.

"Oh, thank you honey."

Returning with her bag, I said, "We'll have to get together again soon."

Hugging me, she said, "We sure will. I don't want to wake Chase, but please give him and the kids a hug good bye for me."

Hugging her back, I said, "Okay."

I waved to both of them as Rob started the car and watched until they disappeared around the corner. I had spent almost 24 hours with her and the only things I learned were that she liked ice cubes in her coffee, didn't talk about herself, and when she got nervous, smoked pot. She had mentioned that she was on her seventh marriage, but was certain this one would last. I was still struggling with my first. Seven was too much to fathom. Time would take its course. I wanted to get to know her better. How much better, I wasn't sure, but I'd give her the benefit of any doubt.

A Love Child's Journey

Chapter Thirteen

Hearing my name paged, I hurried to my desk to take the call. "This is Colette."

"Your mom's here!" Mom whispered into the phone.

"Mom?" I said. "Why are you whispering?"

She continued to whisper, "Your mom is here at the house."

"My mom. What do you mean my mom? Aren't you my mom?" I joked.

"Your other mom. You know… Lacy," she murmured.

Shocked, I said, "Oh… that mom."

"Yeah… that mom and she don't look too good."

"What do you mean?"

"Her eye is bloodshot and the side of her face is all black and blue. It looks horrible. I think she said she had a fight with some guy or something like that."

"How did she get to your house?"

"She said she came from Idaho and used her last twelve dollars on a cab to get here."

"It had to cost more than that to get here from Idaho."

"I didn't ask. I fixed her some coffee and said I'd give you a call."

"Okay, let me think a minute."

123

"There's nothing to think about. You need to come and pick her up."

"Okay... you're right. I'll see if I can get off work early."

"Sounds good. See you when you get here."

"Sorry, Mom," I said.

"It's fine. Just get here as soon as you can."

"I will."

I slowly put the receiver back on the telephone. Was Pandora's box creeping open? Why was Lacy showing up now? What was I going to do with her? It had been over eight months since I'd heard from her and just over a year and a half since she came to my house. At first, we exchanged letters every week or so, but the weeks turned into months and then I didn't hear from her at all. Her last letter mentioned that she'd be moving and would let me know her new address when she settled. I thought she was moving to somewhere in California. Later Mitch told me she had gone to Idaho, divorced Rob and was getting ready to marry some other guy named Rob. At least she didn't have to worry about getting their names mixed up. The new Rob would be her eighth marriage. Even though it wasn't highly acceptable, at that rate, if I was her, I think I'd live with them rather than marry them.

I'd been preoccupied with sorting out my own life; I didn't dwell on the fact that I hadn't heard from her. I figured she'd write me when she could. The last letter I sent her, I mentioned that I was thinking of separating from my husband. Not knowing if I had, that's probably why she went to my parents' house.

It was unsettling that my parents had to deal with Lacy under these circumstances. I could hear in Mom's voice her discomfort with the situation, but she didn't sound upset with me. That had been a concern when I was searching for Lacy.

My son and I had been living in a condominium during the divorce process. At times it was difficult, but I felt happier. My life had turned into a smooth ride down a newly paved highway. I wasn't expecting to hit a pothole.

I glanced over my door and saw my boss working at her desk. Embarrassed, I didn't want my co-workers to know what was happening, so I called Sandy on the telephone.

"This is Colette. I have a little problem and need to leave early, if possible."

"Is everything okay?" she asked.

"I hope so. My biological mother showed up at my parents' house after someone beat her up."

Hesitating, she asked, "Are you in a position with your work where you can leave?"

"I have one thing to take care of, then I will be."

"Okay, well... be careful and I'll see you Monday."

"You too and thank you."

I was glad it was Friday, and the weekend my son would be going to his father's. I didn't want him to see Lacy's black and blue face. Actually, I didn't want to see it either.

* * *

Leaving work, I didn't know whether to drive fast or slow. Mom wanted me at her house immediately, but I was uncomfortable with the situation too. I brought Lacy into our lives so it was my responsibility to take care of this. I just didn't know how or what to say to her.

Why hadn't she gone to Mitch or Allaine? Allaine was closer in actual distance than any of us. Lacy must have been desperate in order to show up at my parents' house. She must be in need of a friend and I'm the only choice she has. I didn't have any other options either.

Concentrating on what I would say made time disappear. I don't remember driving. My car was on autopilot until it stopped at my parents' house. I grabbed my coat and got out. It was late October and falling leaves swayed back and forth in a gusty breeze before landing softly. I stopped and waited for the next gust of wind. It swirled around me, refreshing and invigorating. Was I windblown or just frazzled? I took a deep breath, let it out slowly then walked to the door.

At my knock, Mom yelled for me to come in. Mom, Dad and Lacy sat around the dining table laughing and drinking coffee. The laughter released some of my tension until Lacy turned toward me.

The look on my face stopped the laughter. Different shades of deep purple covered the right side of her face. Her right pupil faded into the deep red color that used to be the white of her eye, as if all the blood vessels had been broken in that eye. I wondered if her cheekbone was broken. I'd never seen anything like this before.

I looked at Dad. He gave me a disappointed glance and shrugged. I looked at Mom; she gave me a reassuring smile and motioned me to approach Lacy.

"Don't worry, I'm fine." Lacy said. "I've dealt with worse than this before."

Studying her face, I asked, "Don't you need to see a doctor or go to the emergency room?"

"No, it'll be better in a few days. I just needed to get away."

"I'm sorry this happened to you," I said.

"It's okay," she said, trying to shift the focus from her. "I'm sorry to hear that it didn't work out with you and your husband, but I'm glad you and Chase are living in a nice condo."

"Yes. It's not large, but I like it."

"Where's Chase?"

"It's his dad's weekend. He'll pick him up from the sitters."

Seeing Dad fidget with his sugar spoon, I knew it was time to leave. He raised one eyebrow higher than the other, a sure sign that he wasn't pleased with the situation. Mom pursed her lips, letting me know Dad was about to say something we would all regret if I didn't act quickly.

Trying to look at her without seeing her injury, I asked, "Lacy, are you ready to go see my condo?"

"Love to," she said, rising.

I waited for her to get her overnight bag or a sack of clothes, or something, but she just had her coat. She must have left Idaho in a hurry.

With a quick hug goodbye, Dad whispered in my ear "Snip, are you going to be okay?"

I gave a reassuring nod before he turned to hug Lacy goodbye.

I gave Mom an extra squeeze when I hugged her. She smiled at me.

I let out a quiet sigh as we walked to the car. Lacy walked better than before and had more balance. She also looked thinner in size since I'd last seen her.

Seated in the car, she said, "Your parents are sure neat people."

"Yeah, they are."

"It's nice to see you again, but I wish it was under different circumstances."

"Me too. What happened?"

"Rob... my husband... not the Rob you met. I divorced that Rob and married another one. He's a good guy, but when he drinks and I happen to say the wrong thing... well, he gets angry."

"Mitch told me that you had divorced and married again."

"Oh... PLEASE... do me a favor and don't tell Mitch about this, okay?"

"I... I won't."

"Mitch said if Rob hit me again, he would kill him."

Those were strong words I had only heard on television or at the movies, not in real life. I didn't think Mitch would actually kill someone, but I didn't know him well enough to be certain.

"He's been hitting you a lot?" I asked.

"Well... There was another time. Mitch told him if he ever hit me again, he'd hunt him down and kill him. The first time was shame on Rob, but the second time is shame on me."

"That doesn't make it right, Lacy."

She shrugged.

"He could have hurt you really bad." I added. "I mean your face looks...well... not too good."

She chuckled, "Yeah, I know."

It amazed me that she didn't seem very bothered by a guy hitting her. I knew in my heart it had to hurt or she wouldn't be here, but she acted like it was ordinary, something that happened all the time. Maybe it did. I felt queasy every time I looked at her face.

"Do you have a store near your home?" She asked. "I need a cigarette really bad."

"Yes, there's one around the corner."

"You know, honey, I hate to ask you this, but I don't have any money."

I already knew she didn't have any money. "Don't worry about it."

"I used what I had to get here. Do you have enough to loan me money to buy some cigarettes? And I really need some tampons. I promise I'll pay you back. If you have a piece of paper I'll write an I. O. U. for you."

"Okay, but don't worry about it. How did you get here?"

"I grabbed my coat and started walking down the road. I thought he'd follow me, but he didn't. My eye swelled up so much I couldn't see out of it. I started hitchhiking and this trucker stopped and picked me up. He felt sorry for me so he drove me halfway here."

"That was nice of him. It would be scary hitchhiking. Weren't you afraid?"

"Oh no. He said he was a man of God. In fact, he was so nice that he gave me $75 when he dropped me off. That made it possible for me to catch the bus the rest of the way."

It could have been true but I found it hard to believe that some guy gave her $75 without receiving something for it. At least his generous 'contribution' got her here safely.

We stopped at the store and picked up the things she needed before driving to my place.

I offered to put an icepack on her face, but she said it had been almost two days and wouldn't help. She was probably right, but I would have felt better doing something to help, whether it did or not.

She got restless and antsy while I was fixing dinner.

"Is something wrong?" I asked.

"I should call Rob. He must be worried about me."

My first thought was ARE YOU CRAZY...? This guy used your face as a punching bag and you want to call him to let him know you're okay? He didn't care if you were okay when he hit you.

"You're welcome to use my telephone, but why call him? It's his fault, not yours."

"I know but I'm thinking I should," she said.

Ambling around to the other side of the counter, she picked up the phone, gave me a lopsided smile and began to dial.

"Would you like me to step outside while you call?"

"No, but I could use some coffee."

I wanted to hear her conversation, but it wasn't any of my business, so I turned on the water to fill the coffeepot. Once the coffeemaker started, I sat down at my small kitchen table and flipped through a magazine. My place was small. I kept turning the pages, pretending I wasn't listening, but straining to catch her every word.

It didn't take long before I heard the words that would change the length of her visit. She was leaning on the counter twisting the telephone cord around her fingers. "I know you didn't mean it," she said. "I love you too. I know you're sorry. I understand."

I gritted my teeth.

During a long silence her head slowly bobbed up and down. I couldn't believe she was being so nice to the jerk. It was as if she was assuring him it was okay to hit her. Sadness swallowed my heart. She must feel she doesn't deserve better. I knew she did, but what could I do?

She hung up and sat down at the table. She seemed to know what I was thinking.

"I know... I know... I shouldn't have let him off the hook, but I do love him, and he loves me too," she protested.

No matter what I said, it wouldn't change the situation. "How about some coffee?" I asked.

I poured us both some coffee and sat down across from her. At first her face had softness about it, but the longer she sat the harder it became.

"I know this may seem odd to you," she said. "But it's my life."

"I understand that."

The telephone rang. I got up and answered it. "Hello."

A deep voice said, "This is Rob. Can I speak with Lacy?"

She must have guessed who it was because she started toward me. I handed her the receiver and returned to the table. As I sat down, she hung up and returned to her seat.

"That was fast," I said.

"Yeah... he started crying and couldn't talk. I think he took a Valium." She said it in a matter of fact tone, as if it was nothing.

I knew it was some kind of drug, but had no idea what it did. "Will he be okay?" I asked.

"Sure, it calms him down. I take them myself if I need to."

Not surprised, I said, "Oh."

She smiled and sipped coffee. The silence was awkward, but I didn't know what to say. The telephone rang again.

"It's probably him. Do you want to answer it?" I asked.

"No. If it's not him they'll think they have the wrong number."

I walked over to answer my phone, saying, "Yeah, that's true."

"Hello."

He sounded like a record that had slowed from 78 rpms to 33.

"Hiiiii... Thisss... isss... Robbb."

It was so weird that I didn't even answer him. He seemed to be talking in slow motion. It would have taken him the rest of the night to ask me to speak with Lacy, so I just handed the receiver to her.

I sat down and flipped through the same magazine I'd already looked through. I turned the pages without seeing them, trying to stay busy and make sense of the craziness unfolding before me.

Lacy eventually returned to the table. "He's going to wire me some money in the morning so I can catch a bus back to Idaho."

"Is that what you want to do?"

"Yeah, I know he loves me and I love him too. I can only go three days without sex," she added.

I could relate to that, although I didn't have any three-day issue.

"Well, I guess we better make sure you get on a bus tomorrow."

"Sounds good, honey."

I think she had expected me to argue against her going back to him, but I knew in my heart it wouldn't matter what I said. That was how she lived her life. No one could have persuaded her differently. She didn't seem to know any other way to live.

*   *   *

In the morning we had coffee, then drove to the bus depot. Rob had wired her a ticket and some money that would be waiting at the depot. Driving to Sacramento was not one of my favorite things, but that's where she had to catch the bus.

Near the depot, she said, "Honey, just drop me off. I don't want you here by yourself."

Looking around, I understood what she meant. There were all kinds of questionable characters hanging about. But what scared me most was the parking. It was all parallel parking.

"But what about you? Will you be all right?"

"This doesn't bother me. Give me a hug. I'll call you when I get home, and write you too."

I hugged her and told her to be careful. Double-parked, I watched her limp to the door. She was right; everyone seemed oblivious to her. She looked back at me, smiled and blew a kiss, then walked inside.

A loud honking horn startled me. I was blocking traffic and had to move. It was difficult leaving her there. I wished it could have been the last time she got hit like that but I wasn't going to hold my breath. I hoped she'd let me know she had a safe trip home.

A Love Child's Journey

Chapter Fourteen

It was mid November when I heard from Lacy again. She sent me a birthday card, and her enclosed letter said how thrilled she was to send another card for my birthday. Our situation made it difficult to find fitting cards, but hers was beautiful. She signed it *with all my love always, Lacy*. I liked that.

She thanked me for helping her out, but didn't say much about her surprise visit! I was glad she had made it home safe. Thoughts about the creepy bus station flashed in my mind: the homeless sitting along the sidewalk and wandering in and out of the station. They would've known immediately I was out of my element as soon as I tried to parallel park. But I was amazed with the comfort she displayed in those surroundings.

She wrote that Allaine was getting married in February to her boyfriend, Kerry. Allaine, Kerry and her son had stopped by for a day back in August, on their way to Disneyland. I enjoyed meeting them, but didn't get to spend much time talking with her. We didn't look alike except for dark eyes and hair. Did she think my features had anything in common with her grandfather, Rodney? I didn't bring it up and neither did she.

Lacy's letter said Allaine and Kerry were having a Catholic wedding and had been sleeping in separate bedrooms and attending the required classes for marriage in a Catholic Church.

To me it was odd that they had lived together for a year, but now had to remain celibate for four months. I guess none of Lacy's marriages had been Catholic, since three days was her limit without sex.

She closed by saying she would be in touch and gave me her new address in Boise, Idaho.

*　　　　　*　　　　　*

Christmas came and went. Lacy, Mitch, Allaine and I exchanged cards. Lacy mentioned that she would send a gift for Chase when she got some extra money. I didn't think it was necessary, but I guess she wanted to. Mitch said he'd be passing through after the first of the year and asked if he could visit for a few days. He would call to let me know when. I wrote back and told him any time was fine. Allaine was getting excited about her wedding and asked if I'd be her matron of honor. I was touched that she wanted me in her wedding. Not knowing each other that well, I had no idea she'd want to include me in her marriage ceremony. She was going to call for confirmation. Just being invited would be a nice gesture. I didn't expect to be a participant.

*　　　　　*　　　　　*

It was cold and rainy outside, so my son and I spent the day inside, much to his dismay. He busied himself with toys while I read. We both jumped when the telephone rang. Chase raced to pick up the receiver and handed it to me. That was all I'd let him do. He felt old enough to answer the phone, but I didn't think he was.

"Hello," I said into the receiver.

"Hi honey, this is your mom."

"Hi Mom. What are you up to on this rainy day?"

"Oh, not too much."

"Same here."

"The reason I'm calling is that you have company," she said quietly.

My heart began to throb as I remembered the last time she called to tell me I had company "You mean like... Lacy company?"

"It's not Lacy, it's your brother Mitch."

"He's not all beat up, is he?" I asked.

She laughed. "No."

"That's good. He did mention he was going to stop and visit me on his way to Idaho. Don't say anything to him about Lacy getting beat up. I promised her I wouldn't tell him."

"I won't. Do you want me to give him directions to your place?"

"If you would, please, and tell him I'll talk with him when he gets here."

"Sounds good. Bye honey, love you,"

"Bye and I love you too."

Hanging up, I glanced around to see if things looked okay. I had cleaned earlier, but wanted to make sure my apartment was presentable.

I hadn't seen Mitch for some time and was looking forward to visiting with him. I hoped he would tell me more about Lacy, too.

Soon a knock at the door brought Chase running down the stairs. Company didn't come often and I doubted that he remembered Mitch from our first meeting.

Peering out the window, I could see Mitch standing in front of the door holding a small suitcase. Faded jeans and a weathered jean jacket gave him a cowboy appearance. He reminded me of a young John Wayne.

Opening the door, I said, "Hi, it's nice to see you again."

I almost asked him where he parked his horse, but wasn't sure how he'd take it.

He reached down to hug me. "Hey Sis. It's nice to see you too."

My other brothers called my by my first name, so the 'sis' caught me by surprise. I enjoyed hearing it again.

"Come on in. You're getting wet."

Looking down at my son, he said, "Hi Chase. Boy, you sure have grown since I last saw you."

Three and a half-year old Chase smiled, then ran and hopped on the couch. I had told him Mitch was my brother, but I think it confused him a little. From his own experience with a half brother, he knew brothers were special.

It wasn't until I put Chase to bed that I was able to talk to Mitch without watching summersaults, hopping on one foot around the room and various toy demonstrations.

Curious if he had heard from Lacy, I asked, "Have you talked to your mom lately?"

He sighed, "Yeah, she's still with Rob number two. Last time I saw her, I was working in Idaho. I stopped by, and both of them were drunk. Mom was sitting on the floor crying, her face swollen and red. I walked over to pick her up and Rob pulled a gun on me."

Shocked, I said, "Wow! That must have been scary. What did you do?"

He shifted in the chair. "I'd seen the gun before and knew he only kept one bullet in it. So I told him he better make it count if he was going to pull the trigger."

"Weren't you afraid he'd shoot you?" I gasped.

"You know... I didn't worry about it. I just wanted to get my mom out of there."

"It sounds like you take care of her a lot."

His forehead wrinkled. "She's not the same since her accident. Before her accident... she would never have tolerated someone hitting her like that."

"I wish I could've met her before it happened."

"Yeah...me too."

Like waiting for the end of a movie, I wanted to know what Mitch did with a gun pointed at him. "So did Rob let you take Lacy with you?"

"Yeah... I picked her up and walked out the door."

Horrified, I asked, "Did you think he would shoot you?"

He laughed. "Adrenaline had kicked in and I didn't care. He was so drunk I don't think he could have hit me anyway. But after I got outside I asked myself what the hell I was thinking."

"Yeah, that would have scared the crap out of me."

"You know the saying, *hindsight's better than foresight*."

I knew the answer but I asked anyway. "And Lacy went back to him after that?"

"You know, she was doing good for about a week. She didn't drink and stayed with me in the motel I rented. Then one day I came home from work and she was gone. I drove over to Rob's and there she was."

"Did you talk with her?"

"Yeah... I tried to, but all she said was that she loved him. I knew no matter what I said, I couldn't convince her to stay away from him."

I didn't say a word about her coming to see me. It would only have made him feel worse. Mitch seemed mature way beyond his years. A kind gentle guy with a rugged edge. I liked him. He was easy to talk with, something I always wished my older brother and I shared.

*   *   *

The following day I showed Mitch the same places I showed Lacy. The home where I grew up, the skating rink and then we stopped at my parents' house. They took to him right away. It was hard not to like him.

"Mitch, do you work or are you a free-loader?" Dad scoffed.

Mitch laughed. "I'm on my way to Idaho to see if I can get some work. I was working in Fresno, but we completed that job."

"What kind of work do you do?" Dad asked.

"I do grunt work for construction companies."

"So you're a flunky?"

Mitch smiled at me. Embarrassed, I wanted to crawl under the table but Mitch held his own with my dad.

"I guess you could call it that, but work's work. I'll do most anything to put food in my belly and gas in my car."

Dad asked, "How long are you going to be around?"

"I'm not sure. I wanted to visit with Colette for a few days. I don't have a job waiting for me so there's no rush."

"Well... instead of sitting on your butt all day waiting for her to get home from work, why don't you come and work for me? I have plenty of grunt work and I pay a decent wage."

Mitch looked at me as if for approval. It was evident that Dad liked Mitch and wanted to hire him. It didn't matter to me because I worked all day myself.

"Mitch, I think it would be great if you want to work for my dad. Plus it'll give you some insight on what it's like belonging to this family," I joked.

Mitch raised one eyebrow in a way that again reminded me of John Wayne. He put out his hand to Dad and said, "You got a deal."

We said our good-byes and headed to my place. Once in the car Mitch lit a cigarette and began laughing.

"Your dad's quite a character."

"That's putting it nicely. But he likes you or he wouldn't have hired you."

"What exactly does he do? I was afraid to ask."

"Yeah, I know what you mean. He can be intimidating. Actually, he scares the hell out of me sometimes. We're used to moving quickly when he talks. To answer your question, he does small reconstruction jobs for insurance agencies.

"I figured it was something like that. I guess he likes to test people to see what they're made of."

"You're right, but it did get me thinking that if you'd like to stay awhile with me and work with my Dad it would be fine. I could use some help with the bills. You can sleep in Chase's room. He ends up in my bed most nights anyway."

He smiled. "That would be fine. It'll be a good way for you and me to get to know each other."

*   *   *

Mitch settled in comfortably at my house and Dad seemed pleased with his work. Mitch had already helped with my grocery bill and was an expert on fixing inexpensive meals. He prepared many of our dinners. I never thought I'd enjoy cold sliced hotdogs on a piece of bread with mayonnaise. They were either amazingly good or I was desperate for cheap dinner ideas.

We had just sat down to enjoy another night of cold hotdogs when the telephone rang.

Mitch said, "I'll get it."

I nodded as I cut up Chase's hot dog. My son wasn't into bread and mayonnaise, but did enjoy dipping his hotdogs into ketchup.

Mitch put his hand over the receiver and mouthed silently to me "Allaine". His... well, our sister.

Hearing his side of the conversation, I knew it was about Allaine's upcoming wedding. Mitch told her he'd be there and wrote something down.

"Allaine wants to talk with you," he said, handing me the phone.

I had talked with her twice and exchanged a few letters, but still didn't know her that well.

"Hi Allaine, how are you?"

Her voice was loud and boisterous. "Okay. I was telling Mitch I'd like you both to be in my wedding. That is... if you want to be."

"That would be great and I'm honored that you asked. How many are in your wedding party?"

"Kerry and I decided that he'll have his best man and I'll have you as my matron of honor. It gets too expensive otherwise."

"I understand. What do you want me to wear?"

"I don't want you to have to go out and buy something. My colors are pink and maroon. If you have a dress with those colors, it would be perfect."

Relieved that I didn't have to buy anything new, I said, "I have a long maroon bridesmaid dress I wore in a friend's wedding."

Excited, she said, "Perfect! You and Mitch can stay here with Kerry and me. Mom's coming up from Boise to stay with us too. We have a huge house with a big basement. It'll give us all a chance to hang out together."

Her enthusiasm must have raced through the line because I was ready to leave for Idaho. "I can't wait to get the chance to visit with you and Lacy."

"She'll be thrilled. This is way too cool. It's nice that Mitch's living with you. ...It's kind of... amazing, don't you think?"

"Yeah, it is."

"It'll be nice. You two can drive up together. I'll keep you posted on everything. The wedding's February 16th. You can come up anytime before that."

"I need to make arrangements with my son's father and my work, but I'll plan on some extra days so we can spend time together."

"Sounds great. Tell Mitch bye and I'll be in touch with any other details as it gets closer."

"Sounds good. I'll talk with you later," I said, and then hung up.

I looked over at Mitch. He had one eyebrow raised.

"So... what are you thinking?" I asked.

"What do you mean?" he asked.

"The eyebrow thing."

He laughed. "The eyebrow thing?"

"Well, in the short time you've been living here I've noticed that when you raise one eyebrow, there's something on your mind."

He let out a loud cackle. "Boy, are you getting to know me."

"So what gives?"

"I was just wondering why Allaine and Kerry were getting married. I don't think she really loves him and I know she's not pregnant because she's made such a big deal about them not sleeping together for the last four months."

"Maybe she does love him. How do you know?"

"Kerry's been my friend for a long time and he's a nice guy. He's not very assertive, but he's good to Allaine and her son from her first husband. Kerry makes a good living too. Oh, yeah and he has a house. Allaine's all about material things and the money."

"Do you think Kerry loves Allaine?"

"Probably."

"Well, then maybe he wants to get married."

"Yeah... you're probably right. Kerry sure wouldn't tell Allaine no, I don't want to marry you."

"But if he really didn't want to, wouldn't he say so?"

Mitch began to laugh again, as if he was snickering about some hidden secret I didn't know.

Annoyed, I asked, "What's so funny?"

139

"You don't know Allaine. You wouldn't want to piss her off. One of the many times she was mad at me, she chased my friend and me with a rolling pin. I know for a fact if she had caught me, that would have been it."

"She wouldn't really have hurt you, would she?"

He smiled "I didn't slow down to find out and neither did my friend. You see Allaine is a mix between Nammie and Mom. The temper and craziness is the Nammie part, but she can turn around and sweet talk you and use you just like Mom."

"And I thought my older brother telling me and the neighbor boy to run while he shot our legs with a BB gun was bad."

"Hey, don't get me wrong. I love Allaine, but she has a nasty temper and she's strong."

"Well, thank you for filling me in on that. I'll make sure I don't upset her."

He seemed to sense my uneasiness. Taking a bite of his hotdog sandwich, he said, "You don't have to worry. She'll want to make a good impression with you. She'll be at her best. Come and finish your dinner while it's still cold."

Laughing, I said, "Yeah, you're right. I wouldn't want my cold hotdog sandwich to get warm."

*   *   *

Allaine's wedding was fast approaching. Mitch and I planned to leave five days before the wedding. My dad had been working in Jasper, Oregon for a few weeks. He and Mom recently bought a house and planned to move there with my younger brother and sister. Mitch and I decided to drive to there, spend the night, and then take off early the following morning. On our way back, Dad wanted me to leave Mitch with him to help on the remodel.

I looked forward to the wedding and spending more time around Lacy, but I was already missing my son. I knew he'd be fine with his dad. My ex wasn't the greatest husband, but he did love our son and took good care of him. I'd never been away from Chase for any extended time, but didn't think a wedding was the right place for him. I'd be busy with the wedding and trying to find out more about Lacy and my biological family.

* * *

I woke up to Eddie Rabbit singing "I Love A Rainy Night" on the radio. Eyes closed, I listened to the music and thought about the trip ahead. When the song finished, I got out of bed. That song reminded me to take my umbrella, but I hoped it wasn't raining. We were going to northern Idaho via Oregon and Washington. Mitch said that at times it did snow in Idaho and Oregon's known for its rain.

Downstairs I could hear Mitch bustling around the kitchen. I put on my robe and joined him.

"Good morning." I said as I poured myself a cup of coffee. "You're busy for this early in the morning."

"I thought I'd fix us some sandwiches for the road. I'm outdoing myself," he boasted. "Are you ready for this?"

Grabbing one of his cigarettes, a habit I had recently picked up, I asked, "Do I have a choice?"

"Hoagie hotdogs. They have lettuce, tomato, onions, mayo and mustard with two, sliced down the middle, hotdogs on white bread. Ooh... and let's not forget the cheese. They looked so good I fixed myself one for breakfast," he bragged.

"How about peanut butter and jelly sandwiches?" I asked. "Did you make some of those?"

"Of course, but they're just fillers, my hoagies are the main deal."

"You're going to eat hotdogs for breakfast?"

He laughed, "I already did. Do you want one?"

"No, cereal's fine for me. I'll wait till we're on the road for the hotdog hoagie."

Smiling, he sat down across from me and took a sip of coffee. "What time do you want to leave?"

"I'm packed. I'll hop in the shower after I eat and be ready to go in less than an hour."

"I'll be ready too."

As promised, I was ready to go in less than an hour with three minutes to spare. Mitch had the car loaded and ready.

Getting into the car, I asked, "Are you ready for this?"

141

He rose one eyebrow "The question is, are you ready for this? I know what to expect, but you have no idea."

"Well… you're right about that. But it's important to Allaine and it'll give me the opportunity to spend time with Lacy."

"Okay, if you're ready, then I'm ready."

A Love Child's Journey

Chapter Fifteen

It took us less than eight hours to get to Jasper. Mitch was right. I was pleasantly surprised how great his hoagie hotdogs tasted, but I enjoyed the peanut butter sandwich as well.

I hadn't seen Dad in a few weeks and was looking forward to that, although if he knew I had taken up smoking he wouldn't be happy. I could always blame the smell on Mitch, a sisterly thing-making him responsible for what I did.

It was misty and dark but good directions made it easy to find their new place. An old jeep parked in the driveway was a dead giveaway. Dad had a passion for jeeps, probably from his military days.

The house had a nice view, but was old and small. Mitch and I grabbed our bags and hustled to the door. It opened before I had a chance to knock.

Bending down to hug me, Dad said, "Hi Snip, how's my girl? You stink like cigarettes. Have you been smoking?"

I looked at Mitch, then back at Dad. "Once in a while," I said, sheepishly.

He turned and walked into the house. "I thought you knew better than that."

Mitch hung back in the doorway with me, whispering, "This is getting off to a nice start. Why didn't you just say it was from me?"

Before walking inside I whispered, "That was my plan, but I couldn't lie to him. My nose turns red if I do."

He laughed and followed me inside. "Your nose turns red?"

Dad overheard and said, "That's right. When you lie to someone, it makes your nose turn red."

Mitch roared with laughter. "Well, I bet people could have called me Rudolph any number of times in my life."

That lightened the mood. Dad showed us where to throw our sleeping bags on the bare floor by the wood-burning stove. The house looked large inside. He was in the process of replacing its exposed walls. Lumber and wire covered most of the floor space, but we each found an open area for our bags.

"You two, follow me," Dad said.

Mitch and I single filed after him out the back sliding door of the house onto a large wooden deck.

"Look at this. Isn't it beautiful?"

Instantly I knew why my parents had bought the house. Even in the dark its view was beautiful. Stars in the clear night sky glowed like vivid flashlights. As far as I could see, trees scattered the plush green grass below the deck. Rushing water from a nearby river made a soothing sound. We stood in silence listening to the night noises of crickets and a frog that croaked in unison.

"How about some grub?" Dad asked. "I have some chili and hotdogs I can warm up for you two."

Mitch looked at me with one eyebrow raised. I figured he was thinking the same thing as me. Chili… and both of us confined to a car the next day driving across two states. It had been a while since we stopped and ate, but for both our sakes we should pass on the chili.

"No thanks, Dad. We ate just before we got here."

"Well, if you want something to snack on later I got some Pogey Bait in the refrigerator." He went into the kitchen.

"Pogey bait?" asked Mitch. That doesn't sound like anything I'd want to eat."

I laughed. "It's candy."

"Oh. I hope it tastes better than it sounds. I figured it was something to put on the end of a fishing pole and cast into that river."

I whispered, "He usually buys good candy and I'm sure we'll be hungry later."

The evening passed and we settled down in our sleeping bags.

Whispering across the stove, Mitch said, "Damn, this floor's hard."

"Yeah, but I'm too tired to worry about it."

"Are you sure your Dad will wake us up early enough?"

"Believe me, that's the last thing you need to worry about. When I was growing up, if we got to sleep in until six in the morning, we were in heaven. Besides, he gets up now and then to put wood in the stove."

"Okay... good night and I hope I can move in the morning."

"Good night."

*   *   *

Dad didn't disappoint me; he had us up at 5:30 and by 6:30 we were on the road heading for the state of Washington. We were both hungry and went to a fast food drive-through. Neither of us wanted to waste time but we were thankful we hadn't eaten beans.

By mid afternoon we approached the place where Lacy went off a cliff in her Volkswagen bug. Mitch wanted to show me and I wanted to see it. He had taken over the driving after a fuel stop in Pasco. The traffic wasn't heavy, but everyone traveled at a high rate of speed. He didn't seem fazed by the speeding cars as he slowed down and pulled my small white hatchback alongside the edge of the road.

"There's the place." His voice was somber.

I looked down over the edge. "That's steep. I can't see the bottom."

"Yeah... it's a long ways down there. The car rolled a lot of times. Being thrown from the car was what saved her. But she broke just about every bone in her body."

"It's amazing that she survived."

"We weren't too sure if she was going to make it. She had a long stay in the hospital and then a rest home. There was brain damage and she didn't seem to be getting any better. She drooled and we couldn't understand what she was saying. She couldn't walk or even get out of bed. Finally, a good friend of hers realized she was being over medicated. Once that stopped, she started improving."

"Mitch, I'm so sorry. That had to be awful for you and Allaine."

"We were glad when Mom's friend stepped in to help us. I had just turned sixteen and Allaine was close to eighteen. I remember when we got the hospital bill. You know how these computer print-out pages that are perforated and accordion together?"

"Yeah."

"Well, her bill was so long that Allaine and I could walk through each room in our apartment unfolding it page after page. It was so overwhelming we just started laughing."

Not sure what to say, I shook my head.

"It was like a joke to us. Where would we get the money to pay that bill?"

"What did you do?"

"The State stepped in and took care of it since we were both minors."

Driving away, I took one last look. Sadness encased my heart, not only for Lacy but for Mitch and Allaine as well. I couldn't imagine going through something like that.

For a while we drove in silence. I wanted to change our gloomy mood.

"What did you mean by your comment when we left my house yesterday?"

"What? Oh... you mean being ready for this encounter?"

"Yeah."

With a deep laugh he said, "Life in northern Idaho is different than what you're used to."

"What do you mean?"

"Well... there's not much to do there. Which means there's a lot of partying."

"I can deal with that. I'm not that straight-laced."

"When there's celebrating, they drink, smoke dope or whatever and it can go on all night."

"I haven't partied much; I don't do well with the drinking thing, but I've tried pot before. And I already know that Lacy smokes pot."

Surprised, he asked, "How'd you know that?"

"When she visited me she was nervous and needed something to relax her."

"Oh, man. She never ceases to amaze me."

I laughed. "I was amazed myself. No... more like shocked."

We both laughed.

*   *   *

We rolled into Lewiston about an hour after dark. Mitch was driving. He knew his way around so we stopped at a gas station to freshen up. I think he did that for me, and I appreciated it. This was Allaine's wedding, but I sensed from Mitch that I would be on display as well. It was their turf and their friends. I figured they all knew about me by now, Mitch and Allaine's older sister who was given up for adoption. I didn't mind. I enjoyed getting to know Mitch and being his sister. He was protective and kind. I wanted the same thing with Allaine. Okay, she didn't have to protect me, but I wanted to get to know her. According to Mitch, I'd be pretty safe hanging out with her.

Mitch stopped the car in front of a nice older home. The large front yard had been neatly mowed. After my first visit with Lacy, in her kitchenette, I wasn't sure what to expect. Mitch grabbed our bags and we walked up to the door. Looking at me, he tapped a few times on the door, then opened it and walked in. I followed.

The room was full of people. Our sudden appearance was like the crash of breaking glass in a busy restaurant, immediate silence, with all eyes on us. Everyone smiled at me as I followed Mitch to the kitchen. Allaine's toddler son, Allan sat in a highchair eating and wearing a girl's powder blue coat with white fur around the hood. He was a beautiful little guy with striking blue eyes and much prettier than most boys. Allan was a little over a year younger than Chase.

Allaine walked toward us saying, "Hey, you guys made it."

Mitch hugged her and looked at her son. "How ya doing?" Looking at Allaine, "Don't you have a boy's coat for him to wear?"

She laughed, "Yeah, that's kind of girlie. But hey, it's a hand-me-down."

"Well, whoever handed it down should have skipped him," added Mitch.

Allaine ignored that and walked over to hug me, "Thanks for coming," she said.

"Thanks for inviting me."

She was taller and larger than me, but nicely portioned. Her long dark hair and large brown eyes looked beautiful against her olive complexion. Like Lacy, her makeup was flawless, but their facial features were very different. She was beautiful, but didn't resemble Lacy much at all. She had a radiant glow and seemed excited, presumably about her wedding.

I hadn't noticed Lacy walking up behind me, "Hey, don't I get a hug?" she asked, putting her arms around me.

Hugging her, I said, "Oh, I didn't see you."

She looked much better than the last time I'd seen her. Her face wasn't bruised, her teeth had been fixed and her stability had improved.

"I was down in the basement. There's a big room down there with a pool table."

"Sounds neat. Were you playing pool?"

"No, just visiting with everyone. How was your trip here?"

"Good. We broke it up by stopping to see my dad."

"Yeah, that's what Mitch said. Are you hungry? We have plenty of food. Allaine and I made enough lasagna to feed an army."

"That sounds great."

She led me to the paper plates and plastic utensils and told me to join her down in the basement with my food. Everyone was friendly and most looked close to my age or younger. Mitch was visiting with friends at one side of the room. I fixed my plate and followed the stream of people going downstairs to what I assumed was the basement.

At the bottom of the steps, I stopped. A cloud of smoke hovered over the entire room. It was like a neighborhood bar. The pungent smell was a combination of cigarette and pot smoke. Most of the crowd had a beer in hand and a couple of guys were playing pool. Lacy sat talking to a nice looking guy. When I got closer, I saw it was Kerry, Allaine's fiancée. I'd met him once quite a while ago.

Walking up to them, I said, "Hi Kerry! This is sure a large basement."

"Yeah, it is," he said. This was my Dad's place. I'm glad you and Mitch came up for the wedding. It's been like one constant party all week."

"Probably because everyone was surprised that you two made it this far," muttered Lacy.

Kerry laughed, "You're probably right."

There were no chairs available. Wanting to get away from the smoke, I said, "I think I'll go upstairs and eat. It's a little smoky down here."

"I don't blame you," said Lacy. "I'll be up soon."

"Okay." I went back upstairs.

After spending time in the basement, I figured my food would taste smoky anyway, but I didn't care. I was hungry. I found an open spot on the couch and sat down to eat, watching everyone talk. The evening settled down and people began to leave.

It was after midnight before Allaine had a chance to show me where I'd sleep. I had my own room, and was so tired it didn't take me long to fall asleep.

*   *   *

The next morning I found Lacy at the kitchen table having coffee with Mitch. Allan was playing near by.

"Good morning sleepy head," said Mitch.

"Sleepy head? What time is it?"

"A little after nine," said Lacy.

"Man, I must have been tired. Where are Allaine and Kerry?"

"Allaine's putting her makeup on and Kerry had to go to work," said Lacy.

"You want some coffee?" Mitch asked.

"Thanks, that would be great."

"I thought maybe later we would go over to my friend, Mary's house," said Lacy. "She's a palm reader. You know by now that I'm into that type of thing. Numerology and astrology too."

"Yeah, that would be fine," I replied. "I don't know much about it, but it sounds interesting."

"As soon as we can get Allaine ready we'll head over there."

"Okay," I said.

"I think I'll go see my friend John," Mitch said. He sounded cynical.

"You weren't invited anyway," snapped Lacy.

Three hours later we all piled into Allaine's small car, including Allan wearing the powder blue coat. Along the way, Allaine and Lacy pointed out different places where they had lived either together or separately. I couldn't imagine moving around like they did, but it didn't appear to bother them.

Lacy was excited. She wanted to introduce me to her palm reader friend and let her read my palm. I didn't understand palm reading, but I was open to new experiences. I didn't understand numerology either, but astrology fascinated me. Not that I understood it, except when I was out socializing and someone would asked me my sign.

Not raised with any religious beliefs, I was open to whatever information came my way. At times I wished I wasn't so ignorant of traditional subjects. It was a comfort knowing that Lacy and I shared unconventional ideas.

Allaine stopped the car in front of a small house tucked back off the road. Rose bushes alongside a walkway led to its faded white exterior. The flowers would be beautiful when they bloomed in springtime.

Lacy's friend Mary met us at the door, "Hi, come on in."

Hugging her, Lacy asked, "Hi honey, how ya doing?"

"Oh, I'm fine and look at you. You look great and you're walking so much better now."

"I am. Mary, this is Colette," Lacy proudly boasted.

"Mary grabbed my hand and gently squeezed it, "Hi. I've heard so much about you."

150

"Well... I hope it was good," I joked.

Leading us toward her kitchen table, "Of course..." she said. "You guys have a seat. How about a soda?"

We nodded our heads yes and she got each of us a soda, then sat down at the table.

"We want our palms read. Are you up for that?" Lacy asked Mary.

"Yeah, we can do that." Mary replied.

"Colette, you go first," said Lacy.

"Are you sure?" I asked.

"Yeah," Mary said. "Allaine's entertaining her son right now and besides, she's had her palm read by me before."

"Okay, if you say so. What do you want me to do?" I asked.

"Give me your right hand."

I turned my palm up and laid it in front of her. She picked it up and began inspecting it. Curious, I leaned down to get a better view of it. In silence, she moved my hand around, then ran her index finger over the different lines on my palm. I wondered what she was seeing. Patiently I waited.

"You have very dry hands," she said at last.

I was expecting something mystical, not mundane. I already knew that. I smiled and nodded so as not to interrupt her concentration.

After a time of silence, she said, "A new man is soon coming into your life... you're healthy and have a generous heart. Your Sun Line indicates that you will have a lucky life with many blessings coming your way."

Where was all that information on those little lines?

"A new man sounds good," I said. "I already feel lucky."

"You are blessed," she added again.

"I'm not sure what that means, but it sounds good. Thank you."

"You're welcome. Just remember that you are blessed."

"I will."

I wasn't sure what to think about her reading, but I'd welcome a new man since I'd been single for the last year. The blessing part sounded good, but I had no idea why she said that or what line on my palm showed it. I decided to take it all with a grain of salt.

I walked into the other room to relieve Allaine of her son so she could have her palm read but she said she'd do it another day.

When we walked back into the kitchen, Mary was finishing Lacy's reading. I wished I'd heard what was said about her life. I had been around her for two days and still didn't know any more about her than from our first meeting. We visited a little longer, and then headed back to Allaine's house.

In the car Lacy asked me, "How'd you like your reading?"

"Well... it sounded good. But I don't know much about it."

"Trust me. She's good."

Allaine didn't say much. She gave the impression of liking Mary, but didn't seem interested in getting a reading.

"Hey, I got an idea." Allaine sounded excited.

"What?" asked Lacy.

"Tomorrow, why don't the three of us drive to Moscow Mall? We can have our makeup done at Merle Norman. Maybe get some ideas for the wedding."

"Sounds fun." Lacy said. "What do you think, Colette?"

"Hey... it sounds good. Anything will be an improvement for me."

"This way we'll all be beautiful for the rehearsal dinner," said Allaine.

We decided to get up early the following morning and have breakfast before driving an hour to the mall. I'd never had makeup done and was hoping I'd look as good as Allaine and Lacy. I didn't know why they wanted their makeup done by someone else when both of them always looked perfect but it did take them a long time to do it. With me, it usually took about two minutes. Allaine used a safety pin to separate each of her eyelashes. No thank you! If someone got that close to my eyelashes, they'd have to deal with them stuck together.

Tomorrow would be the last day I could spend time with Allaine. The day after was her wedding and she'd be too busy being a bride, and then off on her honeymoon. I looked forward to just the three of us spending some time together.

152

A Love Child's Journey

Chapter Sixteen

We had a great time at the Moscow Mall getting our makeup done. I didn't want to disappoint Lacy or Allaine, but my makeup turned out horrible. Every time we passed a mirror, I did a double take to make sure I was looking at myself. I had enough on to last me through the rehearsal dinner and the wedding the following day. Lacy's and Allaine's didn't look that great either; they did a better job on their own. But it was more about enjoying the day together and it was a nice day with just the three of us. Conversation was light as we browsed the mall stores, had lunch and returned to Lewiston.

*   *   *

The small quaint church was just right for the wedding Allaine had in mind. She told me it would be a shorter version of Catholic weddings. I was glad to hear that, having already experienced the long version for a friend a few years earlier.

With only four people in the wedding party, including the bride and groom, rehearsing didn't take long. We piled back into the car and returned to Allaine and Kerry's house for our rehearsal dinner. This was the first rehearsal dinner I'd attended at someone's home. Kerry's mom and sister had prepared casseroles, salads, appetizers and desserts that covered the dining room table. Familiar faces began showing up at the door. The rehearsal dinner didn't seem much different from the first night we arrived. I avoided alcohol, to prevent a hangover. Not that I had to do anything for the wedding, but who needs to feel lousy? And I wanted to be at my best for Allaine on her special day.

*   *   *

She was right, the wedding moved quickly. The ceremony was in Latin so I didn't understand much besides 'I Do', but everyone was pleased and ready to move on to the Moose Lodge for the reception.

Maroon and silver streamers gave a festive flair to the stark white walls at the lodge. Bouquets of balloons in the same colors sat in the center of each table. Caterers were setting up food and the DJ was organizing his music. Most of the guests had arrived. There was no special place for the wedding party, so Mitch and I found a spot and sat down. Lacy walked in with a large, white-haired guy.

"Mitch, who's that?' I asked.

"That's her husband, Rob."

"I didn't notice him at the wedding. So... that's the guy who likes to hit her?"

"Yeah, that's him. He drove in from Boise for the wedding."

Walking over to our table, Lacy introduced me to him. He was sickening sweet to me. He knew that I knew what he'd done to her. Wanting to be sociable for Lacy's sake, I was polite, but barely. I had no desire to talk with him. What I wanted to say he wouldn't want to hear. Mitch felt the same. Lacy knew better than to sit with us, so they moved on to another table.

Allaine and Kerry started dancing to the song 'Brick House'. It's a great song, but not what I expected to hear for a bride and groom's special dance. It must be very special to them.

The reception ended. Kerry and Allaine said their goodbyes and took off for a local hotel to enjoy their wedding night. I didn't know how long it might be before I'd see her again. Mitch and I went back to their house. Lacy and Rob followed us, but Lacy was the only one who got out of the car. She passed his goodbye to us and said he needed to get back to Boise. Mitch and I were thankful he wasn't staying. Cars began stopping in front of the house before we made it to the front door. I realized the reception wasn't over. After a few glasses of wine and champagne, I was relaxed and willing to continue a good time.

It didn't take long for everyone to gather down in the basement, *the party room*. People lined the floor drinking beer and taking hits off the pot being passed around. I was sitting on the floor next to Lacy drinking a beer. Well, I was holding a beer but not really drinking it. I didn't like beer. I was still lucid but feeling the affects of the alcohol I drank earlier. I watched Lacy take a joint from the person on the other side of her. She didn't look at me as she brought it to her lips and took a long drag. Holding her breath, she handed it to me. Not wanting to seem naïve, I did the same and passed it to the next person. My eyes burned as I tried not to think about how many lips it had touched. At least I didn't choke or cough in the process. She still didn't look at me. It seemed cool. I mean, here I was smoking a joint with my mother. No... actually, it was ludicrous. I couldn't imagine smoking anything with or in front of my adopted mother and living to tell about it.

I wasn't sure where the old joint stopped and a new one began, but there seemed to be a continuous joint going around the room. After a few hits, I started to feel the effects.

"Lacy," I said. "Tell me about being a call girl."

She laughed softly. "There's nothing to tell."

"Well, you know... like something special you'd do for a guy."

As the words left my mouth, I realized how dumb they were, but I was intrigued by her previous lifestyle. Not the usual topic between mothers and daughters but maybe she could give me some pointers. Suddenly I knew she wasn't going to answer me. She didn't want me to see her in that light. I felt bad about bringing it up.

"Sorry I asked you."

"It's okay. I prefer to keep my personal life my business."

"Yeah... you've told me that." Wanting to lighten the mood, I asked, "Do you want another beer?"

"That's a great idea."

When I returned with her beer, she had moved to another part of the room and was talking with some of Allaine's friends. I walked over and handed it to her. She smiled her thanks and continued the conversation. I went upstairs feeling lousy. I blew the one chance I had to ask her something by asking the wrong thing. Why didn't I ask who my father was? What was I thinking? The disappointment sobered me right up. I hoped she wasn't as upset at me.

I found Mitch in the kitchen. After explaining what I did, he told me not to worry about it. He said she just wanted me to see her in a more motherly way. I told him it was difficult to see her that way while she was smoking pot. We laughed, and decided to call it a night. We'd be driving to Oregon in the morning to drop him off at my Dad's place. He'd be working there for a few weeks.

*   *   *

I woke to Mitch banging on the bedroom door. "Are you awake?" he asked.

"I am now," I said. "I'll be right out."

I hurried and dressed. Lacy was fixing breakfast in the kitchen. Now that looked motherly.

"How bout some coffee?" she asked.

"That would be great, thank you."

"I thought I'd fix you two a nice breakfast since you have a long drive ahead of you."

"That's really nice of you," I said. She seemed fine.

"That's what mom's do, right?" she asked.

"Yes, they do," I answered.

Mitch was right. She wanted me to see her as a mother. And I wanted to reassure her that I did, whether it was 100% true or not.

We finished breakfast and packed our things to go. Mitch and I hugged Lacy goodbye and said we'd write her and hoped to see her soon. She stood in the doorway and waved as we got in the car.

"I think she's sad to see us go," I said.

"Yeah... I think you're right, but I'm glad it's over."

"Me too... I guess. I just wish I could have talked more with her."

"She's always said that her life is her own business. Though there have been times when she wanted to share some call girl stories with me but I didn't want to hear them."

"I can understand that."

We drove back the same way we came and passed the place where Lacy went off the cliff. Neither of us commented on it. We took turns driving and by late afternoon arrived at Dad's. I visited for a short while before driving on to California. I was nervous driving the mountains in the snow, but I missed my son and wanted to get home.

The steady fall of snow made it difficult to see. I held the steering wheel so tight my hands ached. It was my first time driving in the snow alone, but I got behind a large truck and followed it until we were out of the mountains. By late night I made it back to my condominium.

* * *

A few weeks later, Mitch and my dad returned to California. I missed Mitch and was glad to have him back.

Sitting at the kitchen table Mitch said, "You know your dad got me up every morning at three to stoke the fire."

"Yeah, that sounds like him."

"He was already up, he could have done it himself instead of waking me up to do it."

I laughed, "That's the kind of things he does. Things like that build *character*."

"And he doesn't drink coffee either, he drinks tea. He had me drive his Jeep with no top in the rain to the hardware store almost every day. One time the cashier was drinking a hot cup of coffee. It smelled so good, I thought about stealing it. The two weeks without coffee was pure torture."

My sides hurt from laughing while I listened to Mitch's experiences over the past two weeks. He wasn't telling me anything new. My experience with Dad was much longer than two weeks.

He didn't say why but Mitch decided to move to Fresno and go to an ironworker training school. I would miss him, but it seemed like a good path for him. Chase and I watched as he loaded his things in his car.

"Give me a hug," he said when he finished.

I hugged him. "It was nice getting to know you and I'm glad you're my brother."

He smiled, patted Chase on the head, and said, "Take care of your mom."

"I will," said Chase.

His saying that to my young son had a lot of meaning. Mitch had taken care of Lacy off and on since he was young. That's what he did best, take care of people he loved, but now he was off to take care of himself.

*   *   *

Lacy's palm reader friend was right. A few months after Mitch left I met a new guy. Allaine wrote to tell me she was pregnant and Lacy was divorcing her husband Rob. I was pleased to hear about that. Allaine said her baby was due around my birthday.

Mitch sent me a letter a few months later. He'd finished school and was working on his apprenticeship with the ironworkers. And he was living with a gal and her two young children. That seemed right for Mitch. He said she was pregnant with his baby and they'd probably get married in a few months.

We all seemed to be getting on with our lives, but as time went by communication dwindled. Dad finished his remodel of the house in Oregon, and my mom, little brother and sister moved up there. It was difficult when they left. They'd been around me all my life and were always there when I needed them. They were no longer a few miles away. I was thankful to be in a serious relationship at that time, but it wouldn't replace Mom and Dad.

*   *   *

In late November, Allaine called to tell me she gave birth to a baby girl on my birthday. She said Lacy was so elated she couldn't stop talking about the matching dates. I had to admit it was amazing. I was happy for Allaine and the baby. She said Lacy had met a new man and was thinking about marrying him. I suggested Lacy should just live with them instead of getting married all the time. Allaine told me she does that too, but marries the ones she thinks will be good husbands. So much for her ability to evaluate men.

We continued to exchange Christmas cards. Lacy wrote me that she was using a different first name. She didn't say why. Did she want to be someone different? I didn't pay much attention to it because she was Lacy to me and that's what I continued to call her. It didn't mean much to Mitch and Allaine either since they called her Mom.

* * *

A few more years passed. Christmas and birthdays were the only time we sent cards and that became sparse too. Allaine did write that she and Kerry divorced. I was sorry to hear it. I was in the process of planning my wedding and it made me uneasy to hear about the end of a marriage. I'd been through that once and didn't want to experience it again.

September rolled around and after five years of dating, John and I finally married. It was a nice backyard wedding. Mom and Dad had returned from Oregon and were living not too far from us. My little brother and sister stayed in Oregon. They were both out of high school and had established themselves there with friends and jobs. I'd invited Lacy, Mitch and Allaine to my wedding, but none of them could make it. It might have been awkward, but not to me.

Mitch now had two sons of his own and two stepchildren. He was too busy working to get away. I understood. Allaine lived in Idaho and had two kids to care for. Lacy divorced the guy I heard she married and was going by her own name again. She'd been in rehab for drinking and was doing well, but couldn't afford to make the trip. It was probably best that she didn't.

* * *

In the spring of 1989, my husband's birthday was a week away. We'd been enjoying the nice weather and waiting until our pool warmed up enough for swimming.

I'd started a new job in a different field, but I liked the challenge.

My telephone rang. I picked it up and said, "Colette speaking."

Her voice trembled, "Hi honey, this is your mom. I hate to bother you at work, but I think your dad had a stroke."

"What? Is he in the hospital?"

"No, he won't go."

"Is he there?" I asked. "Let me talk to him."

I could hear her fumbling with the telephone.

"Hi Snip," he said.

"Dad you need to go to the hospital?"

"I'm fine. I just got a little dizzy."

"I'll come by and see you after work, but consider going to the hospital at least to be checked out," I begged.

"We'll see."

"I'll see you later."

I couldn't concentrate the rest of the day. After work, I stopped by their motor home. Dad had been working on their commercial building for a few years in order to generate income after its sale fell through. His 6'3" slender frame looked healthy, but stress and high blood pressure don't mix well. He had both.

He was sitting in his chair watching television when I arrived. He said his head hurt and he would have it checked the next day. I was glad to hear him agree to see a doctor.

I stopped by the next night and the doctor had given him strong medication that knocked him out. All I could do was look at him sleep. Mom seemed to be holding up well. She'd been painting walls inside the commercial building. She was tired and I could see the worry in her face. It scared me. I told her I'd stop by the next day when I went on my walk. My husband and I had stopped smoking a year earlier and I took up walking.

The following morning I stopped by on my walk. Dad had a bad headache, but was lucid and wanted to talk. Mom went inside to paint. Dad and I talked about everything. It was the first in-depth talk I'd ever had with him. We reminisced about camping trips, jeep rides and my husband and I buying a motor home of our own. What surprised me was when he started talking about God. He'd always said he didn't believe in God, but when he started talking about God taking care of everything I wondered why he said one thing, and believed another. But I didn't question it. I just listened. Although his head hurt him, we talked for nearly two hours. Mom came back from painting. I hugged them both and went home.

    I hadn't been home long when I got a call from the police station telling me to go outside and speak with an officer. I walked outside and there was my policeman friend who had helped me with my search for Lacy. He told me my dad just suffered a stroke and was on his way to the hospital by ambulance. I could hear the siren. I thanked him and ran back into the house for my purse and keys. Chase stayed with my husband John as I headed for the hospital.

Dad died early in the morning two days later on my husband's birthday. My little brother said it best. He had to get us up early one more time. I wished he hadn't died on my husband's birthday, but Dad would have found that funny. It was unexpected and fast. I felt bad for my siblings. They didn't get to say anything to him before the end, but I had those two wonderful hours.

    Mitch, Allaine and Lacy called with condolences. It was nice to hear from all of them. Lacy said she wasn't happy in her marriage and was divorcing the guy she had married only six months earlier. I hadn't met him or the previous husband. Which number husband was this, anyway? It really didn't matter. She wasn't married to them anymore. She said she was moving to Spokane and would send me her address when she got a place to live. Allaine was doing well and Mitch now had three boys. He was working long hours to support his home and family. It sounded overwhelming. I think I'd be overwhelmed supporting five kids and a wife too!

    *   *   *

Not long after my father's death. I quit my job. Mom and I opened a gift shop in her commercial building so I could help her with the tenants. I hadn't heard from Lacy or Mitch, but Allaine sent me a Christmas card with pictures of her kids. It surprised me when my husband said Allaine had called and it was important for me to call her back.

I waited until after dinner before calling her.

"Allaine, this is Colette. Are you okay?"

"I'm so glad you called. I'm fine, but Mom's not."

"What do you mean?"

"She's at the Sacred Heart Hospital in Spokane."

"Did she get hurt?"

"No… she went to sell her blood or platelets and they wouldn't take it. She was told it was very important she go to the hospital."

"She sells her blood?"

"Yeah, but the bad thing is that they discovered she has acute leukemia."

"She's not going to die, is she?"

Choking back tears, Allaine said, "According to the doctor, it doesn't look too hopeful, but Mom thinks she's going to be fine."

"Have you called Mitch?"

"Yeah, he didn't take it well. I think he's under so much stress trying to take care of his family that this is just too much for him."

I didn't want to think about Lacy dying. I was still struggling with my dad's death.

"I'm driving up there tomorrow. I'll know more about what's going on when I can talk face to face with the doctor," said Allaine.

"Okay, I'll wait to hear from you tomorrow. Thanks for calling me Allaine. It means a lot."

"You're her daughter too."

"Thanks for that. Talk with you tomorrow."

It was something I liked from the beginning. Mitch and Allaine treated me as if I'd been around them their entire life. As far as they were concerned, I was part of their family. It was a nice feeling. I knew the seriousness of acute leukemia. We had a close family friend die within two weeks of finding out she had it.

I'd wait to hear from Allaine. I wanted to call Mitch, but decided to wait.

*   *   *

It was early evening when I heard from Allaine. She had just gotten home from Spokane. She said that they were giving Lacy radiation, but she was told not to get her hopes up because it was a serious disease. Lacy was very tired and slept most of the time. Allaine would call Mitch after she hung up. It would be two days before she could go back there again. It was a two-hour drive for her, and I was glad she was close enough to go.

I waited two days and then called Mitch.

"Hey Mitch, have you heard from Allaine?"

"No, she hasn't called. You know... it's that damned boob job she had. She's had problems with them leaking for a long time. Now it's in her system and making her sick," he said in anguish.

"I didn't know they were leaking."

He calmed down. "Yeah, she just can't afford to get them fixed. That's why she stays in cooler climates."

"Are you planning on going to see her?"

"I want to, but I'll have to check with my boss. I got my wife and the kids."

"Well, I'd wait until we hear from Allaine. But if you go up, I'll go with you."

"Okay... that sounds good. I need to see what I can do around here to make it easier for my family to manage while I'm gone."

"I'll wait to hear from you."

Allaine called me later that night and said Lacy was a little better. It relieved me to hear a bit of good news. I asked Allaine if I could call Lacy in the morning. She thought that would be a good idea. It was difficult to sleep that night. I thought about Dad then Lacy, back and forth. I knew Mitch and Allaine were scared, not knowing if Lacy would make it through this. Statistics were not in her favor. The thought of dealing with another death was overwhelming. Finally I drifted off to sleep.

*   *   *

The next morning was a beautiful sunny day. I waited to call Lacy from my gift shop. Nervous, I didn't know what to say or what she'd say. Slowly I dialed the number Allaine had given me. I was surprised to hear Lacy's voice. She sounded good.

"Hi, this is Colette. How are you feeling today?"

"I'm feeling great. I should be out of here in no time."

"I'm glad to hear that," I said, elated that she sounded so good.

"Tomorrow's Chase's 12th birthday. One more year and he'll be a teenager," she said.

I couldn't believe that in her condition, she remembered my son's birthday. "Yeah, he's excited about it. But I think he's more excited about summer vacation getting here."

"I don't blame him there. When I'm out of here, maybe we can get together. It's been a long time since I've seen you. Did you know I got married last month?"

"No, I didn't."

"He's a good guy. He just walked in."

"I'm happy for you. Well, I'll let you go so you can visit with him."

"Okay, honey. I'll talk with you then. Glad you called."

"Me too."

Feeling some relief that she was doing better, but I couldn't believe she married again. Allaine had told me it was her eleventh marriage. Lacy seemed happy about it. I think she passed Elizabeth Taylor's record a few husbands ago. I didn't know anyone else who had been married that many times.

*   *   *

The next afternoon Allaine called.

"Colette, Mom's not doing well at all."

"But… she sounded really good yesterday when I talked with her. What happened?"

"I'm not sure. I just got here and she's bleeding everywhere. Her nose, ears, and eyes, who knows where else. She's really out of it."

Shocked, I didn't know what to say. I thought she was doing better, but I didn't understand the disease or how it affected people.

"Do you want me to call Mitch?" I asked.

"Would you please? I'm going to see if I can get hold of the doctor."

"I'll call Mitch, then wait to hear from you."

I didn't want to be the one to tell Mitch that Lacy wasn't doing well, but Allaine had enough to worry about. I called and talked to his wife and she said she'd have him call me when he got home from work.

I didn't hear from Mitch until after 8:00 in the evening. He had already talked with Allaine and Lacy was worse. He said he couldn't leave until the day after next. I told him that would be fine. Allaine would call tomorrow and let us know how Lacy was doing. My heart was heavy. I wanted to reassure Mitch that she'd be fine, but I couldn't even convince myself.

Unable to escape the thoughts of Dad and Lacy made it impossible to fall asleep. She was only 48 years old, too young to die. Yet thinking of our family friend, she was in her twenties when she died. Age didn't matter with this disease.

The following day my heart sank every time the phone rang. It was about 2:30 in the afternoon when Allaine finally called.

"Hi Colette."

"I've been waiting for your call. How is she?"

Allaine's voice trembled. "She's gone."

"She's gone... you mean she died?"

She started crying. "Yeah... I just got here and they said she died about twenty minutes ago."

I was speechless. "Allaine, I don't know what to say."

"I know. I'm dreading the call to Mitch. I don't think he's home from work yet."

"I don't think so either. He wanted the two of us to drive up tomorrow."

"That would still be good. I can make the arrangements and it'll give us a chance to go through her things together."

"What about her new husband? Does he know?"

"Yeah... he was here. He just left."

165

"I'll wait to hear from either you or Mitch."

Hanging up, I couldn't believe she was gone. The last time I'd seen her was at Allaine's wedding. At that time, I had no idea it would be the last time I'd see her.

A Love Child's Journey

Chapter Seventeen

Mitch showed up at my house around eight in the morning. My husband had gone to work and my son was at school. They'd be fine while I was away. This trip to Idaho would be very different from our last one.

Mitch left his home early for the three-hour drive to my house. He parked his truck in my driveway and loaded our suitcases into my car. I asked if he was okay and he said he was. He then filled his thermos with the remaining coffee from my coffeepot.

We decided to drive through Nevada this time. He said it would be faster. On our way, we talked about the hardships and sadness in Lacy's life, especially having the three of us at a young age. But we were thankful she did. That thought made me feel better. He said my finding her was the most important thing she'd wanted in her adult life. We laughed about her getting married the previous month and figured she could be in the record book for the most marriages.

We moved on to update each other on our own lives. He seemed unhappy and he had lost his spunk. It was a sad trip, but probably good for Mitch to get away from his daily responsibilities.

We filled-up with gas, bought coffee and ate fast foods. We did have relief stops because of so much coffee drinking. I was on caffeine overload. Usually I got a headache for being under my coffee quota. But with too much, my head felt like it would explode.

We arrived at Allaine's around two in the morning. She lived in a little two-bedroom house. The three of us hugged, and tip toed around to avoid waking her kids. She had the sleeper couch folded out for me and Mitch had the bottom bunk in her son's room. Wired on coffee, I didn't know if I'd ever fall asleep, but finally I did.

I woke to bustling and shushing sounds from the kitchen. Allaine was busy getting her kids ready for school. My body ached but my head felt much better.

Walking into the kitchen, I greeted everyone.

Allan, almost ten and Nicole, seven, both said good morning. It was the first time I'd seen Allaine's daughter. Allaine's wedding was the last time I'd seen her son. Both kids had sandy brown hair with blue eyes. They had different fathers, but neither of them had Allaine's coloring. They were nice looking kids.

"I'll be right back." Allaine said. "I've got to run them to school."

"Sure... no problem."

Besides knick-knacks, she had a lot of family pictures on her shelves and hanging on her walls. I picked up a large photo of a man in a suit.

"That's Allaine's dad," Mitch said.

Startled, I turned around. "I didn't hear you get up, but I figured that's who it was." I studied the picture again. "Her dad, that is. She sure looks a lot like him."

"Yeah... she does. Kind of like my biological dad and me. Allaine's dad lives in San Francisco."

"So he's alive?"

"Yeah. It's another one of those weird situations."

"Let me get this straight. Allaine looks like her dad and you look like your dad, but I don't look like either Rodney or Lacy."

"Well, I've told you all along, I don't think you're Grampy's daughter."

"Yeah, I know... but in a round-about way, Lacy said I am."

Bringing up her name made us pause. Mitch appeared in control, but I knew that inside he was wishing we'd come earlier, before she died. I wished the same. Allaine returned and sat down at the kitchen table with us. We sat in silence for a few moments.

Then Allaine got up and grabbed a piece of paper out of a drawer. "I wrote her obituary. Do you want to read it?"

Mitch and I read it. She had done a good job and picked a beautiful picture to go with it. She wrote that Lacy had three surviving children. It was the first time I'd seen my name written as her daughter. Seeing it like that made it more real somehow.

Allaine had taken care of all the arrangements. Lacy was cremated and the service would take place the next day. After her service we would drive to Lacy's storage unit and pick up her things.

"Allaine, did you call Nammie and Laura?" asked Mitch.

Allaine looked disgusted. "Yeah... but I don't think either of them are going to come. You'd think if your sister and daughter died, you'd at least want to come to her service and pay your respects."

Mitch said, "I didn't think Nammie would come, but I thought Laura would at least try to make it."

"She said something about not having the money to get here. Her and mom weren't on speaking terms, but that shouldn't matter. Nammie said she was heading for Yuma."

"It's about what I expected to hear," Mitch said. So who's going to be at the service?"

Allaine shrugged. "Well, my friend Debbie and her kids. Rick, Mom's new husband... maybe his mom and us. I did put it in the newspaper. Others will probably show up."

It saddened me to think that not only close family members but also close friends might not come. She did move around a lot; and perhaps her friends changed every time she married someone new. The funeral home would be bursting if all her husbands and their extended families showed up. I hoped she had new friends with her new husband and their family would support him at this time.

We spent the day sharing stories of Lacy. I didn't have many, but both Mitch and Allaine got a kick out of my reaction to Lacy's pot smoking. It was nothing new to them. Most of their stories weren't typical mother stories. They told me about the time she let the two of them drive themselves from Idaho to California when Allaine was fourteen and Mitch was twelve. Allaine had an Idaho license. On the way they were pulled over by a policeman who thought they'd stolen the car. After the officer got hold of Lacy at the local tavern, she told him they had her permission because they wanted to see their grandparents in California and she couldn't go with them. The officer was shocked. It was getting dark so he made them sleep in their car at the police station. We laughed, but they both knew it wasn't something a parent should let kids do at that age. Lacy always said she was a woman first and a mother second.

*   *   *

The following morning we were on the road early. It was a two and a half-hour drive to the funeral home. Allaine was tense but looked beautiful, her makeup perfect. Mine, well... you couldn't really see if I had any on, but it worked for me. Nicole rode with Allaine's friend. Allan, Mitch and I piled into Allaine's car. My heart throbbed and I dreaded every mile we covered. I should have been thinking about Lacy, but thoughts of Dad consumed me. We didn't have a service for him and his death the year before was still fresh in my mind. It seemed like yesterday. Lacy was too young to die, but I didn't have the privilege of knowing her as I knew my dad. Ever since finding her, I wished I knew more about her, but this day I was glad I didn't. It was sad, but if I had the same intense emotional ties with her, it would have been unbearable.

Mitch and Allaine seemed strong and composed. I couldn't let myself fall apart. Distractions helped. I sang songs in my head, and thought of fun things I've done. I didn't dare think of Mitch and Allaine's pain. Or the fact that Lacy was gone.

At the funeral home Alliane realized her friend's car was no longer following her. She was irritated, but her friend had the address and we hoped she'd find her way.

My heart pounded as we entered. It was large and beautiful inside. Pews stretched the length of the room with aisles in the middle and along the sides. It looked like enough room for a few hundred people. Allaine placed a large picture of Lacy on a lace-covered table near the podium. The same picture she used for the obituary notice, the photo of a beautiful woman. She arranged flowers around it. Lacy had brought the three of us into this world, yet her life had been sad and tragic.

Allaine paced the floor waiting for her friend to show up with Nicole. Mitch, Allan and I sat quietly in the second pew. A guy and two older women entered and sat a few pews back from us. Allaine walked over and spoke briefly to them, then came and sat down by Mitch.

"I don't know where the hell Debbie is with Nicole," she whispered, "but she's going to miss this. I want my daughter here for her grandmother's funeral."

"Allaine, you know how Debbie is," murmured Mitch.

"I know and I'm going to be pissed if she makes my daughter miss this."

"Hey, is that Mom's new husband who just walked in?" he asked.

"Yeah. The older lady is his mother and the other one's a friend from the bar. He doesn't look much older than us, does he?"

Mitch laughed. "No, he doesn't."

Allaine walked outside to look for her missing friend. I turned around to check out Lacy's husband. He looked straight at me. I smiled and turned back. We were the only ones there for Lacy's funeral. I wondered if her short life had been that insignificant. Did she treat people she met with surface only conversation? Had she been hurt so much and let down so often by the people she loved that she allowed no one to get close enough to know her? Did only her family know the good and the bad, her unhappiness and joys? What about the ten other guys she married? Her inability to go without sex for more than three days must have been the lure that caught them. That may be the reason that none of her marriages lasted long, with one exception, JL's. He was one of Lacy's ex-husbands who she stayed married to for over ten years. According to Mitch, he had a drinking problem but Lacy loved really him.

Sitting down next to Mitch, Allaine whispered, "She's not here and they want to start because they have another funeral right after this one. We can't delay any longer."

"She'll show up."

The service didn't take long and I tried to think of other things. I didn't want to hear anything that would make me cry. I was afraid that once I started I wouldn't be able to stop.

Afterward the seven of us were ushered out to the reception area. Allaine introduced Mitch and I to Lacy's husband and his mother. I didn't know what had happened to the other lady, but she was gone. After an exchange of condolences he and his mom left. We stepped outside to wait while Allaine retrieved Lacy's ashes. Allaine's friend finally drove up with Nicole.

Mitch bent down to the car window and said, "If I were you, I'd stay put. Allaine is not happy."

"We just stopped to get an ice cream and then... I got lost. Has it started yet?" asked Debbie.

"It's over," he said.

Nicole got out of the car. Debbie asked Mitch to tell Allaine she was sorry, but thought it best not to stick around and upset her friend even more. Mitch agreed.

When Alliane returned carrying Lacy's ashes, she walked right to Nicole. "Where have you been? And where's Debbie?"

Nicole stiffened. Mitch said, "She apologized. She stopped to get the kids ice cream and got lost. She said she was sorry. She'll call you later."

Alliane's face was beet-red with anger, but there was nothing she could do about it.

Turning to Mitch and me, she said, "I got the key to Mom's storage from her husband. I want to go by and get her things."

"What things?" Mitch asked.

"I'm not sure, but I know there are pictures and her sewing machine. Her husband has no use for them."

"Okay," he agreed.

We all piled into Allaine's small car. She placed Lacy's ashes on the front floorboard between Mitch's feet. He didn't look too comfortable with it, but didn't have much choice. Space was limited. Whatever Lacy had in her storage that Allaine wanted had better fit in the trunk. There was no extra room in her car.

We arrived at an old two-story warehouse of sheet metal and wood only a few blocks away. One puff from the big bad wolf could have blown it down. The shabby structure of the building didn't seem to bother Allaine or Mitch.

Allaine went into the office and returned saying the manager told her to take the freight service elevator to the second floor and turn left.

I'd never been in a service elevator and wasn't sure I wanted to be in this one. Mitch reached down and pulled up the latch on the screened door. He waited for all of us to enter, and then closed it with a bang. He pushed the up button. With a loud screech it jarred and jiggled us upward before stopping.

We followed Allaine down a narrow plywood hallway. I was thankful for the skylights that let in enough sunlight to see. Allaine unlocked the padlock and walked inside. We followed. The room was about eight feet wide by ten feet long. On the right sat some boxes, a lamp and the sewing machine Allaine wanted. Sorrow swept down on me like a shadow. Her things didn't cover more than a third of the storage space. That was her life. These belongings were her only possessions at the end of forty-eight years. We all stared at the boxes in silence.

"Not much here Allaine," said Mitch.

"Yeah... sad isn't it?"

"Well, what do you want to do?"

"I want the boxes and the sewing machine. You never know, maybe she has something about Colette filed in one of those boxes. We won't know if we don't check."

I perked up. "I never thought about that."

"Okay," Mitch said. "Let's take the boxes and the sewing machine. Leave the lamp for her husband."

We hauled the four boxes and the sewing machine to the car and left for Lewiston.

Half way back Allaine asked Mitch, "Do you want some of Mom's ashes?"

"What?" he asked.

"I said, do you want some of Mom's ashes?"

"So... what parts did you want to give me? A leg... maybe? Or an arm? No... I want her to stay whole. At least whole in the box."

"Okay... okay, I was just asking. I didn't know."

"That's one thing I don't want to share," he added.

"How about you, Colette?" asked Allaine.

Pleased at being asked, I said, "Nah... she's fine just the way she is."

We all laughed.

*   *   *

That evening after dinner at Allaine's house, the kids went to bed and we sat down to go through Lacy's boxes. There were a lot of photos, some that Allaine and Mitch already had and some they'd never seen. I was surprised how they shared the pictures with me. I hadn't spent very many years with them, but they treated me no different than each other. They divided the pictures equally. I was disappointed at not finding any mysterious letter about my origin or me. But Lacy had kept the bible she was given at the home for unwed mothers. Allaine and Mitch both agreed I should have it because Lacy was pregnant with me then. I graciously accepted. Opening it, I noticed different passages she had underlined. But what caught my attention was her list of all but her last two marriages in the middle of the book under a Marriages column. There were too many to fit, so she marked out the Deaths column on the next page and wrote marriages instead. Allaine added Lacy's last two marriages for me. I hadn't heard about the two before her current husband. Widower, that is.

There were pictures of Vietnam and cards from her last husband with explicit lovemaking messages that Allaine read aloud to us. They laughed and said—that's Mom.

"It doesn't bother you reading those things about her?" I asked.

Mitch laughed. "We're used to it. She used to tell us about her tricks with her johns and sometimes a lot more than we wanted to hear. How you came about was the one thing she never discussed, though."

"We've always known about you and every time your birthday came around we knew she'd get so depressed that it scared us, but that's all we know," said Allaine.

Mitch added, "And whenever we'd see a red-headed girl about your age, we wondered if maybe it was you."

I laughed. "As you can see, I have no red hairs."

"Yeah. That's why I know you're not Grampy's," said Mitch.

"I wish I'd asked her more questions. Well... besides asking her to share some of the techniques she used while working."

Allaine laughed loudly. "You asked her that?"

"Yeah, at your wedding."

"She didn't want you to see her as a call girl," said Allaine.

"I realized that after the fact. I guess it's why she didn't tell me anything."

We finished going through her things and went to bed.

*   *   *

Mitch and I left for California the following morning. It had been a quick sad trip, but spending time with Allaine and Mitch comforted me. I wanted to be there for them and Lacy.

We drove home the same way we came, with minimal stops and driving straight through. Mitch had to get back to work. He and I promised to stay in touch and visit each other when we could.

*   *   *

A few years passed. Mitch and I had less contact, but Allaine decided to move to California. I liked that until I heard she was going to move in with the crazy grandmother, Nammie, a.k.a. Wilma. She had no choice. She needed a place to stay while looking for an apartment. I told her she'd have to visit me at my house until she found a place. I wouldn't go to Nammie's.

She rented an apartment. It was still a drive away, but much closer than Idaho. We visited once in a while but she was busy with her kids and working. I was busy with Chase and working, but we stayed in touch.

175

She started dating a guy who after a while became abusive. She decided to move back to Idaho. In helping her move, I heard more Lacy stories. They weren't very different from the others I'd heard. Lacy seemed to have followed a road of constant self-destruction. Mitch and Allaine had difficulties, as most people do, but appeared to survive life in general. Lacy would have been happy about that.

*   *   *

The years clicked by. Mitch had long since divorced and was living in Monterey with his boys. Allaine and her son were finishing college as her daughter was beginning it. My son had finished his education, found work and married. I was a proud grandmother of two. My husband had retired and life was great.

Out of the blue one day, I got a call from Mitch. He had moved to Sacramento. He said he wanted to be closer to me. I missed him and was pleased that he would live near by.

*   *   *

Mitch and I met and caught up on the missing years. Over lunch we started talking about Lacy.

"Mitch, I remember you saying so many times that you never thought Grampy, a.k.a. Rodney was my father."

"Yeah... I never did think that."

"Well... why not?"

"The obvious thing is that you don't look anything like him. Not at all. I can see a little of mom in you, but look at Allaine and me. Mom's genes just weren't very dominant. We look like our dads. You probably look like your dad. The other reason is that JL said you belonged to some local Italian boy."

JL was the guy who'd been married to Lacy the longest. They were together ten years and then off and on again between her other marriages. He was the man Mitch considered his dad.

"I might go and see Wilma. What do you think of that?"

"It couldn't hurt. I think she knows the truth. Remember what she said to you when you first saw her? You didn't look like anyone in her family and that was good. That right there tells you that you aren't Grampy's."

"The Nammie stories from you and Allaine had me afraid of her, but Allaine told me she's blind now."

" I didn't know that, but I think she'll be okay with you. You don't have the history that Allaine and I have with her."

"Yeah... and since she's blind I could probably outrun her. But it's been over twenty-five years since I've seen her and that was the only time. What do I say? I've been busy, and Mitch and Allaine scared me by saying you're crazy."

He laughed. "Just take her something, like flowers, candy or pictures. That works well with her. If you bring her something, she gives you something in return. I think she has a lot of information hidden in her brain or her house. I bet she knows who your father is. One last thing, don't tell her you've seen me."

I made up my mind; when I got home from lunch I'd call Wilma.

*   *   *

I sat with the telephone in one hand and Wilma's phone number in the other. My heart drummed, and my stomach danced to the beat. I didn't know what to say to explain why I hadn't called her before now. The worse she could do is say no, I don't want to see you. There's no way she could hurt me. But I had a hunch she was my only hope in finding the truth about my biological father. It was something I'd been thinking about more and more since Lacy's death.

I pushed the buttons. The other end of the line rang, then stopped.

There was a raspy hello.

"Hello, is this Wilma?"

"Yes. Who's this?"

"This is Colette, Lacy's daughter."

In a salty tone she said, "Well! I haven't heard from *you* in a long time."

"Yes, I know. I'm sorry about that. I've been caught up with my everyday life, working and raising my son. I was wondering... would it be okay to come and see you?"

She paused. "Well... I guess it would be all right."

"How about this Saturday?"

"That would be fine, but I have a different address."

She gave me her address and said she would see me on Saturday.

I felt half excited, half scared. I needed to get as much information as I could from her, so I would take Mitch's advice and bring her something. Maybe, a whole bunch of things.

A Love Child's Journey

Chapter Eighteen

I planned to arrive at Wilma's home around eleven that morning. Taking Mitch's advice, I gathered some family pictures along with current photos. On the way I stopped and bought her a box of candy. I'd wait on buying flowers in case there was a next visit. I was hoping to get the information I wanted in one visit.

I had many questions for her, but knew I'd have to take it slow. According to Mitch, she wouldn't air *dirty laundry*. I wanted the truth about what really happened to Lacy when she got pregnant with me.

Thinking back on the first time I saw Wilma, she said I didn't look like anyone in her family. I wondered if she remembered saying that to me. I had wished I asked her more questions then. She told me a dress salesman had raped Lacy, but now I knew that wasn't true.

Her trailer park was close to the freeway. As I turned into it, my hands began to sweat. I drove slowly down the narrow street to her address. Sparse red roses covered a small trellis on the weathered green doublewide trailer. A small cement walk way led to four steps in front of her door.

Grabbing the pictures and candy, I went up the walk. I had to remind myself that she was almost blind and I could outrun her. Taking a deep breath, I knocked on her door.

"Just a minute," she yelled.

I swallowed as I heard her making her way to the door. For a split second, I wanted to run. Instead I yelled back, "Okay."

"Who is it?" She asked behind the door.

"It's Colette."

She opened the door and said, "Hi, come in."

Entering, I noticed some of the same pictures from my first visit.

"Thank you," I said.

"You were about twenty-five the last time I saw you. Why did you stay away for so long?"

"I'm still not sure. I guess the rush of ordinary life just sort of takes over everything until you wake-up one day and realize a lot of time has passed. Still I want to learn more about where I came from. I don't know the truth and I need to know."

"Did you bring pictures?" she asked.

"I did and I thought you'd like some candy, too."

"Oh, how nice. Is it See's?"

Wishing I'd bought that kind, I said, "No... I wasn't sure what you liked."

"That's fine." she said, "Let's sit over here where the light's better." She led me to the left side of the room and we sat down on a large white couch. Everything in her home was white, including the clothes she was wearing. She either liked white or could see it better than colors. It was a little too much white for me.

"You get around pretty good," I said.

She laughed. "As long as I'm in my own house I do fine. I know my way around it. Now, where are the pictures you brought?"

She had a difficult time seeing my photos. I explained each one the best I could, but realized she couldn't see much at all. Not even white.

"Now that I'm older," I said, "I've thought a lot about Lacy. I wished I'd asked her more questions when she was alive. I was hoping you could tell me what she was like as a child."

Staring at the floor, she said, "Lacy was such a beautiful sweet child. I loved her so much. She was a shy little girl."

Wanting to hear more about when she got pregnant, I asked, "What was she like at twelve or thirteen?"

With a sarcastic tone, she said, "She didn't want anything to do with me then. Rodney and I did the best we could for her. I made her clothes and she had nice costumes for parties, but I got back at her one time. There was a tea party for mothers at her school. She didn't invite me, but I got wind of it and showed up anyway."

I didn't know what to say to that. After the stories I'd heard about Wilma, I probably wouldn't have invited her either.

I figured I'd better take her side, and said, "That must have been upsetting."

She turned her face away. "It was."

For a brief moment, I felt sorry for her. She was visibly upset.

To lighten the conversation, I asked, "Do you hear from Laura?"

"Oh yeah, she writes me and sends me cards saying she loves me. She doesn't love me. Did you know she tried to have me committed soon after Rodney died?"

Surprised by her question I asked, "She did?"

"It didn't work though. She just wanted money. You want to go to lunch?"

"Yeah…sure, that would be fine."

The short time I've been around Wilma, and Mitch and Allaine's stories, Laura's actions didn't seem that odd.

I hadn't met Laura, Lacy's sister who lived in Oregon. I wanted to write her, feeling Lacy would have told her the truth about my father.

Wilma's mood changed like a swirling wind. She went from mad to sad in seconds. Mitch and Allaine were right. This woman was wacky.

She took my arm once we were outside. On the way she told me a gal came by every other day to take her to doctor's appointments, shopping, and help with meals. It was obvious she was lonely.

After eating, she became more talkative. She told me about different towns she and Rodney traveled to and how much they loved Lacy, but not much about Laura. She said that Rodney hadn't wanted Laura, but in order to get Lacy, they had to take

Laura too. She never forgave Rodney for what he did to Lacy, but she seemed to blame Lacy too.

I listened to one story after another, none of them giving me the information I wanted. But I hoped to eventually hear something of use, so I listened.

Driving back to her trailer, I could see she was tired.

After parking I asked, "Do you think I could have Laura's address?"

"Why do you want her address?" she snapped.

"I thought maybe she could tell me what it was like being Lacy's sister. You know, childhood memories."

"Laura was always in Lacy's shadow. She wasn't as pretty."

"You mentioned earlier that they got along okay. I'd really appreciate it," I said, practically begging.

"I suppose that would be all right."

"Thank you."

I helped her into the house to what seemed to be her favorite chair and she asked me to turn the television on. The sound level made me jump. Not only can she not see, she can't hear either. Laura had recently sent her a card and it was lying on the chair next to her. I wrote down the return address and said I'd like to come back and visit again. She seemed pleased that I wanted to return. What I wanted was more information. The only thing I got from this trip was Laura's address. The rest I already knew. Maybe the address would turn out to be a key to the truth.

*   *   *

The next day I wrote Laura. I told her about my life and my family. I wanted her to know that I had a loving family, but didn't believe that Rodney was my father. I asked her to find it in her heart to have compassion for me. I just wanted the truth. Then I asked her if I could either call or come and see her. I explained as I did to Wilma why I hadn't contacted her earlier, hoping she'd understand. I mailed it the same day. I tried not to get my hopes up, but if Lacy told anyone what really happened, I thought it would be her sister.

*   *   *

Weeks passed with no word from Laura. I called Wilma and said I'd like to see her again. She sounded eager. I drove up the following day. This time I took her flowers and See's candy, anything to get her to tell me something truthful about my father.

Her house seemed no different from the last visit and she was wearing white again. We sat down on the same couch in the same spot, but this time she had boxes of pictures beside it. She seemed happy with the flowers and candy, but did mention that roses were her favorite. I had brought her carnations.

"I thought you could go through some of these pictures and pick out the ones you want and we'll go make copies of them," she said.

Surprised and pleased, I said, "That would be great. Thank you."

Although she couldn't see the pictures, as soon as I told her a small detail of each one, she could describe the place and approximate date taken. I was amazed at her memory and enjoyed looking at pictures of Lacy when she was young. Neither she nor Laura smiled in any of the photos. Two sad little girls.

We dropped the pictures off at a one-hour photo shop, and went to the same restaurant as before.

Curious about her fetish with white, I said, "You sure look nice today dressed in white."

"Well, white's my favorite color. It's so clean and pure."

"Yeah, I like it too."

Mitch told me how she had dressed him in white all the time, then beat him if he got dirty, so I figured she had an obsession with cleanliness.

She couldn't see the menu, but ordered the same thing as before. You wouldn't know she was blind by the way she ate. She explained that she could see through a small pinhole from one eye.

Half way through our meal I finally got the courage to ask her about Rodney.

"So... you think Rodney's my father?" I asked.

"He *IS* your father, but it hurts me to think about it."

"Do you remember what you said to me the first time you saw me?"

"No, it was a long time ago."

"You said I didn't look like anyone in your family and it was a good thing."

"Well, you don't."

"So you don't think I look like Rodney?"

"No, but I know what he did to Lacy."

"Maybe... Lacy was with someone else?"

"No, no, no... she was a good girl."

Thinking she probably made Lacy wear white too, I said, "But look at Allaine and her dad, Mitch and his dad. They both look like their dads. And I don't look like Lacy at all."

"You did some when you were younger."

"But don't you think I'd have some of Rodney's features?"

"I don't know and I don't want to talk about this anymore."

"Okay, I just needed to ask."

"You'll have to accept the fact that Rodney's your father."

"But I don't."

We sat a few minutes in silence. I didn't want our visit to end on a sour note so I began asking questions about her and her siblings. She enjoyed talking about herself, but liked only one of her four siblings. She made it clear that she hated the brother who was Lacy's biological father because he was mean to her when they were young.

We picked up the copies of the pictures and went back to her home. I thanked her for them. Once I got her settled, I told her I'd like to visit again. I wasn't sure how she'd react after our minor tiff at the restaurant, but she said she'd like that. I believed this woman was hiding a lot of information from me and carefully doling it out a little at a time. It could be a long and expensive process. Next time I would bring her roses. Darn! I should have found out her favorite color of rose.

* * *

A few days later I got a call from Allaine. She had taken a teaching job in Kuwait and flew home to Idaho for the summer. She wanted to visit me. I told her I'd been visiting Wilma and she asked me not to tell her grandmother that she was coming to see me. Allaine wanted no part of her. I told her I'd written a letter to Laura asking for information about my father. Allaine thought it was a good idea. She would fly down to see me the next week.

*   *   *

Each day the mailman came, I hoped for a letter from Laura. Finally one arrived.

Colette,

I received your very nice and thoughtful letter. I've read it several times. I'm so glad you have loving parents, siblings and also a great husband, children and grandchildren. You were adopted into a family of love. This would have made my sister extremely happy. She wanted you to have a good family and you do. I have no answers to any of your questions. My life is serene and beautiful and I have worked very hard to get here. I'm sorry, but please leave me out of your life. I'm not being mean or nasty. I just want you to stay with the loving family you have. Please, it's for the best.

Thank You,
Laura

P.S. If Lacy had wanted you to know who your father is, she would have told you.

My heart sank. She didn't know me but thought it best for me not to know something very important about myself. Who was she to make that call? It sounded as if she might know the truth. Her loyalty to Lacy was touching but I wished she would talk with me. Hurt and disappointed I wrote her back thanking her for responding and made it clear I wouldn't contact her again. What I really wanted to do was drive to Oregon, knock on her door, look straight into her eyes and say TELL ME THE TRUTH! It was one of those times when I cursed my parents for teaching me to be so dammed respectful and polite to my elders. Being mad was better than crying.

*   *   *

It was great to see Allaine. Teaching in Kuwait had matured her. She seemed to appreciate life more in general. She was reading the same types of books as me. We were both interested in John Edwards, Sylvia Browne and other intuitive people. Before she had been focused on traditional religions, but had made a shift in her beliefs. She was exploring and learning more about her spiritual path. The same as me.

We went to a mystical store and found intuitive readers. We were out to enjoy our day and decided to have a reading. Allaine went first and was amazed at the accuracy. I wasn't sure what to ask. Then it came to me—ask about my biological father. I'd tried everything else. I had even thought of taking the crazy grandmother, Wilma, and turning her upside down to shake information out of her. Her hearing aids would probably be the only thing to shake loose. So... it couldn't hurt to ask the intuitive.

We sat down and she asked me to say my whole name out loud three times. I watched as she closed her eyes and took a deep breath. Then she told me to ask her questions.

"Well... I'm searching for my biological father. I don't think Rodney's my father."

She sat motionless. Taking another deep breath, she said, "Rodney's not your father. He's ashamed of what he did, but he's not your father."

Relieved, I said, "I didn't think he was, even though he messed with Lacy. I don't look anything like him."

She took another deep breath, and then said, "I see dark hair, and it's cut very short. He's maybe Greek, Armenian, or Italian. He could be in his twenties, but his energy is very immature."

"So you're confident that Rodney's not my father?"

"Oh yeah. This person I'm seeing is very remorseful too."

"Sounds like an older guy. I was thinking maybe someone could have raped her or maybe an older guy sweet-talked her. Is there a name?"

"I just get immature energy."

Pleased so far I asked, "Do you have anything else for me?"

"You're an advanced soul on the right spiritual track. You've been around many lifetimes and you're coming into your own spiritual enlightenment."

"Huh... I am?"

"Yes, you're very intuitive. Go within and you'll find some answers."

"I took a dowsing class and enjoyed it, but I've only used it to find my mom's keys. Maybe I should practice with it more. Maybe I'll learn something about my father."

Then she said, "Don't be too surprised by what comes from it."

I thanked her and went up front with Allaine to pay. A guy kept looking at me. Not directly, but all around me. I turned my head to see what he was looking at, but nothing was there. While paying, I asked about him. He was an intuitive reader.

Allaine and I exchanged our readings and were both amazed.

"I like that place," I said.

"Me too."

"Hey, did you notice that guy looking all around me?"

"No. Was he checking you out?" Allaine teased.

I laughed. "No not at all, but it was like he was seeing something around me."

"Does he work there?"

"Yeah, they told me he was a reader too."

"You just might have to go back and see him."

"You know, I just might do that."

*   *   *

Allaine stayed a few more days. She felt certain Wilma was hiding something from me or had hidden paperwork in her house about my father. She urged me to keep visiting Wilma. I enjoyed

Allaine's stay and was looking forward to the following year when she would visit again. I did remember to ask her Wilma's favorite color of rose. It wasn't white, which would have been my guess. I wanted to get something right for the next visit. Who would have thought it was red. Maybe deep inside her there was love after all.

A Love Child's Journey

Chapter Nineteen

Around Halloween, I made my third visit to Wilma. Leaves dotted the lawns of houses I passed along the way. Now and then I glanced to my right, checking the roses propped against my purse. I was bringing her three fragrant red velvet roses in a small green vase garnished with sprigs of baby's breath. She might not be able to see them, but she would smell them. I'd thought of getting more, but decided to start out small. I could add to the number each visit and throw in an occasional box of See's Candy between roses. I didn't know how many roses it might take to get the information that I wanted.

I had called her earlier. She said she didn't feel like going out to eat and asked me to stop on the way and get her a hamburger and vanilla milkshake from a nearby burger stand. I liked that better. She made me nervous when we went out. I was afraid she might trip and fall.

When I got to her mobile home, I heard her television blaring. I knocked loudly but nothing happened.

After knocking a few more times, I checked the door. It was unlocked. My imagination went into overtime. What if she'd fallen and was unconscious? My heart beat faster. Slowly I walked in. The television was loud enough for the whole trailer park to hear.

There she sat in her old brown chair wearing a polyester white jacket, a child's white sweater yellowed with age wrapped around her neck and a red blanket over her lap. The front of her hair poked through the top of a tattered white hair net. I could only hope she wasn't dead. As I stepped closer, I could see the front of her jacket move with each breath she took.

Relieved, I yelled, "Wilma, are you awake?"

She opened her eyes. "Colette, is that you?"

"Yeah, it's me. Are you okay?"

"Oh sure, just didn't get much sleep last night."

It took her a few minutes to wake up and I handed her the roses. She sniffed them. "I just love the smell of roses."

Pleased, I hoped my efforts would pay off and she'd give me some new information. I didn't want to be too selfish about it, but I wasn't above bribing her.

I waited until she finished her hamburger before I asked any questions. I knew not to push her and started out easy. She seemed to enjoy talking about her travels with her husband, Rodney. I started with that, hoping to end up at Forest Glen, my place of conception. She repeated the story when Rodney surprised her with a new travel trailer, then told her to pack because they were heading for New York. She enjoyed all the different people she met in New York and referred to their trailer as a motel on wheels. After letting her talk for a while, I tried to change the direction of our conversation. I knew Wilma was sharp. And she knew I was there for information. She was slowly doling it out to ensure my return for more. I felt like a dog at dinnertime given a few scraps of fat from my master's steak but what I really wanted was the whole steak.

It wasn't as if she had many visitors. I thought I might be her only one. She was careful not to tell me too much, her words guarded. I was tempted to say that if she wanted more roses, she'd better drop a little more steak off the table. But that wouldn't work.

Kicking the covers off her lap, she said, "Follow me."

She stood up abruptly and wobbled a little before gaining her balance. I considered helping her but decided she might be insulted. She walked toward the back bedroom. Her back slightly

190

hunched over allowed her to watch the ground as she took each step.

I was thrilled that she wanted me to follow her. Was she going to show me something that would tell me who my father was? Anxious to see what she wanted to show me, I followed her slowly as she went to the closet. My heart skipped a beat for joy. This is it. I was going to see some paperwork that has the truth imprinted on it. She slid back one side of a mirrored covered closet. I held my breath. I could see two large metal trunks. It was like finding a buried treasure.

Pointing to the green one, she said, "That's Lacy's trunk. Come over here and open it up." Her tone was more demanding than friendly.

Hardly able to contain my excitement, I walked over and unlocked the trunk. The key was in the lock.

Slowly I opened it. It was half full of papers, greeting cards, miscellaneous envelopes and two high school yearbooks.

"Do you see the yearbooks?" she asked.

"Yes."

"Grab them, then shut and lock the trunk back up."

No, wait, my inner voice screamed. I needed to see the letters and cards. I wanted to see *EVERYTHING* in the trunk. I've already seen the yearbooks.

Disappointed, I slowly shut and locked the trunk. Was this a game? Was she teasing me by allowing me to see the possibility of more information about my existence?

Wilma waited until she heard me slide the closet shut. Then she shuffled back to her tattered brown chair.

Holding the yearbooks, I sat down in a small rocking chair next to her.

"I thought you might want to look in Lacy's yearbooks. You're welcome to take them home if you promise to bring them back."

Surprised that she trusted me to take them home and return them, I said, "I'd love to. Thank you."

What I really wanted, she wouldn't give me. I would need to earn more than just her trust.

It was time for boldness, "Did Lacy have a boyfriend or any boy she liked around the time she became pregnant with me?"

Clearly uncomfortable with the question, Wilma straightened her back before answering. "Well, I asked her if she went too far with David."

A name! She said a name. "Who's David?" I asked. My heart pounded with anticipation.

"He and his family were at one of the job sites. His dad worked on the tunnels with Rodney. On occasion, we would have dinner with his family. He was a few years older than Lacy."

Feeling brave, I asked, "What's his last name?"

"Gilbert. David Gilbert. He was a detective and then became an accountant after he was injured. His dad's name was Hap."

Snickering, I asked, "You mean like in Happy?"

She frowned. "What? No! His name was just Hap," she replied sharply.

I hoped mentioning the word happy might change her disposition but she didn't seem to have much of a sense of humor.

"So... Lacy liked him?" I asked.

"She said he never touched her and that they were just friends, but I had to ask her."

"I understand. Was the Gilbert family in Forest Glen?"

"What? What did you say? I don't know. I'm getting tired and don't want to talk about this anymore," she snapped.

I must have gone over her limit of giving. "Okay. Maybe I better go and let you get some sleep. I'll be back soon and bring the yearbooks with me."

"Thank you for the hamburger and I want to see you again, but I get tired easily."

"I understand. I'll let myself out."

Outside I quietly jumped up and down. I had a name! Someone who knew Lacy around the time she got pregnant. Maybe, this was the guy I was looking for. The red roses seemed to have worked. Next time I'd bring her six, but not until I've seen where this name leads me. She hadn't given me a clear answer about the Gilbert family being in Forest Glen and didn't like the fact that I even asked. But I had the name of a boy. David.

*   *   *

At home I went straight to the computer and looked for a David Gilbert. His name showed up right away, but it listed him in two different states, Arizona and California. I was certain I had the right guy because his California address was in the Unger area near Oildale, and his age fit. But I had no way of knowing which address was current. His telephone numbers showed as unavailable. I sat at my computer contemplating my next move. I wasn't sure what to ask him, but at least I'd know which address was current. I wanted to see him in person. Study his body language and see what he looked like. I wanted to find out if I could see a glimpse of me in him.

I'd go back and ask the intuitive I spoke to when Allaine was visiting. I could also get a reading from the guy who was looking at me in an odd way. At this point I was game for any help I could get.

*   *   *

It was early January before I could meet with both readers on the same day. I was okay with that because the holidays kept me busy. I learned that the guy I wanted to see was Michael.

The scheduled day was gloomy and gray. Rain drizzled down the entire drive to the Twilight Greetings store. It didn't matter to me. My excitement cancelled the doom and gloom of the weather. I had no idea what I'd be told, but my mind was open for anything. Well, anything that sounded semi normal from an intuitive reader. Was it normal going to see not one, but two readers to find out who my dad was or where he lived? I didn't want to answer that.

Through pouring rain, I hurried across the street and into the shop. Burning incense and Enya music filled the store. Immediately I found myself relaxing. I walked up to the counter feeling good. My first appointment was with Angel. I thought it best to start with her.

While waiting I strolled around the store browsing through the clothes, books and spiritual paraphernalia. Someone tapped my

193

shoulder. As I turned, I saw Angel with her vibrant dark red hair and shimmering eye makeup that sparkled as she smiled.

"Colette?" she asked softly.

"Yes."

"Please follow me to my table."

The arms on her black blouse fluttered like bat wings as she made her way to a small table with a crystal ball on it. She motioned me to sit on a small chair across from her.

Her friendly demeanor was comforting and she remembered me from the previous summer. She asked me how Allaine was doing and then moved her crystal ball to the middle of the small table.

"How can I help you today?" she asked.

"Well... I'm continuing my search for my biological father."

"Oh, yes. I remember. Your grandmother keeps saying her husband's your father, but... I remember saying he's not."

"Right. She did give me the name of a David Gilbert. She said he was friends with my birth mother at the time she got pregnant."

"Let's see. I need to take a moment and connect with my guides."

She closed her eyes and put her hands on the small crystal ball.

"Please say your full name three times."

I said my name three times.

She took a few deep breaths. "I'm not getting that David Gilbert is your father."

"Really?" I said surprised.

"He did know your mother, but I don't get that he's your father. Just a minute." She took more deep breaths. I waited for her to speak.

"I'm seeing that your father is sick. Depressed, and the possibility of a problem with alcohol."

That stunned me. "You do? He's not dying, is he?"

She shook her head. "No, I don't get that, but he has some problems."

"Well... at least you think he's still alive. That's good. The drinking thing I'll deal with when the time comes. Lacy had that problem too. Besides, I don't want to judge him. I'm just disappointed it's not this David guy."

"Spirit tells me he's not, but it can't hurt to talk with him."

"Do you have anything else for me?"

"You are evolving spiritually, you are an old soul. "

I thanked her and got up. "I have a reading scheduled with Michael too."

"It's always good to get information from different readers," she assured me.

At the desk I let them know I was done with Angel and ready when Michael was available. I wondered what he'd say about David Gilbert. Not that I doubted Angel, but it would be nice to have confirmation. I didn't put a whole lot of faith in what Wilma told me. She got flustered when I asked if David's family was in Forest Glen.

I circled the store as Michael finished a reading in the middle of the room. A few minutes later he walked over to me and introduced himself.

He used the Irish pronunciation of my name. A clean-cut man with graying hair, he looked in his late fifties. Something about him reminded me of an accountant or maybe an engineer. Not the typical appearance I'd expect of an intuitive reader. His vocabulary made it obvious he was well educated. I guessed that the spirit world really wasn't concerned with outward appearance as long as they could bring information through them.

Michael had his own small table. I told him that I just had a reading with Angel. I mentioned being there the previous summer, but he didn't remember me. I explained that I was looking for my biological father and had a name but wanted to know what he thought of it. I told him what Wilma said about my father and other information I thought would help. I didn't tell him anything Angel told me.

He closed his eyes and took a deep breath, then sat silently for a few seconds.

He opened his eyes. "Okay, I'm ready. Ask me what you want to know."

He didn't even ask me to say my name.

"First of all…" I asked. "Is Rodney, Wilma's husband, my biological father?"

"I'm getting a definite no. He did things to her that were inappropriate, but he's not your father."

He got that right. I felt more confident with him now.

"What about David Gilbert? Is he my father?"

Michael closed his eyes and raised his index finger in the air as if to say wait a minute. I sat motionless waiting. The seconds seemed like hours.

Slowly he lowered his hand down. "No, David Gilbert is not your father, but it probably wouldn't hurt to contact him. I'm getting he doesn't have much to tell you."

Disappointed again, I said, "That's what Angel told me too."

He raised his finger again. "Just a minute. My guide is trying to tell me something."

His finger moved slightly up and down. He nodded. "Does the name Gary Smith or Jerry Smith sound familiar?"

"No, not to me."

"My guide is telling me the last name is Smith, but went by the name Smitty as a nick name."

"Wow. Really?"

"You might want to ask your grandmother about that name."

"I'm not sure what she'll say because she keeps telling me Rodney's my father."

"That's because it's easier for her to accept. Less disgrace as far as she's concerned."

Which didn't make sense to me. Why would incest be better than rape or being with some other guy?

"So you think this Gary Smith is my father?"

"That's what I'm being told. He's either your father or has had some connection with your father."

"That's great," I said excited. "It gives me another name to check out. Is that all you have for me?"

"Well, did you know you have the energy form of a young person hanging off your left shoulder?"

"Really?" Turning left, I looked around. "No... I... didn't know that."

"It's probably a young child. It's not hurting you, but would you like me to try and get it to go away?"

Uneasy about carrying an invisible child on my shoulder, I said "Uh… sure… I guess."

He told me to stand. His hands about eight inches from my body he moved them all around me. I felt his movement but his hands never touched me.

When he was done, I thanked him and said, "I'll be back."

I couldn't wait to visit Wilma and ask her about this Gary Smith or Smitty guy, but wanted to check out David Gilbert too.

*　　　　　*　　　　　*

I waited until mid February, closer to Wilma's birthday, before seeing her again. I bought her a music box and a nice card along with a bouquet of flowers. They weren't roses, but I thought she'd like them with the other gift. I hoped she'd enjoy the music box because I had more questions for her and I remembered to return the yearbooks.

I could hear the television blasting as I approached the door.

I banged on her door hard and hoped she could hear it.

"Just a minute," she yelled.

When she opened the door, I smiled. "I have some flowers and a special gift for your birthday."

"You do?" She sounded surprised.

"I do. I have your yearbooks too."

"Oh, wonderful. I'm glad you brought them back."

I was glad I hadn't forgotten them.

She ambled over to her brown chair. She had on a light purple polyester jacket. I thought she had nothing, but white clothes. Setting the yearbooks and flowers down I handed her the gift bag.

"Oh my, I have another gift?"

"It's almost your birthday isn't it?"

"In few more days I'll be 88 years old. I want to live until I'm ninety."

"Well, you look like you're doing fine to me."

I helped her open her gift and watched a rare smile light up her face as she listened to the music play. I wondered when she had last received a birthday gift. At that moment, I felt sorry for her. She had created her life, and been cruel to everyone who loved her

197

but it was still sad to see. Allaine once told me Rodney predicted Wilma would die a lonely old woman because she chased off all the people who loved her.

When I offered to return the yearbooks to the closet trunks for her, she refused. It made me wonder even more if there was something in that chest that would answer my questions.

Deciding to be bold, I asked, "Wilma, was there any people in the Forest Glen area with the last name of Smith? Maybe a guy they called Smitty?"

She immediately answered, "No."

Her quick response made me suspicious, but I'd wait a while before bringing it up again.

"So, who did Lacy hang out with when she was in Forest Glen?"

"I can't remember what she did. She was so secretive... There was this one girl. She was older than Lacy, but not a nice girl. I used to give her rides into town for her beauty school training and she'd holler at the boys along the way. I told her mother I wouldn't tolerate that kind of behavior; she'd have to find another ride."

"What town did you give her a ride to?"

"I don't remember. Why are you asking me these questions?"

"I'm just trying to find out about Lacy's life."

She frowned. "Where did you get that name Smitty?"

I didn't want to freak her out, but wanting to be honest, I said, "An intuitive reader."

She looked startled. "You did?"

Curious about her thoughts, I waited for her to say more, but she didn't. "Yeah, I did. Do you believe in psychics?"

"I'm not sure. There might be something to it."

That surprised me. I sparked her curiosity. Maybe we do have something in common. I thought about telling her that I dowsed with a pendulum, mostly for missing items, but I didn't. Mentioning psychics was enough.

"I was told that a Gary or Jerry Smith who went by the name Smitty was either my father or a clue to my father."

She bowed her head. "There was a boss that worked with Rodney. They called him Smitty."

That excited me so much it was all I could do to stay seated in the chair, but I remained outwardly calm. She tipped her head up as if trying to remember something. I didn't want to push her too much.

"It was his daughter that I stopped taking to beauty school. She was no good."

I tried to get the girl's name out of her, but she said she couldn't remember. She didn't remember Smitty's first name either. I was pleased with the information that I had received. I wasn't sure how much was true, but at least she said there was a Smitty in the area who had worked with Rodney.

She immediately changed the conversation and told me stories of making clothes for Lacy and her sister when they were very young. Mostly Halloween costumes or Easter dresses. She did mention a beauty contest they both participated in and won first and second place. But she avoided the time frame of when Lacy first became pregnant with me. The one thing she did recall pleasing about Forest Glen, was the painting class she gave to wives in the area at that time.

I left that day with confirmation; there was a Smitty. Having two names to check out, I was finally making progress. It gave me hope that I would find the truth. I couldn't wait to tell Michael that Wilma validated the name Smitty.

A Love Child's Journey

Chapter Twenty

At the Twilight Greeting store, I could see Michael in the middle of a reading. Pretending to browse, I paced the opposite side of the store waiting for him to finish. Excitement got the best of me and I headed for the restroom.

On my return, Michael was walking to the counter with his client. Now it was my turn. I never thought I'd be so thrilled to give money to someone, but he was giving me information I didn't know how to get any other way.

We exchanged greetings.

"Are you ready for your reading?" he asked.

Ready for my reading? I was so ready I was about to dump his previous client on the floor and take her seat.

"Yes," I said containing my eagerness.

He sat down at his table and asked, "How's your search going?"

My heart raced with excitement. It felt like I was telling a dirty secret. "Smith is a valid name. You know, the Smitty name."

"That's great." His voice hardly fluctuated.

Hoping for a little more enthusiasm, I asked, "So what do you think?"

"Let me go into my space."

He closed his eyes and took deep breaths, again raising his index finger in the air. I wondered if he did this to all his clients or just me. I had a tendency to ramble during readings, but his ritual had been the same each time.

"Go ahead and ask me questions."

"Wilma, the crazy grandmother told me there was a boss her husband worked with. His last name was Smith but I couldn't get her to tell me his first name. They called him Smitty. He's the father of the girl she gave rides to. I came up with the first name of Linda and her current last name as Homes. Then I got the name Peter. Any thoughts on that?"

"How did you come up with those names?" he asked.

"I dowsed using an alphabet chart. I thought it couldn't hurt to try and get information by spelling words."

"Did you know that dowsing is another avenue for speaking with the spirit world?"

"I hadn't thought of it like that, but somebody or something has to be giving me information. It works great when I misplace my keys."

He laughed. "So... you want me to ask if Linda Homes is the name of this girl who's Smitty's daughter?"

"Yeah... and while you're at it, could you ask what town they live in?"

He paused, "Well... I'm getting a yes, the name's right and the town is Ukiah."

"Ukiah isn't too far. What about the Peter name?"

He paused again. "Yes, check him out too."

I thanked Michael and told him I'd check the names out. I was thrilled at having more names, and equally thrilled that my dowsing had been corroborated.

That evening I searched the Internet and to my surprise found a Linda Homes in Rumsey, not far from Ukiah. But there was a Linda Homes listed in Hayward too. Hayward was near San Francisco. I couldn't tell which address was current. I found a Peter Smith in Ukiah. He had many addresses in Ukiah, but at least they were in the same town. I had to be on the right track. I dowsed and got that Peter Smith was a cousin of Linda's. I

201

wanted to talk with Wilma one more time, before setting off to look for these people. Maybe Linda Homes was my half sister.

*　　　　*　　　　*

A few weeks later I was on my way to Oildale again. Hoping to get new information from Wilma or at least some clarification with the Linda name, small bunch of flowers and a couple of individually wrapped truffles took the ride with me.

I followed the same routine as my last few visits. Each trip I was glad to see her still alive. This visit, she was feeling better and wanted me to take her to her favorite restaurant. Of course, she liked the truffles and flowers. During lunch we talked about what she had been doing the last few days, which exhausted the topic of medical appointments. Having her hair done seemed to be the highlight. But she didn't like the way her hairdresser had done the front of her hair and wasn't pleased with the color used.

Knowing she couldn't see her hair, I asked, "How do you know what color it is?"

Irritated, she shouted, "Because my hairdresser told me and I don't like that color. Never have. She knows it too."

To lighten the mood, I said, "I think it looks real nice. You better watch out or one of these older guys around here might want to take you dancing."

"Which old guys?" she quipped.

I'd forgotten she didn't have much of a sense of humor and I said, "I was trying to make you feel good, but I agree that your hairdresser should use the color you prefer."

Agreeing with her issues satisfied her and settled her bouts of irritation.

We sat in silence for a while. If I asked her directly, I don't think she'd tell me the truth about the name of Smitty's daughter.

Acting as though she had already said the name before, I asked, "Did Lacy spend a lot of time around Smitty's daughter Linda?"

She hesitated. "No, not much, but Lacy spent the night at her house once."

Lightly tapping my feet on the floor in a victory dance, I was elated that she didn't correct the name. "So you didn't like Lacy hanging around Linda?"

"No I didn't. That girl was too wild for my liking."

I wasn't having much luck on getting her to say Linda's name, but she didn't dispute it either.

Treading on thin ice, I asked, "Was Smitty home when Lacy spent the night there?"

Visibly agitated, she snapped, "What do you mean? Why are you asking me about this?"

"I wondered if Smitty worked out of town a lot. I thought maybe that's why you had to give Linda rides to Beauty College."

"I suppose he did at times. I'm ready to go."

I took her back to her house and got her settled in her favorite chair with a truffle. I thought about swirling the truffle around her nose so she could smell the sweet scent of chocolate, then quickly pulling it away. *Give me information and I'll give you the delicious creamy chocolate!* But that would be cruel and probably wouldn't work. I turned the television on, setting the sound so her neighbors could hear it, and then headed for home.

Truffles and flowers were a good trade for getting the Linda name confirmed, even indirectly. Now two names came from intuitive sources that Wilma unknowingly verified.

*   *   *

I had been dowsing on a daily basis and came up with more information. Linda worked at a K-mart near the town of Hayward. I wondered about accuracy, but it was important enough for me to make the drive.

By enticing Mom with a nice stay in San Francisco and a promise to stop at all Indian casinos on our route, she agreed to go with me. She continued to be as supportive of my search for my biological father as she had been with Lacy's search. Now in her early eighties, she looked forward to any kind of entertainment and gambling happened to be a favorite.

It rained continuously on the way to San Francisco. I had always loved going there and so did Mom. I wondered what to say to Linda and I'm sure my mom was wondering when we'd hit the first casino. I had planned a big circle, first going to Hayward, then winding up the Napa valley to Ukiah, and of course stopping at all Indian casinos we came upon. Thanks to mapquest.com, we found plenty.

The next morning we headed for the K-mart closest to the town of Hayward. I was uncertain if Linda's last name had changed, but through dowsing, I learned she was a manager and started work at noon.

It was afternoon when we reached the store.

As I parked, Mom asked, "Do you know what you're going to say to her?"

"Well... I've been thinking about it and decided just to be truthful. Start out asking about Forest Glen, then go from there."

"That sounds good. I'll browse around the store while you talk with her."

My heart sped up and my hands got clammy. It was comforting to have my mom in the store while I searched for a complete stranger who might be my sister. It was important for me to do this. I just hoped Linda didn't think I was some crazy woman.

I checked with Customer Service and asked if their manager named Linda was working. Told yes, a surge of heat rushed through me. I felt as if I was floating like a helium balloon in the breeze. Pacing the main aisle, I waited for her to emerge from the back. A young employee stocking shelves asked if I needed help. I explained that I was waiting for the manager Linda and continued to pace up and down the aisle.

"Excuse me Ma'am."

Turning around, I noticed the girl that was stocking walking towards me, "Yes?" I answered.

"Linda's out from the back now. I just saw her walk by."

I stopped pacing and began to tremble I couldn't tell if it was excitement or fear.

"Could you point Linda out to me, please... without being too obvious?" I asked.

"Sure," she answered.

I followed her down the aisle. She stopped just short of the end, and in view of the Customer Service desk.

"There she is... at Customer Service," she said.

Seeing only one person there, I asked, " Is Linda on the outside of the Customer service desk?"

"Yeah, that's her."

My balloon that was victoriously floating in the breeze suddenly punctured and made a devastating decent to the ground.

I thanked her for helping me, and stood there like a statue after she left.

I didn't look anything like Linda. She was pretty, but our ancestry was totally different. I wasn't sure what mine was, but I knew that it wasn't African American. I was dismayed at not finding the right Linda and disappointed in my dowsing. Some information turned out right and some didn't. Why was that? Had my Linda worked there at one time? I still had the house address in Hayward to check out.

*   *   *

We found the house in Hayward and I parked across the street. Mom waited in the car. It wasn't a favorable area. I joked that if I didn't come back in a few minutes, she might want to call the police. It was a standard tract house weathered by the ocean air. The lawn or maybe weeds in the front hadn't been mowed for quite some time. A dilapidated car sat in the driveway. From the street I couldn't see the front door of the house. Knocking on it, I heard rustling inside. Finally the front door cracked open, a pungent odor seeping out. A half-awake guy in his thirties with tattoos' covering the upper part of his shirtless body stood there staring at me.

"Yeah?" he asked.

"I'm looking for Linda Homes."

"She don't live here no more."

Somewhat thankful, but hoping he might know something about her, I asked, "Do you know where she moved?"

"No, but I think it was somewhere north."

I thanked him and headed for the car, hoping that north meant Rumsey.

Although I was eager to reach Rumsey before dark, I wanted Mom to enjoy a few casinos. We stopped at three, and actually won some money. We had a great time and I was grateful she came with me.

The sun was setting as we rolled into Rumsey. There wasn't much to it. Small houses and mobile homes sporadically lined each side of the road. A small marina with a few fishing boats sat at one end. The street I wanted was off the main road behind the local bar. Right after turning, the pavement ended and dirt took over. Ahead to our right, an older motel appeared to be used for long-term living. I parked in front of the office, again leaving Mom in the car. Old stoves, tattered mattresses and rusty bicycle parts littered the grounds.

Inside the office, stale cigarette smoke made it difficult to breathe. Beside a bell on the counter, a note read, "Ring for assistance". Pictures of fish and deer hung on the dark paneled walls. Off in a corner sat a black vinyl chair. I tapped the bell a few times and a woman puffing a cigarette emerged from a back door.

"Can I help you?' she asked.

"Yes, I hope so. I'm looking for Linda Homes."

"I know Linda and Dick. I bought this place from them about a year ago."

Sensing that she was skeptical about my inquiry, I told her a little about my search. Giving vague details, I saw her eyes soften. She explained that Linda still received some mail there, but traveled in a motor home and was living down south toward Los Angeles. She was battling with cancer and receiving chemotherapy.

Saddened by the news and thinking that something could happen to her before we met. I felt shamed by my selfish thought. I wasn't even sure I had the right Smith. I gave the manager my name and phone number and asked her to give it to Linda or Dick if either should call.

It was too late to go to Ukiah and check out Peter Smith, so we drove home. I did get some information about Linda, but nothing to lead me to her or confirm that she was the person I needed. Living in a motor home makes it difficult to find someone, but traveling in a motor home or a trailer was something the Linda I was looking for did while growing up. Her father worked in the construction business.

*   *   *

Two weeks passed and I was on another search, looking for Dave Gilbert. Instead of my mom, I enlisted the help of my dear friend Beth. She wanted to spend a day with me and I convinced her it would be an interesting adventure. Knowing about my search, she agreed.

I had three California addresses collected off the Internet, two addresses in Oildale and one in Unger. One Oildale address was on the far end of town. I had the same problem searching for Linda; not knowing which one was current.

We picked the address in town first. It was about two miles from Wilma's house. That was the first time I had been to Oildale and not visited her. Even with Mapquest.com directions, the house was difficult to find.

Beth waited in the car while I went to the door. The yard and house look well maintained with trimmed rose bushes and a chain link fence that surrounded the property. A new pickup truck sat in the driveway. Before I reached the door it opened and a young man in a mechanics uniform came barreling out. Seeing me, he stopped.

"Can I help you?" he asked.

"I'm looking for Dave Gilbert. I have this as his address."

"He and Paula haven't lived here for about five years. If you're speaking of the Dave Gilbert I know."

Wanting confirmation, that I had the right one, I said, "His father's name was Hap."

"Yeah… that's the one I know."

"He was a childhood friend of my mom. Do you know where he lives now?"

"Dave and my father were friends. I know he was living on some property that belonged to a friend of his, but that's been a while. I think his son lives in Unger, but I'm not sure. I wish I could help you more, but I'm on my lunch hour and need to get back to work. I normally don't come home, but forgot my lunch today."

I thanked him and thought it odd that I happened to get there on the day he forgot his lunch and had to go home for it. At least I knew it was the right Dave Gilbert, even if he didn't live at that address anymore.

The Unger address might be better, especially since he said Dave's son might live there. Unger was only about fifteen minutes from Oildale. Beth directed me toward the Mapquest address. We reached our destination, in the parking lot of a Pancake House. At first glance, the restaurant and strip mall behind it seemed newly built, but a second look showed it might have been there awhile. We sat in the parking lot wondering why this would be listed as his address.

Pointing off to the left, Beth said, "Hey, look!"

Following her finger I noticed the Mail Box Etc. "Oh my gosh. That's why."

"Yep. I bet he gets his mail there."

"Well, there are no houses in this area, so that has to be the reason for this address."

"We headed for the next address."

* * *

The more we drove the more beautiful the countryside became. The houses were farther apart and most of them newly built with fenced acreage. It took us about thirty-five minutes from Unger, but we enjoyed the ride.

Beth, a great navigator, found the address with ease. White ranch style fencing bordered the dirt road and a scatter of fruit trees grew beyond the fence. It looked nice. From the main road we couldn't see a house. Slowly making our way up the driveway, we could see a farm tractor slowly approaching. I stopped and got out of the car.

The tractor stopped in front of us, its operator was tall and tanned with a slight muscular build. Strands of dark hair fell to one side of his face when he removed his straw hat revealing blue eyes.

"Can I help you?" he asked from up on the tractor.

Trying not to stare, I said, "I hope so. I'm looking for Dave Gilbert. Does he live here?"

"He did at one time. His son is a friend of mine and Dave and Paula parked their motor home on my property for a while."

"Do you know where he is now?"

Apprehensive, he asked, "Why are you looking for him?"

Beth got out of the car. I wasn't sure if she did it for my reinforcement or a better view of the handsome farmer. Either way, I appreciated her standing by me.

I explained why I was looking for Dave Gilbert. The farmer never budged from the tractor, but listened intently. Maybe he decided no one could make up a story as preposterous as mine unless there was some truth to it. He asked for my name, address and phone number. It would have been flattering, but I knew it was to protect his friend's father in case my story wasn't true.

I think he had some empathy for me, which made him even more handsome.

"Dave and Paula live in Arizona for the winter, but come back in the spring and park their motor home in an RV park somewhere on the outskirts of Oildale," he reluctantly said.

From my visits to see Wilma, I remembered passing a couple of RV parks, but thought it best not to ask him more. Instead, I thanked him for the information.

He put his straw hat on and tipped his head, waiting for us to get into the car. As I backed down the driveway, he did the same in the other direction.

I was on top of the world. It was early March and I had a place where Dave Gilbert stays in the springtime. I didn't have a strong sense that he was my father, but according to Wilma, he knew Lacy around the time she became pregnant with me, so he might have known my father.

* * *

It took about a half an hour to reach the first RV trailer park. It was small, but had an office. After a brief conversation with the manager who didn't know a Dave or Paula Gilbert, I knew it wasn't the right RV Park. The manager suggested trying the RV trailer park down the road about five miles. I remembered seeing a small nine-hole golf course with trailers off to the side.

The next RV Park had a large office building surrounded by tall birch trees. Motor homes and RV trailers parked on strips of green lawn. Some looked as if they had been there for a long time.

We parked and walked inside the office. There, behind the long counter was a young woman in her early twenties.

"Welcome," she enthusiastically said.

Cautious, I asked, "Have Dave and Paula Gilbert arrived yet?"

"No, not yet," she answered.

Surprised, I asked, "So you know them?"

"Yeah. I've been working here for over a year. I met them last season. I can look and see when they'll be here, if you'd like."

Shocked by her eagerness to share, I said, "I know they come here from Arizona in the spring, but I don't know exactly when."

She walked over to a desk and thumbed through a large ledger.

Closing the book, she said, " They'll arrive around the first week of May."

I didn't move, but my insides were jumping up and down. Beth looked at me with wide eyes, as if we had hit the jackpot.

That bit of information boosted my confidence.

"Do you have a current phone number for Dave and Paula?" I asked.

"Yeah… I'm pretty sure we do. Let me check."

We watched her thumb though the same large book as before. Beth put her hand to her heart. I did the same.

The young woman approached the counter.

"I have his current number, but I can't give it out to you. It's part of our privacy policy."

"I understand."

She must have noticed my disappointment. "Is it important?" She asked.

I told her what I told the farmer. She too must have thought no one could make up a story like mine.

"Wow, so you found your mom and now you're looking for your dad?"

"Yeah... that's why I need to speak with Dave. He knew my mom and maybe can help me find my dad."

"Hey, I got an idea. Why don't I call Dave and then you can talk with him from here?"

Thrilled at her helping me when most likely she shouldn't, I said, "That would be wonderful if you could."

She dialed the number and I hoped he was home. Otherwise I'd have to wait until May to talk with him.

I went numb when I heard her say hi. Then she said, "Someone wants to talk with you," and handed me the telephone.

Nervous, I took it and said, "Hello Dave, this is Colette Cooper, Lacy Fisherman's daughter. Do you remember Lacy and her sister, Laura?"

Hesitating, he said, "Yeah... Rodney and Wilma's daughters."

Relieved that he remembered, I said, "Yes... did you know that Lacy had a child soon after turning fourteen?"

"No, I didn't know that." He sounded surprised.

"Do you remember her in Forest Glen? That's where she lived when she got pregnant. I'm the child she had."

Suddenly his voice hardened. "My family never lived in Forest Glen. When Lacy was around ten or so our families got together once in a while, but after that we moved to Wildwood and my dad and I worked in the tunnels there."

Confused by his reaction, I asked, "So you and your family never actually lived in Forest Glen?"

"No, but my dad did work some with Rodney before we moved. I'm not your father, if that's what you're implying."

"No, I'm not. I just thought you might have known some of Lacy's friends at that time."

"I wasn't around her then. I don't think I have any information to help you."

"Do you remember a boss that worked in the tunnels called Smitty?"

"Yeah, he was the boss at Wildwood. What about him?"

"Was he ever at Forest Glen?"

"I don't know."

211

"Do you know his first name and what he looked like?"

Sounding irritated, he said, "I only saw him in the tunnels and it was always dark. Everyone wore a hard hat. He had a mustache is all I remember. Everyone called him Smitty; I never heard his first name."

I thanked him and asked if I could have his phone number in case I had more questions. He preferred I didn't. I thanked him again and said goodbye.

I thanked the young gal who made the call and offered to pay for it. She said it was fine and wished me luck with my search.

Puzzled by Dave's information, I tried to put together what he said with what Wilma told me. Why would she have asked Lacy if she and Dave went too far when he wasn't even in Forest Glen? Was she trying to throw me a curve or sabotage my search? At my readings with Michael and Angel, both stated that Dave wouldn't be much help.

One thing he did, was confirm the existence of a guy named Smitty. And he was a boss as Wilma had said, but he couldn't have been at Wildwood and Forest Glen at the same time. That didn't make sense.

I had to find Peter Smith in Ukiah. Being related to Linda, well, hopefully related, according to my dowsing, he should know how to get hold of her. Next trip, Ukiah.

A Love Child's Journey

Chapter Twenty-One

I hadn't made it to Ukiah, but kept it in the back of my mind. After the Hayward trip, I was hesitant about another road trip based on intuitive information

It was the first week in June. Allaine, who taught school in Kuwait, e-mailed that she had written Laura to try and get information about my biological father. Laura wrote back saying only that her oldest son had died of cancer in January. I hadn't met him but felt sad for her loss and understood that my search wasn't a priority to her.

Allaine asked if I would tell Wilma of his death. Not that Wilma was close to Laura's children, but he was her grandson. I said I would. It had been a while since I'd seen her.

I also wanted to stop on the way and introduce myself to Dave Gilbert. He and his wife were scheduled to arrive at the RV Park soon. Seeing me in person and talking with me, he might realize that I'm sincere in my search and not a fruitcake, well... not too much of one anyway.

* * *

Mom and I headed for Oildale the following Saturday. She'd discovered that Oildale had two Indian casinos and wanted to check them out.

Uneasy I pulled into the RV Park, remembering that Dave Gilbert hadn't been thrilled talking with me on the phone. Maybe he had something to hide. I wondered what he looked like. He said he'd never lived in Forest Glen, but I still wanted to see him.

At the front office I checked to see if Dave had actually arrived. He had and the gal who helped me before told me where he parked his motor home.

I was nervous about meeting him. Both Michael and Angel had said he wasn't my father, but what if they were wrong? What if I looked like him? What would I say? I decided to leave the car by the office and walk to his motor home. It wasn't far. The walk gave me time to calm down my nerves.

At his motor home, the door opened before I got there and out stepped a guy over six feet tall. He had sandy brown hair intertwined with gray and tired blue eyes. An attractive man, but after studying his features, I knew he wasn't my father. Not looking much like Lacy, I expected some resemblance to my father. But there was none at all with him. It was a little disappointing, but I'd been told he wasn't the one. I held on to the hopes that I looked like my father, but there was a possibility that I didn't.

"Can I help you?" he asked.

"Are you Dave Gilbert?"

"Yes."

"I'm Colette Cooper, Lacy Fisherman's daughter. I spoke with you in March. I wanted to introduce myself and thank you for taking the time to talk with me."

"I've told you all I know," he said, turning away to watch his wife come out of the motor home.

My presence seemed to make him nervous and defensive. I didn't think it had anything to do with Lacy or me. Maybe he and his wife had issues.

She walked over and stood next to him. He turned back to me. "We're getting ready to go eat. I wish I had more to tell you, but as I said before, me and my family weren't in Forest Glen at any time."

His wife grabbed his hand in a possessive way. She acted threatened at my being there. It was time for me to leave.

"Well... thank you for talking with me. I really appreciate it. Sometimes on a search the wrong roads are as important as finding the right ones."

I said good-bye and walked to my car. I had hoped to get more from him, but it was obvious he didn't want to talk with me. I was a little disappointed, but at least meeting him helped eliminate him as a likely father.

The next stop was the Indian casino, then the drug store to buy Wilma something. I wanted to get her something different.

After the casino, I browsed the drug store looking for a gift that Wilma might like. Her blindness made it difficult. I found a small ceramic heart with a thoughtful saying on it. I could read her the message. For backup, I bought a small box of soft chew chocolates. Just in case the ceramic heart didn't go over too well.

We went through the same arrival ritual as before and I gave her my gifts. She seemed to like them, but whenever I brought up her years in Forest Glen, she changed the direction of our conversation. This time she talked about her school years and how she and her brother would alternate days attending school. She loved school and he hated it.

I knew better than to tell her about my visit with Dave Gilbert. She wouldn't like my having told him that Lacy became pregnant at thirteen. She had made it clear she didn't want anyone to know.

I told her about Laura's son dying from cancer. It saddened her, but she said she didn't know him that well. Then she blamed Laura for being jealous of her having raised Lacy's kids. Wilma hadn't seen Laura's children since they were small. I wondered if they knew how fortunate they were to have been spared the wrath of Wilma. Although, I'm sure Laura did.

I visited for another hour, listening to the stories of her life and the good and bad times with her husband, mostly bad. She enjoyed traveling to new places with Rodney, but wished he'd told her he loved her. He never did. The person she loved the most was her mother. But her father was mean and selfish and she didn't care for him.

I was disappointed at not getting any new leads or clues from her. She knew I was there mainly for information and she hoarded it like a miser so I would have to come back. Maybe she didn't like the gifts I brought this time. She did mention again that Rodney was my father. I wished I could read her mind. Did she honestly believe that or was it just easier to throw the blame at him? I didn't understand why she was hiding the truth from me and secretly hoped she would eventually let me look in those trunks in her closet. Maybe there was something about me in one of them. She never budged from her recliner, but seemed pleased with our visit.

I told her it would be a while before I could visit her again. Allaine was coming from Kuwait to visit me in a few weeks. She didn't want me to tell Wilma. She had no desire to see her grandmother. I explained that my husband and I would be spending time in our motor home in the mountains. She said she understood and would see me when I could make it.

*   *   *

Allaine stopped in Idaho, her home base in America, before coming to see me. It gave her a chance to rest from the long flight, visit friends and take care of any business she had in the States.

I met her at the bottom of the Sacramento airport escalator. I enjoyed her visit the year before and she was eager to see Angel for another reading. Between last year's visit and our year of emailing, we had become quite close.

She caught me up on recent events of her travels and I filled her in on my latest visit with Wilma. We mapped out our itinerary for the following week. We would visit her dad in San Francisco and then see Angel. It would be my first time meeting Allaine's father. I wondered if Lacy had said anything to him about me. She had run away to San Francisco at sixteen, met Allaine's dad and became pregnant right away. At the time, he was divorced and had two young children. He married Lacy, but she had their marriage annulled shortly after Allaine was born.

The next morning we headed for San Francisco. I never wanted to live there, but always enjoyed visiting. We arranged to meet in front of the Flamingo motel because Allaine couldn't go to his home. He had remarried his first wife and she didn't want any part of Allaine.

A small elderly man stood near the motel's curb, tufts of steel gray hair protruded from his wool duffer's hat. He wore a matching cardigan and dark gray slacks. When I stopped, Allaine got out and hugged him before he got in. She followed and introduced us. I was amazed how much Allaine looked like him. She had some of Lacy's features and had become even more beautiful with age, but there was no question that he was her father. For a moment I was a little envious. They didn't have much of a relationship but at least she knew he was her father.

It had been over seven years since Allaine had seen him. He directed us to a small diner, his favorite restaurant. After Allaine updated him on herself and her children, they ran out of things to say. Taking advantage of the silence, I asked him if Lacy had mentioned me to him. He said he didn't know I existed until Allaine told him that I was the one driving her to San Francisco. So much for that, he couldn't help me out. I was a secret to some and not to others, but my biological father was a secret to all.

We drove him back to the same motel. As he got out, he gave Allaine a wad of money. She gave it right back to him, explaining that she didn't need or want it. He threw the money in my lap and hurried away down the sidewalk. He was spry for eighty-three.

"He wants you to have this money, Allaine."

"I know, but why? I told him I didn't need or want it."

Handing her the money, I said, "I think its guilt money. It probably makes him feel better. He didn't say much, but seemed very proud of you and your teaching accomplishments."

Opening the wad of money and counting it, she said, "Oh my gosh, there's a THOUSAND dollars here."

"Wow... he must feel *really* guilty."

217

Tearing, she said, "Well, maybe I'll see Angel for a half-hour instead of fifteen minutes when we go to Twilight Greetings tomorrow. That was so nice of him."

Allaine thought maybe I was right. He couldn't have a relationship with her while she was young, but wanted to make up for it with money. That was all he could give. I hoped that when I found my father I'd be able to see him for more than a quick lunch.

*   *   *

Allaine and I were both excited to see what Angel had for us. Allaine went first while I browsed around the store. She sat with Angel for a half-hour and had a big smile on her face as she went to the counter to pay. She seemed happy with her reading. Now it was my turn.

Angel sat down at her table. My excitement puzzled me. There was no reason for it.

"How's your search going?" she asked.

"You were right, the Dave Gilbert guy isn't my father. You and Michael both told me he wasn't."

"I vaguely remember talking about that. So what can I help you with today?"

"Well... how about just tell me whatever comes up. I'm still on my search, but just tell me what comes through from Spirit."

"Okay."

After I said my name out-loud three times, she went into her space. I wasn't sure where that was, but when she was silent, that's where she went.

"Um... that's odd," she said.

"What's odd?" I asked.

"I've never got this before."

Uneasy, I asked, "What are you getting?"

"Spirit is telling me that you need to go to Ukiah and find a gypsy reader. She has information that you need to hear. Her skin is tanned; she's a foreign gypsy reader. Another woman will help you find her."

"That's odd because Michael told me I need to go to Ukiah too. You know the Smith name. I dowsed that Peter Smith lives in the Ukiah area."

"Spirit is saying that's where you need to go. In all the years that I've been doing readings, I've never been told to send someone to another reader."

"Wow... maybe this is my big break. My big clue on finding my father."

"It seems important for you to go," she added.

Thrilled, I thanked her, then paid and caught up with Allaine. She smiled at my excitement. We waited until we were outside before comparing notes.

"You had a good reading too?" she asked.

"I did. How about you?"

"Yeah... it seems that I'm finally going to get on with my life."

Knowing that readings are personal, I didn't want to probe, but said, "So, you felt good about what you heard?"

"Definitely."

"Well... she told me that I needed to go to Ukiah and find a gypsy reader. A tanned foreign gypsy reader, she has information for me. And also some other lady who will help me find her."

"That's kind of cool. Where at in Ukiah?"

"Uh... she didn't give me that part of it."

"So you're supposed to drive to Ukiah and find a tanned gypsy reader who has information for you?"

"Yeah."

"Hey... maybe that's why I received money from my dad."

"What does that have to do with a gypsy reader who's supposed to be in Ukiah?"

"I have extra money. I can extend my stay and we can go to Ukiah together."

"Great! I've wanted to go to Ukiah and find Peter Smith. I have addresses for him. Are you sure you want to pay extra to extend your stay for what might be a wild goose chase?"

"Why not? Maybe you can dowse about it and get more information. We can leave early tomorrow and spend the night."

"Did I tell you about the last trip I took trying to find Linda Smith?"

"Yeah... but it'll be fun no matter what happens."

"I guess you're right. It could even be the lead I've been looking for."

Allaine extended her stay three extra days. Like Angel and Michael, I had dowsed and been told to go to Ukiah. It was a long way to go just to find a tanned gypsy woman we didn't know. That evening I dowsed that the gypsy woman was located on the outskirts of Ukiah. I didn't know if she lived there or had a business there. The only shop we found that might have readers was a place called Moon Crest. It was quite a way from Ukiah. Angel had said the gypsy was in a small place tucked away. I wondered if it was the gypsy's home.

I printed the three addresses listed for Peter Smith. Time permitting we would stop in Rumsey to see if Linda Smith Homes had called.

*   *   *

In the morning we headed for Ukiah. Stopping at Rumsey, we inquired about Linda Smith Homes, but the motel owner hadn't heard from her. We continued toward Ukiah, looking for little mystical shops tucked back off the road. We didn't find any.

In Ukiah I was more interested in finding Peter Smith than the tanned gypsy woman. We had the three addresses mapped out and headed for the first one. Finding it wasn't difficult. An old mailbox on the street had its street number, but there was no house, just an empty lot.

We both laughed about it and headed for the next address, an apartment complex. Allaine waited in the car as I went to the door. Sweat beaded on my forehead. As many times as I've gone to stranger's doors, I would have thought I'd be more comfortable with it by now, but I wasn't. It was still nerve wracking.

A man about my age answered the door. I studied his face. He had no idea I was looking for some resemblance of myself in him.

"Sorry to bother you, but I'm looking for Peter Smith."

"I'm not Peter Smith and I've lived here four years. If he lived here it was before then," he said.

I wondered if he was being truthful, but I couldn't see anything of myself in him. He could be right considering how old some of Dave Gilbert's addresses were. Disappointed, I thanked him and returned to the car.

"Any luck?" Allaine asked.

"No."

"There's one more address. It could be the one."

"It's not looking too positive," I added.

Allaine directed us to the next address. It was getting late and I got more discouraged as the day dragged on.

At a four way stop sign Allaine yelled, "Look! There's a place called Mystic Earth. It looks like a mystical type of store and it's tucked back off the road. Turn around and let's check it out."

"But... don't you think we should go to this last address first?"

"No, just turn around and let's check it out."

Reluctantly I turned the car around. I was surprised the shop was still open. It sat between houses and it was a few minutes to five on a Sunday evening.

Inside the store we realized it was the type of place we'd been looking for. It was smaller than Twilight Greetings but it had the same sort of merchandise. The sales person, a young woman, was waiting on another customer. Allaine began looking at the stones and I checked out the artwork.

Engrossed in paintings, I didn't see the sales person approach me.

"Welcome to Mystic Earth. Can I help you find something?"

"I hope so. Do you have readers here?"

"Not today. Sometimes on Saturdays we do. Did you look at our bulletin board by the door?"

"No, I didn't see it."

I followed her to the bulletin board covered with business cards.

Pointing to a card, she said, "This gal is really good."

Somehow, I knew it wasn't the person I needed to see. "I don't think that's the right reader."

"Well... who are you looking for?"

Allaine was walking toward us and yelled, "She's looking for a gypsy woman."

I followed with, "Yeah...um... a tanned foreign gypsy woman?"

"Oh... I know exactly who you mean."

Simultaneously, Allaine and I said, "You do?"

We hadn't been sure the person even existed and now this woman was telling us she knew her.

The young woman went behind the counter to search through a Rolodex.

"Oh my God," whispered Allaine.

I whispered back, "This is too wild. I have goose bumps."

"*ME TOO.*"

The young woman said, "I'm not sure if I have her number here, but if not, I have it at home."

I wasn't worried as long as she had the number somewhere. We had planned to stay the night in Ukiah anyway. Maybe I could see the gypsy woman in the morning.

"I found it," she yelled.

"Wow!" said Allaine.

"Yeah, but she never answers her telephone. I'll leave her a message and hopefully she'll call me back tomorrow."

I was sitting on pins and needles. The gypsy must have important information for me about my father. I said a small prayer while she dialed the number. Every inch of me had goose bumps. I kept reminding myself to breathe as I watched her punch each number. I turned toward some stones nearby but my vision seemed blurred. All my senses focused on her fingers. Hearing her speak, I thought I was going to faint. I looked over at Allaine. She had her hand over her mouth.

The young woman told the gypsy about me. I wondered if the gypsy would see me or at least talk to me. I was willing to drive anywhere for information about my search.

The young woman motioned for my attention and handed me the telephone. "She wants to talk with you."

Shocked I took the receiver. "Hello?"

In broken English a woman said, "My dear friend says that you have been sent to me. You know, I never answer my telephone, but I did today. It is meant for you to hear what I have to say."

She was difficult to understand, but it was like... talking to God with a very heavy European accent.

My voice shook. "I would really appreciate hearing what you have to say."

"I'm from Germany. I have traveled the world. I have sat with Dalai Lama, and Shaman in the Arctic, also been to all Holy lands. I have been on both coasts and people have come from all over the world for my readings. I was music teacher at University. I have knowledge on all religions and do not do readings anymore, but you have been sent to hear what I have to say."

Not knowing how to respond, I said, "Yes."

She asked me my full name and date of birth. She said she would sit at midnight by the stream near her house. Her name was Satrie and she lived in a small place on the outskirts of Ukiah. She gave me her phone number, which surprised me. She said she would send me two tapes and it would be the reading of a lifetime. I asked her the cost and she said eighty-five dollars, but that was just for good faith. She told me not to send it until after I received her tapes.

I gave her my address, thanked her for her time and said I would wait for the tapes. We bought some stones and thanked the young woman for her help.

Allaine and I were jazzed. We had found the tanned gypsy woman, but it still didn't seem real. We headed for the last address of Peter Smith.

It was right down the road from the Mystic Earth. A young gal answered the door and said she never heard of Peter Smith. Back at the car I told Allaine it was odd. We had three addresses and a name, but couldn't find the guy; yet after one accidental stop on the track of a foreign gypsy reader, whose name we didn't know or certain she even existed, we found her. That was too bizarre.

I wasn't disappointed about not finding Peter Smith; because it was obvious I was to find Satrie. If we hadn't been looking for Peter Smith's address, we might never have found Mystic Earth.

It was late, but with no reason to stay in Ukiah we headed home. Allaine and I were both overwhelmed by our experience. We thought the trip would give us time to talk and enjoy each other's company, but neither of us expected actually to find a gypsy woman. Foreign or otherwise, but I forgot to ask the young woman if Satrie, was tanned.

We sat in silence for a while, both of us thinking about our lucky encounter. "Hey," I said. "Do you want to see if we can find Lacy's brother in Trenton?"

"What?"

"Larry Burnell, he's supposed to be a Reverend in Trenton. I have a phone number and an address. Of course, it could be like Peter Smith's addresses. I haven't had the courage to go on my own, but you and I can go together. I've been wanting to meet him, if he's still in Trenton."

"I met him when I was about nine," Allaine said. "But I can't remember anything about him. Nammie always said he was no good."

"Well... you wouldn't expect her to say different, would you?"

"No. Um... why not? Let's do it. I don't leave until the day after tomorrow."

"We can sleep in tomorrow and still have plenty of time to drive there and back."

"Boy, talk about going from one extreme to the next."

"What do you mean?" I asked.

"You know... the intuitive reader to the Reverend."

"If we happen to find him, I don't think we should mention what we did today."

"Probably not a good idea."

A Love Child's Journey

Chapter Twenty-two

Ready for another adventure, whatever the outcome, Allaine and I decided not to call Lacy's brother until we reached downtown Trenton. We wanted to meet him, but after our visit to Ukiah, we had to prepare for any encounter.

We drove to Trenton, a small town located on the California Nevada border. Quaint tourist shops lined both sides of a two-lane road, with occasional glimpses of railroad tracks off to the right.

"Wow. There are some cool little shops here," Allaine said. "We should check them out if we don't find our uncle."

"Yeah... did you see the Chocolate store?"

"No, I missed that. Pull over when you get a chance and I'll try his number."

On the next block, I parked off the side of the road. Allaine began punching the number into my cell phone, and said, "Cross your fingers."

For a moment an uneasy pang of doubt raced through me. We had no idea what we were getting into. Looking at her, I took a deep breath. Even though it wasn't my first time at this, I was glad to have her here with me. She had met him once when she was nine years old.

Eyes wide, she mouthed, "Ringing."

My fingers crossed, I heard her say, "Hello, is this the Burnell residence?"

She looked at me and nodded her head up and down. I couldn't believe it, we had the right number and he was home. I stared at her the cell telephone planted tightly against her ear as she explained who we were and what we wanted. She wrote down an address and directions to their house, saying we weren't too far away.

Closing the phone with a goodbye, she said, "Oh my God. He wants to see us. His wife answered and she told me her name's Sue and they were preparing and decorating their house for their son's wedding reception. She said Larry would want to see us and then she called him to the phone."

"What did he say?" I asked.

"He was excited and told us to come on over. He gave me directions."

"Did he sound nice?"

"Yeah."

"Uh… did he sound normal?"

"I don't know. Did I sound normal?"

I laughed. "I already know you're normal, so I wasn't paying attention to you."

"We'll just have to wait until we meet him."

The directions he gave made it easy to find his house. Four or five years earlier I had camped not far from the turn-off to his house. I wondered if he was living there at the time.

"Turn right, here," said Allaine.

"Which side of the street is it on?"

"Slow down. I think that's it. See the green truck?"

"Yeah. The yard's nice and green and the house is nice too."

"Yeah… it is." She agreed. "It looks… normal."

"Good sign, don't you think?"

She smiled as we parked and got out of the car.

The two-story A-frame reminded me of a country cabin. I imagined the beauty of it surrounded by snow. It looked cozy and normal, but still wondered about the people inside.

Before we reached the front door, a handsome dark haired man in blue jeans and a plaid shirt stepped out to greet us. He was average in height and had blue eyes, but not as brilliant as Lacy's. Although there was no doubt that he was her brother. His warmth and kindness was overwhelming. The soothing tone of his voice seemed fitting for a Reverend. He invited us inside and his wife met us at the door.

Sue was bubbly and welcoming. Her blonde hair had been pulled back, but strands fell to each side of her face as if from some busy task. She explained that Larry had tried contacting his sisters many times, but eventually gave up. He didn't know Lacy had died and seemed deeply saddened by the news. He had seen Lacy when she was pregnant with Allaine, but hadn't been told that she gave an earlier child up for adoption. He remembered visiting Wilma and Rodney when Allaine was young, but didn't see Lacy at that time.

I listened to their excitement as he and Allaine talked. Although he was getting his house ready for his son's reception, he seemed pleased that we had stopped to see him. He took the time to show us pictures of Lacy's parents, our biological grandparents and great-grandparents. It was the first time I'd seen pictures of them. Our grandmother had curly hair and so did Lacy, a trait that affected all of us, but neither Allaine nor I had any other noticeable traits of our biological grandparents or great-grandparents. Lacy resembled both her parents and her brother.

Time passed quickly and we stayed longer than we meant to, but Allaine was leaving the next day for Kuwait and wouldn't be back for another year. So much time had passed and it was difficult to make up for it all in one visit. I told him I'd be back and bring the pictures I had of Lacy.

He walked us to our car, hugged us, and said a prayer for our safe trip home. We were his sister's children, part of his family, something he thought he'd never have the opportunity to experience again.

Overjoyed at his acceptance, and reflecting on our conversation that had taken place, I said nothing as we headed home.

Allaine broke the silence. "Wow... that was amazing."

"Yeah... it was. They're wonderful people."

"Isn't it weird how our grandmother gave up both daughters and led a life of men and drinking and then died in a car accident?"

"A lot like Lacy's life," I added. And both had been in a bad car accident. The one positive thing was that Lacy didn't die in her car accident."

"But, she wasn't the same after it."

"I don't know how she was before, but she had a remarkable recovery from all the severe injuries. They both seemed to have the same self-destructive behavior."

It was amazing how much Lacy was like her biological mother, especially since Lacy was adopted at the age of two. I felt thankful that neither of our lives mirrored theirs.

*   *   *

A few days after Allaine left for Kuwait, my tapes arrived from the tanned foreign gypsy woman. My husband and I were going to the mountains for a long weekend, a good place to listen to her tapes.

At our camping spot I hurried to unpack, stretched out on the chaise lounge under the beautiful pine trees, then turned on my tape player. She was difficult to understand but educated in spiritual beliefs and religions. She explained Hinduism, Christianity, Buddhism, and Shamanism, to name a few. I knew nothing about any of them.

She told me that I was an enlightened being and referred to me as a Bodhisattva. I had no idea what that was, but she made it sound like a good thing. I liked hearing it. Not until I bought The Everything World Religions book did I learn what it was. A Bodhisattva is a soul who has already reached enlightenment, but because of compassion decides to postpone ascension into nirvana in order to work toward the salvation of others.

In other words, I was here to help other people. She continued to tell me how blessed I was and that great things were coming my way. She told me to read many books, such as, A Course in Miracles, poems by Rumi, Findhorn Gardens in Scotland and talks by Krishnamurti. I thought my tape player would give out; I had to rewind so many times, hoping to better understand what she said and then try and figure out what it meant.

One subject caught my attention in a very profound way. I had only given her my name and birthday when we talked, but listening to her tape, I heard these words—*You are a love child. You were not raised by your biological parents, but you were a child conceived in love. You were a wanted child.*

I was amazed. It comforted me to hear that there was love attached to the emotional pain Lacy endured. Maybe that's why she returned to Fairhaven home to try and get me back. Maybe she truly loved my biological father, which would have made her situation more painful.

I stared at the trees wishing I could have just one more conversation with her. Then it occurred to me. Try dowsing and ask her to talk with me. I had nothing to lose.

In the motor home, I grabbed my pendulum, dowsing book, pen and paper. I turned to the page with letters. I was pleased that I was excited rather than scared. I planned to try to communicate with someone who was no longer alive, at least not on the physical plane, but decided not to think about it like that.

I asked permission to dowse and then asked questions as if Lacy was sitting across from me.

Q. Lacy, may I ask you questions about my father?
A. Yes.
Q. Can you tell me about him?
A. There were two brothers.
Q. What did they look like?
A. Dark skin, maybe Italian, I'm not sure. The younger one liked me, but I liked the older one.
Q. Did you have intimate relations with them?
A. Only the older one.

With that answer, a strong sexual surge pulsed through me like a bolt of lightening.

Q. Did the younger one know you liked the older one?
A. No.

The door of the motor home opened and in walked my husband. He had always been supportive of my dowsing, but I didn't want Lacy to leave.

"What kind of perfume are you wearing?" He snarled. "It smells like you sprayed the whole bottle on yourself."

Unable to smell anything, I asked, "What do you mean? I'm wearing the same kind I always wear. The one you buy me."

He had always been very sensitive to perfumes and because of that, I had worn the same one for years.

"For a minute I thought your mom was here," he said.

Then it hit me. My mom was there, just not the one he was referring to.

"I bet you're smelling Lacy?"

"What?"

"I've been dowsing and talking with her. I can feel her presence. Maybe you can smell her perfume and I can't."

"It's pretty strong."

"Well... I guess she's making her presence known."

"You might want to mention that the next time she visits, she could wear less perfume."

"I'm not sure it works that way."

He smiled and walked back outside.

I was hoping she was still around. I had a few more questions I wanted to ask. I held the pendulum in the center of the letters.

Q. Lacy, did you love my biological father?
A. Yes.
Q. Did he love you?
A. Yes.

My body flushed and my heart picked up its beat. I wondered if that was an indication of the love she felt for him. It was amazing.

Q. What was his name?
A. A common name, like Mike.
Q. Is his name Mike?

A. No.

My pendulum began turning in a circle. Maybe I wasn't supposed to ask, but it sure would have made my search a lot easier if she'd just spell his name out for me. Maybe it wasn't the way to find out about him. I was overjoyed at feeling her presence and not being frightened by it. Then the presence faded and she was gone.

*   *   *

The following week I called Wilma to arrange another visit, she sounded upset. She had received a letter from Laura who had inoperable pancreatic cancer and had decided against chemotherapy treatments. She hadn't seen Laura in thirty years. Wilma had felt guilty not seeing Lacy when she was dying. Hoping not to make the same mistake, she wanted to see Laura before her death. I couldn't fathom not seeing your own daughter for that long, but she seemed genuinely sad. I decided to put my search on hold and take her to see Laura. I knew Laura didn't want me in her life, but from the letters she had sent Wilma, I was sure she'd want to see her mother. I could drop Wilma off and then come back and pick her up if necessary. It wasn't as if Wilma could hop in a car and drive herself three hundred and fifty miles. She was eighty-eight years old and blind.

"Wilma, do you want me to take you to see Laura?" I asked.

"You mean, you'd do that for me?"

Wondering what I might be getting into, I said, "Yes... I think you should be able to see your terminally ill daughter."

"That would be wonderful. When can we go?"

"How about I pick you up early Friday morning around nine?"

"Oh, thank you so much. I'll be ready."

Hanging up the phone, I wondered if my offer was based on my selfishness. Was I hoping that if I did something really nice for her, she'd give me the information I wanted? I decided not to ask her anything about my search or myself. Her daughter was dying and that was more important at the moment.

231

*   *   *

Friday morning I arrived at Wilma's house shortly before nine. She was sitting in her chair, dressed and ready to go. Her caregiver had helped her pack two mid sized suitcases. I thought about my small overnight bag in the car, wondering if she and I had the same thoughts about the duration of our visit. I had planned on her spending the afternoon with Laura and then heading back home. Laura was sick and neither of us knew the stage of her cancer.

I loaded the suitcases and then retrieved Wilma from her chair. She said she was tired and didn't feel well. She had fallen earlier that morning, but said she was okay. I settled her in the car, laid the seat back, and covered her with a blanket I'd brought. I told her to try and get some rest on the drive. She thought that was a good idea and closed her eyes.

*   *   *

We were approaching the town of Castella when Wilma woke up.

"Pull over, I don't feel good." She yelled. "I'm sick to my stomach."

"Do you normally get car sick?" I asked.

"Sometimes, but I've felt sick all morning."

I didn't know she had trouble with motion sickness, but if I had closed my eyes on a ride and didn't go to sleep, I'd probably have difficulties too. Maybe being blind intensified it. I pulled over, but the freeway shoulder was slanted and covered with stones the size of golf balls. There was nothing around except trees and rocks. I was worried about her stability, but didn't want her throwing up in my van.

Helping her out, I asked, "Are you okay?"

"I don't know. I feel sick. I need to walk."

I held her arm as she took a few steps. It was evident she couldn't walk on the rocks. I was afraid she would fall.

"My legs are giving out and my chest hurts," she cried.

Suddenly I realized her condition was more than carsickness. My heart started pumping so fast it was hard to breathe. Trying to calm down, I took a deep breath. The last thing I wanted was for her to collapse and fall on the rocks. "We need to get you some medical help." I told her.

I held her tight as she staggered back to the van, then got her into the seat and took off like a bat out of hell. We weren't far from Castella, but it was about three miles to the next exit off the freeway. I looked for any type of business or even homes, but it was barren. We eventually came upon railroad tracks and the beginning of a town. I seemed to be in a fog while someone else was driving the car. I looked over at Wilma; she was white as a ghost, but still coherent and hadn't thrown up yet, which I was thankful for.

There was a small coffee shop off to the left and an open parking space in front of it. That amazed me because parked cars filled both sides of the street. I made a U-turn and took the open spot. I got Wilma out of the car and headed to the Coffee shop.

"I'm going to be sick and I need a bathroom," she said.

"This is a Coffee shop. I'll take you to the restroom."

Inside the place, people were standing around. Within seconds, all eyes swiveled to us.

I yelled, "Where's your restroom?"

Everyone pointed to a small doorway at the back of the shop. It was all I could do to get her back there. Two women about thirty were talking at a corner table near the restroom. The shop being old, there was only one unisex bathroom that happened to be occupied. I sat Wilma down at the table nearest the restroom.

"I need something, I'm going to throw up," she insisted.

I ran to the front and yelled that I needed a bucket or something. Someone handed me a small plastic tub. I ran back to Wilma who amazingly, hadn't thrown up yet. One woman from the corner table was sitting with her.

"I think she's having a heart attack," the woman said. "Do you want me to call for help?"

"I think you're right. Would you, please?"

At that moment, a girl came out of the bathroom and I ushered Wilma in while holding the plastic tub in front of her. After she

233

used the toilet, I helped her with her pants and noticed a large bruise on the side of her leg. I didn't say anything figuring that it would stress her more. Suddenly a loud bang jolted the door.

"OPEN UP, IT'S THE PARAMEDICS."

Wilma whispered, "Don't open the door until you help me get my pants up."

She was probably having a heart attack but she was worried more about covering her private parts. I understood her embarrassment but didn't want her to die in the bathroom.

"UNLOCK THE DOOR OR WE'LL BREAK IT DOWN!"

Struggling to pull up her pants, I yelled back, "Okay, we're just trying to get her pants up."

"UNLOCK THE DOOR NOW!!!"

Sitting her back down on the toilet with her pants on more or less, I unlocked the door. In barged three paramedics. The last one in told me to leave the room. I was relieved they were there. Not all of us would have fit in that dinky room anyway.

People gathered around the bathroom. The woman who had called for help stood by me as they wheeled Wilma out. She was still lucid and I walked beside her to the ambulance. I told her I would follow her to the hospital in my car.

My heart sank as I watched them speed away with her. Just then, I felt a hand on my shoulder.

"Are you okay?" the helpful woman asked.

"I think so. Thank you so much for calling the paramedics."

"You're welcome. She's your grandmother?"

I wasn't sure how to answer that. I hadn't thought of her in that way. She was Lacy's adoptive mother so I guess she was my grandmother.

"Yes, my biological mother's mother, if that makes any sense."

"Yes, it does. My name's Kelly," she said.

"Hi, I'm Colette. We were traveling to Oregon to see her daughter who is dying of cancer."

"Take my phone number, call me and let me know how she's doing. Or if you need anything."

She gave me directions to the hospital, then hugged me goodbye. How nice it was to have someone be so kind at such a time.

* * *

I was still trembling when I entered the hospital emergency room. After explaining that I was Wilma's granddaughter, they led me back to her. My relief at finding her alive was huge. I felt some responsibility for this. Maybe I should have realized she was too old and fragile for this kind of trip. I thought it would be good for both Wilma and Laura to see each other, but it didn't look like it was going to happen.

She had a lot of tubes and wires hooked up to her, but she was alert and told the doctors I was her granddaughter. One of them pulled me aside and said she was in the middle of a heart attack, but they had given her medication to help stop it. He said that she needed to be air lifted to Eureka Hospital for a heart stint. They didn't have the facilities to handle that type of emergency, but it had to be done right away or she might die. He asked me if she had been under any stress lately.

Tears welled up in my eyes. I told him where I was taking her and why.

He must have sensed that I felt responsible for her condition, and made it clear that her heart problems were long standing. It was only a matter of time before she had a heart attack and he said I should be grateful to have been there for her when it happened.

* * *

At the Eureka hospital, they had already completed inserting the stint and had her sedated. They were more concerned with her bruise than her heart because a blood clot had formed. She'd be sedated all night.

They set me up in hospital housing. It was nice. Like a motel, and felt safe. Once settled in, I decided to call Kelly.

"Kelly, this is Colette Cooper from the coffee shop."
"Oh, hi! How's your grandmother?"
"They've inserted a stint and she's resting."
"Good."

"It's kind of a strange situation. She and I don't really know each other that well. What I mean is... I was adopted and she's my biological grandmother, but really my great-aunt. It's confusing."

"So... your biological mother was adopted by her aunt and you were given up for adoption?"

"Yeah... my biological mother isn't alive anymore and now I'm trying to find my biological father. So... I started visiting Wilma, my grandmother, sort of."

"What was it like being adopted?"

Surprised by her question, I said, "Great. I had a great life. I was loved and I have other adopted siblings. I always knew I was adopted. All of us were considered special. I was so fortunate to find my biological mother and now I want to find my biological father."

"She didn't tell you who it was?"

"No. I'm not sure why, but the subject was off limits and I didn't push it. Now I wish I had."

I waited for Kelly to say something. The silence was awkward. I wondered what she was thinking, but decided to wait before saying more.

"You know... I had a baby at a young age... and gave it up for adoption."

Sensing the pain in her voice, I said, "That must have been hard for you."

"Yeah... it was a long time ago, but sometimes it seems like yesterday."

The telephone fell silent again. I waited for her to speak.

"Tell me all the good things about your life and your feelings about being adopted," she asked.

I realized that my experience as an adopted child gave her some idea of how her own child may be living. She never said if it was a boy or girl. I don't know if she knew. Not that uncommon for the women and young girls who gave up their babies.

This young woman, a complete stranger was there for me in a crisis and I was here to help her deal with the grief of adopting out her baby. Although she seemed to feel it was best for her child, it was apparent that it wasn't best for her. I admired her love. She wanted a better life for her baby. I felt certain that she and Lacy shared the same emptiness in their hearts.

I talked about my adoptive mother and father being able to love and enjoy a baby because someone like herself gave them that chance. I mentioned the time my mother confided the ache and emptiness in her heart over failed pregnancies and her gratitude to Lacy for giving me up. To her, a baby was the perfect gift for any woman unable to have a child and desperately wanting one.

Instead of opening up and sharing her personal experience, Kelly said quietly, "Thank you."

I told her I would call in the morning and update her about Wilma. She invited me to the Abbey on the outskirts of Castella and said I could meet the Buddhist monks after their ceremony. Buddhist monks? Abbey? I had enough going on right now with Wilma. I told her I might drive up in the morning after checking on Wilma.

*   *   *

The next day Wilma was still sedated. They wanted her to rest and stay calm. They were more concerned about her bruise, but said her heart was fine. I asked them to call me if anything changed and said I'd be back later.

It took about an hour to get to the Buddhist Abbey. I had no idea what to expect, but thought maybe I was supposed to be there. An elderly lady noticed me walking onto the grounds, and asked if it was my first time there. I think she knew it was, but was being kind.

She showed me where to go. It was like church on Sunday, fifty years earlier. The monks in their robes and shaved heads were a mix of both males and females. They all looked alike, which I guessed was the intention. Most were older and had duties to perform in the ceremony.

Kelly was nowhere to be found and I wondered what I'd gotten myself into, but decided to follow the group. Everyone was kind, so I felt safe. I had never bowed so much in my life.

My new elderly friend, whose name I never did hear sat me down beside her, handed me a songbook and told me to follow her lead.

I stood when she did, bowed when she did and sang when she did. I watched as the monks completed their trips up to the large Buddha statue, bowed, then returned to the back. Words were said, but I didn't understand them. Eventually, I saw Kelly come in on the other side of the room. She nodded at me and sat on the floor.

I had been there about two hours and sensed that this was going to be a long ordeal. I was concerned about Wilma, so when the next break came, I left. Unfortunately, I didn't see Kelly to say goodbye.

I drove back to the hospital but Wilma was still in and out of a sleep state. The nurses weren't sure when she would be released. Not having planned to be away more than a couple of days, I said goodbye to her and headed home. I told the nurses I would call and check on her.

*   *   *

The following afternoon the hospital called. Wilma was being released. If I had known that, I would have stayed. I called her caregiver, who Wilma was more comfortable with to see if she could go pick her up. She said she couldn't. I asked her to please stay with Wilma a while when I got her home. Reluctantly, she agreed.

My little sister drove with me to pick Wilma up. It was a nice time for both of us, but close to nine o'clock in the evening when we reached the hospital. Wilma was very weak but seemed eager to get home.

We got her into the car and headed for the freeway. I don't think I drove three blocks before she said she was feeling sick to her stomach. Déjà vu! I took deep breaths, telling myself not to panic.

Thankfully, we had a large plastic bag from the hospital for her personal things. Wilma threw up before we reached the freeway.

My sister's quick action with the bag saved most of my van. It was going to be a long drive home.

Wilma thought the medicine they gave her was causing her to have an allergic reaction but wasn't sure. She didn't want me to take her back to the hospital though. Bless her heart, she was sick off and on for the entire drive home. I was beginning to wonder where it was coming from. I drove faster than I should have. Fast or slow didn't seem to make a difference, she just kept throwing up, but didn't want me to stop or take her back.

My sister and I felt sorry for her, but I was thankful that we both had strong stomachs. We arrived at Wilma's around midnight. Her caregiver met us there and I explained the medicines. It seemed selfish of me to leave her. I was her granddaughter, more or less, but we were still halfway strangers to each other. She would be more comfortable with her caregiver who had cared for her the last three years than with me. We hugged Wilma and headed home with the van windows wide open.

A Love Child's Journey

Chapter Twenty-three

I continued to check on Wilma's condition and visited every few weeks. Her heart attack seemed to be a turning point in our relationship. Not that I was given new information regarding my father, but she seemed to trust and actually like me. Having been with her during the heart attack and shown concern for her health, I was no longer that baby girl from Sacramento. Now I was her granddaughter.

My heart did go out for her, although sometimes I recalled the stories I heard of her verbal and physical abuse to all the people who loved her. But I didn't have those experiences embedded in my heart, which made it easier to see her in a kinder light.

I had always prided myself on viewing individuals based on the treatment I received from them. She had become so frail and helpless. When I'd visit her, all I could see was a sick elderly woman who longed for someone to take a few minutes and talk with her. Wilma hadn't given me what I wanted, but she always expressed her appreciation when I visited. I had to allow time for her to get better before I prodded her with more questions about my father.

During one of my visits, Wilma asked me to help her write a letter to Laura. She wanted her daughter to know that she had tried to come and see her, but suffered a heart attack on the way.

Her letter was short and she ended with "I love you, darling." I never saw her shed a tear, but the tone in her voice left me with no doubt that she loved Laura and was concerned. She understood that Laura's condition was serious and the survival rate for pancreatic cancer was slim. She said she didn't want to lose another daughter to cancer.

My eyes welled up writing the letter for her. I wondered if she had become callous over the years or just too stubborn to share her guarded feelings. I felt sad for her. I knew in her heart she wanted to see Laura before she died, but she also knew that most likely she wouldn't. I wished I had some comforting words for her.

*   *   *

Christmas had come and gone. Wilma's strength was slowly improving and her eighty-ninth birthday was the following week. I had plans to visit her the Sunday before. Allaine once told me that Lacy would occasionally bring Wilma Chanel No. 5 perfume. As a remembrance, for her birthday gift I bought her a small bottle of it. Roses would have been cheaper.

I arrived shortly before noon. The door was unlocked. I knocked, yelled out her name, and then walked in.

"Colette, is that you?" she asked.

"Yes, it's me."

"Oh, have a seat here by me. I have something I want you to read. It's in the chair."

There was a letter in the chair next to her. I picked it up and sat down. The return address was a preprinted label with Laura's name and address. Opening the envelope, I realized it was the letter Wilma asked me to write Laura a few months earlier.

My heart sank as I read the chilling words underneath Wilma's sign-off: I love you darling, Love Mom
LAURA FAY DIED NOVEMBER 5, 2006.

Nothing else was added, no signature, nothing. The icy information was beyond cold. I didn't know how to react. I wasn't surprised at Laura's death, but it would have been nice if the guy, her husband, or whoever wrote that had called Wilma or written something more, even a cliché like—sorry to be the bearer of bad news.

Wilma explained that her caregiver had read her the letter. She was disappointed at not seeing Laura before her death, and wondered what Laura had told her husband about her. Wilma assumed it wasn't pleasant. She said it wasn't right that both her daughters were gone... yet she didn't cry. I hadn't even met Laura, but I was fighting to hold back tears.

Wilma and I sat in silence a few moments. I hoped she was reflecting on fond memories rather than disturbing ones.

"What about the service?" she asked.

"Maybe he didn't have one for her."

She bowed her head and said, "You know, I wasn't invited to Lacy's service when she died and I was so good to those baby girls."

I knew that she had been invited to Lacy's funeral because Allaine told me she was. Not that she needed an invitation. Allaine had hoped that Wilma would show up out of respect for her daughter and grandchildren, but she didn't. I thought it best to keep quiet.

I had begun to see a pattern in Wilma's personality. All the misfortunes and unpleasant situations, like Lacy pregnant with me at thirteen, seemed of concern to Wilma, but only for how they affected and reflected on her, not for the people themselves.

Hoping to cheer her up, I said, "I have a gift for you."

"You do?"

"Your birthday is in a couple of days," I said jubilantly.

"Yeah... I hope I live to be ninety. That's my dream."

"You will. You're getting stronger every day."

"I don't know about that."

I knew. She was too mean and spiteful to die. It wasn't a kind thought, but it felt true. Selfishly, I hoped she would give me some hint of information before dying and I wanted it before she turned ninety.

I gave her the bag and she reached inside. I explained what it was. She was thrilled and told me that Lacy had bought it for her too. She felt the bottle and tried to spray it, but couldn't push the sprayer down far enough. She had no strength. I should have gotten her flowers.

I reached over and helped her. She smiled as the mist lightly touched her skin. Maybe it was a good thing. I hoped she wouldn't spray it in her eyes.

"Hand me my purse off the floor," she demanded.

I did, wondering why she wanted it. Maybe she had something about me hidden in it.

I watched her dig around in the purse. Handing me a key, she said, "I want you to have a key to my house. That way I don't have to keep the door unlocked on the days you visit."

Shocked with disbelief that she trusted me, I said, "Thank you. I'll be very careful with it."

"I know you will. That's why I'm letting you have it."

I thanked her again, but I really wanted to say—just tell me some information about my father instead. Like what really happened when Lacy got pregnant or what you thought happened. Or let me go through those trunks in your closet. I'd trade the key in an instant for any of those things.

The key did give me access to her house, but I knew I would respect her personal things. Evidently she thought so too.

We visited a little longer before I left for home with her house key in hand.

*   *   *

I had been doing a lot of dowsing and meditating with hopes of getting some information about my father, since I wasn't getting anything from Wilma. My meditations had been very interesting. I started an early morning ritual of meditating 20-30 minutes, then dowsing right after. Often it was difficult to quiet my thoughts and at times, I'd fall asleep, but lately I had images from different historical eras. It seemed as if I was watching movies while playing one of the characters in each movie. Sometimes what I saw in my meditations didn't seem to have any connection to my dowsing, but I found both very intriguing.

I had decided to see Michael again and share the information from my meditations and dowsing. Maybe his guides or connections to the spirit world could make sense of what I was getting. I was game for anything that might give me some direction with my search.

*   *   *

The following Saturday, I made an appointment with Michael. When I got there, he had just finished a reading. Angel was there giving readings too. Thinking two heads were better than one or maybe two psychic minds were better than one, I considered talking with her after Michael.

I sat with Michael and watched him go into his place. I'd learned to be quiet when he closed his eyes.

Putting his hand on the table, something he did each time, he asked, "Did you have questions or do you want to hear what my guides have to say?"

"Well... both, but I have a lot of questions about my meditating and my dowsing."

"Okay, let's start with your meditations."

Hesitating, I wondered how much to share. I didn't want him to think I was weird, but given that I was there and he was a psychic reader eased that thought. I was sure he'd heard a lot of unusual experiences.

"Well... I keep having visions that I'm in different historical times. Sometimes I'm a male and sometimes a female. What's that about?"

Michael closed his eyes and pointed his finger in the air. "Yes, these are true events. You are going through the Halls of Time. You're simply getting a glimpse of your past lives. It's your way of coming into mastery. It's your venture on Earth, which is wound through time. Finding your past is who you are in this lifetime and what you are here for."

"Well, this morning I was in the ocean somewhere and I drowned. It was calming. I could see bubbles, but I knew I was drowning and I seemed fine with it. I was watching myself from above."

My drowning story didn't faze Michael. Since I was sitting in front of him, he most likely assumed I was alive.

Michael closed his eyes. "You are on a unique mission as a healer. To heal you have to have the ability to see and sense other past lives. It's a major gift on your part. It's like a therapist who works with someone for years, except you have the ability to help in a few sessions. Bring them into wholeness. This could be later in this lifetime or your next. You're in training and you're humbly going through the learning process."

"Wow... I feel like when I first learned CPR. The need to go out and save a life."

Michael chuckled. "Your vibrational frequency is rising, but there is no loss of who you are as an individual."

"That's good. But I still think I'll be careful who I share this with."

"Reincarnation does not only affect a selected few."

"Yes, I know.

"Anything else?"

"Let's talk about my dowsing information. I'll summarize what I've received lately and maybe you can either verify it, tell me what it means or tell me what to do with it."

"We'll hear what my guides have to say about it."

"I received all this information dowsing. Remember I came up with the name Michael? I got this Michael Carney and that he now lives in the state of Oregon. His wife's name is Jocelyn. I got that he is my father or knows my father or is the person who could lead me to my father. What do you think about that?"

Eyes closed, he said, "I get the name Spear or Spears, some combination of that name. Big clue... he is the controlling answer to your riddle. He knows it all. Find him and solve the mystery. The state of Oregon is correct. He is the key that will lead you to your father. My guide says you should check out the census records around 1930."

"But... I get that he was born around 1938 or 1939."

"Check anyway. You might want to check with the Church of Latter Day Saints too."

"Why the Mormons?" I asked.

"They are big into genealogy."

"Okay... oh, I also got that this Michael guy was into motorcycle racing."

Eyes closing, Michael said, "Was, but not now."

"So... I'm on the right track. I just need to find this Michael Spear or Spears guy in the state of Oregon."

"Yes. You have chosen this journey to find your father as your path to spiritual enlightenment. The larger purpose is your inner knowing."

"I wish my inner knowing could avoid all the obstacles and lead me directly to my father."

"Remember, the journey is the key."

I thanked Michael and searched the store for Angel. I received validation from Michael, but a second opinion would make me feel that much better.

Angel and her guides mirrored Michael's spirits and my dowsing. The one thing she was adamant about was that my father was young energy. She confirmed the 1939 birth date.

When I left the store, I was confident that I needed to find this Spears guy. If I found him, what would I say when he asked how I got his name? Would I tell him—through psychic readers? Oh... and by the way, I dowsed some of the information too. If he had any type of religious upbringing or ties, he would think I was the devil without a red suit. I needed to think about that.

When I got home, I searched the Internet and found a lot of Spears in Oregon, but couldn't tie any of them to Forest Glen or the Eureka area.

*   *   *

I wasn't sure what to do with all the information, but I wasn't ready to drive to Oregon and start knocking on the doors of the entire Spears group. I could check to see if anyone named Spears lived in Forest Glen between 1954 and 1955.

I went online to find the library nearest to Forest Glen. The best choice was the main library in Eureka. I called to ask if they had information regarding the Forest Glen area and high school yearbooks for students in that area during the 50's. The gal that I spoke with thought I would have better luck contacting the Eureka Historical Society. I called the number she gave me and they had the yearbooks as well as information about Forest Glen.

I made plans to drive to Eureka on Friday and be there when they opened their doors at 10:00. Then I would drive to Forest Glen.

*   *   *

I made it to Eureka and found the Historical Society address right before they opened. Besides the yearbooks, I wasn't sure what I was looking for. Names of people who lived or worked in Forest Glen at that time might be helpful.

The Eureka Historical Society reminded me of a library. Shelves full of books and artifacts sparsely displayed. All the workers were elderly and volunteered their time. One thing that caught my attention was a large map of the area and smaller ones too. I had always been fascinated with maps.

A gentleman showed me the articles they had about Forest Glen, but they were years before Lacy and her family lived there. He proceeded to read me its history. I wasn't interested in what happened in Forest Glen before Lacy was there, but I listened not wanting to be unkind. They had yearbooks, but not the ones from Channey High School, which is where the workers believed kids from Forest Glen attended.

The volunteers were helpful and nice. They each sat down at the table by me, wanting to help. I explained what I was looking for and told them my story. Well, minus the psychic part.

One of the ladies said, "Hey, why don't we call Cheryl, she's the Post Master in Forest Glen. She may have some ideas. Her mom has passed, but she lived in Forest Glen her whole life and so did Cheryl."

That perked me up. It was like hitting the jackpot. I waited as she made the call. She wrote down something.

After hanging up, she walked over to me.

Her face beaming, she said, "Cheryl thought you might want to talk with her aunt. She's in her eighties, but has been in Forest Glen since she was very young. She said to give her a call. Her name is Hattie Campbell. Here's her number."

Hugging her, I said, "Thank you."

Using my cell phone, I called Hattie. I was delighted when she told me I could see her, but preferred it to be later that afternoon. After writing down her address, I told her I'd see her soon.

I was glad she wanted me to come by later because I wanted to go to Channey High School to look at the old yearbooks.

The gentleman who helped me gave me directions to the high school. I thanked them for all their help and headed for the school.

His directions were great. It had been a long time since I had been in a high school setting. My son had graduated eleven years earlier. I got the location of the school library from a student. It was a small library with the librarian sitting behind a glass enclosure.

I waited at the counter until I got her attention. She looked too young for a librarian or maybe I was just getting old. The students looked young too. I asked if I could see the old yearbooks. She handed me a small Xeroxed form to sign that stated I would return them undamaged. She then went into an adjacent room and returned with the yearbooks. Pointing to a nearby table, she informed me they could not leave the room. I thanked her and sat down.

I enjoyed looking through the books. I wondered if anyone I was looking at was my father. I thought he may have been older, but remembered Angel insisted he was young. I didn't find any Spears, but did find some Smiths. I searched for Linda Smith, but didn't find her. I was disappointed that no one jumped out at me. I wrote down a few names and returned the books to the librarian.

It didn't take as long as I'd thought. Eager to talk with Hattie Campbell, I decided to head for Forest Glen. I just knew something good would come from our meeting.

A Love Child's Journey

Chapter Twenty-four

I passed a few small towns, the houses sparse along the road between them. Enjoying the scenic mountain drive, I wondered how sound Hattie Campbell's memory would be. Over fifty years had passed, a long time to remember events and people, and she was in her eighties. She did live alone, and if she was capable of taking care of herself, maybe her memory was intact as well.

A warm wave of excitement rushed through me when I saw the road sign: Forest Glen, 15 miles, and an arrow pointing to my left. Forest Glen—that's where it all began. Where I began, my conception. I smiled and turned left down the curvy two-lane road.

Beautiful cedar and pine trees shaded the road as it wound down around the mountains. Afternoon sunlight reflected through the trees. The brisk air was refreshing and the weather perfect for a mid February day.

Hattie had told me her street was right off the main road before the elementary school. I passed a few houses and roads. Forest Glen seemed farther than fifteen miles from the main highway. I thought about road conditions fifty years earlier and was glad for the smooth drive now.

The curving road gradually straightened out as I approached a street sign beside a dirt road. To my surprise, it read Pioneer

Lane. I couldn't believe it. Pioneer Lane was the name Wilma used when she talked about Forest Glen. She said that's where they had lived.

I drove on, looking for the elementary school and Hattie's street. Passing a few more houses, I had to be getting closer to town. About a mile later, I found Hattie's road and off to the left the elementary school. I had an hour before my meeting with her.

The school was small, but looked in good condition with tan bricks around the office entrance. It had a large wooden sign that read: Rock Creek Elementary School. The school Lacy had attended when she became pregnant with me.

I pulled into the parking lot in front of the school and watched a man park a school bus in a large metal shed. There was time, so I decided to ask him some questions. He looked older than me. Maybe he knew Lacy or someone who had known her. It couldn't hurt to ask.

Up close, I realized he wasn't much older than me, but decided to tell him what I was doing in Forest Glen. I had nothing to lose, and was willing to ask anyone for help. His name was Steve and he was the school bus driver and maintenance man for the school. He had lived in Forest Glen all his life and attended Rock Creek Elementary. He said a few rooms had been added on to the building, but not much else had changed. He didn't recognize Lacy's name. I asked about school records and he said school was over for the day, but some of the staff was still inside.

I followed him in. Off to our left a hallway led to the classrooms. Excitement rushed through me as we entered the hall. It was Lacy's school. She walked this hall every school day for two years. I could touch the walls she touched on the way to her classroom. I could almost feel her presence guiding me down the hall like a small child eager to show off her work.

Steve led me to the teacher's room. A woman in her late thirties was bustling around the room.

"Pam, this is Colette. She's looking for some information about her mother who went to school here in the mid-fifties," he said.

I explained to Pam, the kindergarten teacher that my mother was in the eighth grade at the time of my conception and I was searching for my biological father.

"Pam, it may be a long shot," I said. "But I was hoping the school had records going back that far."

"Aren't there old records in the vacant classroom?" she asked Steve. "In those boxes against the wall?"

"There might be. Let's go check," he said.

I followed them to the vacant classroom. They walked over to a stack of large cardboard boxes. Steve lifted a few boxes and set them on top of a long narrow table. Pam pulled out a few folders from one.

"These are the old records," she said.

I couldn't believe it, remembering when I wanted Lacy's high school records, and they were on microfilm in the basement storage of the high school and I had to wait for them. It took a few days.

The boxes were neatly stacked, but unsealed and most of them wide open. They held information over fifty years old. And there it all sat right before me. Definitely better than those chests that Wilma won't let me look in.

Maybe a small town creates a trusting environment or maybe they couldn't afford to do anything different. Either way, I was glad the records were there.

"What years are you looking for?" asked Pam.

"1954 and 1955."

Steve asked, "What grades?"

"Eighth grade. But I guess that would be fall 1954 and spring 1955."

"What name are you looking for?" asked Pam.

"Lacy Fisherman."

I watched Steve place another box on the table. Pam fanned through it, pausing at each folder.

Pulling out a large folder, she said, "Here it is."

I could hardly believe it. "You found it?" I asked.

She handed me the folder labeled Monthly Attendance Record, Record for the Fiscal Year beginning July 1, 1954 and ending June 30, 1955. Each page recorded all the student's activity for a school month. Seventh and eighth graders shared the same teacher. Lacy and her sister Laura were in the same classroom.

I still couldn't believe my luck. I was looking at Lacy's daily school activity. When she was late, had the mumps and had a dentist appointment. (If she went to a dentist in Eureka, it had to be a long torturous ride.) There were only seven eighth graders, two girls and five boys. Remembering that the psychics described my father as young energy, I studied the names of the boys wondering if any of them was my father or knew him. I believed my father was older than my mother.

"Pam what's the large 'L' mean next to Laura's name on January 17, 1955?" I asked.

Pam looked at the 'L', she said, "That meant she left the school."

"You mean... for good?"

"Yeah... it looks like her last day was January 14, 1955."

I remembered Wilma saying that she and Laura moved to Oildale in early spring. January isn't early spring. I flipped the page to February. There it was. Lacy's last day at Rock Creek School was, February 18, 1955. She must have become pregnant with me either the prior week or that weekend. Maybe my conception was on Valentine's Day. The tanned gypsy woman said I was a child conceived in love.

I checked my watch. It was almost time to meet with Hattie Campbell. Pam made me copies of Lacy's records. I thanked them both and said I'd keep them posted on my search. I was so grateful for their time and help.

*   *   *

I turned down Hattie's road looking for her house. She had explained it was right before all the electrical towers. Scattered houses and trailer homes lined the left side of the road. When the paving turned into dirt, I could see the towers getting closer. How safe could it be living near to so many of them? She was in her eighties, so I guess she was fine.

The last home on the right was hers. I couldn't tell if it was a house or a trailer on a foundation, but it didn't matter. Three small chairs sat on the wooden porch near the door. Two broken down cars guarded the house, one near the side and the other in front. Old tires and boxes covered the grounds. There was no grass, just dirt. I almost expected Jed Clampett from 'The Beverly Hillbillies' show to come out the door after a hound dog started barking at me, but instead Hattie emerged from behind the house. A swirling gust of wind blew her thick silver hair in her face.

I parked and watched her walk toward me. Her confident gait showed that she was stable on her feet. There was no snow, but she wore snow boots and a warm sweater. I could see smoke coming from a stovepipe on her roof. It was probably her only heat.

Getting out of the car, I said, "Mrs. Campbell?"

In between the dog's howl she said, "Just call me Hattie."

"Thank you for taking the time to see me."

"Oh… I don't mind. I don't have many visitors."

I sensed she was lonely. Explaining about Lacy and my search, I told her of the possibility of rape by my biological father.

"I remember Wilma Fisherman, but I never heard about no rape," she said.

Excited that she knew Wilma, and still not convinced that Lacy was raped, I said, "You do?"

"Yeah, I took some paintin' classes from her. I can show you where she used to live… if you want."

"That would be wonderful. I'd really appreciate it."

I opened the passenger door for her, and then got back into my van. Wilma told me that she had given painting classes to the women who lived around Forest Glen.

"Turn around and head back towards town," she said.

Toward town? I never did actually see a town.

After a while we turned left onto a dirt road. We hadn't gone far when we came upon an old tin building on the left near an open field. Two houses on the right sat back off the dirt road.

"Stop here. See those houses…? Well, that's where the bosses lived."

"Were any of them named Smitty?" I asked.

"No, not that I know of. The only Smitty I knew was Roy. Roy Smith, but they called him Smitty."

Smitty was the name Michael got during a reading. I also remembered that when I was dowsing, Lacy mentioned meeting my father at a matinee. "Was there a movie theater around here?" I asked.

Hattie pointed to an open spot near the tin shed, "There was a building that sat there. They would show movies every once in a while inside. Mostly matinees.

That validated Lacy's information she communicated to me. I didn't know what excited me more, that I was in a place where Lacy had spent time or that I was communicating with her in spirit form. And Hattie knew a Smitty.

"Do you want me to show you where the Fisherman's lived?"

"That would be great. Just let me take some pictures before we move on."

After taking my pictures, we continued on the dirt road. I was disappointed that Hattie couldn't remember Lacy or Laura. She thought her niece Daisy would have been around Lacy's age. Unfortunately, Daisy had died from cancer a few years earlier.

We drove up a small hill and off to the left were some houses about a hundred yards away.

Hattie pointed to the right side of the road. "Right there. That's where Wilma lived. There used to be a house there, but it was torn down."

"A house? I thought they lived in a trailer."

"No... they lived in a house. I came here for my paintin' classes and it was a house."

I remembered Wilma telling me that Lacy's rape happened in their trailer, but she didn't tell me the truth about much. I didn't think Hattie had any reason to say different than what she seemed certain of. I decided to ask Wilma about their house in Forest Glen.

"Do you want me to show you where Smitty lived?"

"Sure. I'd like that."

Following her directions, we were heading away from Forest Glen into the mountains. All the dirt roads looked the same. I had no idea how to get back to where we started.

Uneasy, I asked, "Do you know how to get us back to your house?"

She chuckled. "I've lived on this mountain for over sixty years. I know it like the back of my hand."

Relieved, I said, "Okay, as long as you're comfortable with it, so am I."

We drove another four miles, turning here and there, and then headed up a long winding hill.

"It's not too far. The Smith's lived near the top. He controlled the water flow."

We passed a small lake. I could see water movement from underground tunnels. That must have been what Rodney, Lacy's father, worked on. The lake was beautiful. I guessed that in summer the kids spent time cooling off in it.

"Stop right up there to your left. That's where Smitty and his family lived."

It was like Lacy's home, an empty lot with a few fallen branches from the surrounding trees. I wondered if Smitty could be my father or have some connection with him. I took some more pictures.

"You know, Gary Smith lives in Bridgeville. He's Roy's boy. I think he would have been about 16 or 17 at the time your mother was here. He was in high school. Maybe you should talk with him."

"Yeah… maybe. He's probably too old to know Lacy or too young to be my father. But who knows? I'll think about it."

We drove a little farther up the road and then turned around and headed back to her house. It was getting late, but she had no problem finding her way back. She invited me inside for a cup of coffee. I had a long drive home, but was grateful for her time so I accepted.

I followed her inside past the howling dog. A narrow pathway worn into the carpet led to a chair where she told me to sit. The inside mirrored the outside. I declined the coffee. An old wood-burning stove with a stack of split wood on one side took up the entire corner of her small living room.

She threw a few small logs in the stove. Family pictures covered the walls.

"That's my husband right there. You never know. Maybe you're a Campbell."

I studied the pictures but couldn't see anything of myself. However, I didn't rule it out.

"There are a lot of Campbell boys. Of course, they're older. Most of them have died, but they were a wild bunch. My brother-in-law sits down by the general store most days. Maybe he might remember something."

"Yeah... maybe I'll check that out before I leave."

I looked at the pictures on her wall. Whoever my father was, it didn't appear that I belonged to this family.

"Let me look up Gary's telephone number for you. He's in the phone book."

"Thank you. I'd appreciate that."

She wrote down his number. I wasn't sure about this Gary, but he was the son of a Smitty. Except this Smitty operated the waterways. I was looking for a Smitty who worked with Rodney. It might be a lead.

I thanked Hattie and asked if I could call her again. She said she'd love to have me call or visit anytime. She reminded me to drive by the general store and talk with her brother-in-law.

*   *   *

It was dusk by the time I left her. She told me the general store would be on my left after passing the school. I followed her directions and pulled into a gravel parking lot. A small tattered green gas pump sat off to the left of the store. I wondered if it worked. The dark wood building sat on a large cement foundation. I walked up the steps and pushed open a heavy spring-loaded door. The inside was surprisingly large and had just about anything needed to get by on, even frozen food.

The clerk appeared to be in her early forties. I asked her about Hattie's brother-in-law. She said he usually sat down at the end of the curb, close to the entrance, but had already gone home for the day.

Hoping for new leads, I told her my story and asked if she had grown up in Forest Glen. But she had only lived there a few years. She asked me if I had talked to Fred Bell. She said he lived in

Forest Glen and drove the school bus years ago. She got out the telephone book and wrote down his name and address for me.

Pleased with her help, I thanked her for everything. It amazed me how helpful everyone had been. I bought a coke and a chocolate bar.

Before leaving, I stopped at the door, and asked, "Does that gas pump work?"

Looking puzzled, she asked, "Yeah… did you need some gas?"

"No, I just haven't seen a gas pump that old in a long time. I wasn't sure if it was just for looks or actually worked."

She smiled. "It works."

Smiling back, I waved good-bye and left.

I would have to talk with Hattie's brother-in-law another time. I wasn't too concerned because I felt certain I'd be back again. But for now I had pictures of Lacy's and Smitty's home sites, school records with actual dates of when Laura and Lacy left Forest Glen. I also had validation about the matinee and the names of two new people to contact.

I was pleased and excited, but felt sad leaving Forest Glen. It had created an unexpected connection with Lacy that I hadn't experienced before. I felt more determined than ever to find the truth.

A Love Child's Journey

Chapter Twenty-five

I had chosen the nicest thank you cards I could find to send to Hattie and the people who helped me at Rock Creek School. I wanted to express my gratitude for their time and help. As I pulled out my notes with the school address, I noticed the retired bus driver's name and phone number from the Forest Glen store clerk. She wasn't sure when he started driving the school bus, but knew it was a long time ago.

Taking a minute to think about what to say, I dialed his number. I wasn't nervous, because I didn't need to tell him everything at this point. First, I wanted to ask what years he was the school bus driver. The phone rang twice before an older male voice answered.

I introduced myself and explained how I got his phone number. I told him briefly about finding my mother, who had passed, and now searching for my biological father. He seemed eager to help, but didn't recognize Lacy's last name. He said he started driving the school bus in 1957. Lacy had left Forest Glen before then. He invited me to his home and said I could talk with his wife. She was much older than Lacy but was a native of Forest Glen.

I thanked him for his time and told him I'd be back in touch. I wasn't disappointed at not getting information from him because I had the feeling I wouldn't. Maybe I didn't have any expectations. That wasn't healthy thinking for my search. A positive attitude would create a better outcome. I had copies of Lacy's school roster and a list of names to check out. I didn't have much enthusiasm in checking out Gary Smith. Yes, he was a Smith, but not necessarily connected to the Smith I was looking for. Hattie said he would have been around seventeen in 1955. I was looking for someone either in Lacy's class or about eight years older. I kept in mind that Lacy stated on my adoption papers that my father was eight years older than she was at the time of my conception. There may be some truth to it, and the year 1939 might be of some importance.

Lacy's attendance records fascinated me. She and Rodney stayed in Forest Glen together a month after Wilma and Laura had moved. The hushed knowledge that Rodney was sexually inappropriate with Lacy made me wonder, what happened that month? She was a child... beautiful and mature, but only thirteen. Had she become withdrawn? Did she threaten to tell on him? Lacy told me, it only happened once with Rodney. That was her only statement to me, nothing more. But was that true? Did he, out of guilt, give her outside liberties he otherwise wouldn't have? Wilma said he was very ashamed of what he'd done. If so, Lacy may have had a lot of freedom at that time.

Fathers, even adopted and step, are supposed to protect their children, not exploit them sexually. She was in the midst of puberty, when most thirteen-year-olds experience hormonal changes in their feelings and bodies.

*   *   *

I spent more time meditating and dowsing in hope of getting new ideas and leads.

I hadn't mastered meditation, but knew it was important and many of my questions would be answered if I did. That became my daily routine. I meditated, well... sat in a quiet room for twenty-five minutes each morning trying to quiet my mind. It was tempting to hurry it and get on with the dowsing, but patience was essential. At times, it seemed as if I was watching a movie in my mind. Why didn't I see the movie that my biological father starred in, complete with his name? Then I'd have my answer, simple as that. But it didn't work like that.

The intuitive reader Michael had confirmed my dowsing information. But I still wasn't ready to take off for Oregon and look for a guy who knew another guy that was into motorcycle racing with a wife named Jocelyn. And just maybe, the guy might know a Smitty linked to my father. That even sounded ridiculous to me. So I'd dowse and hope to get more practical information.

My standard practice when dowsing was first to ask permission to dowse. Then I'd ask if there was information for me. The information that came to me had nothing to do with my search. The information was spiritual and compelling, but wasn't what I wanted to receive. I could ask to speak with someone else. I think that would've been fine except I had no idea who was giving me information to begin with. But I was grateful for it and figured I needed to hear it. I'd try again the following morning.

*   *   *

A few days later I kept hearing the name Mike during my meditation. I remembered Lacy in spirit form telling me my father's and his brother's names were common. Mike was common, but the guy from Oregon was named Mike too. I didn't know what it meant, so I continued with my dowsing.

Q. How can you be sure Mike is my father?
A. Mike lived in Bridgeville.
Q. How did he know Lacy?
A. They met at the matinee.
Q. In Forest Glen?
A. Yes. Mike lived on the mountain.
Q. Did he live alone?
A. No. He lived with his family.
Q. Did he work with his family or father?
A. Yes.
Q. What is Mike's last name?
A. Mad… something.

Q. Mad what?
A. Madsen or Madison.
Q. Anything else?
A. Ponder his work.
Q. What do you mean?
A. He works in Unger at Lumberyard.
Q. Do you have another clue?
A. Look in telephone book under lumber.
Q. Can you please narrow down the lumber area in the telephone book?
A. Mike's in a Lowe's in the Paint department.
Q. Which Lowe's?
A. Unger.

I went on line and looked for a Mike Madsen or Madison. I checked every name in that area starting with Mad and got nothing. Maybe it wasn't a name. Maybe it meant angry or crazy. I had no idea, but I needed information. So, I continued dowsing.

Q. I can't find Mike Mad... anything in Unger. Can you help me with that?
A. Mike lives in Eureka.
Q. You're confusing me. Mike lives in Eureka now?
A. Yes.
Q. Where does he work?
A. Mike works at Lowe's in the paint department.
Q. In Eureka?
A. Yes.
Q. You say now that he lives in Eureka and works in Eureka?
A. Yes.

There was more information about his job in the paint department. I was confused. Why did the paint details matter? Again, I didn't feel confident enough to go to Lowe's in Eureka just yet. Something had to be missing, but I didn't know what.

*   *   *

I continued dowsing and again got information about my father being in the paint department at Lowe's. According to the information, the man I was looking for had two daughters and was going to Wyoming in late August or early September. That made no sense to me. Was the man my father or someone else? I hoped that eventually this would all make sense.

I had visited Wilma a few times, but didn't mention having gone to Forest Glen. I wanted to, but felt it would be best to wait. She'd begun to trust me and feel comfortable with me, yet the chests in the closet remained off limits. That bothered me more than anything. What big secret was she hiding? At this point, nothing would have shocked me about the family. Or was she just pretending to have more secrets to keep me visiting her?

*   *   *

Allaine was coming soon from the Middle East. We always had a lot of fun and I was a little more adventurous with her around, remembering her last visit when we found the gypsy woman. Maybe we'd go look for the guy at Lowe's. Maybe he's my father.

She planned to spend two weeks with me. The first week her daughter flew in from New York to stay with us. We hit every intuitive store between my house and San Francisco. The three of us enjoyed being together, but I didn't have time to concentrate on my search until Allaine's daughter flew home.

That evening Allaine looked at me and said, "Hey, why don't we go to Lowe's tomorrow?"

I laughed. "You mean the Lowe's in Eureka?"

"Yeah… we did find the gypsy woman."

"Yes we did and we didn't know if she actually existed when we started out. Okay, let's go."

That night I dreamed of a man in a plaid shirt with salt and pepper hair slightly receding on the sides. He was at some sort of amusement park. I told Allaine about it and she thought I should dowse before we left for Eureka to see if I could get more information about the Lowe's man.

I did and came up with the name Joe, a plaid shirt, khaki pants, mustache and Bridgeville.

"What do you think the Joe is about?" asked Allaine.

"I don't know. I thought I was looking for a Mike."

"Well… we'll keep an eye out for a clue or sign about Joe."

The day was warm, beautiful and sunny. Not too hot for July which made the drive to pleasant. Butterflies began swirling in my stomach as I exited the freeway into Eureka.

"Allaine," I asked. "What if my father's really there?"

"Well… you ask him are you my D-a-a…ddy?"

We both started laughing, which helped ease my tension.

"You sounded like a sheep," I said.

"But you're like a little lost sheep looking for her D-a-a…ddy."

We parked at Lowe's, freshened our makeup and looked around for some clue about the name Joe, but didn't see anything guessing something may come up later.

"Are you ready to go in?" She asked.

"I don't know. I'm so nervous I feel like throwing up. Look at my hands… they're shaking and I'm not sure what to say."

"Like I said…"

"I know, I know. Are you my D-a-a…ddy?"

"Take a deep breath. You'll be fine."

Walking across the big parking lot brought me to my senses. I'd been dowsing about this guy in Lowe's for months. The guy in the plaid shirt, khaki pants and oh, let's not forget the mustache and salt and pepper hair, working in the paint department. The more I thought about it the more ludicrous it sounded, but we were at Lowe's and thoughts of the gypsy woman flashed in my mind. It's a good thing I didn't share this with anyone but my family or I might've been locked away.

The lights inside the store were almost as bright as the sun outside. We stopped and looked for the paint department sign.

I gasped! "There it is."

I could walk to the paint department and check out the workers without saying anything to anyone. As we got closer, my hopes dwindled. Three younger ladies were working in the paint department. Maybe he wasn't working that day or was on a break.

We walked up to the counter and a worker came to help us. I asked her if Mike was working today. She said they didn't have a guy named Mike working there. Only females worked in the paint department. I asked if she knew an older guy named Mike who worked in any area of the store. She didn't. I asked her if any older guys worked at Lowe's at all. I was grasping for anything. As crazy as it seemed, my hopes were high that I might find my father there. The help I got from the spirit world or whoever, was at times off, but right now I wanted it on. I'd waited six months for this trip. The spirit world had plenty of time to set it all up.

The young woman at the paint counter told me that the oldest men working were in the next two aisles. I thanked her and we turned and headed to our right.

We saw the two older guys, who seemed to be in our age range. I looked at Allaine and said, "If this is her definition of old, we're screwed."

It was hard to hide my disappointment. "I can't believe we came all this way with all these clues and he's not even here."

Allaine was optimistic. "Why don't we check all the aisles just to make sure?"

"Maybe we could use their PA system and page the guy with a mustache and salt and pepper hair wearing a plaid shirt and khaki pants. It would save us a lot of time."

"Come on," she said. "Let's start down here."

We walked to the last aisle on our right, only three down from where we were. The first aisle had no one in it. Allaine and I about had heart attacks when we looked down the next aisle.

"Oh my Gosh. There he is, looking at the molding," she said.

My mouth gaped in disbelief. Slowly I said, "Yeah... older man, plaid shirt, khaki pants, salt and pepper hair with a mustache."

"I have a plan," she whispered in excitement.

"Okay... but what if he really is my father?"

"That would be good... wouldn't it?"

"Yeah... I hope so."

"Let's pretend we're looking at molding for our house in Forest Glen. Maybe that will spark his attention. You check the molding, I don't know anything about it."

"It's not as if we're going to buy some, but sounds like a good plan."

I walked slowly toward him. My face and ears felt on fire. Warm moist sweat beads formed on my forehead. I could only see his profile. I strained to see myself in him. He wasn't very tall, a good sign. His plaid shirt wasn't as dark as the one in my dream, but it was definitely plaid. Everything seemed to fit. Was this the father I'd been searching two long years for? Here, in Lowe's? I wondered if his name was Mike and if he was kind. My head spun with anticipation and my legs were on auto-pilot as I continued walking toward him.

Trying to act nonchalant, I kept my eyes on him, and stopped about three feet away. He looked at me and smiled. I smiled back. He seemed nice. Nice hair and the right age range. He looked back at the molding.

Allaine, in an increasingly loud voice said, "DO... YOU... THINK... THAT... MOLDING... WILL... BE... GOOD.... FOR... OUR... HOME... IN... FORRESST....... GLENNN?"

It was hard to keep from laughing. I'm sure he heard her. Probably people in the other aisles heard her too, but it didn't faze him. He continued inspecting the molding without looking up. I couldn't turn around or I'd have busted into laughter. He might have been hard of hearing, but he didn't appear to have any issues with understanding what was being said. I wasn't sure why Allaine did that, but the humor of it calmed me down.

I edged myself closer to him, less than an arm's length away, and leaned over to get a better look at his face. I'm sure he was wondering what in the world I was doing. Maybe he thought I was trying to flirt or something, but he didn't move. I tried hard to see some part of myself in him. He had light brown eyes. I decided I either needed to start talking with him or totally block his view from the molding, which I had already partially done.

Feeling brave, I asked, "How are you today?"

He looked at me. "I'm okay and you?"

"Fine," I answered.

He focused on the molding again. I needed to be braver and ask him some questions before he started feeling uncomfortable. I was standing practically on top of him.

"Do you live in the Eureka area?"

"No. I live in Bridgeville."

I turned and glared at Allaine. Her eyes were bigger than silver dollars. Bridgeville was one of our clues. A man with plaid shirt and khaki pants drove from Bridgeville to the Lowe's store in Eureka and we were here at the same time. Bridgeville was an hour away. Was I looking at my biological father?

"Do you mind if I ask your name?"

"Willy. Well, it's really Edward William, but I go by Willy."

Disappointed that it wasn't Mike, I still felt there had to be a connection to this guy. Maybe I had the name wrong. I decided to tell him why we were there. I had nothing to lose. Worse case, he might just think we were crazy.

I introduced Allaine and myself, explained to him that I was searching for my biological father and had found information that led me to Lowe's. I explained that I was conceived in Forest Glen and my biological father may have lived in Bridgeville.

He smiled. "So you think I may be your father?"

I hesitated. "Well... I did wonder."

"How did you get your information?"

"Meditating, praying, dowsing, divine help, some friends call it my *airy fairy* information."

He laughed. Good, I thought. He didn't call for security. Confronted by two women, one who thinks he might be her father because a prayer or pendulum told her so, and he was just trying to buy some molding. The whole thing sounded crazy, but he didn't budge.

"Well... I'm sorry to disappoint you, but I know I'm not your father. My wife and I moved from back east to Bridgeville three years ago and I have only one son, here, in Eureka. We moved to be closer to him."

His voice was so kind and he seemed to feel my disappointment. Why would I be directed to this man? He fit all the details, but he wasn't my father. His coloring was right, but I couldn't see anything of myself in him. He did have nice hair though.

After an awkward moment of silence he said, "If I were you, I'd go to Bridgeville and check the Chamber of Commerce and the

Bridgeville Library. Maybe you'll find something in one of those places."

I had mentioned about looking for a Smith or Smitty guy, but the name didn't ring a bell for him.

"It was nice talking with you gals and I wish you luck in finding your father, but I've got to head over to Home Depot to see if I can find the molding I'm looking for."

I thanked him for his help and watched him leave.

"Wow, that was wild," said Allaine.

"Yeah it was. Interesting that he told us to go to the Bridgeville Chamber of Commerce and the library.

"I think he was here to make us go to Bridgeville, so let's go," Allaine said jubilantly.

"I think you're right. It's an hour away, but we might as well. It seems we're being directed to go there."

A Love Child's Journey

Chapter Twenty-six

It felt good heading toward Forest Glen. I was hoping we'd have time to go there later, but our first destination was Bridgeville.

"I haven't been to Bridgeville before, have you?" I asked Allaine.

"Yeah... when I was thirteen. Nammie wouldn't let me change my clothes for a whole week as punishment. I ran away to my friend's house. I didn't even get out of Oildale. She had the police pick me up. The whole ordeal backfired on her and she had one of her screaming crazy episodes at the police station. After that they wouldn't let me go home with her. Mom had to come down from Idaho and get me. It was hard leaving my friends in Oildale, but more than anything, I wanted to say goodbye to my boyfriend, Hank. He'd just moved to Bridgeville. Mom drove me there to say goodbye to him."

"Wow! That was nice of her to do that," I said. "Did you know the Forest Glen exit is right off this road?"

"Really? I always thought it was off Interstate 80."

"Yeah, me too, but during one of my first visits with Wilma or Nammie, she told me it was off this road."

"Well, at least you got something from her. That blows me away. Mom, Mitch and I drove all this way to Bridgeville. A hundred miles out of the way so I could say goodbye to my boyfriend on our way to Idaho. We drove right past this turn off to where she had lived and you were conceived without saying a word."

"A little odd, don't you think?"

"Yeah, I do."

"That's what makes me think that maybe she cared very deeply for my father. I mean... think about it. She drove a hundred miles out of the way to give you, at the age of thirteen, the opportunity to say goodbye to your boyfriend. Remember, that Wilma didn't let her go back to Forest Glen because she felt Lacy was acting too grown up."

"That's right. I remember you telling me Nammie mentioned seeing her panties. That's too weird. Nammie's such a prude, I can't believe she told you that."

"Well... she was talking as if Lacy had been raped, but no one did anything about it. I think she realized Lacy had had sex so there was no way Wilma was going to let her go back to Forest Glen. Lacy didn't have the opportunity to say goodbye to whoever got her pregnant."

" Pretty sad. She told me things about her "job" things that you don't tell kids, but nothing about Forest Glen or how you truthfully came about."

"There's a good possibility she really loved my father."

"I think so too."

We stopped at a turnout right before descending the mountain to Bridgeville. It was a beautiful view. Allaine took her usual pictures. She enjoyed taking pictures everywhere.

We were both hungry and decided to get something to eat. Before entering Bridgeville, a large sign read Joe's Pizza. Allaine and I saw it at the same time. It wasn't hard to miss, since there was nothing else around it.

"Did you see that sign for Joes's Pizza?" she asked.

"Yeah, that's a little freaky."

"We have to eat there," she said.

"Is that why we came to Bridgeville?"

"Sure. To have lunch at Joe's and be there when your Da-a-a....dddy comes in."

"Sounds good to me."
"To me too."
"The pizza or my dad?"
We laughed. At least our sense of humor was in tact.

Joe's Pizza was at the far end of Bridgeville. We passed the Bridgeville Chamber of Commerce, so we knew where to go when we finished eating.

It was a small quaint restaurant operated by two older women. One made the pizza, and the other was cashier. Allaine and I were the only ones in there, so I didn't have to look around for my dad.

We fantasized my father walking through the door, but that was wishful thinking. Allaine and I tried to figure out the Joe name. What part of my search did it connect with? We decided not to over-think it and enjoy our lunch. Moments before we were done eating, I heard the squeaking of the entrance door. Allaine and I both turned our heads. A young man with two small children entered. A father all right, but I was old enough to be his mother. Not our guy. Before leaving, we spoke briefly with the cashier. She hadn't lived in Bridgeville long, and was unable to help us. We left Joe's Pizza disappointed at not getting new information or more clues.

We parked on the main street in front of the small Chamber of Commerce. It appeared to have been a small house at one time. Its grounds were beautiful. Flowers lined a walkway leading to a bench on freshly mowed grass. People were coming and going. Inside we talked to a woman about our age. We asked for any information about the businesses there and some history of Bridgeville or Forest Glen. She handed us a small telephone book, some brochures and told us we might want to go to the library around the corner for more history information.

She gave us directions to the library, only a few blocks away.

The library wasn't much bigger than the Chamber of Commerce, but it had been built like a library. Inside, a large fluffy cat lay sprawled across one of the two tables.

I whispered to Allaine. "I guess we move the cat if we want to sit down and look at a book."

"It appears so, but it's kind of cool."

A woman with short blonde hair asked, "Can I help you find something?"

"I hope so," I said. "We're looking for some history of the Bridgeville and Forest Glen area and the names of people who may have lived here in the mid fifties."

She showed us where to look. There wasn't much to find, mostly small pamphlets, but they were chronologically dated back to the forties. Allaine took the 1954 pamphlets and I took 1955. We sat down by the cat, which didn't move. Allaine didn't find anything helpful, but enjoyed petting the cat. I found the family of a guy named Garold Smith. His family eventually moved back to Eureka. Maybe this was the guy. Michael the intuitive said I was looking for a Gary or Jerry Smith. Maybe his name was Garold and he went by Gary.

Looking through the small telephone book, Allaine said, "Hey, here's that Gary Smith guy you said the elderly woman told you about. It has his phone number and address. Maybe we should go see him."

"I'm not sure he can help us. Besides, I found this guy named Garold Smith in Eureka. I think we should go back there. We aren't having much luck here."

"But, Gary's very close to Jerry, and you're here in Bridgeville. It can't hurt to see him. Get this, he lives on Juniper. You know, the same street the Lowe's is on. There could be a connection. There's a map of Bridgeville in the phone book that shows where Juniper Street is. I say, before we head back we should go see this Gary guy. You never know, maybe he's the Smith you're looking for."

"Yeah... maybe you're right. For all I know, he's the reason we were led to Bridgeville. Maybe he's the guy with two daughters who's going to Wyoming in August since it wasn't the guy at Lowe's like I thought. But what'll I say? What would you say to him?"

"I don't know. You didn't seem to have a problem with the guy in Lowe's."

"That's true, but I was scared and nervous. You're right though. We're here, so I should at least talk to him. He did live in Forest Glen at the right time."

*   *   *

Juniper Street was less than a mile from the library. My stomach started to rumble and my heart beat faster. I didn't want to be nervous, but my body must have felt differently. I kept thinking, this guy will wonder what space ship I got off of and might suggest I get back on it.

"There it is," yelled Allaine.

"Third house from the corner. Nice house and the lawn neatly manicured."

I was surprised. Maybe I was thinking about when I found Lacy and expected someone less fortunate like her. Could this guy be my father or maybe another brother? I'd have to wait and see, but it made me tremble. Either way, if he was, my search could be over. The hole in Lacy's heart and soul would mend. I studied the house and the large tree in front. Had he lived there a long time?

Allaine, said, "It looks like you'd better park across the street. You don't want to park on his grass."

I parked across the street. A truck sat on the right side of the driveway.

"It doesn't look like anyone's home," I said, after parking.

"You never know. Just go knock on the door and see."

I felt certain no one was there, but I got out and knocked on the door anyway. With the front window draperies open, I could see inside and through a sliding glass door. It was nice and neat, but no lights were on. I could see part of a neatly mowed back yard and a travel trailer parked off to the side. It didn't look like the people who lived there would be gone long. I ran back to the car.

"No one home?" asked Allaine.

"No, but maybe they'll be back soon. Let's drive around the back."

"Why?"

"I don't know. I just think we should."

We drove around to the backside of the house. Country style apartments began at the edge of his property. We pulled into the apartments and parked.

"I think we should wait here for a while," I said.
"Okay. Let's use my new Doreen Virtue oracle cards that I got in San Francisco and see what they say."
"Can't hurt. We've done everything else."
I watched as Allaine read about how to use her cards. She tapped on them three times, and then began shuffling them.
"I'm going to ask what we should do now," she said.
"Good idea, because at this point I have no clue."
She pulled a card from the deck and said, "Meditate. I drew the card that says Meditate."
"Now? I have a hard enough time meditating at home when it's quiet and I'm alone."
"Let me read it to you."
"Okay... it's not like I have a better suggestion."
"This card is a call for you to meditate regularly. Your path, body, and soul are asking for quiet time to reflect, think, and receive insights."
Allaine stopped reading. "What do you think?"
"Well... I've been thinking and reflecting about this for a few years, but what we do now, at this moment, I have no idea."
"I think we need to pray and do a little meditating while we wait. Pray for this Gary Smith to come home."
"Great idea. I think that's about all we have right now."
I closed my eyes and asked God and everyone in the spirit world to help me. To please have Gary return to his home before we had to leave Bridgeville. We sat quietly for a while longer. Finally, we decided to leave. I drove slowly past the Smith's house. Much to my surprise there was a car parked in their driveway that wasn't there earlier.
"Oh my God, someone's home," gasped Allaine.
"I see that."
My heart was pounding so hard; it was like a train rumbling faster and faster on its track. I drove down Juniper, made a U-turn, and parked across the street from his house.
"Don't forget your pictures." Allaine reminded me.
"Aren't you going with me?"
"No. I'm waiting in the car."
"Chicken!"

She laughed. "It's your search."

"Thanks a lot." I teased.

I grabbed my pictures and went to the door. Everything seemed to blur. So far, everyone had been kind, but would he? Was there a possibility he was my father? My head was spinning with thoughts. I looked back at Allaine in the car. She motioned me to ring the doorbell. Easy for her, she's in the car, far from the door.

I took a deep breath and pushed the doorbell. The door opened almost immediately. There stood an attractive, slightly rounded woman with light brown hair in her early sixties.

"Hi, my name is Colette Cooper. Does Gary Smith live here?"

She backed away from the door and yelled to her husband. I could hear his footsteps as he neared the door.

"I'm Gary Smith. Can I help you?"

A tall, slender man much younger looking than I expected stood in front of me. His voice was deep but soft. He had dark receding hair and dark eyes. I studied him, but couldn't see any resemblance between us.

I explained briefly to both of them about my search and how, since he had lived in Forest Glen in the fifties, I was hoping he might have known Lacy and her family.

Gary and his wife Diane invited me into their home and I felt welcomed. They listened intently to the rest of my story, including Lacy's supposed rape, which I didn't believe was true. Gary didn't remember hearing of such a thing. I showed them pictures of Lacy, myself and my son, school records and my adoption papers.

"How did you get my name," Gary asked.

I wanted to be truthful with these wonderful people, but didn't want them to think I was crazy. Nevertheless, I still thought that honesty was the best no matter what the outcome.

"Well... actually, I got the name Smith or Smitty from an intuitive. But Hattie Campbell gave me your name last February when I was in Forest Glen. I didn't contact you then because I didn't think you were the right age or the right Smith."

I wondered when I finished that sentence whether they would ask me to leave, but they didn't. These people were amazingly kind.

"Colette, we consider ourselves open-minded and try not to judge what other people do or believe," said Diane.

"There were other Smiths in that area as well as my family, but we weren't connected to any them," Gary said.

"I realize that Smith is a common name. I've been on some wild excursions looking for someone in another Smith family who worked with Lacy's father, but not in Forest Glen. I just want to know who my father is."

"If I were you, I'd want to know too," Gary said.

"Colette, what age range are you looking for?" asked Diane.

"My birth mother stated on my adoption papers that my birth father was eight years older than her."

"Do you think she was telling the truth, especially when you say other things she said aren't true?"

"I'm not sure. I keep coming across the year 1939, in my search, but I don't know if it means anything."

"Is someone in the car waiting for you?" she asked.

"Yes, that's my sister, Allaine. My birth mother's other daughter."

"Well, have her come in."

I ran outside to the car and gave Allaine a quick run-down about the Smiths who wanted her to come in and join us, and how kind and compassionate they'd been.

After introductions, Allaine backed up some of what I had told them.

The pictures I took in Forest Glen surprised Gary. I told him Hattie had shown me where his house had been.

His voice soft but stern, he asked, "Colette, do you think I'm your father?"

"Not now, but I wasn't sure when I knocked on your door. I was told that a Smitty was either my father or would lead me to my father."

His voice still soothing but matter of fact, he said, "One thing a guy knows and that's who they've done, and I didn't do your mother. She does look familiar. I might have seen her at a party

275

or something, but if I thought there was any possibility, I'd say let's do a DNA test."

"Thank you for that, Gary."

"You know, there's one thing we could do that might help you out. We're going to Wyoming in a month or so to visit some of my close friends. They lived in Forest Glen when we were young and we get together each year. I could ask them if they knew your mother or have any ideas or information that may help you."

"Gary, I'd appreciate that so much."

"Maybe you could send us some copies of your pictures and information so we could show everyone. You never know, maybe one of them will know something," said Diane.

"I'll make copies and send them to you right away."

Diane said, "Colette, we feel it's important for everyone to know where they came from."

It was all I could do to hold back my tears. I wished Gary was my father. Their kindness and empathy was overwhelming. Here they were, willing to help a perfect stranger find her father. If everyone opened their hearts the way these people did, the world would instantly be a better place.

Hugging them goodbye, I asked, "Do you have children?"

"Yes, we have two daughters," said Diane.

I shot a look at Allaine. Her eyes were wide with shock.

"Is something wrong?" Gary asked.

"No... it's just that some of my information had me looking for a man with two daughters, but I'd forgotten about it until now."

They both smiled. We exchanged address and phone numbers. I thanked them again for their hospitality and interest.

Allaine and I couldn't get to the car fast enough to hash over what had just happened.

"WOW...WOW... WOW. This is wild," said Allaine in the car. "Colette, he's your guy, he's the one who is suppose to help you find your father."

"I know. I know. When I first got his name I didn't act on it, so God and the spirit world sent me to the man in Lowe's wearing the plaid shirt and khaki pants who directed us to Bridgeville. Then I was ready to leave Bridgeville, but you said no, let's go see this Gary guy first. Thank you so much for being here with me."

"You know... our energy together is pretty strong. Remember... we found the gypsy woman, so we're going to find your father too."

"I feel strong about it too. I think it's meant to be."

"But, I wonder, what's the connection with the name Joe?"

"I don't know. The Smith's didn't say anything about it when I mentioned it. We'll have to wait and see. I bet that name will come up again."

"Well, that seems to be the way your search has been going. Just like today. You get clues that don't make any sense, but later they do. It's like one giant puzzle."

"Boy, it sure is. Michael is going to be pleased that he was right on target with the name Smitty.

"That's great validation for him as an intuitive reader. "

"Yes, it is. I need to get the pictures off in the mail tomorrow."

"I'll be interesting to see what the Smiths come up with from their friends in Wyoming."

A Love Child's Journey

Chapter Twenty-Seven

The next day Allaine and I made copies of all documents related to my search. She helped me pick out pictures. Oddly enough, knowing my pictures would be seen by a lot of people, I wasn't too concerned with how good I looked in them. It didn't matter. I wanted the Smiths to present their friends with as much information as possible. Anything that might help wrap their memory around my birth mother and possible father.

I wasn't as beautiful as Lacy, and actually didn't look much like her at all. I still didn't know if I resembled my father. Was he ugly, handsome, or in between like most people. I wasn't an ugly duckling, just not a beauty queen like my mother. I hoped someone would recognize either me or my son in somebody from their teen years in Forest Glen. My son looks a great deal like me and I thought it might be easier to recognize another male with similar characteristics.

Earlier I called Michael to tell him I might have found the right Smith or Smitty with a close first name Gary instead of Jerry. He was elated. It's important for intuitive readers to hear validation for correct or helpful information from their readings. I appreciated validation on dowsing. Michael reminded me his guide had channeled the information. I told him to thank his guide for me. He laughed.

I scheduled a reading for Allaine and I the following evening. I couldn't wait to hear what he had to say, or rather, what his guide had to say. I'd listen to whoever would talk to me as long as I could get information leading to my biological father.

I was more convinced than ever that it was meant for me to find my birth father. God and the spirit world were working with me and I truly appreciated it. Listen and pay attention the keys in my own dowsing. I thought about the guy in Lowe's. It was amazing, unbelievable and helpful, to say the least. I still didn't understand the whole paint department deal. The guy I found was buying molding, not paint. But that's what I was told—by my spirit guides or whoever talks to me. Whenever I pay attention and listen, I seemed to get pointed in the right direction.

*   *   *

Michael was waiting for us at Twilight Greetings. Allaine went first. I paced the store waiting for my turn. I always seemed to be in such a hurry to give away my money there. But to me, it was a bargain. I wondered what Michael's guide would say today. Although Gary Smith was a quiet man who kept his thoughts to himself, I believed he was the key to my father. I wasn't sure in what way, and he seemed unsure himself, but I felt strongly that he was my link. His wife knew many of the people from Forest Glen, but lived in Bridgeville as a teenager. Gary had lived in Forest Glen at the time of my conception.

My turn with Michael finally came. I didn't want to rush Allaine. She was leaving in a few days for Kuwait and wouldn't be back for a year. Kuwait wasn't a place to get readings. I could get a reading every day if I could afford it. Michael reminded me that I really didn't need to keep coming back, that I was getting information through my own dowsing and I was very intuitive. But I lacked confidence and needed validation and confirmation. I got that through Michael and Angel.

I gave Michael the details of the trip to Lowe's and Bridgeville. He smiled in amusement but not surprised.

"So what do you think?" I asked. "Or what does your guide think about all this?"

"Let me go into my space."

Familiar with his ritual, I sat back in my chair and relaxed. I had learned not to talk until he tells me to. That was a feat in itself.

Michael opened his eyes. "What do you want to ask?"

"Well... this Gary Smith. He's not my father and his father's not my father, but they called his dad Smitty. Why was I led to him?"

He closed his eyes again. "He is one you are here to heal."

"Oh yeah... I remember you told me about this healing I'm supposed to do. But, what connection is he to my father?"

"Your biological parents are not the most important. Many past lives connect."

Maybe he or his guide doesn't think it's the most important thing and maybe it sounds selfish, but right now it is to me. Michael paused, and let me think about what he'd just said. My journey was to help heal Lacy and find the truth about her becoming pregnant at thirteen. She kept it so secret it must have been dear to her heart and so painful that she buried it deep within her soul. I couldn't deny the selfishness of wanting it for myself. I needed to know who I came from, but mostly I wanted the truth to be known... no more secrets.

Michael continued. "I'm seeing a map. Is Bridgeville north of here?"

"Yes."

"I'm seeing a road leading to southern Oregon."

"Lacy's sister Laura, lived in Oregon, but she passed."

"She knew."

"You mean Laura knew who my father was?"

"Yes, Lacy told her and she didn't have a high opinion of him. Was Laura jealous of your mother?"

"I heard she was. Lacy was a beauty. Why are you asking?"

"Your mother and her sister are reconciling on the other side. Laura says Lacy was an ass or her behavior was that of an ass."

"Yeah... that could be true."

"Laura wants to help you now. There's a lot of healing going on."

"That's great... but could you mention that I'd really appreciate it if they'd move along with their clues?"

He smiled. "You will find your father, but not right now. The clues you'll need will appear in your dreams and all is in divine order. Keep communicating with this Gary. By Christmas this year, you will know who your father is. And then... you'll become a healer through spontaneous healing."

"That sounds encouraging. So I'll know who my father is by the end of the year?"

"That's what my guide's telling me."

"That would be wonderful. Thanks, Michael. You know I'll be back."

Allaine and I shared our readings on the way home. She was as excited as me and got a kick out of Laura seeing Lacy's behavior as that of an ass. She understood why Laura made the comment.

* * *

Allaine left a few days later and I felt a little melancholy. That feeling became more the norm after her yearly visit. There had been such a close connection between us, and my heart ached when she left. She was like my partner in crime, my backup companion in my search. In the last few years of her visits, amazing things always happened and our bond became stronger. We hadn't been raised together, our ties began much later in life, but most outsiders would never have guessed. Finding the gypsy woman, then finding the Smitty or Gary Smith. Things just seemed to propel forward when she was here, but now she was back teaching in Kuwait. There was no doubt that I would continue my search. I was excited at the possibility of finding my father by Christmas, my favorite holiday.

* * *

My spirits lifted when I got a call from Diane Smith. Gary had called one of the friends they were planning to visit in Wyoming and asked him about Lacy. The friend knew who she was, but had moved away before she became pregnant. She gave me the man's name and number, and said he was fine with me calling him to ask questions.

I wanted to leap through the phone and give her and Gary both a big hug. It was hard for me to comprehend the help they were willing to give me. Their kindness was amazing. I'm not sure I'd have been willing to help a stranger who showed up on my doorstep with some offbeat story. They were non-judgmental people, a rare trait. I thanked her and told her I'd call him later that evening.

I wasn't sure what to say to the guy, but felt relieved that he knew Lacy and about my search for my father. I began tensing up as I dialed his number. I was certain he wasn't my father, but he remembered Lacy. I slowly entered the numbers on the telephone, while my heart rate increased as usual. I took a few deeps breaths.

A deep gruff voice cheerfully said, "Hello."

"Hello. This is Colette Cooper. I got your number from the Smiths in Bridgeville."

"Oh yeah... Lacy's daughter."

Relieved by the friendly tone in his voice, I said, "Yes."

"You know I'm not your father, right?"

"Yes. I realize that."

"Your mom was my girlfriend, well... I called her my girlfriend when she was in sixth grade and I was in the eighth. She was very quiet. Her sister Laura was more outspoken, but Lacy was such a beauty. She was a nice girl too. Years later, I thought I saw her in San Diego, but didn't get a chance to confirm it. Always wished I had. The Mackenzie family lived across the road from Lacy. There was only about half-a-dozen houses around at that time. Daisy Campbell seemed to be her closest friend. You might want to talk with her. And rest assured if I thought I was your father I'd have no problem taking a DNA test. But we moved away from Forest Glen right after I graduated from the eighth grade. I wasn't around when Lacy became pregnant with you."

"I appreciate your taking the time to talk with me."

"Lacy was something. I wish you luck in finding your father."

"Thank you."

As I hung up the phone, I felt warm heat slowly work its way all through me. It was comforting to hear nice things about Lacy. Although he didn't say anything about it, I think he was sad knowing that she had passed away, which I assumed Gary must have told him.

*   *   *

Over three weeks had gone by and I hadn't heard from the Smiths. Each day I struggled with the desire to call them, but realized my priority was not theirs. They were busy getting ready to go to Wyoming. I did want to make sure they received the package I sent. I didn't want them annoyed at my impatient behavior.

Meanwhile, I made another visit to Michael the reader. I'd been meditating or working on meditating along with dowsing. But all the information I received was about my spiritual path or what to do after I found my father. I was to become a soul healer. It was a good idea. How wonderful to help people, but my present goal was still to find my father. Like Michael, I couldn't direct the information coming to me, but I continued to try. It must have been a spiritual joke to whoever was giving me information.

Michael's guide must have been working with whoever gives me information. His reading was more of the same. He said my gift is to work with soul genealogy, then he explained it.

Eyes closed and forehead wrinkled he said slowly, "The genealogy of a parent does not always destine the child. Say the father was a doctor and wanted his child to become a doctor, but the child is actually connected to a long line of soul artists and not doctors. This child's soul is drawn toward being an artist, who is not understood by the child's doctor father and creates unsettled issues in this lifetime."

"Makes sense. It would be great to help people."

"People will be placed in front of you who need your ability."

"Well, could you ask them to place my father in front of me too?"

He laughed. "It's all about the journey. As we were told before, divine timing."

283

"Yes, I know. Patience must be something I'm supposed to be working on, because this search requires a lot of it."

*   *   *

I'd waited long enough and decided to call the Smiths. I wanted to make sure they received my package of information.

Diane answered. She confirmed that they got it, but hadn't had a chance to go through it. She was surprised I hadn't received the e-mail she sent a week earlier. They were having trouble with their Internet and she promised to re-send the message.

"Colette, the information from our "network" came up with Suzanne Mackenzie Daniels. She lives in Eureka, but her family lived across the road from Lacy. I believe she was a few years older than Lacy, but the closest in age. One of her older brothers Roscoe was a best friend with Gary. They moved from Forest Glen, but I'm not sure when."

My heart began bouncing like a rubber ball, "That's a good lead. Who's the "network"?

She chuckled. "Oh, I just call them that, but it's the people we're still in contact with who lived in Forest Glen while we were growing up."

"That's pretty amazing after all these years that you have kept in contact."

"It is. Anyway, I sent you her phone number and address via e-mail. Gary feels certain that Roscoe isn't your father, they were glued at the hip, but there was an older brother out of school. We thought maybe Suzanne might remember Lacy or be of some help."

"Thank you so much, Diane. You and Gary have been more than kind and so helpful."

"Colette, Gary and I both feel that everyone has a right to know where they came from. So... we want to help you as much as we can."

A lump filled my throat as I hung up the phone. It took a few deep breaths to hold back my tears that had welled up in my eyes. I wished Gary had been my biological father. I could only hope that when I found the real one, he would be as kind.

Excited, I tried calling Suzanne right away, but no answer. I tried a few more times, but kept getting her answering machine. We were heading to the mountains for a long weekend, so I decided to wait until we returned home. Maybe she was on a vacation herself. Based on the answering machine message, I had the right phone number for her.

*　　　*　　　*

I enjoyed relaxing in the mountains. A place my husband and I went every summer. It was less than an hour drive away, and we kept our motor home there. Having bought a new one, the previous year made our stays longer and more enjoyable. It was like a first rate hotel on wheels. The mountains were a wonderful place to meditate and dowse.

My sister-in-law and her husband joined us with their trailer. During dinner one evening, my sister-in-law, soft spoken and quiet asked how my search was going. I filled her in on my trip to Bridgeville and meeting the Smiths. She told me about a friend of hers who lived in Bridgeville, but grew up in Forest Glen. The friend was close to my age, but might be able to help me in some way. I was amazed. What were the chances of one of my relatives having a good friend living in Bridgeville who grew up in Forest Glen? She told me she'd call and give me her friend's number when she got home.

I was paying attention and help was all around me. Who would have thought our once a year camping get together with my sister-in-law would give me a lead in my search? I was grateful and thanked God and the spirit world immensely.

*　　　*　　　*

Home from the mountains, I tried calling Suzanne Mackenzie Daniels again. Waiting a few days made it easier to call. I didn't have my usual nervous jitters.

Someone answered. A soft-spoken woman said, "Hello."

"Hello… my name is Colette Cooper, I'm looking for Suzanne Mackenzie Daniels."

In a more assertive tone, she said, "I'm Suzanne."

"I understand your family lived in Forest Glen around the first part of the year in 1955. And you have a brother older than Roscoe who lived with you too."

"Why are you asking these questions?"

"Do you remember Lacy Fisherman who lived near you in Forest Glen?"

"Vaguely. The name sounds familiar."

She seemed uncomfortable with our conversation. "She became pregnant with me around mid February of 1955, she's no longer living and I'm searching for my biological father."

"I can't help you. We moved long before that."

"But, don't you have an older brother, older than Roscoe?"

"Yes." She sounded irritated. "But he was away in the military at that time. I can't help you with this. I wasn't in Forest Glen at that time. Goodbye."

It felt like she couldn't get me off the phone fast enough, as if she was trying to hide something or I was invading her privacy. It was clear she didn't want to be involved with this search or contribute anything.

I kept her number just in case. I got the impression she didn't believe I was connected to either of her brothers.

An hour after my conversation with Suzanne my sister-in-law called. A positive twist, I thought, hoping her friend would be more helpful. She told me her friend's name—Stephanie—her number, and told me to say hi from her. I didn't know what to ask. I figured I'd start with my search information and see where the conversation ended up. I was certain I was supposed to talk with her.

I waited until evening to call, giving her a chance to settle from her day and have dinner out of the way. I didn't know what if any information Stephanie could have. The fact that she grew up in Forest Glen was a good friend of my sister-in-law and now lived in Bridgeville, seemed like a good connection.

The telephone rang two times before a cheerful woman said, "Hello."

"Is this Stephanie?" I asked.

"Yes… I'm Stephanie."

"My name is Colette. I'm Rhonda's sister-in-law. She gave me your number."

"Oh yeah...Rhonda. How's she doing?"

"She's great and says hi. She thought maybe you might be able to help me."

I told her a short version of my story, the progress with my search and about meeting the Smiths. She knew Gary. He was retired, but they'd worked for the same company. She said he was a nice man. I agreed.

"How did you get all this information?"

Hesitant to admit how I received my information, I paused. "Well... actually, a lot of it through intuitive readings and my own dowsing."

Half expecting her to hang up or tell me she'll get back to me later or don't call me, I'll call you, but she didn't.

Her voice pitched up in excitement as if she just won a jackpot of gold, "I know who you need to talk with."

Caught up in her excitement, I said, "You do?"

"Yeah. Dick Thomas. He's a dowser and works with electromagnetic energies. He's helped us. You never know, maybe he can help you. I did grow up in Forest Glen, but I'm around your age. A different generation from what you're looking for. I think you should call Dick. Would you like his number?"

"That would be wonderful."

I waited while she searched for his phone number. Maybe Dick was the reason I was directed to contact her. It was another lead, regardless of what Dick could do for me. I was very grateful.

She gave me his number. I thanked her and said I'd be in touch.

*   *   *

The following day I called Dick. He owned a barbershop in town and said he dowsed for wells, dealt with noxious energies and electromagnetic energies. He was fascinating to talk with. I explained about my search and asked him if he'd have time to see me. He invited me to his home on the outskirts of Bridgeville where he and his wife lived. He gave me the days that would be good for him and I told him I'd call back to confirm a day.

Diane and Gary wouldn't leave for Wyoming for another two weeks. I had more information and pictures for them, and tapes of Michael's reading they wanted to hear. I e-mailed Diane to tell her about Stephanie and Dick, and that I'd like to see her and Gary again.

She e-mailed me back saying they'd love to see me and anytime within the next week would be fine. They knew both Stephanie and Dick and considered them good people. The next part of the e-mail seemed odd; she asked if my son or I had any artistic or musical talent. I didn't question why she asked and later forgot about it.

I called Dick and asked if the coming Saturday would be a good day for our meeting. He said it would be fine. I e-mailed Diane that I would like to see her and Gary after my meeting with Dick on Saturday. And my mother, Mom wanted to try her luck at the local Indian casino while I was visiting. I mentioned my son was musical and played the saxophone. I played drums as a teenager, much to the distress of my parents. And I enjoyed writing stories and throwing pots on a pottery wheel.

Her return e-mail said they were looking forward to seeing me. I wanted to visit Gary and Diane again, but I was excited about meeting Dick.

A Love Child's Journey

Chapter Twenty-Eight

Mom and I left early in the morning to ensure our arrival in Bridgeville at noon. I'd be meeting Dick at the barbershop he owned.

The days had been warm lately, but fall was just around the corner. Driving to Bridgeville with my mom was enjoyable. No matter how long the time we spend together; we never run out of words. Especially me. I was the talker and she the listener, a good match. Talking was never my problem, only stopping.

Mom had turned eighty-four a few months earlier, but had no trouble getting around. She had a passion for gambling and she could afford it so that became her hobby. She continued to be supportive of my search. Sure, she found it intriguing and wanted to know the answers, but more importantly, she wanted it for me. She was so happy for me when I found Lacy. She hoped the outcome would be just as welcoming when I found my birth father. Every passing day I felt more grateful for her and my wonderful family. My mother's love and support had been unconditional.

Eighteen years ago my dad passed, and at times, I really missed him. Maybe missing my dad enhanced the desire to find my biological father. One thing for sure, I continued to have a nagging pain in my heart to find my birth father. He didn't define who I was, but it was important to know who I came from. I wanted to know him; I wanted him to know me. The person he helped create and the person I had become. Nothing more, but nothing less.

We had an enjoyable ride despite gray skies from the smoke of wildfires burning throughout the state. This year had become one of California's worst fire seasons.

*   *   *

It didn't bother Mom that we arrived too early to check into our hotel. She wanted to start gambling. Not far off the main road, the casino wasn't large, but she didn't care. Built like a large exhibit barn at the state fair, but if it had machines with money slots and handles to pull, Mom would be happy. It was a nice town, but I wanted to make sure there was some type of security inside. She was tough, but not that tough.

"Just drop me off at the front door," she told me.

"Mom, don't you think I should check it out? At least make sure you're okay with it before I just leave you here."

"Oh... I'll be fine."

"Okay, then I'll use the restroom."

"Suit yourself."

Mom gave me her *I told you so* look when a man in a security uniform opened the door for us. Inside there were workers all over. Nothing fancy about the place but it had lots of slot machines, security, a place to eat and places to sit down and relax. Those were Mom's only requirements when gambling.

I used the restroom, wished her luck and headed for Dick's barbershop.

*   *   *

Dick was right, his shop wasn't hard to find. I parked on the side of the main road, unsure why I needed to meet the man, but he sounded fascinating. He'd been a dowser for a very long time and was a few years older than Mom. Dowsing is an ancient practice.

I brought along all the information gathered from my search. I'd wait and see how it went before bombarding him with questions, so I left the paperwork in the car.

The heavy door squeaked as I pulled it open. A man in a blue barber smock sat in one of two barber chairs reading a newspaper. I remembered my dad taking me with him to get his hair cut. That was before he'd taught me to cut hair with clippers. Dad had a few bald spots before I got the hang of it, but that didn't seem to bother him. It was the same attitude he took about his socks matching. Mom said the sock issue was because of being colorblind. Mix matched socks didn't matter, but he could feel where hair was missing. After I finished he always said it looked fine.

Large mirrors covered the walls behind the barber chairs. A coat rack and a few wood chairs lined the opposite side of the room. Old pictures of the town hung on dark wood walls along with a few that looked like family photos.

"Dick?" I asked.

He got up. "Yes, and you must be Colette."

"I am."

We shook hands.

"I'm done for the day and I was thinking that maybe we could get a sandwich and go to my place. I promised my wife I'd bring her lunch. I don't live far."

"Sure, that would be fine with me."

He was tall and medium built with a very mischievous grin for an old guy. Well, maybe not that old, but he looked old to me. Mom would have thought him the cat's meow, as she would say. His dark brown eyes smiled when he talked, his hair neatly slicked back over the crown of his head. Good advertising for a barber.

I followed him to the sandwich shop where he bought me what he claimed to be the best sandwich in town. Then I followed him to the post office while he got his mail. I stayed in my car for that stop, and then followed him to his home.

He had a beautiful place on a large parcel of property. Scattered trees embraced the mountainous view. It was quiet. His wife was resting and would eat later. We sat outside on his back porch, which extended the entire length of the house and ate sandwiches without saying much. It was a great sandwich.

Busy trying to keep my barbecue sauce in one place, I looked up when he whispered, "There they are."

A doe and two fawns walked toward him from the trees.

"They want something to eat. See papa back there making sure they're okay? Sometimes he comes up, too."

Looking at the direction Dick pointed, I saw a small buck hiding in the trees. It amazed me that they would get so close to people. Dick had gentleness in the way he fed them tortillas.

He handed me a tortilla. "Here, you feed them."

Copying him, I slowly stuck my hand out. The doe took my tortilla. I was relieved she didn't take my fingers with it.

The deer left when the food was gone.

Dick said, "Follow me."

I followed him out into his yard. He took a pendulum on a chain from his pocket, and said, "Stand here, put your arm out and hold this pendulum."

I did and to my surprise, the pendulum lifted straight out.

"What's making it do that?"

"A vortex. It's like a whirlpool deep in the earth."

"That's really amazing."

"Follow me."

He led me into his garage and showed me various dowsing instruments. Some he made for his seminars and some he used in his work. His job involved finding water for wells or re-directing negative energies on individual's property.

He showed me his awards and gave me a few of his dowsing tools and some lecture material. Thanking him, I was grateful for all the information but still wondered why I was there. How could he help me?

"Let's go sit down and talk about you."

It felt like he read my mind. On the porch again he grabbed a chair, placing it in front of me, facing away from him.

"You told me you're looking for your father."

"Yes."

He sat down on a chair behind me. "Write down some questions you want me to answer. Ask either yes or no questions. Tell me when you're done."

He was going to dowse for me. I was thrilled, but thinking of useful questions was harder than I realized. Thoughts whirled in my head. I didn't want to ask unnecessary questions. After a moment, I wrote some down.

"I'm ready."

In a matter of fact voice, he said, "If the question is not asked specific enough, I'll ask you to reword."

"I understand. Okay... was my father eight years older than my mother?"

"No."

"Does Lacy's mother know who my father is?"

"Yes."

"Did my biological father live in Bridgeville?"

"Yes."

"Does my biological father know Gary Smith?"

"Yes."

"Is Gary Smith the key to my search?"

"Yes."

"Is my biological father alive?"

"Yes."

"Is his first name Mike?"

"No."

"Will I find him?"

"Yes. Are you done with your questions?"

I wasn't, but I could tell he was. I wished I'd had time to think and ask more. My mind was racing and I wasn't even close to the finish line. But I was thankful for what I got from him.

It was getting late and I had to meet with the Smiths in the next hour, but wanted to check on my mom before that. I thanked Dick and asked if I could call him with more questions. He said I could call him anytime. That made my day.

*   *   *

It didn't take long to find Mom. She was having a great time and had met a new friend. He had told her he'd watch out for her. She said he was harmless and kind and told me to enjoy my visit with the Smiths.

Walking out of the casino beside two other patrons, they remarked to me that the smoke was horrible. I agreed and said it was just as bad where I lived.

"Where do you live?" asked the woman.

"Sacramento area," I answered.

"Our son lives there. Did you come here to gamble?"

I laughed. "No. I'm here visiting some friends that lived in Forest Glen and they're helping me find my biological father."

"I grew up in Forest Glen," said her husband.

I stopped walking and faced him, "You did? Did you live there in 1955?"

"Oh yeah. If you don't mind my asking, who are you seeing that lived in Forest Glen?"

"Gary Smith."

"Oh yeah, Gary. He's a good guy."

I told him and his wife briefly about my situation and my search. They seemed eager to help and thought it was important for me to find my father, but he didn't remember Lacy. He was older, like Gary.

"Did you know anyone who was into motorcycle racing? I asked."

"A guy named Huckabee, but he didn't live right in Forest Glen. He was into motorcycle racing though."

Excited...maybe that was a clue. "Can I get your name and phone number?" I asked. "In case I have any questions? I'll give you mine in case you remember anything that could help me?"

"That would be fine. I'll do some thinking about it and call you if I come up with something."

I thanked him and we exchanged information. He told me to tell Gary hi.

Almost in tears, I got into the car and sat there. So many people had been amazingly kind and helpful during this search. Casual conversation about the smoke-filled skies prompted another person to offer to help. I was, as my reader Michael said, a truly blessed person. Again, I was grateful.

*   *   *

I walked up to the Smith's house much more relaxed than the time before. They were expecting me. Their house was as clean and orderly as the first time I saw it. I hugged Diane at the door as Gary emerged from down the hall. It was so nice to see them.

I told them about my visit with Dick and he dowsed questions for me. Neither Diane nor Gary knew he had any psychic abilities beyond dowsing for water, but were glad that he helped me.

"Diane, you know how you get this feeling that my father may be closer to my mother's age? Well, Dick came up with a younger person too."

"Colette, I'm not for sure, I just feel that."

"That's okay. Most of my information comes from a feel or what some call a knowing. At this point, I will take anything."

They laughed. I told them about the man at the casino and Gary said he knew him and the guy was closer to Gary's age rather than Lacy's. The Huckabee guy, Gary wasn't too sure about. He had lived at Beaver Camp, by the turnoff to Forest Glen, about 15 miles away. A long way for kids to try and get around back then, but it might be worth checking out.

I brought them more pictures and a couple tapes of Michael's readings. They enjoyed listening to them. I wanted them to hear how I was getting some of my information along with my own dowsing. We spent the next few hours talking. I shared all the information I had, explained Lacy's mother's attitude about my search and that I felt sure there was some clue in her house about me, and maybe in one of her closet chests. The ones I couldn't look in.

Gary said he was constantly thinking about it and trying to rack his brain to come up with something for me. All I could say was thank you. They'd already done more than expected and in a few days they would take all my information to their friends in Wyoming. Maybe one of them would remember something for me. Their help was astounding.

It was time to go but I hated leaving them. I wished they were both my birth parents. I felt so welcomed and wanted. If Gary were my father, Diane would be another mother for me. One thing I knew for sure—we had room in our hearts to love as many people as we wanted. From our first meeting, Gary and Diane had touched and entered my heart.

They both thought I should check out the Huckabee guy and Diane suggested trying the names on Lacy's school roster.

We hugged goodbye and Diane said she'd call me as soon as they returned from Wyoming. If there were any major information to report, she'd call from there. I couldn't wait for them to leave and get back.

The following morning Mom and I had breakfast at the local diner, which gave me the chance to talk with the friend she met while gambling. The little guy who kept an eye on her. It also gave me something to tease her about. We continued to talk about the previous day's events. She was as excited as I was about all the wonderful help I had gotten. After breakfast we headed home. Mom had a great time but her wallet was a little lighter. I had information confirmed by Dick and a couple new names to check out.

*   *   *

I thought it best to dowse for information about the Huckabee guy. That told me he wasn't my father and didn't know my father through motorcycle racing. Motorcycle racing had been a clue for me earlier in my search, but my dowsing was saying no to this guy. Although my dowsing wasn't always right.

I decided to see what Michael's guide could came up with, because my sources, whoever they were, sometimes gave me conflicting information. One time Huckabee knows my father, and then he doesn't. Another time, he lives in Bridgeville in a trailer park, and then he doesn't. I understood that the information comes through when the divine timing is right, but my guides or angels needed to be a little more certain before giving me any information. They could say—take a break and when we get this all organized we'll get back with you, but they don't. Not that I'm sure I'd take a break anyway, but all the conflicting information was driving me crazy.

A week went by before I could see Michael. The Smiths had left for Wyoming. I happened to pick a time when Michael was less busy. He sat motionless and listened about my trip to Bridgeville, the Huckabee guy and my frustration with my own dowsing. As usual, he went into his space. I needed to get into my own space. I knew I had one; I just wasn't sure how to get there. Michael said my dowsing was like my space, but I wanted a space where I could ask a question, then get the answer right then. I knew what it took to access that space, but I hadn't mastered it yet.

I asked Michael about the Huckabee guy. His guide said it could be a way to proceed, but overall I was on the right track. He's just an outside party.

I was neutral on that comment. Maybe it was a new lead. Maybe that's why I kept getting conflicting information when I dowsed about it.

Michael did his usual gesture of holding up one finger. I waited, watching his eyes squint and forehead wrinkle, as if he was trying to read something far away.

Then he opened his eyes. "I'm seeing the name Jim Sommer written out."

"Jim's a common name." I said. "Based on information I already have, I'm looking for a common name."

"Something close to the Sommer name. I'm not sure, but the first name is clearly Jim. My guide says Jim is the jackpot. He's the one who knows. A final assistance."

"So I need to find this Jim Sommer?"

"Yes. You're closing in. Either October or November."

"Michael, is my father married?"

"Was, but no longer."

"How about other children and will he be happy to meet me?"

"Yes for both."

"I hope he's like the Smiths."

"You should bring up Jim Sommer to Gary Smith. Gary is the key to finding Jim. The Smiths will get the connection. These clues will get you to the green near the hole. One more person for the connection."

"So... I'm very close and I don't need to contact this Huckabee guy, but the Smiths will have a clue from the Jim Sommer name?"

"Yes. You're very near to crossing the finish line. This is what you've chosen."

"What do you mean?"

"Your path to enlightenment."

"Ah yes... I think I should have picked something a little easier."

Michael laughed. He always made me feel confident about my search and confirmed that I was doing what I was supposed to do. He gave me the Smith name, and I found them, so I was certain there would be something to this Jim Sommer guy and I'd find him too.

A Love Child's Journey

Chapter Twenty-Nine

I stared at the Rock Creek School roster. The first name listed in Lacy's eighth grade class was James Ellyson. He might have gone by Jim, but the last name was far from Sommer. Michael wasn't as sure about the last name, but he was sure about Jim.

Doing a name search on the Internet, I found a James Ellyson in the state of Oregon. His date of birth was listed on the roster, and the age for the Oregon Jim matched the one on the roster. I was thrilled. It had to be the same guy. I'd found someone, providing he was alive, who'd been in school with Lacy at the time she became pregnant with me. Maybe he'd remember her friends and possible boyfriends. It might be a long shot, but what else did I have? I needed to organize my thoughts and questions. At least I had the roster so I didn't have to say his first name came from an intuitive reader.

I would run this name through the Smiths. Michael said it would ring a bell with Gary. Diane had told me she'd call as soon as they returned from their trip. They'd been gone over a week and a half and I was disappointed at not hearing from her. I guess she wasn't having much luck with my pictures and information.

Studying the roster, there were only six boys and two girls in Lacy's eighth-grade class. Of the six boys, there was only one

James. In my heart, I was certain he had to be connected in some way to my search.

The next day Diane called me. They had returned the day before, and were busy unpacking.

"Colette, we talked with the "network" and all of them said that they'd be willing to take a DNA test and the wives said they would welcome you into their family, but none of the guys had been with Lacy."

"Well... did they have any ideas?"

Diane was silent.

Grasping for some bit of news, I asked, "Diane, remember when you asked me about whether my son or I had any artistic or musical talents?"

"Yes."

"You must have had someone in mind when you asked that question."

"Well... we think there's a possibility that you're either an Ellyson or belong to the oldest Mackenzie boy."

My heart pounded with excitement. Two possible families; I would have been ecstatic with even one.

"So, which one do you think it is?"

"Gary thinks it might be the older Mackenzie boy, because some of the Mackenzies had moles like you, but they have lighter complexion."

"According to his sister, they moved a year before Lacy's pregnancy and her older brother wasn't living there," I said.

"Yes, that's true. However, Gary says he remembers him riding the bus into Eureka, not to school. But his father drove the school bus at that time. Gary's not sure, it's just one of two possibilities."

"That's interesting you brought up the Ellysons, because my intuitive reader came up with the name Jim. There was a James Ellyson in Lacy's class."

Diane asked, "Colette, do you know who Joe Ellyson is?"

I thought for a moment. There's that Joe name I dowsed. I thought it meant the pizza place in Bridgeville but I had no idea who Joe Ellyson was.

"No, I don't."

"I want you to hang up and Goggle him on the Internet, then call me back."

That seemed odd, but I was curious enough to try it.

"Okay...I'll check it out."

I got on the computer and Goggled Joe Ellyson. Immediately a list of Joe Ellyson names popped up, all for the same guy. I checked them all out, staring at the screen in disbelief. I was familiar with his work, but never knew his name. It was very strange to think that this man might be my birth father. My birth mother, a call girl and my possible biological father a famous landscape artist. It didn't seem real. Did the spirit world have a warped sense of humor? The thought of him as my father was exciting, but might turn into a difficult situation. During my search, I expected to find him living in a trailer park. I didn't have any problem with that, but the other extreme was overwhelming.

I called Diane back.

"Hello," she said.

"That's just too weird, Diane."

"Yes it is, Colette. That's why we waited and checked out everything we could, but feel there's a strong possibility you belong to the Ellyson family. We're still not sure, but you have some resemblance to their mother. Gary's dad Smitty was best friends with Jim and Joe's father."

"So Gary's dad, Smitty was the connecting factor to the Ellyson family. That's why Michael's guide gave him the Smitty name for me."

"Maybe."

"The Internet says Joe lives in France. That could make it difficult to get in touch with him."

"Yes... it could.

"That's why the spirit world directed me to Jim. Joe's too far away and I needed someone in the U.S. who remembered Lacy."

"It makes sense," she said.

"Do you think there's a possibility that I'm Jim's daughter?"

"You can't rule it out. Not yet. There's a brother older than Joe too, but Gary doesn't think it was him."

"I've been thinking about calling Jim, but wanted to run it by you and Gary first. So what do you think, should I call him?"

"I think it would be a good move. Do you have his number?"
"Not yet, but I can get it."
"I have it here."

I wrote down his number and thanked her for everything the two of them had done. I tried to tell her how much I appreciated their caring and helpful attitudes. They waited until they were almost certain before passing the information to me.

"Colette, we know you appreciate our help. Gary and I have always believed you have a right to know who your father is and we know when you find him, he will be proud that you're his daughter."

"Thank you Diane and please thank Gary for me too."

*   *   *

Butterflies and bees swirled in my stomach as I thought about calling Jim. He could be a major milestone in my search and possibly my father. I didn't want to stumble or make a mistake. I took a deep breath and slowly punched his number on my phone. Hearing it ring made me shiver.

"Hello," said a stern female voice.

"Yes," I said quickly. "I'm Colette, Lacy Fisherman's daughter. Jim was her classmate in Forest Glen. May I speak with him?"

"Just a minute."

I heard her lay the receiver down and begin yelling for Jim. I began to shake. I forced myself to breathe deep and not hyperventilate. My ears began to ring.

"Hel...lo," said a loud raspy male voice.

He sounded like a longtime smoker.

"Hello, Jim. I'm Lacy Fisherman's daughter, Colette. She lived in Forest Glen."

In a softer raspy tone he said, "No kidding. I remember Lacy, how's she doing?"

"Much to my sadness, she died of leukemia in 1990."

"I'm sorry to hear that. She was a beauty. My brother Joe thought she was about it."

Surprised to hear him mention Joe's feelings, I wondered. Were they the two brothers my dowsing told me about?

"Did you know that Lacy got pregnant in the eighth grade?"

He was silent, then said slowly, "Noooo... I didn't know that. I'm sorry to hear it. Lacy was a good girl. She wasn't like that. There were others that were, but not her."

"Yeah... but she did get pregnant and I'm the baby she had. She put me up for adoption. I found her when I was twenty-four, but never questioned her about my biological father, so now I'm searching for him."

In his raspy good old boy voice, he said, "I did all kinds of things with Lacy and her sister Laura. We danced, well... I danced with Laura too because she was like a wallflower and I felt sorry for her. Lacy was so beautiful, but not poor Laura. Don't get me wrong. Laura was nice. The other girls liked Lacy, but were jealous. Yeah... we skated and watched matinees at the Community Center. I guess you could have called Lacy my girlfriend but we just kissed, that's all. I never touched her. I mean... it's not that I didn't want to, but I didn't."

I told him Lacy's adopted father, Rodney had molested her, but he wasn't my father and about Wilma's reaction to Lacy's pregnancy. Lacy said she was raped by a dress salesman, but Wilma didn't seem to believe it."

"I don't mean to be rude, but Lacy's mother, Wilma was a B..., if you know what I mean."

I laughed. "That seems to be the general consensus."

He told me he and his wife, Jocelyn had lived in Oregon for years and he talked about his brothers. His oldest brother had married young and was into motorcycle racing. Motorcycles were something they all enjoyed. He recalled carving his and Lacy's names on trees and he enjoyed being around her. He liked Forest Glen and agreed with his siblings that it was the best place they lived while growing up. How refreshing to hear nice stories about Lacy and that she enjoyed her childhood. At least, before she became pregnant.

"Well... hey, are you as pretty as Lacy?"

I laughed at his brashness. Not sure how to answer. "No, but I hold my own."

I wished I was as pretty, but I really didn't look much like her at all. None of her kids did. We all seemed to look like our fathers; Mitch and Allaine did anyway, so I assumed I did too.

Jim and I talked a long time. He mentioned the different kids in their class and the area. I was a talker, but this time I just listened. Accurate or not, I enjoyed his childhood memories and was amazed that he remembered so much from so long ago. He seemed pretty sure that his brother Joe hadn't had any type of physical encounter with Lacy.

He took my phone number and said he'd call his older brother Frank to see if he recalled anything else. If he did, Jim would call me back.

Although it was late when I finished talking with him, I called Diane. I knew she'd be waiting to hear what he said. She thought what Jim told me about Joe's feelings for Lacy was something to think about. Maybe Jim didn't know about anything going on between the two.

I agreed but was disappointed. Did I find the right family? The clues didn't direct me to anyone in the Mackenzie family. So much information from the spirit world led to the Ellysons. The motorcycle racing connection, living in Oregon, Jim's wife named Jocelyn, and a brother named *Joe* who thought Lacy was about it.

"Colette, you might want to give Jim time to think about it. Maybe he'll contact Joe, and he'll remember something."

"You're right. I'm sure he was doing a lot of reminiscing. It was nice he thought so highly of Lacy. You never know, maybe he'll come up with something. He seemed to want to help me."

"I think he would if he could. It's getting late, so I'll let you go."

"Thanks for everything, Diane. I'll talk with you in a few days."

I hung up thinking it wasn't as if I had a choice of who my father was. Actually, I didn't care who it turned out to be, as long as I found the right one.

Because Jim had taken the time to talk with me, I sent him a thank you card. I'd done that with everyone who tried to help me. My husband, John, my biggest support during the search for my birth father, suggested I enclose in the card some of the same pictures I had given the Smiths. Jim might think that either my son or I resembled someone he knew in the past. It was a great idea and I was glad he thought of it. I added a note to the photos asking if he thought I looked like anyone he knew from Forest Glen.

*   *   *

Diane had said the older Mackenzie was living in Wyoming. It didn't take long to find his phone number, but I decided against calling him. It didn't feel right. I was certain that God, my guides and all the spiritual world that seemed to be helping me out wouldn't give me wrong information, even if they had a weird sense of humor. I didn't believe it worked that way, and neither did my family or friends who knew about my search.

As usual when I got stumped, I made a trip to see Michael, my intuitive reader. Since he had a direct tap to his guide, couldn't he ask my guides to be more specific and help me out by cutting to the chase? Forget the detours.

Michael did some energy work on me, saying only I seemed tense. I'm sure he knew why. He had me stand and I watched as he swished his hands up and down around me. I didn't feel any different when I sat back down, but figured he did something and I'd soon relax.

He went into his space and asked his guides about my call to Jim.

"You're reaching the end of the trail. You're going to a more advanced state of mind. You are becoming whole. Make a choice to lead healing circles. Relax and enjoy."

Relax and enjoy? His guide couldn't have been talking with my guide because I can't relax until I find out who my father is.

Michael continued, "How do you want to approach the Ellyson brothers? What questions do you want to ask them?"

I shrugged. "I've already talked with Jim and he says he's not my father and is certain his brother Joe isn't, so why am I directed to this family? You or your guide came up with the Jim name. He remembers a lot about my mother, but as I stated, he said he didn't have sex with her and was sure Joe didn't either. I'd still like to talk to Joe myself. I feel drawn to him and I don't think it's because he's a famous landscape artist, intriguing as that is. I don't understand it myself."

Michael's eyes closed, "You know he's the one. There will be a natural shake out, a process of elimination. Do you want the middle brother to be the one?"

"It doesn't matter as long as I get the right one. The clues point more to the middle brother, Joe but that makes it more complicated. The Smiths are subtle and cautious, but think he's a possibility."

Michael's guide concluded, "Go on. It will sort itself out soon. It's all coming together. You'll be crossing the finish line with your hands up."

"Well... I'm definitely ready to cross that line. I'm tired of being the turtle in this race. Slow and steady doesn't seem to be getting me anywhere. The waiting and wondering is sometimes almost unbearable."

Michael said I should continue with the Ellyson family and the final pieces of the puzzle were coming together. He suggested a visit to Wilma to question her about the Ellysons.

*   *   *

The next day I called Wilma. She hadn't been feeling well. She seemed to enjoy my visits. So I asked if I could come and see her. I wanted to drive up the following day and she said she'd look forward to it. Mom was always happy to accompany me on my visits. She would spend the day in the Indian casino near Wilma's house. I enjoyed her company on the drive.

Before leaving the following morning, I took time to dowse for answers.

After asking permission, standard protocol, I asked:

Q. Should I ask Wilma about my biological father today?
A. Yes.
Q. Will she give me any clues about him?
A. Yes.

Pleased with the answers, but not wanting to push my spiritual help, I didn't ask anything more. Not that I knew if I could, but I didn't want to push it. Receiving clues was the most important for me. I planned to be extra attentive to what Wilma said.

A Love Child's Journey

Chapter Thirty

After letting Mom off at the casino as usual, I drove to Wilma's. She had asked me to call her Nammie, but at times that seemed odd. At least I'd graduated from that baby girl from Sacramento to her granddaughter. On my part, I made an effort not to refer to her, as the *crazy grandmother* however there seemed to be some truth in it.

At her door I knocked and hollered her name.

"Colette, is that you?" she yelled.

The door was unlocked so I didn't need to use the key she'd given me.

She was sitting in her chair, wearing an old tattered white hairnet that clung to the side of her head. It looked uncomfortable and I wondered if she could feel it hanging there.

"Yes, it's me. How are you today, Nammie?"

"Oh... I'm fine. Just a little sleepy. I'm having a hard time keeping my head up."

I sat down in the rocker next to her. Forgetting that she didn't like to be made fun of, I joked. "It's probably your hairnet. It's a little lopsided. Maybe that's why your head falls to one side."

Reaching up to straighten it, she chuckled. "Oh, you're probably right."

Ah… she did have a sense of humor after all. Up until now I was certain it had been surgically removed or never existed. I wanted her in a good mood: happy, talkative and informative. A tall order, especially since she didn't like me asking about my birth father. I tried to make a conscious effort to call her Nammie. That would make her happy.

"Nammie… do you really believe I'm Rodney's daughter?"

"I told you I did," she said sternly.

Hoping to divert her from getting upset, I asked, "Yes, you did… What nationality was he?"

Agitated, she quickly said, "I'm not sure. Irish, I guess. He had red hair, green eyes and freckles all over. We didn't talk about it."

To calm her down, I changed the direction. "Well… remember me saying I have a few intuitive friends I consult?"

"Yes, I remember and I told you I believe there might be something to their abilities."

"My friend Angel is a direct intuitive and she said there's a possibility I'm either Portuguese, Italian or Armenian."

She didn't say a word.

"Do you think I look like Rodney?" I asked.

Her voice trailed off in disappointment. "No… no you don't."

"That's good though, right?"

Her words full of anger, she said, "Lacy was a good girl and what Rodney did was wrong."

Even though, Rodney had molested Lacy, I felt certain I wasn't his daughter. "She was a good girl."

I remembered reading about young unwed mothers in the 1950's. Scorned by society, many of them thought being pregnant without a husband was a fate worse than death. That was hard for me to understand, but I hadn't experienced their situation and didn't know how they felt.

I had upset Wilma. Mentioning the Smiths would either intrigue her or send her over an angry edge. She had no problem telling me what she wanted to hear, so I was sure she'd tell me if she didn't want to hear something. In all our earlier conversations, she appeared curious about my search.

I told her about meeting the Smiths this past summer, but didn't mention Allaine being there. That would have put her over the edge. Allaine was spending much more time with me than her grandmother. She had visited Nammie for one short afternoon but it had been a few years before that. That was enough for Allaine. I wasn't ready to tell Wilma I had spoken with Jim.

"The Smiths talked about the Mackenzie family and Ellis family."

She corrected me. "You mean the Ellyson, not Ellis."

I'd said Ellis by accident, but was ecstatic that she corrected me. She knew them.

"Right, Ellyson."

"I have a painting done by one of the Ellyson boys," she told me. "Either Jim or Joe. I think it was Joe. He was quite an artist. It's a beautiful tree with a young girl leaning up against it. It's somewhere in the bathroom closet. He came with his mother to my house when I gave my art classes to the local ladies. I loved giving my art classes."

She sat motionless with her head turned away from me, as if teaching those classes again in her mind. But I found it hard to contain myself. That had to be my clue. She knew the Ellysons. They had been in her house. Angel, my intuitive friend said all along that Wilma had a clue to my biological father in her house. Maybe the painting by Joe was my clue. I thought the clue would be in one of those chests she wouldn't let me look in, but maybe not.

It was hard but I didn't ask about the Ellysons. She said nothing else about them.

Disappointment nudged my heart. Joe's painting seemed unimportant to her, but it might be everything to me. There was a chance the young boy who painted that picture was my father.

*   *   *

My friend, Debbie and I planned to attend the 20th anniversary party at the store where my intuitive friends gave their readings. Both Michael and Angel would be there.

310

Entering, the store's dimmed lights created a party atmosphere. People crowded around long tables filled with appetizers and most held a plastic champagne glass. Michael was chatting with guests and Angel waved from a distance, a night off for the intuitive readers.

I hadn't been there long when my cell phone rang. To my surprise, it was Jim Ellyson.

His raspy voice seemed to tremble, "Colette, I got your pictures and I don't know how to tell you this, but you're an Ellyson. And you're right. You don't look like Lacy. But you're pretty. And Rodney is not your father. There's no doubt you're an Ellyson and I think you're my daughter."

My heart raced, my face flushed, and my ears rang. I heard his words, but couldn't seem to wrap my mind around them. My mind switched to slow motion. I couldn't think beyond the words —you're an Ellyson. He said that. Finally, after three years of searching, I had the name of the other family I came from.

Hesitant, I said, "Jim, are you sure I'm your daughter?"

His voice had conviction. "Yeah I'm sure."

"But you said you never touched Lacy." I was confused. "You remembered so much about her. I think you'd remember something that intimate."

"I know, but it was a long time ago. I still think I'm your father. I should fly down and do a DNA test."

I couldn't argue the fact that it was a long time ago. For the first time in my long search, things moved too fast for me. I needed time to digest what he said and time to think about it. Circumstances had suddenly reversed. In the past, I'd been the one who asked if someone was my father; I didn't expect someone to tell me he was. The timing was amazing too, especially him calling me at store where I received my intuitive readings and some of the clues for my search. I was excited and overwhelmed.

"Jim, I'm not at home right now. Can I call you tomorrow?"

His raspy voice had calmed down.

"Sure, that would be fine."

"Thanks so much. I'll call you tomorrow."

Debbie patted my hand and asked if I was okay. I told her what Jim said and she was happy I'd finally found my dad. It felt good having her there. I found Michael and Angel and told them about my call. They too were excited for me, but sensed my concern. I kept recalling Jim saying he never touched Lacy in that way. He wanted to but didn't. I loved that he remembered so much about her but that statement made me skeptical of his claim to fatherhood. I could easily be an Ellyson, but was I his?

* * *

I woke the following morning feeling tired, as though I hadn't slept much. Jim probably felt the same. He wanted to fly down and do a DNA blood test. I wasn't sure how it worked, but would research it later on the Internet. What I wanted was a reading with Michael before calling Jim. Maybe his guides from the spirit world could advise me what to do next.

Michael seemed as excited as I was, but not enough to give a free reading. He'd been on this journey with me and hoped I was near the end.

He went into his space, and I remained quiet. I curbed my talking with patience, quite an accomplishment for me.

When ready, he recapped my conversation with Jim from the night before.

"So this Jim has two brothers, Joe and Frank, and you want to know which of the three is your father?"

"Yeah, that's my main question. Jim says he's my father, but I'm not sure. He should have remembered if he really was. But he's adamant that I'm an Ellyson. It's nice and I think he could be right about that, but I want the *right* Ellyson."

"My guide says you are correct. You are an Ellyson, but this will be complicated. You need to continue and Jim can be helpful."

"He wants to do a DNA test."

Michael eyes closed. "Do the test. The journey is discovering the truth, a process of elimination. Remember you are a healer while this is playing out."

"So your guide is certain I'm an Ellyson?"

"Yes. You are very close now, go through the steps."

"Michael, it would be nice to skip the in between steps. Can't your guide get with the right dad's guide and save me some time here? Especially since it appears we have the right family."

Michael smiled. "As you know, it's never that simple. Remember—divine timing. Just relax. You've come a long way on this journey. It's almost complete."

"I just want the truth Michael. I want to know which one is my father."

"You will soon know."

I thanked him and said I'd let him know how it all turns out.

*   *   *

I waited until evening before calling Jim. Both times I talked to him had been easy and comfortable. I had doubts, but couldn't rule out the possibility of him being my father. He was friendly and likeable, if he was my father, I felt sad that he couldn't remember it happening. They were very young for an intimate situation, possibly the first love encounter for both. 'First' sexual experiences, whether good or bad, tend not to be forgotten. I believed Lacy loved my father and hid those feelings deep in her heart. For my father not to even remember the incident made it seem ordinary and nothing special. I had hoped it meant something to my father, whoever it turned out to be.

His phone rang. Then stopped.

"Hel...lo," said Jim.

"Hello Jim, this is Colette."

"I've been waiting for you to call."

I knew he had, but didn't want to tell him I had to consult my intuitive reader before calling him back. He would have hung up on me for sure.

"Sorry about that. It's been a hectic day," I said.

"I think we should do a DNA test, don't you?"

"Definitely. We both need to know for sure. Then we can go from there. Tomorrow, I'll check it out and see what we need to do."

"That's fine, then you can let me know. My wife Joyce is happy for me. She said you look like my oldest daughter."

Hearing the name Joyce jolted me. I had wanted to confirm it. "Your wife's name is Joyce?"

"Well, it's Jocelyn, but I call her Joyce."

I was speechless. Jocelyn was the name I had dowsed, the wife of the person I was looking for. I had the right family so it had to be Jim. If he was my father, I wished he could remember the fathering.

"Colette, are you okay?"

His question brought me back from my thoughts. "Sure... just amazed at all this."

He agreed and started telling me about himself, his retirement from the construction business and his kids and grandkids. I did the same. Then he began to talk about his siblings. His brother, Frank had retired from the fire department with no major injuries. Joe traveled all over the world selling his paintings, was famous and internationally known, which I already knew. He settled in a small town in southern France, but Jim either didn't know or wouldn't say which town. If the family was so close, it seemed odd he wouldn't know the name of the town his brother lived in. I guessed Joe wasn't accessible to the general public and at this point, I was considered general public.

He told me how many children each of his siblings had and how important family was to all of them. He spoke highly of each. A nice family was very comforting. Diane and Gary had said they would be. I wanted to hear more. Was I searching for a glimpse of me in each of them? I wasn't sure. It's not that I needed a new family. I loved every bit of the one I had, but I wanted to complete the whole puzzle of me, no missing pieces. Time flew by while we talked and it was late. I told Jim I'd call him after I had information about the DNA test. He said he'd find pictures of himself and have Joyce send them to me. His demeanor and tone had drastically changed from our first conversation. Now he sounded like a caring father. He loved his family. It was nice to hear. I liked him.

*   *   *

I walked around in a daze with thoughts of pinching myself to see if I'd been dreaming. Did last weekend's events really take place? They did and I had no intentions on creating external pain by pinching myself.

I thought I'd be able to relax for a change. Do a DNA test and go from there, but as much as I liked Jim and as nice as he was, it didn't feel right. Call it a gut feel or intuition. My heart wasn't convinced that he was the one. A DNA test would be the key and as I was told, it was a process of elimination and I couldn't go forward without it.

I found a company to do our test. I ordered the home kit and within a few days, it arrived. I sent Jim his, explaining that once they had both swabs, it would take a week or so for the results.

The DNA test was simple. Swab the inside of each cheek with what looked like large Q-tips let them dry and mail them back in the envelope they provided. Which I did.

A few days passed before Jim called to say he had his kit. He said he'd have Joyce help him with it. I explained that it was simple, but he insisted it would be best if Joyce helped him. She must take care of all their business and this was important business. It was fine with me. He said he'd call and let me know when he sent it.

I decided to write a letter to Jim and the Ellyson family telling about my life and how I found them. Minus the intuitive part of course. I didn't know where I fit with the Ellysons but I didn't want to get thrown out of the family before I had a chance to be in it.

The letter explained my search for Lacy and now my father. I started it by telling them about the wonderful parents and siblings I was blessed with. Although my life was happy, I told them I felt a hole in my heart not knowing the truth about my biological father. That it was very important for me to know and I was grateful to have found their family. Based on Jim's comments, any of the three brothers would be fine for a parent, but I wanted to find the one who actually was my father.

*   *   *

I called the Smiths to update them on my progress. They were happy that things had moved forward.

Diane asked, "Colette, do you plan on contacting the oldest Mackenzie boy?"

"I thought about it, but I haven't received any clues or information to steer me in his direction. Speaking of clues, did you know that Jim's wife's name is Jocelyn?"

"No, I didn't know that."

"That's the same name I got when I was dowsing about the wife of the guy I needed to find to help me with my search."

"That is amazing."

"Yeah …it is. Diane, there's been so many clues pointing me to the Ellysons. It has to be one of them. After Jim saw my pictures, he insisted that I was an Ellyson."

"Did he say who he thought your father would be if it wasn't him?"

"No and I haven't asked him yet. He seemed to care for Lacy a lot. If he's not my father, I think he might feel hurt and betrayed if one of his brothers is."

"Yes… that could be possible. You'll have to wait and see."

I promised to call her when I received the DNA test results.

*   *   *

A week had passed since I sent my DNA samples and I hoped Jim sent his. The testing company had a website allowing clients to check the progress of their tests and approximate completion date. They had received mine but not Jim's.

I didn't want to bother him, but it was important to me. I would have thought he'd want the test done right away.

I called later that afternoon. He had received my letter and loved it. He suggested I send a copy to his sister Lynda who lived on the northern coast of Oregon. He gave me her address and I told him I would.

"Jim," I finally asked. "Have you sent your DNA test in?"

"Nah... not yet. Joyce has been too busy to help me. A lot going on at work, she's too exhausted when she gets home. But we're going to get to it soon."

"I understand. I thought the company misplaced it or something."

What I wanted to say was that I'd been waiting a long time for it. Too long. He could do his own swabbing. It's like brushing teeth. But he wasn't in any hurry. For all I knew, maybe he liked being my dad even if it was just for a short period.

"You need to come up to Portland. Bring your husband if you'd like. We have plenty of room and would love to have you."

"My husband was helping a friend with a house addition, but maybe I could fly up for a day or two. I'd like to hear more about Lacy."

"Check it out and let me know. I'll see if Joyce and I can get that DNA test in the mail in the next few days. In the meantime, try and arrange to visit us. We would love to meet you."

I felt special being invited to his home, although at this stage I'd prefer a hotel. My husband liked the idea of a visit. If Jim wanted me to send a letter to his sister Lynda, he wanted her to know about me. I sent one the following day.

Thanksgiving was fast approaching, so I thought it best to visit before the holiday. I picked out two different flight days, then called Jim to see which fit their schedule. There was no answer so I left a message.

Later that afternoon Joyce called and didn't sound happy.

Without even a hello, she asked in a furious tone, "Colette, what was your message about? Where were you going to meet Jim?"

It was a surreal moment, like Dorothy stepping into Oz. Time stood still. What answer did she want? I graciously replied, "Your... house."

Her voice trembled, but she lowered her tone, and scorned, "Don't you think you should wait for the DNA test results before visiting. You don't even know if you belong to this family. Just because you look like someone doesn't mean you're related to them."

Confused by her hostility, I paused to answer.

She calmed down. "It's not that I mind that you visit, but I think you should wait for the test results. Don't you?" she snapped, anger sneaking back into her voice.

Was that a trick question? Did she honestly think I'd want to visit now, after her far from welcoming comments? She made it sound as if Jim and I planned some rendezvous, which was absurd. He talked to me like father to daughter, but Joyce seemed jealous. Maybe in the past Jim had given her reasons to be. She was far from warm and fuzzy, more like prickly.

I tried to be congenial. "I think you're right. It's best to wait for the DNA test results before I visit."

"I'll make sure Jim gets it done tonight and sends it off tomorrow."

"Thank you, Joyce. I really appreciate it."

The telephone clicked. She hung up without another word.

Disappointment hit me like a burst of cold rain. I'd been looking forward to visiting Jim and hearing more stories about Lacy. In Joyce's defense, maybe she had heard the Lacy stories too many times or maybe she wasn't prepared to deal with a stepdaughter. I wasn't convinced I was Jim's daughter, but I was pretty certain of at least being his niece. Time would tell.

318

A Love Child's Journey

Chapter Thirty-one

I continued to check my e-mails, hoping to find that Jim's DNA had been received. After the fifth day it showed.

The following day Jim called to tell me that he had completed the test and Joyce had mailed it. I explained that a confirmed receipt already showed up on my e-mail.

If Jim knew Joyce had called me, he didn't mention it. I told him it would be a while before I could visit. He said that might be for the best. I sensed some interesting dynamics in their relationship and didn't want to cause them problems.

"Jim, can I ask you something?"

"Sure."

"Are you still 100% sure that I'm an Ellyson?"

"Yes. There's no doubt."

"What If it turns out… that I'm not your daughter, then who would I belong to?"

Without hesitating, he answered, "Joe."

"Are you sure? What about Frank?"

"I know you're not Frank's." His voice lowered, "If you're not mine, then you're Joe's. He's the only other one you could belong to."

"How do you think Joe would feel about me? I mean…. would he want to meet me?"

319

"Oh yeah. Joe would want to get to the bottom of this. He'd want to know the truth."

His words comforted me and I hoped that if Joe were my father he'd be as kind and helpful as Jim.

I held back the urge to ask him about Joe. That could wait until after the DNA test. If by some slim chance Jim was my father, I didn't want him to think that I preferred one brother to the other. In truth, I didn't care which one it was, although I liked Jim and thought that if Joyce got to know me, we'd get along fine.

Jim and I spoke every few days. It was refreshing that he wanted to know all about my life and everyone in it. I was the same with him, wanting to hear all about his life and family. He had a great sense of humor and I had no doubt he loved his family, but I sensed sadness in him. He claimed to be the rebel in his family. Didn't mind what they did, but liked doing his own thing, and at times, he had a hot temper. He didn't give me any examples, but I guessed he didn't always agree with the rest of them. He was proud of Joe being famous, but he was his brother. They had grown up together and as far as he was concerned, they were equal, one no better than the other.

*   *   *

Once they received both samples, the DNA lab would take seven to ten days to complete the testing. I checked my e-mails hourly for a week, and on the eighth day, I got their e-mail. There it was, in bold letters: DNA TEST RESULTS.

I envisioned myself as a ravenous animal suddenly given food, but it wasn't like that. Instead, apprehension and then warmth hovered around me. I thought of my first meeting with Lacy. The excitement and fear of what lay ahead and the worry over whether I made the right decision to find her. But now I know the results of that uncertainty. I met the woman who as a young teenager became pregnant by the young boy she loved and was sent away to a home for unwed mothers. The one, who carried me in her womb for nine months and had so much love for me, gave me a chance at a better life by giving me up for adoption. Yet, despite marrying and two more children, to her dying day she never seemed to recover from that first loss. I now have another brother and sister to add to the ones I have and my love for them grows deeper with each passing day.

Regardless of the DNA outcome, I was certain I'd done the right thing. The e-mail said child and alleged father. It seemed odd being referred to as a child, but that's what I was in this case. I checked the numbers, then scanned to the bottom of the page where it read—Probability of Paternity: 0%. I wasn't surprised, but disappointment jabbed my heart. I liked Jim and would have been happy to have him as my father. He'd probably be disappointed too. I'd hoped I'd come to an end with my search, but I wanted the right guy, the young teenage boy Lacy loved. The one she kept secret in her heart and took to her grave. Jim had said if not him, then Joe. All indications pointed that way.

*   *   *

My family's reaction mirrored mine. They believed most of my leads and clues pointed to Joe, but after hearing all about Jim, they had come to like him too.

I didn't want to keep him waiting any longer so I called him.

He answered with his usual rasp. "Hel...lo."

"Hi Jim. It's Colette." I tried to sound upbeat.

"Oh... hey, how you doing? Did you get the DNA results yet?"

"Yes, I just got it."

I hesitated. He really wanted to be my father, a wonderful compliment, but he wasn't and I had to tell him that.

"Jim, I'm sorry, but according to the test, you're not... you're not my father."

He didn't immediately respond. I guessed he was taking it in.

In a somber voice, he quietly asked, "Are you sure? Could they have made a mistake?"

"Unless there's been some kind of contamination, they're pretty accurate. I was careful with mine and I'm sure you were too."

"I'm not sure I trust those tests," he said, sounding bitter.

Hearing the disappointment in his voice, I said with reluctance, "There is no in-between on a paternity test. Jim... do you still think I'm an Ellyson?"

"I do," he answered immediately.

"So... in that case, you're... my uncle, right?"

Sounding a little upbeat, he said, "Yeah... that's right. I'm glad to be your uncle, but I was hoping to be your dad. I don't know if I agree with that test."

"I'm disappointed, too. I would've loved having you as my father, but I want to know who my biological father is. Can you help me get in touch with Joe?"

"Him being in Europe or France most of the time, I don't talk to him much anymore. We just wait for him to call."

"You don't have his phone number?"

"No...I don't. I used to, but not anymore."

Surprised, I asked, "But what if you had an emergency? How would you get hold of him?"

It may not have been an emergency to him, but that's how it felt for me. I'd been on this search a long time. I wanted to cross the finish line and I wanted the prize. But with every hurdle the finish line shifted and changed. I keep running and thinking I'm getting closer, but am I?

"Well... call my sister. I'm sure she has Joe's number. She talks to him more than I do. You sent her pictures and the letter, so she knows about you. Wait until tomorrow before you call, though. That'll give me a chance to talk to her first."

He gave me her number. I thanked him before saying goodbye and repeated my disappointment that he wasn't my father.

Jim's feelings seemed to run deeper than he let on. Not only was his brother a wealthy and internationally known landscape artist, but it appeared that Joe swooped up one of Jim's first loves and got her pregnant right under his nose. Maybe he was more hurt than disappointed.

*   *   *

Later that evening I called the Smiths to tell them the test results and Jim's suggestion that I call his sister. Diane didn't seem surprised that I wasn't Jim's daughter. She said Gary knew the sister well and she was a kind person. The Smiths thought I should call her.

"Diane, I was thinking I might check out the high school yearbooks at the Historical Society in Eureka. I looked at them when I was there, but didn't know who I was looking for."

"That's a good idea. You'll need to check both high schools. Gary went to Trinity and so did Jim's sister. After they graduated kids were still bussed into Eureka, but they went to Channey High School."

"I remember you telling me that. I'll check out the Mackenzie family as well."

"Good idea."

"Diane, since I'm going to Eureka, do you mind if I stop by and visit for a while, maybe talk some more with Gary? He might think of something else."

"You're always welcome at our house."

"Thank you. You and Gary are so special and will forever be in my heart."

"We're glad you're in our lives too."

I told her I'd call and let her know what Jim's sister had to say. Diane and Gary both seemed to think Joe was my birth father. They seemed as anxious as me to find out for sure.

*   *   *

I thought all afternoon about what to say to Jim's sister. The bottom line was that I wanted to reach Joe and ask if he was my father. If he thought Lacy was just about it, wouldn't he remember a lot about her, like Jim did?

At least the sister knew about me and had pictures, so I wasn't catching her off guard.

I dialed her number.

"Hello." The inflection of her voice was soft and pleasant, as I had imagined from Gary's comments about her.

"Hi. This is Colette. I'm the one Jim's been talking with. I sent you the letter along with pictures of me and my family."

"Yes. I spoke with him last night. He's very disappointed he's not your father."

"Yes, I know. I am too. But he still feels very strongly that I'm an Ellyson."

She didn't say anything. Like a radio with no music, the air was dead. I waited wondering what her thoughts were.

To break the silence, I asked, "You've seen my pictures and the information I sent. What do you think?"

The softness in her voice remained, but she seemed very careful selecting the words she used.

"I'm not sure... I can see... some of my mother in you, but... I don't know. Jim really wanted you to be his daughter."

"Yes, I know. He's been so kind. But I need the right brother, which brings me to Joe. Jim told me if it wasn't him, then it had to be Joe. Do you agree?"

"I don't know. I don't know who either of them associated with or what they did when they were young teenagers. I was busy with my own friends."

"I understand. But... is there any way you could call Joe. Ask him if he remembers Lacy or maybe ask him to call me?"

Her voice a little more assertive, she answered, "I don't feel comfortable talking to him about that sort of thing."

She didn't feel comfortable. Did she realize I wasn't asking her to get details of their intimate encounter? I just wanted to know if they *had* one. There are appropriate ways to present that.

Hoping for a solution, I said, "Could you ask him to call and talk with Jim about me? Since they're both guys, it might be easier that way."

Again, silence. My heart bounced harder with each passing second but again nothing. I didn't dare ask what she thought.

"Please?" I asked.

Assertiveness swallowed her softness. "Let me think about this. Don't call me... just let me think about it... I'll let you know."

There was nothing I could do but agree and thank her, so I did. That's the only choice I had. I was the one asking her for help. Her stipulation was—don't bother her. The finish line moved farther away, but I wasn't going to stop running toward it. The positive note in our conversation was her comment about me looking a little like her mother.

I called Jim in the morning and told him about my conversation with his sister. He sounded glad that I called her. But when I raised the question of him getting Joe's number from her, he ignored it. At times he confused me but he remained adamant that I was an Ellyson. Occasionally, I had the need to ask that for reassurance. He said he'd try and talk to Joe for me, but didn't know if Joe would talk with him. He didn't explain that and it wasn't my business, so I didn't ask.

Jim seemed uncomfortable about calling his brother, yet had only good things to say about him. Some families have these contradictions. He was sad I wasn't his daughter yet certain I was an Ellyson and belonged to his brother, but was reluctant to contact him. There had to be more to their relationship than I knew, but being genetically connected didn't give me the right to ask about any of it.

I changed the subject. "Jim, I'm going to visit the Smiths this weekend."

"Hey, maybe you could take some pictures for me?"

"Sure. Be glad to."

He gave me the locations of trees, bridges and buildings where he had carved his and Lacy's name. He wasn't sure if they'd still be there, but wanted me to look. A long time had passed, but I hoped I could find at least one. Not only for Jim but also for me to have a small remembrance of Lacy's younger happier life.

"Jim, I'm going to stop at the Historical Society and look at high school yearbooks. I see the picture of Joe on the Internet, and I know you're going to send me some pictures, but I want to see a younger Joe. Maybe I'll look at the Mackenzie family too."

"You don't belong to the Mackenzies. I guarantee you that."

"It doesn't hurt to look. And I don't know what else to do. Your sister wants me to give her time to decide whether she'll contact Joe about me, and you don't feel comfortable getting his phone number, although you feel he's my father."

He let out a deep sigh. "Let me see what I can do."

Relieved, I said, "Thank you."

* * *

The November rains drizzled down the entire trip to Bridgeville. It didn't bother Mom who only wanted another chance at an Indian casino, but I wished it would stop. Thoughts of trampling around in the mud and rain to take pictures didn't thrill me.

Mom gambled while I visited the Smiths. I enjoyed seeing them again. None of us had new information to share, but the visit was nice. They liked the idea of me checking out the high school yearbooks to see what everyone looked like. Diane did have an old picture of the Mackenzie boy who was Gary's friend. I studied it but couldn't see even a remote resemblance with my son or me. But I still wanted to look for pictures of his sisters. Diane reminded me that sometimes we don't necessarily look like others in our families. I knew that, but in my case there were three generations in a direct line that resembled Joe. She agreed that it was probably enough confirmation, but it wouldn't hurt to check every possibility. Gary gave me directions to the places Jim had mentioned, including where the Ellysons had lived.

The next morning we headed for Forest Glen. It rained hard the night before, but had stopped by then. Mom, jubilant from her luck at the casino, enjoyed the drive and looked forward to seeing where Lacy had lived when she became pregnant with me.

Forest Glen was fifteen miles down a canyon from the main road. A warm sensation filled me each time I drove it. The first time I thought it was the excitement of a new lead, but later realized it was more than that. It was once the home of Lacy and my father. I walked and drove on the same roads they used years earlier. Being there somehow connected me to them in a way that not much else did, and it felt good. The feeling confirmed what my heart felt, that at the time of my conception, they truly loved each other. As all my intuitive readers told me, I really was a love child.

I took pictures of the Community Center, fences and bridges, but I couldn't find any of the carvings Jim mentioned. The wood on the bridges had been replaced and fences blocked access to the trees. But at least I had pictures of Forest Glen.

*   *   *

We arrived at the Historical Society right before noon. Their elderly volunteers were eager to help but didn't have Channey yearbooks. They had Trinity yearbooks but Channey's were at the school in the library.

Joe had attended Channey. It was the Monday before Thanksgiving, and schools had closed for the holiday week. Frustration fluttered through me. The drive from my home to Eureka seemed to get longer each time and I didn't know when I'd get a chance to come back.

We looked through Trinty yearbooks, and I was glad to find Jim's sister. I took pictures of her and the older Mackenzie girl. As with her brother, I couldn't see any similarities between the Mackenzies and me.

Getting into the car, I said, "Mom, I know kids aren't in school because of Thanksgiving break, which means teachers won't be there either, but my gut feeling tells me to drive to Channey. Maybe some of the office staff is there."

"It can't hurt, especially since you're in the area."

"That was my thought too."

When we pulled into Channey High School the main gate appeared locked, but the parking lot had a handful of cars. I drove around to the side of the school and noticed that there was an open gate. I parked near it.

"That gate's open so I'm going in through there."

Mom looked uneasy with the situation. "I'll sit this one out and wait in the car."

"That's probably a good idea. If I don't come out soon, it could mean I've been arrested for trespassing on school property and they've hauled me off to jail. I'll leave you the keys in case you have to come and bail me out."

"Oh, great."

"I'm kidding... well maybe not, but it's probably best if you stay here. I may have to run."

I hurried through the gate and found an open door into the school. The long hallway had several turns leading to more hallways. Student lockers lined one side. A man carrying the tools and materials of an electrician walked toward me. I started sweating and expected him to tell me to leave because the school was closed. He smiled and walked by. Since my presence didn't bother him, I called after him to ask where the library was. He pointed down the hall and told me to take a left.

I hurried down the hall and turned left. Each room door had a sign above it. Secretary, Principal…oops, I hurried past that one. I didn't want to go there again… although sneaking in here may have guaranteed it. Finally I saw the library sign but the lights were off and the door locked. I heard talking coming from the teachers' lounge. It was a toss-up whether I'd get help to open the library or get a personal escort off the school property.

As I walked in, two men in what looked like maintenance uniforms stopped talking and looked at me. A woman filing papers into a partitioned mailbox cabinet didn't notice me.

"Can I help you?" said one of the men.

"I hope so. I'm doing some research and hoped to get into the library to look at some old yearbooks between the years of 1955 and 1959."

"I think the only person who could help you has left. We aren't authorized to do that."

The woman turned and looked at me. "What's your research?"

I blurted out brief details of my search and that I was from out of town on limited time and would be grateful for any help. They were silent. It was quite a bit to process at one time.

The woman finally said, "Let me see if I can get a hold of someone who has the authority to get in there."

"Thank you."

I listened to her page a few people, but no one responded. She told me to wait; she'd be right back. The maintenance men left and I was alone in the teachers' lounge. I crossed my fingers hoping she'd find someone to open the library. I was so close, but not close enough to see the yearbooks.

Antsy, I stepped out into the hallway. The same woman approached me with what looked like yearbooks tucked under her arm.

Walking ahead, she said, "Follow me."

Without a word I turned and followed her into a small office.

"This is my office," she said, closing the door.

I smiled as I looked at the yearbooks.

She spoke quietly. "I couldn't find anyone to open the library, so I unlocked it myself and got the books."

She placed them on a small table and pulled a chair up to it. "You can look at them here."

I was so grateful for her kindness and understanding, I wanted to hug her. Tears formed in my eyes. "Thank you," I said. "I can't begin to tell you how much I appreciate this."

In a compassionate tone she said, "I do understand. I too was adopted and searched for my biological family. I understand your journey and the importance of knowing."

I couldn't believe it. Was I receiving spiritual help? I wondered. She understood my feelings.

"Was it a pleasant reunion when you met your biological family?"

"It was awkward at first, but nice. I have a lot of siblings now."

"That's great. We can never love too many people."

I opened the yearbook and immediately found Joe's picture. I could have been looking at my son. I remembered Diane saying you can't always go by looks, but this was hard to deny. I checked out the other Mackenzie sister and again saw nothing remotely close in looks. The woman never asked the name I was looking for, as if she must have considered it my business, my journey.

Handing her back the yearbooks, I asked, "Were you supposed to be here today?"

"Funny you should ask. No, I wasn't. What I'm doing could have waited until next week when school's in session, but I felt compelled to come in and do it today. I'm not sure why, I just did."

I knew why. She was there for me, and I was grateful.

"I can't begin to express my gratitude to you."

329

"No problem. I'm glad I could help."

Pure joy surrounded my heart as I walked to the car. I'd seen the pictures and I was still in shock that the person who helped me had been adopted too. All these wonderful people popped up to help me with my search.

Mom glanced at me as I got into the car. "I thought I was going to have to come looking for you."

"Yeah... I figured you'd begin to worry, but boy, you aren't going to believe the help I just received." I told her all about it.

She was amazed as well.

A Love Child's Journey

Chapter Thirty-Two

Jim was disappointed that I hadn't found any of his carvings, but glad that I took pictures of the area. "It was a long time ago," he said. I mentioned getting pictures from the yearbooks, but didn't go into details. He didn't ask about them.
I thought about having a DNA Kinship test and wanted Jim's permission before hand. When asked, he was fine with it and called it *a good idea*. I explained it would only take a week because they already had our DNA. He said he was still trying to get Joe's telephone numbers. I didn't know why it was such a problem, but I hadn't heard from his sister either. If Jim's family knew I was genetically related to him, they might be more helpful. I wanted to know too. I called the DNA Company, and requested a Kinship test. Again, I was in the wait mode.

*   *   *

Waiting would make me crazy. I made an appointment to see Michael my intuitive. Michael's guide confirmed my dowsing. I had the right family, the right guy and I was close to the end of my search. He said it was important to keep knocking on doors. I'd been knocking for a long time but no one had answered yet. Be patient, he concluded, but I was tired of being patient. Patience hadn't produced my father. But that's all I had, so I'd wait.

* * *

"I got it," Jim told me when he called one day. He sounded pleased.

Bursting with excitement, I said, "You got it... you mean you have Joe's telephone number?"

"Yes, I do," he said with victorious conviction.

"Thank you, Jim. I'm not going to ask where you got it. I'm just... so happy you did. But... what do I say to him when I call? Could you call him for me? I'll pay for it."

"No. I don't think I should call. You'll probably get his personal assistant. His name is Henri, but I call him Ornery. I have a hard time understanding him when we talk. He gets mad when I tease him about brushing up on his English. I remind him that Joe's family speaks English. Then he reminds me that Joe lives in France."

I laughed. "Thank you so much, Jim. I hope Joe's okay with this."

"He will be. He'd want to know about you."

It was comforting to hear Jim say that Joe would want to know about me, but I was still nervous about calling. I loved France and French was one of my favorite subjects in high school, but I never could grasp the elegance of spoken French. I couldn't get past greetings.

The time zone in France was important. The last thing I wanted was to call in the middle of the night, which might make Henri very ornery.

I checked the time lines on my world map. France was ten hours ahead of us. Calling when it was their morning seemed best. They'd be fresher and we could talk before their day got busy.

I decided to call that evening at ten. The day dragged. One minute I was glad for the slowness, the next I wished it would speed up. Eating was out of the question, too many butterflies in my stomach and no room for food. I rehearsed all day what I would say to Joe. What would he say to me? All indications pointed to him as my father. I wondered if he even knew about me. Through my dowsing, Lacy said he did, but maybe he didn't.

I waited until ten sharp, and then slowly dialed his number. My heart boomed as if trying to escape my chest. The ring tone sounded like a buzzer.

"Bonjour, c'est Henri," said a young man's voice.

Now that's what I called French. His speech had a savory eloquent flow.

I stammered, "Ah... Henri... I'm Colette... from the United States. Jim, Mr. Ellyson's brother gave me your number."

He answered with a concerned French accent. "Ah oui, Monsieur James, is he okay?"

"Yes... he's fine. I would like to talk with Monsieur Ellyson, please."

He quickly answered, "Monsieur Ellyson has left for Paris and won't be returning for a few days. Is there something I can help you with?"

"It's personal."

"Oui?"

Thinking I should tell him the nature of my call. I decided to let Henri be the one to tell Joe he may have another child. "I'm looking for my biological father and... there's a possibility that Monsieur Ellyson might be my father."

"Ohh...oui, oui."

I wondered what he meant by that. Did he understand what I said? But oui oui! How do I respond to that?

Finally, he said, "Ah... family."

"Yes. Oui. Maybe you could have Monsieur Ellyson call Monsieur Jim and he can explain it to him."

"Oui, I will speak with Monsieur Ellyson regarding this matter when he calls."

"Thank you... Merci. I'd really appreciate it. I will let Monsieur Jim know that he will be calling."

"Oui, Avoir.

"Avoir."

It was exciting talking with someone in France and using a little high school French. But I hoped I'd get to talk with Joe. If he didn't know about me before, he would soon.

333

The next day I checked e-mails and found to my surprise, I had received the Kinship test results. I hurried and opened it, but after reading it, I went numb. This didn't make sense. Jim was less than one tenth of a percent under the possibility of being my uncle. Although close, it still said that I wasn't related to Jim. Did that mean I wasn't an Ellyson? All the clues and information leading me to them and Joe now meant nothing. Was this a joke from the spirit world? I knew that in my heart it didn't work that way, what about the physical resemblance between my son and grandson and me? Tears trickled down the sides of my cheeks as I thought about all the time and effort it took to get the wrong family. I had no other clues. Where would I go from here?

My husband suggested calling the DNA Testing Company to clarify the results.

I called and after explaining the results of my Kinship Test, asked if that meant I was no relation to the Ellyson family. They put me on hold.

"Hello. You were wondering about the Kinship Test?" The woman sounded young and direct.

"Yes. I'm right under the percentage that states I am kin. Does that mean I couldn't belong to a sibling?"

"No, not at all. The Kinship test is for personal use and as it is stated at the bottom of the page, it cannot be used as legal evidence of identity or familial relations. You could have a test with five different siblings and each one could be different. One test might say you're kin and one might say you're not."

"So, what's the point of the Kinship test?"

"Truthfully, nothing. The only way you know for sure what family you belong to is having a positive DNA test with your biological parent. That *is* the only way."

Wanting to make sure I fully understood, I said, "So, the kinship test means nothing and I could still be the daughter of one of the siblings?"

"That's correct."

I thanked her and hung up the phone. The Kinship test was a complete waste of money, but at least there was still a possibility I was an Ellyson and Joe was my father.

Jim didn't care about the Kinship results and reassured me I was an Ellyson and that Joe was my father. He looked forward to Henri or Joe calling him. I had passed the buck, because I thought Joe would respond better to Jim than me.

*　　　*　　　*

Christmas was fast approaching and I hadn't heard from anyone. I called Jim and neither Joe nor Henri hadn't contacted him. Waiting was torturous but maybe they were busy. I decided to let the holidays pass before calling Henri again.

*　　　*　　　*

The first of the year came and went with no contact from anyone. I called France. Not as nervous as before, I was uncertain if that was good or bad. I'd become a little irritated by the lack of communication. I wasn't looking for money, just the truth and validation. Was he my father or wasn't he? A simple DNA test would reveal the truth.

At ten that night I made my call, and again Henri answered.

"Bonjour," he said, very cheerfully.

"Henri, this is Colette from the United States."

"Oui… Oui…"

"You remember me?"

He chuckled. "Oui. Monsieur Ellyson is amused that you are not Monsieur James's daughter."

Some one had talked with Joe. He knew I wasn't Jim's daughter; it had to be their sister, Lynda.

I didn't understand why that would be funny. Was it French humor or one of those sibling things?

"So… Henri. Does Monsieur Ellyson remember my mother?"

He didn't answer my question, but asked in broken English. "Monsieur Ellyson would like to see pictures. Could you send them via the Internet?"

I tensed up. Joe wanted to see pictures of me. He hadn't asked to speak with me, but at least he wanted pictures. He must think there was some chance of being my father, otherwise why would he want to see pictures of a stranger's child? I knew Lacy was no stranger to him.

Henri gave me the e-mail address to send the pictures. Before the day was over, I had e-mailed them to him.

Days rolled by without any word from Henri. I e-mailed to confirm that he received them, but no response. I didn't understand what was happening. Maybe they hoped I'd go away or were having trouble deciding how to deal with me. I wasn't being difficult, but they didn't know me, or the type of person I was, so I understood their apprehension. A simple DNA test would resolve the whole thing. Was he or wasn't he? What did he think? Jim continued to insist that I was an Ellyson and seemed certain his brother would want to know the truth. But Joe's actions said something different.

Joe's notoriety and wealth seemed to have created a major barrier in my search. I couldn't walk up, knock on his door and talk to him. Well, in his case I'd have to fly over to France first and then knock on his door, which according to Jim was a football field away from the gate entrance. He wouldn't hear the knock anyway, his staff would. I had no idea what kind of consequences my existence could create in his life, but I believed in my heart that I had the right to know if he was my father. I had thought he would want to know too, but that impression was quickly fading.

Two more days passed without a response. Weary of waiting, I called Henri. I thought of addressing him as Ornery because of his aloofness. The number I have is his cell phone. For all I know he could have been standing by Joe when I talked with him. Would that have been his doing or Joe's? It was hard for me to accept my possible father being that heartless.

According to Jim, Joe's four children, two boys and two girls, were close to their father and visited him often at his villa. Jim referred to the villa as a large resort. I honestly didn't care if he lived in a tent. Where he lived didn't define him, but his actions did. And so far they weren't very favorable.

"Bonjour," Henri said.

"Bonjour, Henri. This is Colette. I haven't heard from you. Did you receive the pictures I sent you and Monsieur Ellyson?"

He stuttered some French words, then said, "Monsieur Ellyson does not think so."

Wishing I understood his rapid French, I asked, "He doesn't think what?"

"Oui... ah... Monsieur Ellyson does not recognize some of the people in your pictures."

I sent a class picture along with pictures of Lacy and myself. I didn't think he'd recognize everyone, but surely he remembered her.

"Yes, but what about Lacy? Does he remember anything about her?"

"I'm not sure. Monsieur Ellyson is in London. We will talk later. Avoir."

The telephone clicked and then a dial tone took over. He hung up before I had a chance to finish. I held the receiver next to my ear as if thinking he was going to pick his telephone up and talk again. What did he mean? And what about a DNA test? He said we'd talk later. Was he going to call me or was I supposed to call him?

My enthusiasm plunged. Pangs of rejection whittled away at my heart. I desperately wanted to understand, but Joe's avoidance was disheartening.

If Joe really thought I wasn't his daughter, why wouldn't he have a DNA test to prove me wrong? But Henri didn't say that Joe was absolutely sure he wasn't.

For the first time in my search, I didn't know what to do. But I wasn't giving up, not yet.

* * *

I went to see my intuitive, Michael. His reading was the same as before: Joe is my father, I'm on the right track and it's all in divine order and divine timing. His guide seemed amused when I asked if he could move the divine timing a little faster. I didn't know what had to be in order, but I was tired of the search and ready to find out who my father was. My own dowsing echoed Michael's guide.

*   *   *

I decided not to call Jim for a while. I had given up on contacting Joe through him. A few months had passed since the DNA test results without him calling Joe. He continued to tell me that I was an Ellyson and Joe was my father, but for some reason he didn't feel comfortable calling him. If it weren't for my other clues and the strong resemblance between Joe, my son, my grandson and me, I'd be suspicious of his behavior.

I thought I had been respectful and considerate to Joe, giving him plenty of time to think about me and get over the shock or whatever feelings he had to deal with. But it had been long enough. Waiting for some kind of response was unsettling. I sent a text message to Henri

> *Monsieur Henri,*
> *Pls Henri, I'm waiting to hear from you.*
> *Does Monsieur Ellyson remember my mother?*
> *Will he submit to a DNA test?*
> *Pls let me know.*
> *Thank you,*
> *Colette*

I checked my phone constantly for a message from Henri. Nothing. A week later, I got a call, but if wasn't from Henri.

"Colette, this is Joyce," she said in a callous tone.

Hoping for news, I cheerfully said, "Hi, Joyce!"

In a loud voice she demanded, "Leave our family alone."

Shocked, I said, "But...."

She interrupting, snapping, "Don't call our house again. I don't want you talking with Jim. The whole family is mad at him because of you. You are not an Ellyson."

The phone clicked. She had hung up. Was the whole family really mad at Jim? The only other family member I talked with was his sister and I did exactly as she asked. Why would she be mad? She was kind and told me if I were her brother's daughter, she'd welcome me into their family. She had to be the one who told Joe about me. Jim was my connection to the Ellyson family, the one who seemed to know and could help me and now I couldn't call him. I wondered if he knew she'd called me. Tears trickled down my cheeks as I tried to make sense of everything. Was Joyce jealous of me? Or jealous of the feelings Jim had for Lacy many years ago? How could she know I wasn't an Ellyson? The rejections from Henri and Joe had been subtle, but she was blatant. Respect and consideration didn't seem to matter. I wiped my tears and vowed to hear it from Jim if I wasn't an Ellyson. But even then, I didn't know if I'd believe him, not with all the evidence I had.

During my search for Lacy and now my father, almost everyone I met had been willing to help. They encouraged me to continue and did what they could to help me. But now that I might have found the right family, some members weren't so accepting or helpful. The DNA test confirmed I wasn't Jim's daughter, so Joyce should have been happy, but she wasn't. Whatever relationship issues they had I didn't want to cause them problems. But I had a right to know who my father was.

In the morning, I took a chance that Joyce might be at work and called Jim.

His raspy tone was comforting. "Hello."

"Jim, this is Colette. May I speak with you a minute?"

His voice became harsh and distant. "Make it quick."

Instantly, I realized he knew Joyce had called me. I fought to hold back tears at his sudden coldness.

"Jim, do you still believe I'm an Ellyson?"

He hesitated and compassion leaked out. "I'm sorry, I can't say."

Tears welled up in my eyes and I was thankful he couldn't see me. Did he hear the crackle in my voice and feel the pain in my heart?

"Do you still think my son looks like Joe?" I tearfully asked.

"Yes... yes he does."

It took all my control just to talk. Tears slid off my checks like raindrops. The thought of not being able to call him again was overwhelming. He had treated me like a daughter and he was the closest connection to my father.

"I'm so sorry I've caused you problems. Thank you for your kindness and help and I hope someday we'll talk again."

"Don't worry about it."

I sat motionless after saying goodbye. Why didn't he stand up for what he believed was true? Why did Joyce act so threatened by me? Why didn't she want me in the Ellyson family? Being objective about the situation, I was a stranger who showed up unexpectedly, but she was Jim's wife and he had to live with her.

*   *   *

I moped around for a few days, indulging in my own little pity party. I had used all the skills taught to me over the years from my parents, but it didn't matter. The Ellyson family had no intention of helping me find my father. It looked like they were protecting Joe. From what, I didn't know, and why, but I wouldn't stop with my search.

A trip to Wilma's was in order. What else could I do? Maybe she'd feel sorry for me and let me look in the chests. Wishful thinking, but it was worth a try.

Within a few days I was on my way north with my mother, Flo. I made the usual stop at the Indian casino where I dropped her off. Then drove to Wilma's.

She was happy to see me and very alert. Each visit her moods varied from cheerful to comatose. Was it medication or her? I used my key and let myself in.

I had just sat down in the chair next to her when my cell phone rang. It was Diane Smith. She and Gary had returned from a trip down south and wanted an update on my search. It was nice to hear from her and I decided to stay in the chair so Wilma could hear the conversation. It was a good way to bring up the subject of my search.

I pretended not to notice Wilma leaning toward me as she listened. I told Diane about talking with Jim and the call from Joyce. Diane was disappointed and baffled but encouraged me to continue and not drop my search. I assured her I had no intention of that and would call her when I had more to tell, then said our good-byes.

"That was Diane Smith. Remember I told you they were trying to help me with my search?"

Wilma's voice was somber. "I've been thinking about it lately and... you know Lacy had a lot of freedom when she got out of school because Rodney was working. She could do what she wanted until he got home from work."

Wondering what she was leading up to, I said, "Yeah... probably."

She continued, "Anyway, you don't look like Rodney or anyone in his family."

She dropped her head. My ears rang as I held on to every word from her mouth.

"You're not Rodney's daughter. I knew that when I first saw you... when you found us. Rodney was inappropriate with Lacy, and I'll never forgive him for that but... she was a good girl."

I wanted to jump up and down. I had known deep in my heart that Rodney wasn't my father, but now I had no doubts.

I took her hand and gently stroked it. I'd waited two years to hear the truth and she finally admitted I wasn't her husband's daughter.

"Lacy was a good girl and a good person. Becoming pregnant with me didn't make her bad. I believe it was meant to be, but I'm sad that her life was so difficult, which started from becoming pregnant with me."

"Yes... you know, I remember Jim and Joe and I believe there's a strong possibility one of them is your father. Lacy started acting all grown up with high heels and makeup. She didn't act or look like a thirteen-year-old. She'd always been more mature than her age. I don't know why she kept your father a secret."

"I don't know either and I didn't ask her about it. I do remember Mitch telling me that JL told him my father was a local Italian boy. But I didn't think anything about it at the time because I thought by local he meant this town, and I knew she didn't get pregnant here."

JL had been married to Lacy for over ten years, considerably longer than most of her other marriages.

341

Wilma's demeanor changed. She seemed relieved that I didn't get mad or upset with her confession. She now seemed to want to help me.

"You know... if Lacy told anyone the truth about your father, it would've been JL. She loved and trusted him more than her own family, although I don't know why."

It was evident Wilma didn't care for JL, but excitement steamrolled through me, a new direction for my search. I jumped up and hugged her. "Thank you, Nammie."

I wanted her to know I appreciated it but didn't want to make too big a deal about it. I still liked her even if it did take her two... long years to admit the truth, a big milestone in our relationship. The next one would be a look inside her trunks, but for now I was happy with what I had.

I'd met JL a few times. He had stopped by once with Mitch and another time I went with Mitch to visit him and his wife. He wasn't Mitch's biological father, but was all Mitch had.

"JL lives here in town. If I were you, I'd give him a call. Maybe you could see him today."

My head buzzed with joy. Was this the same woman I'd been visiting for two years and who wouldn't talk to me about my origin, but now wants to help me? I wasn't going to question it, only appreciate it.

I found JL's number in the phone book. I flicked a pencil back and forth listening to the rings. I crossed my fingers hoping he'd be home.

His voice was gruff and he coughed every few words, but seemed delighted to hear from me. He invited me to stop by that afternoon and gave me directions.

I was anxious to go to JL's, but visited with Wilma a little longer. Something had shifted in our relationship. Calmness hovered over us as we chatted like a grandmother and granddaughter should. I hugged her goodbye and headed for JL's.

A Love Child's Journey

Chapter Thirty-Three

Potholes dimpled the dirt road leading to JL's house. A chain link fence bordered the large lawn that hadn't had its first spring mowing. As I walked to the door, a small dog barked inside.

I stopped at the screen door, and JL yelled through the open doorway, "Come on in."

The dog continued to bark after I walked in. Cigarette smoke lingered around the dimly lit end table lamps by matching recliners. JL sat in one, and his wife, a petite older woman, blanket on her lap sat in the other. She shoved something in the dog's mouth and after a few more barks it stopped and settled down in a dog bed. I didn't know what she gave him and thought it best not to ask. At least we didn't have to talk over the barking.

JL had combed hair and clean clothes. I remembered him as a nice looking man, but the years of drinking had taken their toll.

"You remember my wife, right?"

Nodding at her, I said, "Nice to see you again."

She smiled. "Same here."

"Thank you for seeing me at such short notice," I said.

Puffing on his cigarette, he said, "Hon, I'm glad to see you. It's been a long time."

"Yes it has."

He asked me to tell him what was going on in my life, which I did, except for my search. I didn't want to influence anything he might have to say. He asked about Allaine and seemed disappointed at not hearing from Mitch for some time. It amazed me that he knew so much about Mitch and Allaine, but what really blew me away was how much he knew about me. He knew Lacy's exact age and the date and time she delivered me. He knew one of the workers at the home made a mistake and brought me to Lacy. That's how she knew she had a girl.

How did he remember all of that? Amazing! The only way he could have known was from Lacy. She must have told him and he retained it. Apparently the drinking didn't affect his memory.

He reciprocated Wilma's poor opinion of him, a mutual dislike.

"I've been visiting Wilma," I said. "Hoping to find out the truth about my biological father. She finally admitted I wasn't Rodney's daughter."

In a loud tone, he said, "Rod's not your father. Who told you that?"

"Well... Lacy did at first, but I didn't think he was." I had to stay cautious. "It's good to have it confirmed."

"He never had actual sexual intercourse with Lacy. She knew who your father was. She told me and it wasn't Rod."

I sat there in disbelief. His straightforward words swirled in my head. Then without a pause he told me all about the inappropriate touching Rodney had done to Lacy.

My head continued to spin. In front of me was someone who Lacy had confided in. My heart ached for her while anger for Rodney filled my stomach like burning acid. How could a father do that to his child?

"Lacy really liked your father. She said he was... I believe a grade above her in school."

Using every ounce of will power to stay calm, I asked, "Who was it? Did she tell you his name?"

"Yeah... he was some local Italian boy. Let me think... oh yeah, Lacy said he liked to draw or paint, something along those lines. He had... a common name, like John or Joe. Something like that. She sure did have some deep feelings for him."

I began to tremble. I didn't know what to say. All my leads and clues had led me to the Ellysons, but I still had some doubt. JL had no idea what information I had received in my search. He was telling me what he remembered without any prompting.

"Lacy and Laura made up a story," he said. "They believed that when you had sex you got pregnant so they conjured up the tale of being raped by a traveling dress salesman."

That comment was like the icing on the cake.

"JL, that's what Lacy told the adoption agency. It's written down in the paperwork I have." Laura was eleven when Lacy became pregnant with me."

"Hum…that had to be Lacy's story then because Laura's first experience was much later with the father of her children."

His comments seemed so casual, as if we were talking about ordinary things, but I was about to have a coronary. I had found some of the missing pieces to my puzzle. He was oblivious to the importance of his words.

I told him about my search minus the intuitive readers and dowsing. Not knowing his beliefs, I decided to skip that aspect of my search. He seemed to think I had the right family and the right person and said he'd do some more thinking about it. I thanked him and said I'd be in touch. Then I drove to the Indian casino to pick up Mom. I couldn't wait to tell her about my day.

*   *   *

After visiting JL, I believed I had the right family. Jim had been eliminated and seemed certain I wasn't the older brother's child, which only left Joe. And he did paint.

I looked on the Internet and found an address in Nice, France. I was certain it wasn't his home address, but if I sent something to him and Henri, he'd get it. It was worth the gamble.

I ordered another DNA kit and had it sent to me. I printed out all the pictures I previously sent to Henri and Joe over the Internet along with a few more. I copied all my adoption papers and the first letter Lacy wrote me, packaged it all together and sent it to the address in Nice, France. It was expensive, but worth it. I didn't want him to think I was a gold-digger or a fake. The only thing I wanted was the truth. With all the evidence that I have presented and he's still certain he's not my father, he'd want to take the DNA test so his attorneys could tell me to go away.

That evening I e-mailed a message to Henri, explaining the contents of the package and where I sent it. To ensure that he checked his e-mail, I sent a text message to his telephone. I wanted him to know that this package would be floating around in Nice. I'm sure Henri was aware of the address. It may have been Joe's agent address, but either way, I wanted him to know.

*   *   *

The next day Jim called to say that Joyce wanted to speak with me. Before I had a chance to respond, she came on the line and yelled, "LEAVE OUR FAMILY ALONE! How many times do you need to hear that you're not part of this family?"

Remaining calm, I said, "You don't know that for a fact and neither do I."

Her angry voice was vicious as she yelled, "You just want money, don't you?"

I couldn't believe what I was hearing, but what hurt was that I knew Jim was listening. I thought he had talked to me enough to realize it had nothing to do with money. Did the wrong assumption come from Joe after my e-mail about the package I sent? At this point I didn't see it was any of her business, but wanted to stay cordial.

Taking a deep breath, I quietly said, "Joyce, this has nothing to do with money. Do you know who your father is?"

"Well of course," she snapped.

"Well, I don't, but it's important that I do. Have you tried putting yourself in my shoes?"

She didn't seem to hear a word I said. "You made Jim take a DNA test," she said bluntly. "And you used him to get Henri's numbers and now his brother won't talk with him and it's all because of you."

Her words were cold, heartless and untrue.

"Listen Joyce, I didn't make Jim do anything. It was his idea to do the DNA test. I did ask him to help me get Joe's phone numbers but he gave me Henri's instead. And he said it was awkward because he and his brother hadn't spoken in a long time, which certainly had nothing to do with me."

Again, she ignored what I said and called me a shameless fortune hunter. It became apparent that she thought I was after Joe's money. I wondered if Jim and Joe's estrangement hampered potential perks. Since Jim wasn't my father, what I did was no concern of hers, but she gave me the odd impression of seeing herself as the victim.

She continued to badger me with hurtful words. I never considered myself meek, but arguing with her wasn't going to change anything.

Finally, I said, "Joyce, this is really none of your business and I don't care to discuss it with you any further."

Instantly I heard a click, then a dial tone. She had hung up on me again.

Why did Jim allow this to happen? Tears flooded my eyes as I tried to make sense of his behavior. I felt that in his heart, he knew the truth, but was unwilling to stand up for what he had led me to believe was right.

My tears kept coming; I couldn't stop crying. I really tried to understand. Did his brother have that much power over him? Or was it his wife? What was wrong with me wanting to know who my father was? Why was this family so against my finding out the truth? Was it about money and wealth? They didn't want to know me or anything about me. I prided myself on the fact that my emotional stability was strong, but this rejection was putting it through a tough test. My painful heart needed a rest, but I was determined not to give up.

*   *   *

I continued to dowse and have an occasional intuitive reading from Michael. His guide told me to keep working on my search and my healing abilities. My dowsing continued to state that Joe was my father and I would become a healer too. Was there some kind of conspiracy going on in the spirit world? Each guide gave me the same information. I asked mine to focus on something other than my search but I couldn't direct the information that the spirit world seemed to want me to hear. My guides kept telling me this summer was going to be key. I hadn't had any more contact with Henri, and nothing from Joyce or Jim. Summer was fast approaching and Allaine would soon visit. The future held possibilities of interesting adventures.

Allaine and I had talked about taking a trip to Sedona, but every time I dowsed, I was told not to go there. Instead, it directed me to Bridgeville and Forest Glen.

I e-mailed Allaine and told her that my dowsing continued to point me to Bridgeville. Although she was looking forward to seeing Sedona, she reminded me about the gypsy woman we found and the man in Lowe's and that I should pay attention to my dowsing.

Relieved that she wasn't disappointed, I added the next bit of information I dowsed. We were to drive to Bridgeville four days after she arrived. She was okay with that too. I explained it was just a gut feeling. I didn't know why. Maybe the spirit world would use some divine timing and place an Ellyson there. I made a mental note to ask, when dowsing, for a congenial Ellyson, if that was the case.

That was our plan. Drive to Bridgeville four days after she arrived from Kuwait and spend three nights there. Check out Forest Glen and wait for an Ellyson to show up. She was agreeable, but suggested we not share our plans with too many others. I agreed.

*   *   *

A few days later my brother Mitch called.

"Hey, what ya been doing?" he asked, cheerful as usual.

It was good to hear from him. Mitch and Allaine had become the next best reasons I found Lacy.

"Not too much. How about you?"

"Well, I was sitting around here thinking that when Allaine comes to visit, the three of us should go on a road trip together. Something small, what do you think?"

I didn't think the road trip Allaine and I had planned was what he had in mind.

"Yeah... Allaine and I talked about that."

"Did you come up with anything? Is it somewhere I could tag along?"

Mitch had encouraged me to look for my father and was open minded when I told him about my dowsing, but up to this point, that's all it had been—me talking and him listening.

"Sure... sure you're welcome to be part of our trip."

"Where are you going?"

I hesitated. "Bridgeville and then spend some time in Forest Glen."

He laughed. "Bridgeville and Forest Glen. What were you planning to do there?"

I let out a deep sigh and he started laughing.

I laughed too. "Okay, here's the deal. When I was dowsing, my guides told me to go to Bridgeville four days after Allaine arrives. So that's our plan."

"Okay, I understand that part, but again, what are you going to do after you get there?"

I said, "I'm not quite sure about that yet. But, hey... we could relax and I can show you where our mom lived and the community center where she spent a lot of her time."

"I didn't realize the house she lived in was still there."

"It's not, but I can show you where the house used to be."

Sarcasm got the better of him. "Yeah, I could see where that would be a lot of fun. Staring at the spot where a house used to be."

"It could be. I think I'm supposed to be there to see my father or one of the Ellyson's."

"Oh, why didn't you say that? So your supposed father and some of the Ellysons are going to be in Bridgeville?"

"Forest Glen, I think, according to my dowsing. But I was told it was important to go there and I'd see an Ellyson or maybe my father."

"Let me get this straight. You and Allaine are driving to Bridgeville and plan on stopping by Forest Glen to see an Ellyson, yet nothing but your dowsing has told you they'll be there?"

It sounded even more ludicrous coming from him, and it was my idea. I remembered Allaine's comment about being cautious. But he was our brother.

"Yeah... that's it in a nut shell."

His laugh turned into a loud roar. "I'm in. I can't imagine missing out on that one."

Laughing with him, I said, "I believe you're making fun of me."

"I am."

He said he'd make our hotel reservations in Bridgeville. Then he'd let me know his flight time on the fourth day after Allaine arrived.

I thanked him for his willingness to embark upon my search and assured him we'd have fun. I told him I'd let Allaine know he'd be joining us. Our first trip together for the three of us and I was certain it would be memorable.

*   *   *

The fourth day after Allaine arrived, Mitch's flight would land right before noon, which was perfect. I had dowsed a list of instructions from... the spirit world... I presumed.   Allaine and I were excited and sure that I would be meeting my father soon.

Nearing the airport, Allaine said, " Do you remember last year there was an intuitive that said to us something about the power of three?"

"Oh... yeah... I remember that."

"I know something's going to happen, because you, me and Mitch are the power of three."

"Ooh...you're right. I remember that. That gives me the chills. Mitch is going to think we've flipped."

"Yeah... probably. So... let's break him in early and go over the agenda you dowsed right from the get go."

"Good idea. He definitely needs to know the dowsing agenda."

Mitch was waiting outside the airport. Allaine and I were glad to see him. He threw his bags in the back of the SUV and hopped in the back seat.

"The first stop," he teased. "I get to ride in front."

We all laughed.

"Hey, you're the youngest," Allaine joked. "You have to ride in back."

I piped in. "I'm the oldest and I say we take turns."

Mitch added, "Good idea. When do I get to drive?"

"You don't."

"So much for taking turns."

"I'm the oldest and I'm the driver."

We laughed some more. It was nice to have the three of us together. Lacy would have been so pleased to see the loving bond that had developed between the three of us. Poor Mitch, he had no idea what his crazy sisters had in mind.

"Mitch, do you want to hear the dowsing agenda?" asked Allaine.

"Do I have a choice?"

"No, so I'll read it to you. But first, we're having dinner with the Smiths tomorrow. Not part of the dowsing agenda. Okay... this is the fourth day after my arrival, and we're on our way, so we're good with that. We have to stay in Bridgeville three days, after arriving. On the third day, we drive to Forest Glen. It's important to be at the community center in Forest Glen by 11:00 in the morning."

Mitch let out a loud cackle, "Wait... wait... wait a minute." Catching his breath, he said, "You got this from dowsing, so now... what do we gotta do?"

Allaine repeated what she had just said, then added, "There's more. We have to wait at the community center for two hours and look for a green car with two people in it."

Mitch snorted and tried to keep a straight face. "So in this green car... is... let me guess, Colette's father?"

Allaine let out a loud giggle, then answered, "Yeah or one of the Ellysons. It has to be something like that. The spirit world has pushed her toward this over the last few months, telling her it was important to be in Bridgeville on this date. What else could it be?"

Mitch retorted, "I have no idea, I'm officially on vacation. So the "dowsing agenda" is fine with me."

We had been driving a while when my cell phone rang. Allaine answered it, shrugged, and handed it to me.

As I listened to the trembling voice on my cell phone, tears filled my eyes and the words echoed in my ears. Numb with disbelief, my heart began to ache. I closed the phone and handed it back to her.

She asked, "Colette, what's wrong? What's happened?"

I tried to speak, but the words stuck in my throat.

I took a deep breath, swallowing and wiping my tears. "It's Gary Smith."

"What's wrong with him?"

Bursting into tears, I cried out, "He died in his sleep last night."

"Oh, no. Oh, my gosh. Poor Diane."

"She'll call us tomorrow night."

"Is… is… this why you're supposed to be in Bridgeville? Gary's death?"

I calmed down. "I don't know. I hope not. This wasn't supposed to happen. He was such a kind man. Even though I didn't know him long, he was very special to me."

"Does this mean the "dowsing agenda" is off?" Mitch yelled from the back seat.

"I don't know what it means, but I think we should stick with the agenda."

Allaine agreed. Mitch felt bad for the loss of my friend, but he hadn't met the Smiths. To him, they were strangers. Gary and Diane were much more than that to me. They were like my surrogate parents. They encouraged me to be positive and understanding with the Ellysons and my search. They never misled me. And continue to tell me that they would be happy to be my parents. But most of all, they never had a harsh word to say about anyone. Gary and Diane each were one of a kind. My heart ached not only for Diane and her family, but for me as well.

Mitch tried to entertain us, but the rest of the drive to Bridgeville was gloomy. Once there, we all worked hard to make the best of it. We had dinner and every time Mitch saw a green car he told me to look inside and see if my daddy was in it. His humor helped. I had a difficult time sleeping that night, wondering how Diane was doing and knowing there was nothing I could do, to make her feel better. I couldn't even make myself feel better.

I didn't have a specific agenda for the second day. We decided to drive back to Eureka and take a walk along the ocean. After lunch and a little shopping, we drove back to Bridgeville. Thoughts of Gary occupied my mind. Diane had called inviting us to stop by the following evening.

The next morning the "dowsing agenda" was put into place. We had breakfast, bought some sandwiches and sodas, and then headed for Forest Glen mid-morning giving us enough time to reach the community center by eleven.

Drifting down a dirt road to the community center, Mitch asked, "Are you sure this is the right way?"

"Yes," I said.

"Do you realize we haven't seen a single car yet?" he teased. "Let alone a green one."

"Yes, I know," I snarled.

"Did you notice there aren't any people around here, either?"

"Oh Mitch, stop," said Allaine.

"Just an observation."

I laughed. "Give it time. We have two hours. Surely something will happen."

He mumbled something else, but I didn't hear him. Two hours was a long time to wait in what seemed to be nowhere. After the news of Gary's death, I wasn't sure if seeing my father was why I'd come. More like a reason to lure me to Bridgeville. We could have picked some place else, but my dowsing was adamant about where I was to be. And, the spirit world put the guy with the plaid shirt and khaki pants in Lowe's at the right time. So, why not put an Ellyson here.

We found some rusty old chairs and sat under a large pine tree off to the left of the community center. Except for an occasional mosquito, it was relaxing. We talked about Lacy and the fact that she had spent a lot of time at the very place we were sitting.

The two-hour wait was almost up and Mitch was getting antsy.

Pointing toward the dirt road, he jumped out of his chair and said, "I think I see a car."

Looking in the same direction, Allaine and I stood up.

"Where?" I asked.

"See it? It's getting closer. I... I... think it's green. Is... is that your Da-a-a...ddy driving it?"

He couldn't keep a straight face anymore and began to laugh. We joined him. There was no car but his joking was priceless. No outside distractions at all, just the three of us, the power of three, but I had hoped to see an Ellyson.

The following day I dowsed about Gary's sudden departure and my dowsing said his work was done. I didn't understand it, and at that point my dowsing confused me. That evening Allaine and I had a tearful visit with Diane.

The trip baffled both of us. On Allaine's last two visits we had amazing adventures, but this one, wasn't what we expected. I didn't understand my "dowsing agenda." The only thing I could figure was that I was to be in Bridgeville the day of Gary's death. And that Mitch, Allaine and I just needed to spend a few days together. That was the only positive outcome.

On our way back, Alliane said, "Hey, I have an idea. Let's visit the other Ellyson brother. He just lives north of Eureka."

Mitch raised his voice. "No... no way. I've had enough of the Ellyson search. Just drop me off at the airport so I can catch the next flight home. Then you guys can do whatever you want."

"That's too far to drive back from," she pouted.

"Well... right now," I said. "I'm not sure where to go with this search. I'm getting so many mixed messages. All the clues led me to the Smiths and the Ellysons and now I'm getting all the blocks. I have no idea what it means. I'm fairly certain that God and the spirit world are a good group, so there has to be some reason for all this."

"Yeah, you'd think so. Maybe you're not knocking on the right door," Allaine said.

"What do you mean?"

"During your search you've knocked on a lot of strangers' doors. Up until lately, you got clues by knocking, so maybe you need some new doors to knock on. And... there are two more Ellyson doors you haven't tried."

"Yeah... you're right."

A Love Child's Journey

Chapter Thirty-Four

Allaine had been back in Kuwait for over a month. Her e-mails kept prodding me to visit Joe's older brother Frank. I leaned more toward paying a visit to their sister first, although she lived further away. But our trip to Bridgeville at the time of Gary's death continued to stay on my mind. I wasn't sure if I was ready to pick myself up off the ground, dust myself off and tackle more rejection and disappointment.

The next e-mail she sent caught my interest. She told me to Google Joe and check out his upcoming events. To my surprise, I discovered he would be involved in two large art expositions, first in New York and a week later in Los Angeles. That meant he would be in the US for at least two weeks. The first event was less than a week away. Maybe I should try to meet him. My heart fluttered with excitement. Was this the divine timing that Michael, the intuitive talked about? What else could it be?"

I considered attending one of the events, but realized he would be busy and his time limited. He had my phone number and address, so if he wanted to see me, he'd have made the effort or had Henri call me. I secretly wished he'd invite me to the LA event and give me a private viewing of his paintings. A big wish, but not very realistic. He had a telephone in France but hadn't called, and several months had passed since he'd requested my pictures. He wasn't leaping through hoops to meet me, but he might need time to process the fact that he'd conceived a daughter at such a young age.

*   *   *

I checked my cell phone at least twenty times a day during his first event, but was only mildly disappointed. If he was going to call, I thought he'd do it when he reached LA. After his third day in LA without a call, my chance of attending had slowly dissolved from my dreams and the chance of meeting him had narrowed.

The last day of his event I carried my cell phone around in my hand. He didn't call. I continued to check my messages for two days after the event. I even gave him the benefit of the doubt, and thought of every excuse for him not calling, from constant meetings with buyers and investors or tied up in negotiations or whatever. Who was I kidding? He seemed to have no interest in acknowledging me and wasn't even curious about me.

That evening in bed, warm tears poured from my eyes as I silently wept in the dark. My husband had been supportive and understanding with my search, but it upset him that he couldn't fix the rejection I was experiencing. I didn't cry often, but at times the rejection become so overwhelming I had to release it. Except for a headache the following morning, crying was the best release.

Maybe Joe was afraid I wanted money from him. Unfortunately, he hadn't given me an opportunity to refute that. Maybe other family members behind doors I hadn't yet knocked on would take the time to talk with me and realize that all I want is to know where I came from.

*   *   *

The Ellyson sister lived by the coast in northern Oregon. All it took to entice Mom was to tell her about a nice Indian casino near our destination. She was game to go with me and knock on the sister's door. Except she preferred to wait at the casino while I did the knocking. Either way, at eighty-five she was willing to ride shotgun on another trip.

Apprehensive and unsure if I was doing the right thing by a surprise visit to Joe's sister, it was comforting to have Mom along.

We enjoyed the scenic drive along the coastal highway. I hadn't been on the coast road since the trip to Bridgeville, when I got the news about Gary. A few seconds after that thought I looked up and saw a billboard with the name of the street he'd lived on. It felt as if he was with me. A few minutes later a large truck went by with the name Frank's Hauling on its door. Frank was the other Ellyson door I hadn't knocked on. We stopped for lunch and a man walked by and yelled the name Joe. I took the coincidences as a positive reassurance that I was doing the right thing.

It was dusk when we arrived at the casino. The sun did a balancing act on the ocean surface and soon it would be dark. We sat a minute and listened to the muffled sound of waves coming in and retracting into the vast sea.

The soothing sound of waves abruptly shifted when we entered the casino. I would have been happy to stay in the parking lot, but Mom's eyes lit up as we walked to the hotel desk. Bells, whistles, smoke and the occasional thrilling scream made her day.

Eight-thirty in the evening was too late to go knocking on a stranger's door, but I wanted to see where she lived. Mom put her gambling on hold and went with me.

Using directions from the Internet, we drove a few miles inland before turning off the main road onto her street. Mid to large size custom homes lined both sides of the street. Yards looked neatly mowed and only a few cars parked along the curbs. Each beat of my heart seemed to slam against my chest as I neared her home, but darkness created a sense of security. The lit street numbers on the houses made it easy to find her tan mid size two-story home with a three-car garage. The house was dark, no lights in the windows. Not even the porch light was on. Either no one was home or they'd gone to bed, which was fine with me. I wasn't ready to knock just yet.

*   *   *

The gambler and I had breakfast together. Then I set off with my pictures and high hopes of meeting an Ellyson. One who would give me the opportunity to explain my intentions and tell me a little something about where I came from. My head buzzed as I rehearsed the best things to say. Use my manners? That's what kept coming up. I already knew that, it worked yet I often ended up begging and pleading my final lines. Lynda had been kind to me when I spoke with her. My heart held on to that kindness; it was all I had.

*   *   *

My hands twisted back and forth on the steering wheel as I made the turn on to her street. Feeling flushed, I glanced in the rearview mirror. Sweat had popped out around my hairline. I hoped they wouldn't run down my face and ruin what makeup I had on.

Mid-morning sun had begun to work its way through the mist. Two young boys raced their bikes down the sidewalk. The sound of a distant lawn mower filled the air as I parked. I picked up my pictures, took a few deep breaths to calm my uneasiness and walked up the neatly trimmed walkway. I rang the doorbell twice, but no one answered. Surely, someone had to be up. Lunchtime was only an hour away. I pushed the doorbell repeatedly, as if it was an elevator button and eventually the door would open. But it didn't. Saturday mornings many people do their grocery shopping after chores. Maybe that's where she was.

I found a coffeehouse a few blocks from her home. I drank coffee and thought about the outcome of our visit. I wrote a quick note asking her to please help me understand the reactions I had been getting from her family. And that I wasn't upset but wanted to know about the medical history as well as the people I came from. I waited an hour then drove by her house. There was still no one home. For a brief moment, I wondered if she was inside but didn't want to answer the door. My common sense returned. I knew better. It was evident that nobody was there. The gambler would want to know right away what happened, so I returned to the casino.

I made four more trips to her house that day, my last one at nine in the evening. Disappointment flooded my heart. What did it mean? Where could she be? Was she on vacation? I had no idea. She and her husband were retired and could have been anywhere. I had tomorrow and that was it. Then I would go back home.

With an early wake up call the next morning I was out the door by seventy thirty. I parked in front of her house again. To my amazement, I wasn't nervous. I'd repeated the same actions for two days with no response, and each time it became less nerve-racking. Maybe I wasn't supposed to talk with her. I had no idea what the spirit world had in mind for me, and I was confused. I felt like I was banging my head against a rock wall. It hurt, but I kept doing it.

I picked up Mom from the casino and we drove farther up the coast. It was a beautiful drive. We shopped, ate and enjoyed being together. We talked about my journey and how fortunate and blessed I'd been with the new wonderful friends it brought me the encouragement and kindness from strangers, the fun and the love and sorrows I had experienced. Although disappointed at the last two days, I suddenly felt good. Mom was right. So many generous people had done everything they could to help me that at times I failed to recognize the goodness all around me. I found it uncanny that the weekend I decided to visit Joe's sister, she was apparently out of town. There were fifty-one other weekends to be gone; why did she pick this one? What was up with the spirit world? Positive clues leading to nothing. It baffled me.

Before leaving, we made one last attempt to catch her at home, but no luck. I left the note on her porch explaining that I only wanted to know where I came from and the family medical history. I pleaded for her help in understanding my rejection by the Ellyson family. As usual, my last line was pleading and begging, but polite.

*   *   *

We drove until we reached California then stopped for the night. Mom didn't get the gambling bug out of her system and suggested that I stop and see Wilma on the way home. Of course I'd drop her off at her favorite casino while I visited. I hadn't seen Wilma for some time and hadn't called her lately. I called her every other night when she had been ill. By mid afternoon we reached the casino and after dropping the gambler off, I went to Wilma's.

I knocked loudly, then used my key to go inside. "Nammie," I yelled.

"Colette, is that you?"

Smiling at the flowered shower cap on her head, I answered, "Yeah, it's me."

Slightly agitated, she said, "I haven't heard from you in a while."

Tired from driving and dealing with the pangs of disappointment, I wasn't sure I was up to appeasing her.

"I went to the Oregon coast with my mom to see Joes's sister, but she wasn't home. I left her a letter. Maybe she'll call me. We changed the route home so I could have a short visit with you."

She smiled. "Your mom's over at the casino?"

"Yeah. She still had money left and it was burning a hole in her pocket."

After a few moments of silence, she looked toward me, her voice warm with empathy. "I'm sorry you didn't get to talk to Joe's sister."

I'd never heard her express so much concern for my feelings. It was genuine. My weariness and frustration had gotten the best of me, and tears filled my eyes, making it difficult to speak.

Fighting to hold back tears, I said, "Sometimes... I wonder... if my desire to meet Joe... is...because... I miss... my dad. The dad that loved me... the dad that wanted me... the dad that accepted me."

I couldn't speak any more. All the rejection and disappointment I had experienced gushed out of my eyes. Wilma looked as though she could see me. She'd never heard me cry, and for an instant she seemed to want to comfort me and make me feel better.

Her voice softened and her words encouraging. "You're lucky you had wonderful parents who adopted you."

"I know. Each passing day I appreciate my mom and dad more and more. There wasn't a day went by that I wasn't told I was loved. So why do I have this nagging hole in my heart? Why do I have this intense desire to know my biological father? I've had a wonderful life and my family loves me unconditionally and he wants nothing to do with me."

Looking down, she said quietly, "I don't know."

I wiped my eyes and nose. "Rejection is hard. It's as if I'm tainted and it's difficult not to take that personally."

"Well... maybe his sister will call you after she reads your note."

"It would be nice."

I visited a short while longer, then headed for the casino to pick up Mom. I didn't tell her about my conversation with Wilma. It would have made her cry she missed my dad too.

*   *   *

The days turned into weeks with no response from Joe's sister. My frustration, disappointment and hurt were unbearable at times. I wondered if there was some horrible story about me passed around within that family. Doubts crept in. Did I really belong to them?

Sometimes I visualized being in their shoes. But not once did it enter my mind to deny someone the opportunity of knowing where they came from. A right that I believed everyone deserved. I wasn't a saint by any means, but I was kind, loving and considerate with people's feelings. I would never intentionally hurt anyone. As Mom had told me many times, "If you can't say something nice, then don't say it at all." And I had been a true believer that you get what you give. What had I given the Ellysons that set them so against me?

*   *   *

My first contact with the Ellyson family had been a year earlier and once again the holidays were just around the corner. For the first time Allaine had planned to visit in America during her

Christmas break. She hinted at a special gift for me. I couldn't wait to see her and hoped whatever adventure we endured together this visit would be better than the last. Her e-mails reminded me that I had one more Ellyson to pursue. Did she have a hunch about that encounter?

It began to look like I might know who my father was, but never meet him. Mom kept reminding me that I'd always said I just wanted to know who he was. And now I did. I should have been more specific about my desires. Maybe added... that I'd like to meet him and that he'd want to meet me; oh... and welcome me. But no... I only wanted to know who he was. Maybe it's a spiritual learning lesson.

* * *

I couldn't wait to meet Allaine at the airport. She waved coming down the escalator. It had been six months since I'd seen her and I missed her.

"This is wild being here in the winter, " she said.

"Yeah, a lot warmer clothes."

"I'm not used to wearing a coat."

We picked up her luggage and walked to the car.

Excited, she asked, "Do you want to know what your Christmas present is?"

Indulging her, I teased, "You don't have my father tucked away in your suitcase, do you?"

"My suit case is heavy, but sorry...I don't. What do we like to do when I come to visit?"

"Are you talking about the weird stuff or the normal stuff? Or maybe the normally weird stuff?"

"Well... I don't think we could say that the things we do are... what someone would call normal. But, they're sort of normal to us."

"Yeah... and that's a little frightening."

"No it's not. Do you want me to tell you about my gift?"

"Yes, of course."

"I went on line and searched for renowned and highly rated intuitives in the US and found one in the Monterey area. Can you believe that? You said you were free while I was here, so I set us up an appointment the day after tomorrow."

Surprised and excited, I said, "Oh my gosh... are you kidding?"

"There are some great comments about her on the Internet. And some of her clients have been on current reality shows."

"Wow. That sounds cool. So... it's like getting to buy a new pair of shoes and going to Nordstrom's rather than Payless."

"Yep."

"Don't get me wrong. Payless shoes are fine, but Nordstrom's is a nice change of venue. Oh, and your gift... it didn't come from Nordstrom's."

We both laughed.

*   *   *

We had the option to have our reading over the telephone, but Allaine and I wanted it in person. It was a five-hour drive so we left my house at six in the morning. Neither of us cared how long it took. We enjoyed it. It gave us time to talk. It wasn't a typical December day. The sun was shining and it was cozy in the car.

We arrived exactly on time. Allaine and I bounced with excitement as she knocked on the door.

A short attractive middle-aged woman with long dark hair opened the door introduced herself and invited us in. Allaine and I decided to do our reading together. After offering us water, the woman seated us in front of her large desk. Autographed pictures of famous actors, singers and comedians lined the wall behind her. Some were more recent than others. But it was evident that she was an established intuitive. I was thrilled at the opportunity to hear what she had to say.

Before she started her reading, she asked for the birth dates of each individual we planned to inquire about. The first date I gave her was Joe's; adding that I was almost certain he was my father. That was something I had planned to ask her. She immediately responded with, "There's no doubt, he's your father." She didn't pull any punches on that, and it was before she started the reading.

Allaine and I asked questions and listened to her answer about our loved ones and our lives. I waited until we were almost done before asking her my last important question.

"There's one Ellyson I haven't approached. The oldest brother," I said. "Should I pay him a visit? Is it the right thing to do?"

Looking right at me, the intuitive said, "Yes. You need to. Do you know why I say this?"

I shook my head.

"Because you aren't going to be able to rest until you've exhausted all your avenues. So... yes, you need to pay him a visit. But I have to tell you, regardless of the outcome of that brother's visit, you will eventually meet your father."

I was relieved to hear that someday I would meet my father, but uneasiness swept through me as I silently replayed her wording "regardless of the outcome." The reading was finished, but I wondered what those words meant.

I thanked Allaine for her gift and told her my gift for her wasn't in the same category. She didn't seem to care. We drove back along the coastline and decided to visit the last Ellyson in a few days.

A Love Child's Journey

Chapter Thirty-Five

We were up early. I took my time with my hair, make-up and clothing selection. It was important to look nice, but I wanted to be comfortable driving. Allaine looked beautiful with her flawless make-up and coordinated slacks and jacket. Her camera, backpack and purse hung over her shoulder. She was ready for an adventure. But, I wasn't sure I was. I didn't have a warm fuzzy feeling about this endeavor. I got a hug from Mom and my husband, both wishing me luck as Allaine and I began a trip up the coast again.

We alternated between talking and quiet time.

Allaine broke the silence, "What are you going to say to him?"

"I'm not sure. I've rehearsed it so much in my mind, then I change it each time."

"Well… you can't ask him if he's your da-a-a…ddy because you should be confident by now that Joe's your father. I mean… I don't know how much more you need to verify that."

"Yeah, I know. It's hard to be positive about this meeting. If you weren't here, I'd probably put it off."

She laughed, "You know our energy, it's strong when we're together, so you'll be fine."

"You're right. So, I'll explain that I thought it would be helpful if one member of Joe's family could meet me and realize that I'm a normal person."

Sounding sarcastic, she said, "I don't think I'd use the word normal."

"Well... you know what I mean. I'm going to introduce myself, be polite, and show him my pictures. Give him a chance to see that I'm an upstanding citizen."

"Upstanding citizen? Are you really going to say that?"

"Well, maybe not. But something like that, I'm not sure. I'll wing most of it. It depends on his reactions and what he says to me."

"Sounds good."

We didn't have to rush. There was no set time we wanted to arrive at his house. I got his address off the Internet. The Ellysons seemed to enjoy the ocean. They each lived by it, although different states.

We arrived in Eureka early in the afternoon. My stomach ached. Was I doing the right thing? Visiting this brother had been on my mind for some time. However, at this point of my journey, I didn't have high expectations. I could only hope for kindness and understanding.

We stopped at a fast food restaurant, used their restroom freshened our makeup and drove to the brother's house. My stomach was in such turmoil that eating was out of the question.

Allaine continued to comfort me with her talk. She reminded me that I had knocked on many doors and this was no different. But I knew it was different. With most of the other doors, I had no idea who or how the person that answered, fit into my journey. But this was Joe's brother and I knew where he fit. At this point, everyone connected to Joe treated me as if I had some infectious disease. It was difficult to believe that Frank might be different.

*   *   *

Allaine navigated us along the coast. We turned away from the shore down a dirt road. Sporadic houses lined each side and a portion of the ocean was still visible. The houses were average sized and some had faded siding. The large yards had wood fences and no sidewalks, but each house seemed well kept and neatly groomed.

The air was cool and misty. Seagulls flew overhead squawking. The scenery was beautiful, but I couldn't appreciate it. I trembled just thinking about knocking on this door.

Allaine yelled, "There it is."

I drove slowly past it. I couldn't seem to catch my breath. "It... doesn't look like anyone's there."

"Go up and turn around," she barked.

As I drove back, a large pickup truck turned onto the dirt road from the coast highway.

Watching the large truck park in front of Frank's house, Allaine yelled, "That's him."

I parked, jumped out and hurried over to the truck. A short husky man helped his petite wife out. Why would someone their age have such a large truck? He looked up at me as I approached.

For a moment I wondered if he'd seen pictures of me. I put my hand out and introduced myself, but he didn't seem to know who I was. Then I explained. And... the walls came crashing down. I tried to tell him I wanted nothing but to know a little about where and who I came from. I was a daughter, wife, mother and grandmother, but it didn't matter what I said. I studied his face, eyes and hair, remembering that at one point I thought he might be my father. It was the first time I had an Ellyson standing in front of me. I tried to see some of me in him. His hands and arms never stopped waving around and his voice became louder and louder. Suddenly, he looked up and around as if someone was watching. I looked around myself, wondering if Joe had put cameras in the trees.

I fought hard to hold back tears. His wife looked at me with empathy. I was sorry for her feeling sorry for me. She seemed to understand what I was trying to say, but he didn't want any part of me. She told me he didn't understand that everyone needed to know where they came from. I used my manners, but I don't think he listened to anything I said. He just kept saying that people make mistakes. I told him I was grateful I was a mistake because I had a wonderful life, but a piece of me was missing.

At that moment, he caught a glimpse of Allaine, standing outside the car taking pictures. He wasn't at all happy. In fact, he was downright furious. I looked at Allaine. She smiled and waved. She wasn't close enough to see us well and had no idea how upset he was. I felt on the verge of crying. Now he assumed I told her to take pictures, which of course I hadn't. He didn't know she took pictures everywhere she went. It didn't matter what I said. He wasn't listening. I realized I should go. I looked at his wife and her eyes were sorrowful. She seemed to feel my pain. She said nothing more, but I think she understood.

Walking back to the car, I didn't know whether to cry or laugh at the thought of Allaine taking unwanted pictures at such a crucial time.

Getting into the car, I looked at her. "Why were you taking pictures?"

Sheepish, she said, "Well, you know how I am about taking pictures and I thought you might want to capture the moment."

I laughed. The moment nearly captured us. "Obviously you couldn't hear what he was saying."

"No, but I could see your upper body and boy, it's a good thing your hands were in your coat pocket. You know how you talk with your hands? So does he. He never put his down. You probably would have knocked each other out."

I smiled. "Yeah, I noticed that."

"I'm so sorry, but why would he be upset with pictures?"

"Uh... because his brother's Joe, a famous person."

"Oh yeah. I didn't think of that."

We drove back into downtown Eureka and parked outside a restaurant. Allaine apologized and felt she'd ruined my chances with him but I assured her it didn't make any difference. It had been time for me to leave and her picture taking put a little humor into a gloomy situation.

I couldn't hold back any longer, tears gushed from of my eyes. I hadn't cried that hard in a long time. Allaine didn't know what to do. She kept saying she was sorry. But between my runny nose and tears, we joked about her pictures.

"Allaine, I'm not mad about your picture taking. In fact, it's funny. Seeing the sad look on his wife's face bothered me more than his rejection. She said we'd talk again, but that can't happen."

"Why not?"

"Because she doesn't even know my name. She doesn't know where I live or my telephone number."

"So? You know where she lives."

"Yeah, I just experienced that."

"I mean, you have her address and... you know her name."

"Okay, your point is...?"

"Write her a letter."

"A letter?"

"Yeah."

I thought for a moment. "I don't want to cause her any problems with her husband."

"Address it to her, but make it look like any other mail. Besides, most women get the mail anyway."

"Yeah... that's true, but I need to think about it."

"Okay, think about it, but I'm hungry, so let's eat."

We had a nice dinner and then began our long drive home.

A few days later, Allaine left for New York to visit her daughter before returning to Kuwait. The last thing she said to me was, "Write the letter." We hadn't discussed it since our trip, but I hadn't forgotten.

*   *   *

Christmas had come and gone and we were in a new year. I'd thought long and hard about writing the letter. One minute it seemed like a good idea and the next it didn't. I chose not to discuss it with any of my family members. It was something I needed to decide on my own. It had to be my letter, from my heart.

Through my dowsing and meditating, it seemed the spirit world thought I should write the letter as well.

The weather had become warmer. Spring was almost here. On a beautiful sunny day, I found myself at home alone, the perfect opportunity for me to write a letter. Thoughts of what I wanted to say had been on my mind, but writing it would be different.

I made myself comfortable. I hadn't bought the fancy paper I planned, so white lined paper would have to do. My final preparation was to place a box of tissues nearby.

Dear Mrs. Ellyson,

First, I apologize if this causes you any problems. That's not my intention. I've thought long and hard about whether I should write you.

Showing up at your house uninvited probably wasn't the best thing to do, but your husband was the only sibling that I hadn't contacted. I didn't know what else to do. I may be wrong, but it seemed, by your comment and the expressions on your face, that you understood how important this is, and realized I was being truthful. Thank you for that.

During my search over the last few years, I've experienced so much compassion and kindness from strangers, that the rejections I have received from your family are hard to understand and break my heart. I haven't been cruel, unkind, or even disrespectful to any family member. But I feel like a boxer who's been knocked out and his opponent starts kicking him while he's lying there motionless. Jim was helpful and kind at first but then he stopped. Why? Why does your family think I'm such a horrible person, when they haven't even tried to know me? It's not as if I'm a secret anymore. I realize Joe is wealthy, but I don't care about that. I don't want his money. I want to know who "he" is. If I share his DNA, I'm a part of him, but know nothing about him. And, I want him to 'want' to know me. To know the person he took part in creating.

It's as if I'm not worthy of his acceptance and he doesn't want his family to talk with me. Do you know why? I've been told that he and my birth mother, although both very young at the time, cared deeply for one another. Lacy never recovered from the devastation of giving me up for adoption, and I believe she would have been deeply hurt at Joe's refusal to acknowledge the daughter they created as young lovers.

I've tried to be content with just knowing his name, and I've tried hard to let go of wanting to know more. But a nagging pain in my heart resurfaces. It's as though I'm still incomplete, like a puzzle with missing pieces. It's been a long emotional journey searching for those pieces. And now I've found them, but can't have them. How do I make the puzzle complete without them?

The family that adopted me, they're amazing. Not a day went by without me knowing I was loved, even when I misbehaved, and there was more of that than I like to admit. They took care of me when I was sick, taught me many skills, gave me my values and work ethics, and participated in my life. But most importantly, they taught me by example to be a good person, to be kind and considerate to others... how to love and what it's like to be loved and wanted. That came from their hearts, not DNA.

With that, I should be complete. What more could a person ask for? But... I think what I received from them makes it harder to understand this type of rejection. We all have so much room in our hearts for love and kindness if our hearts are open.

I'm not looking for Joe to replace my dad. When I found Lacy, she told me, "You will always be my daughter, but your adoptive parents will forever be your mom and dad." Then added, "but there's no reason why we can't be friends."

I'm not sure what you can do, but I would appreciate any information about your family and some insight on Joe's refusal to acknowledge me as his daughter. Thank you so much.

Sincerely,
Colette Cooper

Wiping my tears away, I picked up the letter and held it in my hand. A high-pitched tone centered in my left ear gradually became louder. As I stared at the letter, I remembered a comment from Michael's guide during one of my readings. "We think we are defined by our parents," he said. "But actually it's our soul's design that comes with us in each life time." I thought about it and I knew he was right. Someday I hoped to meet Joe, but I realized that his acknowledgement of me didn't define... who *I* was.

Slowly I folded the letter, gathered my used tissues, and walked over to my dresser. Opening the bottom drawer, I placed the letter neatly toward the back. Shutting the drawer, I realized the letter was meant for me... not the Ellysons.